"I loved it! . . . [obscured] that pulls you out of the everyday . . . I recommend *Damsel in Disguise*."

—*Romancemama*

"Every page turns into a delight from this fantastic author who has an extremely quick wit. Not only is this book a great find for the romance readers out there who simply love historical novels, but it's also filled with the twists and turns that adventure fans crave . . . [Heino] definitely has a gift, and readers will be glad that this author has chosen to share that gift with the rest of us."

—*Night Owl Romance*

"Passion, deception, disguises, and mayhem all combine in *Damsel in Disguise*. Susan Gee Heino has penned a story that's almost Shakespearean in its plot, with lords and actors, villains and rogues, mysteries and a heroine who cross-dresses to rescue her hero . . . I like that Ms. Heino's characters are unconventional, and her writing style definitely appealed to me."

—*Joyfully Reviewed*

"A fun comedy of errors." —*Midwest Book Review*

Mistress by Mistake

"A funny, sexy romp! Destined to become a reader favorite."

—Christine Wells, author of *Sweetest Little Sin*

"Sparkling with superbly crafted characters, humor, and deliciously sexy romance, Heino's debut . . . is splendidly entertaining."

—*Booklist*

"I loved . . . *Mistress by Mistake*." —*Romancemama*

"An amusing Regency romance . . . A wonderful historical."

—*The Best Reviews*

Berkley Sensation Titles by Susan Gee Heino

MISTRESS BY MISTAKE
DAMSEL IN DISGUISE
TEMPTRESS IN TRAINING

Temptress in Training

SUSAN GEE HEINO

BERKLEY SENSATION, NEW YORK

THE BERKLEY PUBLISHING GROUP
Published by the Penguin Group
Penguin Group (USA) Inc.
375 Hudson Street, New York, New York 10014, USA
Penguin Group (Canada), 90 Eglinton Avenue East, Suite 700, Toronto, Ontario M4P 2Y3, Canada
(a division of Pearson Penguin Canada Inc.)
Penguin Books Ltd., 80 Strand, London WC2R 0RL, England
Penguin Group Ireland, 25 St. Stephen's Green, Dublin 2, Ireland (a division of Penguin Books Ltd.)
Penguin Group (Australia), 250 Camberwell Road, Camberwell, Victoria 3124, Australia
(a division of Pearson Australia Group Pty. Ltd.)
Penguin Books India Pvt. Ltd., 11 Community Centre, Panchsheel Park, New Delhi—110 017, India
Penguin Group (NZ), 67 Apollo Drive, Rosedale, Auckland 0632, New Zealand
(a division of Pearson New Zealand Ltd.)
Penguin Books (South Africa) (Pty.) Ltd., 24 Sturdee Avenue, Rosebank, Johannesburg 2196, South Africa

Penguin Books Ltd., Registered Offices: 80 Strand, London WC2R 0RL, England

TEMPTRESS IN TRAINING

A Berkley Sensation Book / published by arrangement with the author

PRINTING HISTORY
Berkley Sensation mass-market edition / July 2011

Cover art by Jim Griffin.
Cover design by George Long.
Cover hand lettering by Ron Zinn.

For information, address: The Berkley Publishing Group,
a division of Penguin Group (USA) Inc.,
375 Hudson Street, New York, New York 10014.

ISBN: 978-0-425-24211-7

BERKLEY® SENSATION
Berkley Sensation Books are published by The Berkley Publishing Group,
a division of Penguin Group (USA) Inc.,
375 Hudson Street, New York, New York 10014.

PRINTED IN THE UNITED STATES OF AMERICA

10 9 8 7 6 5 4 3 2 1

To my parents, Edwin and Blanche Gee.
You trained me to respect God, love other people,
and never be tempted to take myself too seriously.

Chapter One

London, England
13 June 1816

What? There would be no usual Thursday orgy? Indeed, this was a relief.

Sophie Darshaw could not be too grateful for a break from her household duties. Tidying up after Mr. Fitzgelder's constant debauchery was quite exhausting. She honestly didn't believe she had it in her to spend another night re-stitching some randy reveler's trousers or hunting down new lacing for some doxy's willfully dismantled corset. After all, Sophie had her own troubles to tend to. She'd learned several long hours ago that a grave error had been made in the design of her latest undergarment invention.

Velvet pantalets, as it turned out, were a decidedly unwise construction. They chafed. Particularly.

This was a problem, and not merely for the obvious reasons. Madame Eudora, her former employer, had commissioned this project and seemed convinced such an object would suit nicely. Sophie would be obliged to send a carefully worded note tomorrow stressing the, er, unfortunate drawbacks.

Would Madame still pay the agreed upon price for the pantalets if she were to fashion them from some lesser, more comfortable fabric? It hardly seemed likely. Or ethical. Sophie couldn't in good conscience allow it. She would simply have to take a loss on this project and encourage Madame Eudora to settle for something a bit more conventional, like those lovely little silk pillows she'd created to fit snugly into Madame's bodice and force the woman's forty-year-old assets back into proper position. Now *that* had been a useful invention, and certainly there would be nothing like this god-awful rash today's endeavor had got her.

It was this problem that she sought to correct when she spied the linen cupboard. Conveniently, someone had left the door ajar. Sophie would just tiptoe in and make use of the blessedly private and unoccupied space. At least, she'd assumed it was unoccupied. How shocking to find it was not!

Sophie was suddenly face-to-face with her horrible employer, the always-eager Mr. Fitzgelder. That fretful chafing was quickly forgotten. Good heavens, what was the man doing in here? Her first impulse was to glance around for whichever of her unfortunate fellow servants the man must have dragged into the small room for unimaginable purposes, but it appeared this time he was uncharacteristically alone.

In his thin, pasty hand he held what appeared to be a locket, hung from a long golden chain. He'd been working the locket, studying it so intensely she could almost believe that little bit of jewelry might hold his attention long enough for her to slide out of the room unnoticed, and unmolested, with luck.

Apparently, though, it could not. He saw her and smiled. The locket was instantly forgotten, folded into his sweaty palm as he moved toward her.

"Well, if it isn't the proper little miss from Madame Eudora's," he said.

His thick, drawling voice irritated like sand in a shoe, and she knew he chose his words intentionally. Mr. Fitzgelder was not about to let her forget where he had found her and, supposedly, rescued her. He didn't have rescue on his mind now, that much was certain.

"Beg pardon, sir," she said, staring at his feet and backing away. "I'll just . . ."

"You'll just stay here with me, little dove," he said, grabbing her wrist and tugging her back into the room.

He kicked the narrow door shut, too. Now it was dark. Just a thin line of light escaped into the room on three sides around the door. Sophie choked on her panic but forced herself to stay calm. She would find a way to get out of this. She had to.

The room was small. She knew shelves lined each wall, piled high with towels. Bedsheets and all other manner of upstairs linens surrounded them—it would be the perfect place for the unpleasantness her master clearly had planned. Even a fool like Fitzgelder would not overlook such a golden opportunity. Lord, but she should have been more careful. She knew what sort of man her employer was.

Well, she was not ready to give up without a fight. Not that she could count on help from anyone outside that cupboard door, of course. No matter what ruckus she might make in here, Fitzgelder's servants knew the force of their master's wrath—they wouldn't dare interrupt. Especially not for the likes of her. Indeed, although she was ostensibly in training as a maid, everyone knew the real reason Fitzgelder had brought her from Madame Eudora's brothel into his home. And it did not include polishing his silver, unless of course one was not really talking about actual silver.

But Sophie was not interested in polishing anything—real *or* hypothetical—for this man. She hadn't spent the last month repeatedly escaping his groping hands and roving eye only to succumb in a linen cupboard, of all places. She'd survived four years as a seamstress—and only that—for Madame Eudora. She was not about to quietly give up what was left of her virtue to a putty-faced, perpetually drunk bastard like Fitzgelder.

And she was certainly not about to let the man find out she'd been wearing velvet pantalets!

"Get off me, sir! I do not wish for this."

"What fine airs you take on." He laughed, his bony fingers digging into her shoulders. She knew it would leave bruising.

"Leave me alone or I'll scream!"

He simply shrugged—she could feel the slight movement in the dark. "Go ahead and scream. I like screamers."

Well, then screaming was out of the question. She'd conserve her energy for other purposes—like scratching his eyes out.

But in the dark she had a hard time finding them. Her nails had barely scraped his pockmarked face when he caught her hands up in his and clenched them tight. She winced in pain and realized things were not going well for her. She shoved against him but it had little effect.

Desperation took over and she slammed her forehead against his chin. Something warm dripped onto her face. Was that blood? *Good.* With luck she'd caused him to bite off his own tongue. If there were any justice in the world he'd choke to death on it now.

But he merely sprayed her with warm moisture as he laughed—actually laughed!—at her fury. With one hand fisted into her hair so she could no longer move freely, he loomed nearer, breathing heavily and filling the room with the smell of whiskey and tobacco. She was hopelessly pinned.

"I'm going to enjoy this," he hissed.

No, she was fairly certain he would not. With every ounce of outrage she felt, she brought her knee up between them. God was merciful and she caught him dead-on, right where she had hoped to. He let out an injured yelp.

"Dammit, you're going to regret that!"

He grabbed at her again, but she moved slightly to one side. In the dark he didn't know exactly where to find her. The room was far too tight to escape him for long, but she'd be damned if she'd make this easy on him. Too soon, though, he had her pinned in the corner. Now her arms were wedged behind her and she admitted he was not likely to allow her a second chance at attack.

Damn those velvet pantalets that brought her in here! And to think she'd hoped the money she earned from their design might be enough to finally free her from this man and his employment. How mistaken she'd been. She should have known a girl in her circumstance would never earn enough honestly to set herself up as a proper dressmaker. It was just a foolish dream that—

She blinked in surprise when the door suddenly came open and light flooded into the cupboard. Fitzgelder released her immediately, adjusting his sagging breeches and disheveled coat. Sophie was torn between hiding from the shame of being discovered like this and rushing out to embrace her savior.

As her eyes adjusted to the relatively bright light from the hallway, she did neither. Instead her words of thanksgiving died in her throat as she recognized the intruder. Good Lord, could it really be *him*? Here, wandering the halls and linen cupboards of Mr. Fitzgelder's home as if it were his own?

How awful that he should see her this way! What must he think? He stood there in the doorway, his tall, elegant form perfectly silhouetted, taking in the full panorama of what he could not possibly mistake as anything other than what it was.

The Earl of Lindley. The finest man she'd ever laid eyes upon and one of the few who'd treated her with something like respect when she'd been introduced to him at Madame Eudora's. Of all the possible rescuers in the world, she was torn between joy and horror that it had to be Lindley to find her this way.

Yet he gave no appearance of shock or surprise or even the least bit of distress at her plight. Lord, but that struck her more than anything. Why on earth was he not distressed?

Honestly, he seemed barely miffed. His voice, when he finally spoke, was disappointingly calm and dripping with ennui.

"I say, Fitz, why did you not bother to tell me the festivities had begun already? You know how I deplore coming in late on the entertainment."

LORD LINDLEY CURSED HIMSELF AS HE PROWLED THE deserted halls of Fitzgelder's garish town house. Marble statuaries peered at him from the crowded alcoves built to showcase them. Reproductions, of course, but still they represented a great deal of investment. Even upstairs the walls were lined with expensive silks and gilded tapestry. All in all the effect was quite overwhelming, but even the casual observer would have to wonder where a shiftless bastard like Fitzgelder came up with the blunt to furnish his home in such lavish fashion.

Lindley was convinced he knew the answer. Fitzgelder tried to pretend his wealth was inherited from his father, but Lindley knew this not to be the case. He'd spent the last year conjuring a friendship with Fitzgelder's legitimate cousin and learned some intimate details of the family's situation. Fitzgelder was a bastard whose father had seen little use for him. He'd died without heir and left his wealth and his title to his brother. Upon the brother's death, the Rastmoor wealth passed even further from Fitzgelder's grip to his younger cousin. This current Lord Rastmoor was not inclined to share.

Yet somehow Fitzgelder did quite well for himself. By all appearances, his bills were paid and he could afford the lascivious life he led. In all his prying, Lindley had found little explanation for this. Clearly, then, that was its own explanation. Fitzgelder was his man.

Frustrated, he couldn't yet move on it, though. Captain Warren would want details, names, places, and proof. Lindley had none of these, nothing more than suspicions and a deep, churning sense in his gut that told him Fitzgelder was rotten. Just how rotten, he was determined to find out.

He supposed another night spent in carousing and false friendship with the man would likely not kill him. Then again, it would probably give him a strong headache in the morning and another load of guilt to carry around. But he was getting used to that now. No matter of guilt for a few lies here and a liaison or two there would ever come close to comparing to the loss that still festered in his soul. If Fitzgelder was his man, by God he'd do what it took to catch him.

Then he'd see him hanged.

First, though, he'd have to find him. Where had the bloody bastard gone? They'd only just returned from that dreadful reading of erotic poetry one of Fitzgelder's tasteless friends had arranged. What a waste that had been.

At least, he hoped it had been a waste. Had the man met with his contact in the dark secrecy of the event? Damn, he hoped not. He'd hung on Fitzgelder like a horse burr for the last two weeks but still he was no closer to confirming his intuition about the man. It would be a damn shame if he had to put up with all this only to miss out on catching Fitzgelder in the act.

So where was the man now? They had returned to Fitzgelder's home to find a parcel waiting for him, delivered by messenger. Lindley had seen the delight written on Fitzgelder's face, yet he'd not gotten any clue who had sent the parcel. Fitzgelder had deposited a frustrated Lindley in the drawing room and instructed him to wait, saying he was off to refresh himself but would return momentarily and they might resume their evening plans.

Well, Lindley wasn't about to let Fitzgelder go off to deal with that secretive parcel alone. By God, if this was the evidence he'd long been looking for, Lindley was going to find it. He had quietly followed the man upstairs but promptly lost him.

So where the devil was he? And what was in that bloody parcel?

A commotion from farther down the hallway snagged his attention. It seemed to be coming from behind a narrow door, probably a closet or cupboard. Lindley heard the low drum of Fitzgelder's voice and the panicked high pitches of a female. Well, it would appear he might yet catch Fitzgelder in the act, although sadly this was far from the act he was hoping for. Apparently the parcel had turned out to be less enthralling than Fitzgelder expected.

Really, Lindley knew he ought to leave the man to his efforts. He'd worked hard to insinuate himself into Fitzgelder's confidence. A good friend would never interrupt a gentleman—or rather, in Fitzgelder's case, a ruddy lecher—who was availing himself of an opportunity for a little tussle with a willing maid. An interruption just now might actually sever what bond of trust had been established between the men. Was Lindley prepared to sacrifice that?

Yet the female's protest and the sounds of struggle were obvious. She was clearly—and not surprisingly—unwilling. Lindley decided he was not game for heaping that guilt upon his shoulders along with all the other. He'd no doubt kick himself for it later, but right now he must certainly intervene.

And he was glad that he did.

Light from the many sconces in the hallway poured into what turned out to be a linen cupboard. Fitzgelder, startled, struggled to right his clothing. Lindley politely averted his gaze. What his eyes landed on made him temporarily forget his disgust, his guilt, and his mission to implicate Fitzgelder.

Sophie Darshaw. Hell and damnation, it was she who had been struggling with Fitzgelder. By the looks of it, she'd been giving the man quite a fight, too. Her clothing was in dreadful disarray, her fair hair was mussed and tangled in clumps, and were those droplets of blood spattered on her pretty, ashen face? By God, he'd kill the man.

No, he couldn't. He'd come too far and had too much at stake. Sophie Darshaw was just a minor player in this, and Lindley reminded himself he wasn't even entirely sure yet what part she played. He'd interrupted and that was enough. He would not give in to ridiculous sentiment when there might still be a chance to salvage things.

He wiped all trace of loathing from his face and carved out a disgruntled pout.

"I say, Fitz, why did you not bother to tell me the festivities had begun already? You know how I deplore coming in late on the entertainment."

"Bloody hell, Lindley," Fitzgelder growled. "What in damnation are you about, tearing in while a fellow's readying to plug himself a little laced mutton?"

Lindley simply shrugged and allowed a lengthy—and welcome—look over Miss Darshaw's disheveled person. It appeared he'd come just in time. The girl was shaking and pale as the crypt, but he was pleased to see a healthy spark of defiance left in her crystal blue eyes. She'd done well for herself, all things considered. Fitzgelder sported a bloody lip while she was merely untidy.

"Well then," Lindley said, unbuttoning his coat and placing his hand as if to begin unfastening his trousers. "If the mutton's willing, I might fancy a go at her myself."

"The mutton most certainly is *not* willing!" Miss Darshaw announced firmly.

She shoved Fitzgelder aside and pushed her way out of the tiny room. Lindley stood aside to let her. He could well do without a bloodied lip tonight, and Miss Darshaw seemed every bit capable of giving him one. Hell, if he hadn't interrupted when he did poor Fitzgelder might have ended up singing soprano. The way Miss Darshaw glared murder at them both he wasn't entirely convinced she had needed his intervention after all. The girl showed ferocity enough to do serious damage.

But Fitzgelder was a fool and paid no notice. He brushed

past Lindley and made as if to follow the hellcat. Lindley latched onto his arm.

"Oh, let her go," he advised, careful to seem unconcerned. "She's not but a little slip of a thing, Fitz. Hardly woman enough for men like us. Come, what more creative pleasures do you have scheduled tonight? It is Thursday, after all."

Miss Darshaw shot him one hateful glance before scurrying up the hallway and disappearing around a corner. Fitzgelder watched after her, steaming. Indeed, he was too proud to admit his frustration, but Lindley knew this matter was not settled. As long as Miss Darshaw chose to remain in this household—whatever her reasons might be—she was going to be her master's choice prey. Clearly this was not something she wished, but at the same time she did not distain it enough to leave. That, of course, must mean something.

If only he could discern what.

"I swear, that minx needs a good thrashing to put her in her place," Fitzgelder was muttering.

"Thrash her later, old man. I'm nearly bored to death after that abominable poetry party tonight. Whyever did you drag me to such a gathering of stiff-rumped nobs? In faith, I could have enjoyed myself more with my Methodist grandmother. You know I come to you, Fitzy old man, to save me from such dreariness."

He glanced back into the cupboard behind them and noticed the wrappings from Fitzgelder's parcel lying discarded on the floor. *Damn!* Whatever had been in it, the man had already taken possession of it. But perhaps there was some clue in that abandoned wrapper. He'd have to get a look at it.

In hopes of distracting his friend, he stepped aside to allow Fitzgelder to leave the cupboard and join him in the hallway. The man did. Lindley casually shut the cupboard door behind them.

"So where shall we be going next?"

Fitzgelder finally took his focus off the direction Miss Darshaw had gone and brought out a handkerchief to dab his lip. "Well, I'm afraid tonight's entertainment might seem a bit tame for your lordship's high standards," he said.

"Nothing aimed to better my mind, I hope."

At last Fitzgelder lost a bit of his anger and made a sound that was likely akin to laughter. "No, nothing like that. I've had my man engage a theatrical troupe to present for us. They should be already preparing for us down in the blue salon, and our other guests should be arriving presently. I suppose we can expect the odd Shakespeare scene, a tableau or two, and the usual buffoonery. Personally, though, I'm quite looking forward to it. Why don't you go do some damage to my brandy while I find my man to put me in a fresh cravat, eh?"

"By all means," Lindley said. "But see that the man ties it with both hands this time, Fitzy. All evening long it's looked wretched, like someone strapped a wet cat around your neck."

Fitzgelder laughed at him. The stupid man actually seemed to enjoy the ridicule Lindley found all too easy to heap on him.

"I'll tell the man you said so," Fitzgelder assured. "He'll be mortified, of course, so perhaps you'll encourage the sluggard to do better. There's no better judge of the complicated knot than the Earl of Lindley, after all."

"Precisely," Lindley agreed.

Fitzgelder left him then, still chuckling—presumably—over the amusing image of a wet cat around his neck. Honestly, the man thought himself quite the fashion plate when really he was a complete gaby. Lindley watched him go. So just what was the mutton-monger up to? Was he really off to attend to his neckcloth or to conduct secret business without Lindley's watchful eye? Or perhaps the bastard was planning to hunt down Miss Darshaw and finish what he'd started.

Lindley would see that it was not the latter. But first things first. The minute Fitzgelder was out of sight, he ducked into the cupboard and retrieved the wrappings. He didn't dare examine them here, but shoved them quickly into his pocket and left the cupboard. Should Fitzgelder come back to look for them, with luck he might assume a dutiful servant had removed them and not suspect Lindley.

Calm and casual, Lindley took himself down to the ground floor. Miss Darshaw was nowhere in sight, so he headed to the room where Fitzgelder indicated the actors would be. He couldn't help but wonder how the hell a theatrical troupe fit into things. Mangled Shakespeare or pirated French farce was a bit tame for Fitzgelder—hardly the usual fare offered at his frequent routs. Could this simply be a cover for something more furtive? Would he be meeting with someone in regards to that parcel? Or were tonight's theatrics to be of a tawdry nature simply to feed Fitzgelder's insatiable appetites? It was hard to say with the fellow. Lindley could only hope he hadn't ruined any hope of uncovering the truth of that parcel by thwarting Fitzgelder's efforts with Miss Darshaw.

Whatever was to come, though, Lindley could not regret rescuing the girl. Surely she was not party to the worst of her master's sins. She must have some simpler, less sinister reasons for being in the man's employ. Perhaps she might not even know the full extent of his treachery. The sooner he learned Fitzgelder's secrets, the better.

And perhaps along the way, he'd learn Miss Darshaw's secrets, as well.

SOPHIE DID HER VERY BEST TO PRETEND THE LAST FEW minutes in that insufferable linen closet had not happened. She was blissfully anonymous here in her master's busy blue room, surrounded by bustling actors and the hectic preparations for tonight's entertainment. She could make herself useful here, blending safely into the hustle and forgetting what had very nearly occurred—and who had fortunately interrupted it.

Heavens, but what was Lord Lindley doing here? Not that she cared a fig for where the man was or wasn't; it simply surprised her, that was all. Just because he'd seemed a decent sort certainly did not mean he was. He'd been in company with Madame frequently, after all. What sort of upstanding fellow would do that? And now here he was with Mr. Fitzgelder. Clearly she'd been grossly mistaken regarding his character.

How ridiculous that she should waste one ounce of brain matter contemplating one of the dissolute blackguards from her former life. Indeed, she'd left her previous situation to prove she could be better than all that, to *become* better than that. She may have not been able to find work for anyone more respectable than Mr. Fitzgelder, but she fully intended to use this as a step in the right direction. She would have that dress shop one day. It merely appeared it would take a bit longer than she'd first envisioned.

Clearly she needed to find a position better than this one. She could be a ladies' maid, for instance. That was a fine, respectable position, and the pay would no doubt be better and put her that much closer to her dream. All she needed was a bit of experience and a reference. Perhaps she could start on that very thing today. It appeared the acting troupe Mr. Fitzgelder had hired did include a lady or two. Well, a *female* or two, at any rate.

She approached a middle-aged actress and offered to be of assistance. The woman eyed her curiously, then jabbed her thumb in the direction of a young woman who was just now entering the room.

"There you go, miss, that's the lady you need to be presenting yourself to," she said with a smile. "That's our, er, Miss Sands. She'll know what to do with you."

Sophie curtsied and thanked the woman, then hurried over to this Miss Sands. She was young and pretty and gave every appearance of being horribly respectable. At least, as respectable as an actress could be. Sophie knew a thing or two of actresses. Hopefully she could use that to her advantage and make a favorable impression on this one.

"I was told you might be needing some help dressing for the performance, Miss Sands," Sophie offered with a cheerful smile.

She watched the young woman bustle about, selecting her wardrobe and giving instructions to other troupe members as they hauled in the various paraphernalia needed for Fitzgelder's entertainment. Thankfully, there was not a single thing that suggested "orgy." *Good.* If she could impress Miss Sands with properly attentive service perhaps this might be just the opportunity she needed to secure a decent enough reference to move on.

Nervously, Sophie smoothed her apron and patted her hair in place. Everyone knew a proper ladies' maid needed to be properly turned out.

"Thank you," Miss Sands said, her focus clearly torn between the lovely blue silk gown she held in one hand and the more elaborate golden one in the other. "I suppose if our host tonight favors the more classical pieces I ought to go with the embroidered neckline, but I do so prefer the blue. Tell me, is your master a great lover of Shakespeare or will he be more inclined to request . . ."

And now the lady finally turned to look at her. *Oh, bother.* By the look on Miss Sands's face it would seem Sophie's hasty attempts to put herself to rights after that dreadful episode upstairs had failed dismally.

"Good God!" the actress exclaimed. "You poor dear! What in heaven's name has happened to you?"

Sophie stared at the floor. "I'm sorry, miss, I didn't realize I, that is, I should go tend to my appearance." She curtsied and tried to leave, but Miss Sands would have none of it.

"Gracious! Are these bruises at your wrists? And there's blood on your apron! Who did this to you, girl?"

Sophie knew it would be the height of impropriety to lie to her mistress, but since Miss Sands was really only a guest in the house, she supposed it was a forgivable offense this time. Besides, Mr. Fitzgelder would likely not take kindly to having his dirty secrets aired for these entertainers.

"No one, miss," Sophie replied. "I fell."

It seemed Miss Sands had brains as well as beauty. "My arse, you fell. Come, my girl, I recognize the print of a man's hand when I see it. Who did this to you?"

"It's nothing at all, miss. I managed to get away."

"Not before he welted your eye!"

"What?" Sophie shot her hand up to her face. Indeed, her eyelid felt puffy and tender. When she slammed Fitzgelder with her forehead she must have also succeeded in bruising herself.

"Come," the actress ordered, pulling Sophie over toward a row of chairs against the wall.

"Truly, I'm quite fine," Sophie explained, politely trying to fend off the other woman's examination.

"This is very fresh, isn't it? Heavens, we'll have to put something on it immediately."

"No, really I don't need—"

Miss Sands cut her off by turning her to face a lovely round mirror that hung on the master's wall. Sophie had no other option but to stare at her own face and catch her breath at the ugly red welt that showed quite plainly at her swollen eyelid. It throbbed. Merciful Lord, how would she ever hide this from the other servants? They would not need to question who had done such a thing, or why.

And they would not be pleased about it, either. If Mr. Fitzgelder was in a foul mood after this—and of course he would be—he'd naturally take it out on the staff. As far as they would care, this injury would be undeniable evidence of her insolence while they would be the ones paying the price. Unsurprisingly, they'd take it out on her.

"Oh" was all she could say as she stared back at her reflection.

"Don't worry, I'll help you," Miss Sands said. "What is your name?"

Her first instinct was not to trust this stranger, not to give any information that could somehow be used to further damage her place in this household. But as she cautiously met the actress's gaze she wondered if perhaps she could indeed trust Miss Sands with something as innocuous as her name. After all, what more did she have to lose?

"I'm Sophie Darshaw, miss," she replied.

The actress smiled. "Well, Sophie Darshaw, you look like an honest girl. I can't imagine there's anything you could have done to deserve such treatment that would leave you like this."

"*He* would clearly disagree," Sophie replied, unable to keep the bitterness out of her voice.

"And who is *he*?" the actress asked gently. "Your husband?"

Sophie was only too happy to set her straight. "No, thankfully he's nothing more than my employer."

"But surely that doesn't give him the right to do this!"

"At least this is all he did," Sophie assured her. "I know how to handle his likes, Miss Sands."

"And just look how he handled you," the actress replied. "You don't need to suffer this, Sophie. No position is worth this. You simply must leave his service."

"Leave? To go live on the streets?" Sophie shook her head, one unruly lock of her disobedient honey-colored hair bouncing loose of the prim cap where she'd tried so hard to tuck it.

"No, I know all too well what leaving would bring, miss. Trust me, I'm better off here."

"Surely there is somewhere you can go?"

"With no references? No, miss. And I assure you, Mr. Fitzgelder is not likely to authorize a reference."

Oddly enough, this statement seemed to have quite the effect on Miss Sands. Her eyes grew suddenly huge and her face paled as if she feared a dragon might suddenly leap out and eat them. Sophie wondered if the woman wasn't going a bit overboard with her outpouring of sympathy.

"Did you . . . did you say Mr. Fitzgelder?"

Sophie nodded. "Yes, miss. He is my master."

The actress appeared as if she were going to be ill.

"I-I'm sorry," Sophie stammered quickly. "Did I, er, did I say something wrong?"

"Your master is called Fitzgelder? But surely not Mr. Cedrick Fitzgelder, is it?"

"Yes, miss. The very same. Do you know him?"

Miss Sands didn't answer. By her nervous hand wringing and the way her brown eyes darted around frantically, she didn't need to. Yes, Miss Sands obviously knew Sophie's master. Apparently her dealings with him had been as pleasant as Sophie's.

Without warning the actress grasped Sophie by the hand and pulled her toward the other side of the room, to the doorway that led out of the salon at the rear of the house. Deciding it might be best to find out what this was about, Sophie went along. They made it to the doorway just as an older gentleman carrying a crate came through it. Miss Sands nearly plowed into him.

Good-naturedly, he urged the young actress to be careful. What caught Sophie's attention, though, was that he did it in French. Such a simple thing, yet her soul reacted. The dull pain of loss throbbed to life, catching her off guard by its force, even after all this time being dormant. How silly that words from a stranger could evoke so much of the past!

She carefully pushed old, best-forgotten feelings back into that dark corner of her heart. Her life today had no room for such memories. Things were as they were and she'd do well to keep her mind on today's troubles, not useless memories of things dead and buried.

Miss Sands was breathlessly informing the man—also in French—what she had learned from Sophie. He appeared similarly affected when Fitzgelder's name was mentioned. He scanned the room, then hurried them into a corner where they could duck behind a screened wall that had been erected for concealing musicians during an entertainment. He lowered his voice and rattled a string of questions. Was Miss Sands certain it was him? Had he seen her? What else did she know?

Without bothering to answer him, Miss Sands responded with a barrage of her own questions for the man. What could he have been thinking when he scheduled this performance? Did he not realize this was London and they should have been more careful? What did he suggest they do now?

From what Sophie could gather from their hurried, harried conversation, the gentleman insisted he *had* been careful. He was quite certain Mr. Fitzgelder's name had not come up when arrangements were made for this event. In fact, it appeared he thought he'd been hired by a man named Smith.

Then he noticed *her*. Miss Sands gave him her first name and explained—tactfully—the reason for Sophie's lamentable bruising. The man's distress was even more pronounced. He swore.

"And you've believed her story?" he asked gruffly, still in his elegant French.

Well, that was far from the sympathy she'd hoped for!

"Of course I believe her," Miss Sands replied. "Just look at her."

"You trusted her, just because of a little bruising?"

The man eyed Sophie with a dark suspicion. She didn't much care for the intensity of this scrutiny. What exactly did he think she had done?

"I haven't told her anything," Miss Sands went on, also in a very cultured French. Sophie got the idea they had no clue she could understand them.

"Good. Fitzgelder could be using her to get information," the man said.

What? But that was ridiculous. Whatever could they be

talking about? She knew nothing about any information. She wasted no time setting things straight, in French.

"Mr. Fitzgelder certainly was not interested in me for information, monsieur."

They seemed surprised.

"You are French?" the gentleman asked.

"My father was French," Sophie responded. "But Mrs. Harwell scolds me if I do not speak English."

"So you understood our conversation," Miss Sands said.

Sophie shook her head. "Not in the least."

"Don't lie to us," the man said, leaning over her so that she was forced to take a step back. "Did Mr. Fitzgelder send you to find out about us?"

"Find out about you? Heavens, if that was all Mr. Fitzgelder asked of me I would not be wearing this," Sophie replied, touching her swollen eyelid. "Besides, you're in his home. He must know about you already, I would think."

"What did he tell you of us?" the man demanded.

"He did not mention you at all! I came to you hoping to avoid him."

The gentleman did not seem entirely convinced. "You had no other reason to ingratiate yourself with my daughter?"

So this was his daughter, was it? No wonder he was concerned. Any father with a pretty young daughter who suddenly found himself in Mr. Fitzgelder's home had good reason to be concerned.

Sophie swallowed and forced herself to meet his flashing eyes as she replied. "Well, I had thought perhaps if I took extra care, Miss Sands might give me a reference so I could find a position elsewhere."

"See, Papa?" the actress announced. "Surely you can't believe she would ever help Fitzgelder. Look at her! We ought to go while we can and take her with us."

The man frowned, his thick brows nearly touching above his prominent nose. "But if we leave, that will only alert Fitzgelder that something is not right. No, we must think through this first."

"It's too dangerous. We must go now!"

"If we go he'll only follow. No, I must think of something else."

They argued a bit and Sophie felt as if she really ought not be privy to their conversation. Clearly these people had some great, dark reason to fear her master, and it did appear as if Mr. Fitzgelder must have lured them here intentionally. She felt sorry for them, of course, but at the same time she couldn't help but realize things would go especially badly for her if she were discovered in their company.

She tried to excuse herself.

"But you cannot go back to work for that monster!" Miss Sands suddenly protested, grabbing at her hand to keep her hidden with them there.

Suddenly Sophie was inclined to agree. She'd barely poked her head out from around the screened wall and quickly ducked back in. *He* was here.

Miss Sands's father noticed and leaned forward to peer through the openings in the screen. Miss Sands did the same, her breath catching in a way that Sophie could truly not find surprising. Women often did that upon sight of the tall, impeccably dressed gentleman and his arguably perfect features.

"Is that him?" she asked with a mix of awe and astonishment. "Is that Fitzgelder?"

Sophie had to stifle a laugh. As if there could be any comparison!

"No, it's someone else," her father replied. "I don't know him."

"Lindley," Sophie informed them. "His name is Lindley."

"The earl?"

Sophie nodded.

"We are in trouble, then," the actor said.

Sophie joined Miss Sands in sending him a curious glance. He ran his hand through his thick, dark hair and sighed. Could these people have something against Lindley, too? Just what sort of actors were these people, anyway? Sophie watched intently as a careful determination stole over the older man's face. His daughter eyed him.

"Papa, who is this Lindley? What have we to do with him?"

"Nothing, *ma chou-chou*. He is merely a friend of Fitzgelder's. But this tells me what I must do."

"It does?"

"Indeed. I must leave."

"No, Papa. *We* must leave. Together."

He shook his head. "No, people must merely *think* we've left together. Remember, *ma belle*, he's never seen you. You must stay here where you will be safe."

"Safe? *Here?* You cannot be serious, Papa!" Miss Sands protested.

Sophie voiced her agreement. "Beg pardon, monsieur, but Mr. Fitzgelder will surely take notice of Miss Sands, even if he does not know her. I cannot think she'll be safe here!"

The actor simply smiled at them. "She will if she gives the performance of her lifetime."

Chapter Two

If *Romeo and Juliet* was supposed to have been a comedy, Lindley could have called the presentation of the balcony scene quite successful. The young man playing Romeo had been nothing short of hilarious. Not that he was trying to be, of course. Sadly, Lindley believed the young pup's nervous posturing, effeminate mannerisms, and the way he continued to recite Juliet's lines instead of his own was entirely unintentional.

Not that Juliet was any better. She was worse, in fact, and no spry young maiden, either. Indeed, Juliet was particularly older and far more world-weary than her tender Romeo. Lindley was not convinced it was merely her shoes that creaked as she walked toward her shifty young man. It did not play well.

What on earth had Fitzgelder been thinking when he secured this bloody theatrical troupe for his Thursday night rout? His guests—accustomed to entertainment that was a bit more titillating—were growing restless. Lindley hoped Fitzgelder hadn't paid much for this mess of a production.

It would seem, however, their host considered whatever he'd paid to be too much.

"This is bullshit!" Fitzgelder erupted as Romeo continued

to rail on and on about the angelic virtues of his grandmotherly Juliet. "What the hell are we watching here? Where is the real Juliet?"

The actors, understandably, were thrown off balance by the interruption. Romeo was especially flustered. It made sense, of course, as he'd been the one to introduce himself as Alexander Clemmons, the unlikely leader of this sad little troupe. Naturally he'd be the first one Fitzgelder had hauled off to jail for impersonating, well, an actor. It seemed he might possibly be considering hiding behind Juliet, which really would not have been an altogether bad idea since she appeared rather formidable with her beefy fists jammed into her hips and her fiery eyes daring Fitzgelder to insult them again.

The man happily obliged. "*This* Juliet is a sixty-year-old hag! For God's sake, where is the actress who ought to be playing this part? I had it on good authority Miss Sands was part of this troupe and that she, at least, could provide some enjoyment!"

The nervous young Romeo darted a longing look toward the door at the back of the room. Would he bolt? Lindley couldn't say that he'd quite blame the pup, but it appeared he chose to weather the storm. Romeo drew a deep breath, smoothed his pitiful—and dreadfully unfashionable—mustache, and stepped forward.

"I'm sorry, sir, but our lovely Miss, er, Draper here," he said, glancing around the room and then nodding toward Juliet, "is well-known for her excellent abilities. She is acclaimed by royalty, applauded by gentlemen, praised by her peers—"

"And too bloody old to play the damn part!" Fitzgelder interrupted. "Where the hell is Miss Sands?"

Romeo was concerned. He looked helplessly off to the side and Lindley happened to catch a glimpse of movement. Was someone there, in that little screened alcove just beside the actors' playing area? Yes, he believed so. Someone was there; someone female, he presumed, as he caught the hint of skirts.

"We have no Miss Sands, sir," Romeo said. "Only the actors you see before you."

And that, of course, was a lie. Lindley had gotten very good at sniffing those out. True, Romeo and his aged Juliet were at center stage, while the three other actors just waiting at the side for their cues to enter were the only ones who had performed thus far, but Lindley had no doubt their young leader lied. Why, Lindley had no idea.

What he did understand, though, was that Fitzgelder hired a troupe that he expected to bring some actress named Sands. No Sands appeared and the troupe leader claimed he had no such person, yet someone was in the alcove wearing a skirt. This smelled of intrigue.

But whose? Clearly it was not a part of any plot Fitzgelder had. The grumbling bastard was most unhappy with the way things were going, that much was obvious to a blind man. Did Romeo have some plot of his own? Lindley had no clue.

But he knew how to find out.

Lindley slipped out of his seat. He hadn't been forced to attend several of Fitzgelder's disgusting Thursday entertainments and not managed to familiarize himself with every inch of the man's town house. He knew if he could leave the room undetected it would be a simple matter of wrapping around through the house to the rear. There he would find the musicians' entrance into that screened alcove.

If Fitzgelder was looking for an actress named Sands and that very woman was in this house hiding from him, then she was indeed someone Lindley would like to meet. Very much.

SOPHIE HID IN THE SCREENED ALCOVE AND LISTENED. The air in Mr. Fitzgelder's crowded salon was close and uncomfortable compared to the damp evening air she'd just come in from. How near she'd been to escaping this place! But things had not gone as planned and Miss Sands's father had sent her slinking back to warn the actress.

Sophie had crept in through the rear of the house and made her way down servants' passages. Certain she'd been undetected, she'd ducked into the alcove through the little doorway meant to be used by musicians. If she tiptoed close to the screen now, she could peer through to see Mr. Fitzgelder and the dozen or so inebriated guests who lounged on chairs facing the small area that had been designated the "stage." Stepping farther back against the wall, she could still be undetected by the audience yet see out around the screen and watch the performance.

It was an odd sensation, being there like that. How many times before had she stood in the wings, peering out onto a stage, watching in awe? Hundreds, she supposed.

Mamma had been an actress; lovely, graceful. Every audience who saw her throughout England was quickly enthralled. Papa had been dashing and handsome, charming everyone and bartering a dazzling wage wherever they might perform. Indeed, the theater had been a place of wonder and fascination for Sophie. It was with many tears and protests that she left it all those years ago when Mamma and Papa decided she ought to have a proper upbringing and sent her off to live with Grandmamma.

Life had begun a downward spiral after that. She sank back into the corner, leaned against the wall, and closed her eyes, shutting out the memories. There was no room in the present to pine for the past. Right now she needed to compose herself and think of a way to get her message to Miss Sands without being seen by Mr. Fitzgelder.

As her body began to calm from the exertion of her hurried return to this house, the irritation from those dratted pantalets became evident once again. She'd not had the chance to remove them. Well, Miss Sands was clearly occupied on stage just now, and it was rather private back here in the little alcove . . . Perhaps she might dare to finally rid herself of the things.

Carefully, she tucked herself as far back into the corner as possible and struggled to keep herself silent—and modest—while reaching up under her skirts to untie the strings at her waist that held up the pantalets. It was awkward, to say the least. And quite disconcerting, given the sounds of actors and audience only a sheer screen away.

She jumped involuntarily, slightly bumping into the screen, when Mr. Fitzgelder's voice boomed from his place in the front row of chairs. He had some very unpleasant things to say about Juliet. Sophie cringed as the horrid man ranted at the unendurable performance and demanded that Miss Sands be presented immediately. He seemed quite unwilling to hear any claims that she did not exist. Indeed, it appeared the girl's father had been correct not half an hour ago when he'd whispered in Sophie's ear that this must be a trap and that Fitzgelder was clearly expecting them. Miss Sands was in danger.

How foolish Sophie had been to involve herself in this! She knew what unpleasantness Mr. Fitzgelder might be capable of. If he had something against these actors, it would not go well for her to be found assisting them. Oh, but indeed it had been a mistake to come back here, even for the worthy cause of warning Miss Sands. She should steal up to her little garret, gather the few belongings she'd left there, and be gone once and for all. Better to be off on her own than to be in the middle of whatever this was.

Heart pounding, she increased her efforts with the pantalets.

The contrary strings were very nearly undone when Sophie's nervous fingers froze. She could hear Fitzgelder's feet pounding the salon floor—he was coming closer, approaching the stage, demanding to know where Miss Sands was. In only a moment he might come charging back behind the alcove to find her, instead. In his state, Sophie trembled to think what he might do.

But Miss Sands, in her new disguise as Mr. Clemmons, held things in control. Sophie heard the woman clear her throat and address Mr. Fitzgelder in a voice that was remarkably calm and almost not feminine. She announced that yes, their patron for the night was indeed correct and there truly had been a Miss Sands in the troupe.

"But she left," the actress-portraying-an-actor made clear. "She is gone."

"Gone?" Fitzgelder bellowed. "When?"

"Some time ago."

Mr. Fitzgelder was not satisfied. "How much time ago? A week? A day?"

"An hour, sir. She left an hour ago with one of our actors."

"Where were they going?"

"I don't know, sir. I only heard of their defection just as we were to begin performing."

Fitzgelder's voice had leveled to a moderate roar, but it was clear he was not entirely ready to believe this story. "Who did she leave with?"

"Er, Miss Sands left with one of our actors, sir."

"You told me that already! Who the devil is he? Where is he taking her?"

Miss Sands hesitated. Sophie held her breath. They hadn't planned on Mr. Fitzgelder wanting so very many details.

"Er, he's a Mr. Chair, sir," the actress said finally, making Sophie wince. Honestly, what sort of name was *Chair*? How could the woman expect their angry host to believe that?

"Mr. Chair?" Fitzgelder gawked. "Miss Sands ran away with Mr. Chair?"

"Er, Chair-ing-don-ton," Miss Sands amended with halting creativity. "George Chairingdonton, sir. I have no idea where they were going."

"Nearest place they could rent a bed is my guess," another voice interrupted. Sophie made out the voice of the older woman who'd been playing Juliet. "Miss Sands is just *that* sort of a person."

It would seem the woman was trying to help by distracting their host from the unlikelihood of there truly being a Mr. Chair-ing-don-whatever. Her methods, however, could not be entirely acceptable to Miss Sands. My, but what an insult to the poor actress! Still, it did seem to divert Mr. Fitzgelder from questioning the man's unusual name long enough for Miss Sands to continue supplying excuses.

"So, since that particular actress is miles away giving entertainment in parts unknown, why don't you just sit yourself back down, sir, and let us make you forget all about that little, er, tart? How about some acrobatics for you, sir?"

Sophie could hear Mr. Fitzgelder's protests, but the mention of an energetic show seemed to have struck a chord with the guests in the audience. The actors quickly joined Miss Sands in encouraging them, and before long Sophie could hear the sounds of furniture being arranged and props moved on the staging area. It would seem an acrobatic display was imminent and disaster had been avoided. The thumping and scuffling of actors tumbling all over themselves and Mr. Fitzgelder's guests cheering them on drowned out whatever protests Mr. Fitzgelder might have been uttering.

Sophie leaned forward just enough to peer around the screen and catch Miss Sands's eye. She hoped to signal her to make the most of things and get away while she still could. Miss Sands, unfortunately, didn't seem to get the hint. Or perhaps she hadn't actually seen it. Her eyes, Sophie realized, were not actually fixed on her but on a space behind her, toward the narrow door leading into the alcove.

Sophie could feel it suddenly, the chill that coursed down her spine. Someone was with her, there in the tiny space. She ought to turn to look but she truly did not want to. The hairs prickled at the back of her neck, and somehow she knew exactly who she would find. *Oh, dear.*

Knowing it could not be avoided, Sophie turned slowly to find the man propped in the narrow doorway, arms folded across his broad chest, violet blue eyes flashing a combination of amusement and ice.

Her quick intake of breath was just enough to loosen the ties on the almost-removed pantalets. They fell to the floor in a warm velvet pile, spilling out from under her skirt and displaying themselves to the world.

Lord Lindley's icy eyes went from her ashen face down to the wilted garment. He cocked his head, raised one brow, and brought his gaze back up to meet hers.

Then he smiled.

WELL, THIS WAS QUITE THE LAST THING LINDLEY EXpected. Sophie Darshaw? Undressing right here behind this screen, practically in public? He watched her, determined he must be mistaken. She couldn't really be hoisting her skirt, working to untie whatever undergarments she had there, could she? It appeared that she could.

And it appeared he was rather intrigued by the sight. He supposed he really ought to clear his throat or tap the door frame to alert her to his presence, but where would be the fun in that? Besides, it was his duty to investigate every remarkable activity going on here tonight, wasn't it? And the two delicate ankles exposed where Miss Darshaw's skirt was raised truly were remarkable.

But Lindley did not have to work to remain undetected by her. The girl, it seemed, was perfectly focused on the action beyond the screen. Keeping her bottom half carefully out of view, she was leaning dramatically forward, peering around the screen and trying to capture the eye of that popinjay Romeo. It made for an even more remarkable view from this side.

However, it didn't last long. Somehow she realized he was there. With something like horror in her eyes, Miss Darshaw turned slowly. Her efforts with the undergarments must have been successful. With the beguiling whisper of fabric against skin, her pantalets pooled on the floor, tantalizingly peeking out at him from under her skirt. By God, were they constructed of *velvet*?

Remarkable, indeed. Could it be he'd gone to all the trouble of rescuing her from Fitzgelder only to have her come down here and cast off her undergarments for a bloody teenaged actor? Infuriating.

Even more so when he reminded himself that finding her here proved her involvement in whatever secret assignation Fitzgelder had been attempting to arrange. She was heavily involved—and velvet clad, on top of it. At least, she had been. He tried to puzzle out how it all fit.

There was no doubt, however, that he'd interrupted more than a simple romantic rendezvous. The look on Miss Darshaw's face confirmed that. Any fool could see by her expression that she was terrified. Clearly she had much to hide and feared he had found it out. That had to mean only one thing—she knew he was more than merely another one of Fitzgelder's cronies.

This insignificant little slip had somehow discovered his ruse. She knew he was here to investigate, and she had things to hide. Damn, he tasted bitter disappointment. Apparently he'd hoped Sophie Darshaw was nothing more than she seemed: a simple little nobody who had left Madame Eudora merely to better herself and take employment anywhere that would distance her from the taint of the brothel. He'd fancied her an innocent, in fact.

Obviously he'd been wrong.

He should have suspected her from the start. All those times he'd tripped over her at Madame's, all those times he'd caught her glancing up at him through her thick lashes as she sat with her mending in the corner of Madame's boudoir, the blushing and deferring murmurs as he passed her in the hallways . . . This whole time he'd allowed himself to believe it was honest. What a simpleton he'd been. Merely because she'd reminded him of . . .

No, he had no use for sentiment. Miss Darshaw might have the face of an angel, but any fool would have known a girl with her background could amount to nothing good. He'd been absurd to think her better than any of the other sluts Eudora pandered in her home. No, he'd been worse than absurd. He'd endangered his goal.

While he'd been happily duped by Miss Darshaw's modest demeanor and appealing form, she'd likely been watching him all the time, perhaps even carrying information about him here to Fitzgelder or his bloody associates. Damn, but that riled. How many weeks had he wasted culturing this sham friendship only to find out now this little hussy may have been informing his enemies all along?

He should be ashamed of himself for letting a pretty face and those deep, dewy eyes deceive him so effortlessly. Hell, he ought to at least have been allowed to bed the chit for all that! Well, she'd soon enough learn how much he enjoyed being made the fool.

Her lips moved as their eyes met.

"Lord Lindley!" She let out a breathy little gasp, then quickly threw her hand over her mouth to quiet herself.

Indeed, it might have all been quite darling if he hadn't been so painfully aware that anyone in league with Fitzgelder was guilty of the man's sin. That—despite the girl's velvet underthings discarded on the floor—was all he needed to be firmly immune to her unarguable charms.

"What are you doing here?" he asked, keeping his voice low so it would not carry above the ridiculous hoots of Fitzgelder's drunken friends and the *hups* and *thuds* of those even more ridiculous acrobatic actors.

Miss Darshaw shook her head furiously, waving at him to be silent. So, whatever her reasons for hiding here she did not wish for them to become public just yet, did she? Indeed, it seemed she had good reason to avoid Fitzgelder. Was that a bruise Lindley detected? The girl's eye was slightly swollen.

So, she'd suffered at the man's hand and still she remained. He needed to find out exactly why. What was her purpose in this house, hiding back here? Was it at the behest of her despicable master, or someone else?

He supposed there was still the slightest chance she might possibly be in the dark regarding his own purpose here. Her expression and obvious nervousness around him made that improbable, but he decided wisdom would dictate that he use caution. There was no sense in giving her any more information than she already possessed. He would play this carefully, cautiously, and see what he could discern.

Besides, not only would a heavy-handed direct interrogation confirm any suspicions the girl might harbor regarding him, it would also be likely to yield little value. Fitzgelder's associates knew full well the pain they would face at their master's hand if they let slip any of his secrets. Vengeance-hungry though Lindley was, he knew he could never compete with Fitzgelder in that arena. Torture was not a skill the earl valued nor possessed. That was Fitzgelder's strength, not his.

Still, he was not without his resources. In fact, he could think of no better opportunity to make use of them, either. The smile that was so often mistaken for charm and wine-soaked amusement slid onto his face, and he took a careful step closer to Miss Darshaw. She was forced to remain where she was or risk exposing herself—and her undergarments—to those on the other side of the screen. She clearly did not want that, and the fear was most plainly displayed on her face. At least the girl's lovely expression gave every appearance of fear. Lindley was not quite ready to believe it.

"I didn't realize you had such an interest in the theatrical arts, Miss Darshaw," he said, careful to slur his words just the slightest bit.

"I don't!" she replied in a quaking, whispered voice that was delightfully enticing. "That is, only recently I do. Fascinating, aren't they?"

"The actors?" He shrugged. "I can think of far better ways to amuse myself, quite honestly. Unless, of course, that is exactly what you had in mind."

He smiled and nodded down toward her pantalets. She reddened but gave no other indication of acknowledging their existence. He'd always loved a challenge.

"Tell me, Miss Darshaw, which one of those actors in particular has been amusing you of late?"

"None, sir!"

She dropped her gaze. The slight tremble in her lip could only be legitimate. So, she was too young, too green to play this game well enough to survive against him long. Likely this was how she came to be useful to Fitzgelder, as well. Poor chit. In all likelihood she truly had once been the innocent, unaffected maiden he'd previously assumed her. But how long had she been corrupted?

"None, you say?" He moved yet closer to her. "Pity. But tell me, which one of them would you *like* to have amusing you? Clearly you were expecting someone."

He reached out his toe and ever so slightly kicked the hint of fabric at her feet. She cringed and bit her lip. It did little to stop the trembling but did much to Lindley's blood pressure.

"I was hoping to be alone, sir," she said quickly, staring at the floor.

"What? With all those healthy, energetic young actors out there? Surely not, Miss Darshaw. Surely one of them, at least, holds something special for you?"

"No! For certain, sir, I'm not even acquainted with them."

"Oh? Well, perhaps I can put in a good word on your behalf, then—especially were I to have some firsthand appreciation for your, er, goods."

He touched her then. It was a soft touch, just a finger laid against her cheek and trailing down to trace the edge of her jawline and along her ivory throat. He'd touched dozens of women this way. The energy that raced from her skin to his, however, was quite out of the ordinary. By God, prying information out of Miss Darshaw would be far more entertaining by miles than anything he'd done thus far at Fitzgelder's house.

Yet she went pale and shook his hand off almost violently. "No, sir! Truly you cannot!"

He was surprised to find that the furtive smile he gave her was, in fact, quite genuine. He moved even closer and deliberately let the warm breath he exhaled rustle the little tendril of blond hair that escaped her cap and hung at that graceful neck. The little throb of pulse at her throat assured him his actions were not ineffective. A delicious pink flush began to creep up from behind her bodice until it colored her pretty cheeks once again.

"I assure you, Miss Darshaw, I have more than a mere good word to put in on your behalf." He let his eyes convey the full meaning of his speech. "So perhaps if you might tell me what your involvement is with these actors—other than the obvious," he said, sending a quick glance down to the pantalets that she could certainly not misconstrue, "I might find a way to be, shall we say, of use to you."

She eyed him for a long moment. Hell, but there was a fire and a will behind those dewy blue eyes he had never expected to find. Lindley had to admit he was both fascinated and a bit disappointed to realize this slip of unimportant female might just perhaps be a bit more proof to his advances than he'd expected.

"I promise you, sir," she began, squaring her shoulders and meeting his gaze with a delightfully firm one of her own. Not the only part of Miss Darshaw that was delightfully firm, he suspected. "There is nothing you can ever say or do that will be of any use to me," she finished. "Ever."

Ah, but that smacked of further challenge. Damn, but he did want to take this up. So what if Miss Darshaw glared at him as if he were the very devil incarnate? He lifted his hand and boldly felt the golden lock of her unruly hair. It slid like fine silk between his fingers as his knuckles trailed a heated path over the delicate throat he would have so liked to allow himself to taste.

Her breath caught. So, he could be of no use to her, could he? *Silly girl.*

"Perhaps, my dear Miss Darshaw," he whispered so she alone could hear, "you simply do not know yet just what it is you need." He gave a meaningful pause before he continued. "I do."

Now he had her. He could see it, the defiance and willfulness in her eyes being clouded by something else. Yes, she was not impervious to a man's caress—to *his* caress. Deny it she might, but Miss Darshaw was well aware of her needs. With luck, he'd not only get the information he was seeking, but he might be able to show the chit a thing or two of his own needs before the night was out.

But first, it would seem, he needed to get his mind back on the business at hand. Not difficult to do just now, considering the petulant Romeo had just left his post presiding over the acrobatics and was now stalking into the alcove with blood in his eyes.

"Is this gentleman offending you?" he demanded in his overly affected little voice, puffing himself up to look impressive. He failed.

With such a young, feminine face it was obvious the lad was hardly out of his teens, if that. Little more than a boy, really. Yet quite ready to do battle for the pretty Miss Darshaw, it would seem.

Well, so was Lindley.

"Do I take it you already have a protector among these actors, Miss Darshaw?" he asked, barely deigning to acknowledge the younger man's presence.

"She does, sir!" Romeo replied, marching to her side.

Bother. It would hardly do to let himself get dragged into fisticuffs with this whelp. No, that would not serve his purposes nor get him any closer to finding out about Miss Darshaw's schemes or Fitzgelder's interest in that missing actress. Very well. He would play nice.

Lindley stepped away from the girl and cocked his head to stare at the young actor. Not much of a protector, that was for certain. Surely Miss Darshaw could have done better for herself. Hell, if things were not the way they were, perhaps even he himself might have considered taking her on. Certainly he could have set her up far better than any suckling actor ever could.

Not that he was interested in setting her up for anything other than divulging what she knew about Fitzgelder's plans. If the chit was involved with this puffed-up puppy, and if Fitzgelder had been expecting said puppy to show up with some actress named Sands, then clearly Lindley needed to figure out just what these actors were doing in this house. And what Miss Darshaw knew about the strangely absent Miss Sands.

But he'd not get that information just now, he could be certain of that. The young actor was far too guarded. He'd be better off to let things go for now. He'd bide his time and try his hand—both of them, perhaps—with Miss Darshaw a bit later. When he could find her alone.

For now he'd do well to get in the actor's good graces.

Swaying just enough to keep up appearances, Lindley smiled at the couple. He would be nothing more to them than just another one of Fitzgelder's drunken revelers, perhaps someone a smooth-faced lad such as this might even look up to. His interest in Miss Darshaw must be seen as nothing deeper than what anyone might expect. With a cockeyed leer, he studied her.

"I say, boy, you're a lucky one," he slurred, deciding on his new tack. "You could keep her all for yourself, I suppose, or you could make a fair profit from the sharing. Seems the sensible thing to do when you've got as fine a doxy as this one."

Romeo's mouth dropped open. "Share her? Are you suggesting men would *pay* me to, er, share her with them?"

Apparently the thought had not entered the young dolt's head. *Hell.* Lindley had certainly not meant to be the one to give it to him. He'd only hoped to flatter the boy and perhaps see what truly held the two together. Damn, but he hadn't meant to put Miss Darshaw up on the auction block here tonight. That would complicate things for certain.

And probably incite him into killing this infantile scoundrel.

"I merely meant to say—" Lindley began, kicking himself for his careless words.

But the actor didn't seem to care what he meant to say. Thankfully, he was chivalrously aghast at the thought of Lindley's suggestion. He held himself straight and glared. Lindley was positive he'd seen that exact posture at a recent cockfight. On the cock that survived.

"Absolutely not, sir!" the young man raged. "This is not some, some item to be bought and sold. Sophie is, er, she is my wife!"

Lindley must have misheard that. "Your *wife*?"

"Yes. We were married last week and have been keeping it secret so she wouldn't lose her position here. However, given how ill she's been treated, I'm convinced she should not remain another day in this house."

The young man stared defiantly at Lindley, as if he expected an argument. Lindley wasn't quite sure what he himself had expected, but surely not this. Miss Darshaw was *married*? Lindley shifted his gaze to her, requiring confirmation of such a far-fetched claim.

After all, how on earth could this be true? She'd spent the last four years working in a brothel, for heaven's sake! True, Madame claimed she was merely a seamstress there, yet she'd made it clear a time or two that if he was interested in the girl she'd be quite willing to arrange things for him—at a price. Due to the special circumstances of the situation, Lindley had declined. When Miss Darshaw left Madame Eudora to come here for Fitzgelder, it appeared perhaps he may have done better to accept. Hell, he should have accepted. Perhaps he'd have some inkling of a clue as to what was truly going on now.

Had the girl really managed to snag a husband? With a past as colored as hers, what would she have been willing to stoop to for the sake of making an honest woman of herself? Indeed, perhaps that was the prize Fitzgelder had used to entice her into his services. Perhaps this ridiculous actor was her reward for helping Fitzgelder continue evading justice.

Lindley was rather inclined to think that must be the case. Surely she could have no other reason to align herself with this . . . this man-child. He watched them closely. The smooth-cheeked actor glanced at his beloved as if for reassurance. Miss Darshaw responded by gazing up at him with those dewy eyes, rounded in concern. Her rosebud lips pursed in a luscious pout, and her thick, dark lashes fanned porcelain cheeks as she blinked up at her gallant protector. In that pitiful cap and faded apron, the girl was indeed the very picture of maidenly virtue. No human man could be immune. Had she but gazed up at her Romeo with those liquid eyes and whispered tender words in her sweet, whiskey-warm voice, Lindley was convinced the young man would have done practically anything for her. Even marry her.

And follow her wishes by aligning himself with a swine like Fitzgelder.

Yet things had not gone according to their plans. Fitzgelder was still howling about the missing actress. It sounded as if he would storm back here and confront the quaking Romeo about it, as a matter of fact. It was quite plain neither Miss Darshaw nor her husband was eager for that event.

"Hurry now, Sophie," the young man directed. "Go. We must leave. Now."

Miss Darshaw hesitated. "But, I came back to tell you that . . . er, we can't . . ."

Her protests trailed off and Lindley could only wonder what they meant. All he understood for certain was that clearly Miss Darshaw was afraid. Lindley could use that to his advantage.

Her husband again urged her to hurry and leave this place, but the girl seemed unable to comply. For just a moment she turned her blue-eyed gaze upon Lindley. He realized her feet were still tangled in the velvet pantalets. Quite a predicament she was in. Lindley smiled. He had no desire to move.

Romeo cleared his throat. "If you would let her pass, sir."

Something crashed on the other side of the screen and Miss Darshaw jumped. The revelers laughed, but Fitzgelder merely bellowed. Apparently the acrobatics had gone awry and things were getting worse. Romeo and his mistress appeared ready to panic.

"Let her pass, damn you!" the young man demanded.

But Miss Darshaw regained her composure and laid one small hand on her husband's soft arm.

"Dearest, this is Lord Lindley," she began. Her careful tone indicated a reminder for her husband to keep his place when speaking to his better. It appeared to have little effect. The actor didn't seem to realize he had any betters.

"I don't care who the man is. I know all about his type." The scowling actor glanced up at Lindley as if he were contemplating an insect. "If you would be so kind, allow my wife to pass. My lord." The last came out more as an insult than a tribute to Lindley's station.

Well, the pup certainly had nerve. He'd not last a moment should Lindley decide to seriously take him on, but of course he wouldn't. A confrontation here would only draw Fitzgelder's attention and make things far more difficult than they already were. Lindley would be farther from gaining any useful information, and Miss Darshaw would perhaps be placed in an even more uncomfortable position. He stepped aside and wondered what she would do about the pantalets.

Nothing, it appeared. Somehow she must have quietly extricated her feet from them. With one last glance up at her husband, Miss Darshaw darted past and out the narrow doorway. The pantalets were left in an enticing heap. Romeo was too busy glaring at Lindley to notice.

Lindley found the whole thing enormously amusing. His gaze followed as Miss Darshaw disappeared into the servants' corridor, her careful footsteps silent as she fled. That left Romeo alone to glower hatred at Lindley, but this was short-lived. The pup's jealously was interrupted by Fitzgelder, storming into the alcove and fuming at the actor. He came up short, perplexed by Lindley's presence.

Lindley figured he'd best explain himself quickly lest Fitzgelder get the wrong idea about his curious prowling, which might, in fact, be dangerously close to the right idea.

"Heard you roaring there was supposed to be an actress here," Lindley explained with a wandering leer and a half-hearted shrug. "Thought I'd nip back here and take first crack at her."

Fitzgelder frowned. "And?"

"Didn't find her. It's just as this fellow said; seems she's long gone. In faith, old man, this entertainment is a bust! Not a pleasing wench within sight."

"No, it would appear not," Fitzgelder reluctantly admitted. He glared at Romeo.

The young man visibly shuddered. "I'm sorry, sir. She always was a most headstrong actress."

Fitzgelder sneered. "Manipulating little whore, more like it."

Romeo stiffened but kept quiet. So he was offended by his patron's words, was he? Odd, considering the little troupe master would likely have much to lose by his actress's abandonment. Lindley might have expected the young man to be first up to lay criticism at the woman's door.

Another crash and the ridiculing laughter of Fitzgelder's guests erupted outside the screen. Fitzgelder snarled at Romeo. "Don't imagine you'll be getting paid for this debacle."

Romeo dropped his gaze and nodded.

"Get out of here," Fitzgelder ordered. "Take your damn horrid actors and get the hell out of my house."

With a disgusted shake of his greasy head, Fitzgelder left the little alcove and stormed back into the salon, reviling the actors and advising his guests to call for their carriages. It appeared they would all be quitting his home and heading for greater enjoyments elsewhere. Romeo gave out a sigh of relief and swallowed back what Lindley supposed was a lump of fear. Not that he actually took note of any lump in the young man's smooth, graceful neck.

The actor gave him one last, suspicious look, then scurried out to roust his troupe into gathering their few things in preparation for a hasty retreat. Lindley watched until he was out of view, his unusual gait suddenly making sense. An amused smile slid over half of Lindley's face.

Indeed, Fitzgelder was a fool. This Romeo was no lovestruck lad. He was, however, a damn fine actress. Which meant, of course, that Miss Darshaw was still quite unmarried but completely involved in some dangerous intrigue.

And that, of course, meant Lindley had good reason to go hunt her down. He scooped up the velvet pantalets—still warm, though he tried to ignore that tantalizing fact—and let himself out into the servants' corridor.

Chapter Three

Sophie held back a sneeze and buried herself deeper behind the thick drapery. She could hear Fitzgelder ordering people about back in the large salon. Clearly the actors were done for the evening. She listened—sure enough, footsteps approached.

Lord Lindley. She feared he might come this way, following her. That was why she'd tucked herself neatly behind the drapes. With luck, the sneeze would not present itself just now and Lindley would go away before detecting her. Heaven only knew what he might do if he found her here.

Had he believed Miss Sands's wild story of them being husband and wife? He'd seemed to; he gave no overt sign of doubting. Not really, at any rate. For a few moments there she'd thought she'd seen suspicion in his eyes, but in the end it appeared he believed. Still, that could have done nothing to increase his esteem for her. He knew where she had come from.

They'd met at Madame Eudora's more than once. Not that he'd ever given indication she had any cause to fear him, but she'd felt his eyes on her when they passed in the hallway or when she'd been sewing in Madame's chamber and he'd come to visit. Thankfully all he and Madame appeared to do was engage in polite and friendly conversation, but she'd blushed and shuddered at thoughts of the man's obvious purpose in the house. She never learned whom he favored among the ladies, but he seemed to appear often. And there was but one reason for that at Madame Eudora's.

Every now and then Madame asked Sophie if she might be interested in meeting some of the establishment's regular clients on a more intimate basis, but Sophie had always firmly declined. She begged to be allowed to earn her keep by simply mending and stitching and tending to Madame's unconventional costume requests. Madame assured her their arrangement was fine, yet she informed Sophie that certain gentlemen had asked after her and that a seamstress could never do so well as a sought-after courtesan.

Sophie had almost been tempted to ask if Lord Lindley could be one of those "certain gentlemen" who might have asked after her. She hoped to heavens her resolve to remain a seamstress alone would not have wavered had she found out he was. She still was not sure that it would have.

Not that her resolve would have mattered much either way to Lord Lindley. After facing his smoldering gaze tonight, she knew he was the sort of man who always got what he wanted. Even drunk he exuded a force too strong to be denied. Heaven help her if he ever did take an interest in her beyond a momentary curiosity. She doubted she would defend herself against him with the same vigor she had shown her employer.

She could hear him. He paused in the tight hallway, standing very near the hangings where she huddled. Oh, but she prayed he might not notice the drapery shaking as a prickling chill tore through her body. It was as if she could almost sense the heat coming off him, feel his deep blue eyes studying her, seeing her even through the thick fabric. She shuddered again and held her breath, willing that blasted sneeze to dissipate.

Then he was moving again. His footsteps sounded on the flooring. Thank heavens, they were moving away. She struggled to calm her pounding heart until she was certain the confident cadence of those footsteps signified he was leaving to continue his search for entertainment elsewhere. They had long echoed off into another part of the house before she dared draw a safe breath and peer out.

Indeed, he was gone and she appeared quite alone. *Thank God.* The sneeze erupted in a half-muffled squawk. Terrified, she scanned the corridor. No one appeared.

Creeping back to the narrow doorway that provided entrance to the screened alcove, she carefully peered in. Was Mr. Fitzgelder gone now, too? Or was he still commanding the actors as they prepared to depart?

Listening, she found his voice at the far end of the salon. He was laughing with his guests, directing servants as they arranged to put everyone back into their proper conveyances to head off for more amusing venues. *Good.* One could only hope they would all soon be gone—those horrible, leering guests, Mr. Fitzgelder, *and* his perplexing friend Lindley.

The voices trailed out of the salon at the opposite end, and before long she could tell only the actors remained, scuffing and grumbling to themselves as they gathered their things. Sophie stepped into the alcove. She went to retrieve her pantalets but was shocked to find they'd disappeared. Heavens, had Lord Lindley taken them? Or worse, had Mr. Fitzgelder found them?

She rubbed her forehead, wondering if she should worry over this or simply be glad to be rid of the damn things. A sound from the actors nearby caught Sophie's attention, and she glanced around the screen and caught Miss Sands's eye. The actress, her mustache decidedly lopsided now, scurried into the alcove to meet her.

"What is wrong? Why are you not gone with my father?" she asked in hushed tones.

"He sent me back," Sophie explained quickly. "He said I must warn you! It was a trap. We were followed by two men; two of Mr. Fitzgelder's men. He must have been expecting you and laid out a trap!"

Miss Sands was nearly frantic. "And Papa? Did they get him?"

"No, he is safe," Sophie was glad to reassure her. "He is clever, your father. He knew how to escape. But when we were safe he begged me to come back to warn you. He feared your disguise would not be enough to protect you. I'm happy to see that it did."

"Only just." The actress sighed. "Where was my father going? Where are we to find him?"

"He said it was too dangerous for you to come to him here in London," Sophie began, hoping she'd remembered all the details correctly despite all she'd been through this awful evening. "He said you should gather the other actors and then go to meet him in Gloucester. He said you would know how to find him there."

Miss Sands bit her lip, but she didn't seem as confused by it all as Sophie felt. What on earth could Mr. Fitzgelder possibly have against these people? Would they be safe from him even now?

"All right," Miss Sands declared, fixing her mustache. "We'll leave for Gloucester. And you, Miss Darshaw, will be coming with us."

This caught Sophie off guard. "To Gloucester?"

"You certainly can't stay here. Have you anywhere else in London to go?"

"No. I haven't."

That, at least, was certain. Even if she could bring herself to go back to Madame, which she could not, she didn't dare for fear of encountering Fitzgelder. Or Lindley. Gloucester seemed as good a place as any to begin her life anew.

"Then you'll come with us. We have our wagons outside. Have you any belongings you need to retrieve?"

"Yes, miss. Up in the garret, where I sleep."

"Fine. Let's finish up here and we'll go get them."

For the first time in years, Sophie found herself wondering if perhaps things around her were starting to get just a bit brighter.

"IT'S RATHER DARK IN HERE," MISS SANDS WHISPERED as Sophie led them slowly down from the servants' quarters, her little bundle of belongings tucked close against her chest.

"That's because the master is out," Sophie replied. "Mrs. Harwell knows better than to waste candles when Mr. Fitzgelder does not need them."

"Seems he might have a care whether or not his staff breaks a leg tending their duties in the pitch black like this."

Sophie just snorted. "I'd hardly say this could be called tending to duties. Heavens, but Mrs. Harwell would throttle me if she found us sneaking away like this! The other girls will surely get their ears boxed if they don't tend to all their work plus mine until a replacement is found."

"That's not your concern," Miss Sands assured her. "Now show the way out. I don't like being here one more minute than I have to. Look, there's a light up that corridor. What is that?"

"That would be Mr. Fitzgelder's study. He must have left it burning when he went with his friends. I'll go take care of it."

Miss Sands grabbed her arm. "You certainly will not! We're leaving. Let it be."

"But someone will be reprimanded for it!"

"Then they should not have neglected to put it out, should they? Show us the door."

It hardly seemed fair to let someone suffer Mrs. Harwell's wrath when it was but a few steps and a simple matter for Sophie to tend to the forgotten lamp. Ignoring Miss Sands's plea, she moved into the corridor and was just feet from reaching the study when she felt her companion's hand clench around her elbow. At the same time, Sophie heard voices in the lighted room. One voice in particular she recognized.

"Damn!" the actress swore beside her, pulling Sophie back against the wall. The voices were accompanied by footsteps—large, male footsteps. And these males were moving in the study as if preparing to leave it. "What do we do? Where can we go?"

Sophie paused just long enough to gather her wits, then dove across the hall and into an open doorway. She dragged Miss Sands with her. Drat, why had she ignored the young woman's warning? She should have taken them straight out to the street when she'd had the chance.

So Mr. Fitzgelder had not gone when all his guests departed, had he? No, he had stayed behind for some reason. That was his voice in the study, Sophie was sure of it. Oh, but if they should be found out here . . . How dreadful! Clearly they had to hide.

But where? There was nothing to hide them in this small room, just a narrow cabinet with some ugly, half-wilted floral arrangement in a gaudy vase. Obviously Mr. Fitzgelder did not spend much time in this room. Hopefully that was a good thing and meant he and his friend would not bother to come in for any reason. Perhaps if Sophie and Miss Sands stayed very quiet they would be safe until the men went elsewhere. Oh, she prayed that would be the case.

"And you just let them go, just like that," Mr. Fitzgelder was complaining. They could hear him quite clearly from where they crouched behind the cabinet.

"I'm sorry, sir," another voice replied. This one Sophie did not recognize. "I don't know how it happened. We was following them real close. That old man moved awfully quick, he did."

"And the actress? Did you see her?"

"Aye, right pretty young thing, just as you said."

"So where did she go?" Fitzgelder demanded. "I told you not to let her get away!"

"I'm sorry, Mr. Fitzgelder, sir. Somehow they just lost us on the streets."

Now a third man spoke up. This one Sophie recognized from earlier. These must be the men who had chased them and very nearly caught them! Their voices were quite near now, probably just inside the study doorway. Sophie sank down even lower and tucked her knees up under her chin.

"Sir, we'll go back out and find them if you like. They can't have just disappeared."

"No, they can't," Mr. Fitzgelder agreed. "And I'll find them, damn it, I will. But for now, I've got something else I need you to do."

Miss Sands leaned in close to Sophie's ear. "Are those the men who were after you and Papa?"

Sophie nodded. There was just light enough from the candle glow spilling in through the open doorway that she knew the actress could see. Not that it mattered. From what the men said, things were pretty obvious. Miss Sands's father had been right; Mr. Fitzgelder had been expecting them, and not to simply invite them for tea.

"So," the first man said, "you still want us to take care of that other little problem for you?"

"Yes. You'll have to leave now to be sure to meet him along the road. And remember . . ." Mr. Fitzgelder's voice nearly sizzled with hatred. "If you botch this and anyone gets wind of my involvement, I'll personally pry your bollocks off and stuff them down your lifeless throats."

The men were understandably silent, and Sophie managed to catch Miss Sands's wide eyes. The actress shrugged.

"I don't care how you do it," Mr. Fitzgelder continued, "but I must remain out of it. Make it an accident on the highway, a tumble off a high building, or a run-in with a jealous husband. I don't care. When he's dead and no one comes 'round asking me any questions, you get your money. Got it?"

Good God! Sophie could hardly take this to mean anything other than the obvious. The two men who had been following them earlier had just been instructed by Mr. Fitzgelder to go commit murder! What in the world had she gotten herself into?

"Aye, we got it, sir," one of the men assured. "I can make it an accident, all right, but are you sure you want this? It's rather permanent, you know."

"Hell, it had better be permanent," Mr. Fitzgelder snarled. "My cousin isn't worth the paper his damn patent comes written on."

Miss Sands drew a sudden sharp breath. Sophie slid another glance her way. The woman's face was distinctly pale in the dim light here behind this cabinet. Sophie could well understand how she felt. She did, however, wish that the actress was not digging her fingernails so sharply into her shoulder where her hand had been resting.

"Well, he won't be enjoying that lofty title much longer now, will he?" One of the murderers chuckled.

Mr. Fitzgelder concurred. "He'd better not. Here, can you read?"

There was the sound of papers shuffling. "I can, some. What's this?"

"It'll give you directions to meet up with him," Fitzgelder explained. "Now I've already helped you by getting things in motion. My cousin's off at some bloody wedding north of Warwick, but very soon I expect he'll head for home. I've made things, shall we say, difficult for his darling mother and simpering little sister. He'll no doubt feel the need to come rushing back to them here. That will be your chance. Get him while he's on the road from Warwick; that's the easiest."

"Shot by highwaymen?"

"Whatever. Just do it. The only way I want Anthony Rastmoor returned to his family is as a corpse."

Miss Sands let out a squeak. Yes, it was indeed disturbing to hear the man speak such horrors, but really, did the actress have to turn to absolute jelly over it? She'd seemed far more formidable than that. Just now it was of the utmost importance they maintain their silent composure. Perhaps the woman needed comforting. Sophie shifted her hand to reach up and touch the actress's, which was still exerting quite a good deal of pressure on her poor shoulder.

It was an unwise move. The bundle of her belongings that she had clutched to her shifted and slipped out of her grasp. It thumped to the floor. The precious scissors she had carefully wrapped inside slipped out and clanged against the cabinet. Instinctively her hand shot out to rescue them, but it could not be done without noise. Too late she realized the voices outside had stopped.

"What the devil was that?" Mr. Fitzgelder growled.

Sophie desperately scanned the little room they'd been hiding in for any way of escape. What she saw made her draw her breath and utter a squeak very reminiscent of Miss Sands's. The distinctive dark form of a man appeared in the far corner of the room and moved suddenly toward them.

Before she could so much as draw breath to scream, light from the corridor fell onto his face. *Lord Lindley.*

He'd been hiding in here with them all along? *Good heavens!* They'd been discovered right from the start! And now he would inform his awful friend.

Yet his eyes met hers and he put one finger to his lips. He stepped past them and into the doorway just as footsteps approached from the corridor. Mr. Fitzgelder and his henchmen were coming!

"Lindley!" Fitzgelder exclaimed. "By God, what are you doing in there?"

Lord Lindley stood in the doorway, securely blocking the view of anyone who might try to peer into the small room. Sophie didn't take much chance, though. She and Miss Sands cowered in the shadows, barely breathing.

Lindley gave a grunt and readjusted his clothing. "I availed myself of one of your little housemaids, old man. Quite accommodating, she was."

Sophie could hear the shifting footsteps. Mr. Fitzgelder was trying to look into the room!

But Lindley just laughed. "Sorry, she's been gone these last minutes. Sent her on her way so I could put things back in order, so to speak. How about you? Got all your business tended to?"

"It will be soon enough, I anticipate," Mr. Fitzgelder said. "My friends here will see to it."

"Ah, good thing. I say a man needs friends he can trust to take care of things for him. Good work there, men."

Did Lord Lindley have a clue at all what he was complimenting here? Could it be he was a party to it? Either way, it was clear Mr. Fitzgelder trusted Lindley and was comfortable with whatever he may have overheard. That in itself spoke guilt for the earl. Oh, how could she have ever thought him anything less than pure evil? He was everything Fitzgelder was and worse, because he was so casual about it.

"All right then, be off with you," Fitzgelder said, presumably to the criminals he'd just been commissioning. "You've got your directions. Now don't disappoint me!"

The men mumbled their assurances, and their footsteps sounded in the corridor as they left to carry out their deadly orders. It was dreadful, knowing that someone would soon perish at their hands. If only there was something she and Miss Sands could do; but of course there was nothing. They'd be lucky to leave here alive themselves, as a matter of fact.

"So, are we off to join the others for some revelry? Where is it we are headed next, old man?" Lindley asked his friend when they were alone.

"Haven't you had enough sport for the night?" Fitzgelder scoffed.

"Hardly! That little maid I found was barely amusing. Honestly, I don't know what you saw in her this afternoon."

"What? You shagged my little seamstress?"

Sophie was quite sure her gulp had been audible to anyone in this half of the house. What on earth was his lordship saying?

"Is that what she is? Well, let's hope she sews with more than a halfhearted effort. Lord, quite enough to bore a man."

Ooo, how dare he! It was bad enough he was accusing her of engaging in illicit intimacies, but he was insinuating that she was not at all good at it! Most insulting and very uncalled for.

"Damn the little minx. She's been denying me since I brought her here!" Fitzgelder grumbled.

"Well, maybe that's the trouble then. She's worn herself out playing hard to get with you, so she had nothing left for me."

"Hell. If you wouldn't have barged in on us up there earlier I . . . Say, you didn't by any chance notice whether the little slut was wearing a rather fine piece of jewelry, did you?"

"What? No, I didn't see any jewelry. Can't say I was particularly looking for any, if you know what I mean. Why?"

"Damn chit stole from me, that's all. No matter. I'll get it back. I'll find her."

"That's right. Let her rest up a bit for you, eh? So come, there are plenty more rabbits to be snared, Fitz. Let's go set up some traps."

Fitzgelder muttered a string of uncommonly harsh profanity, yet Lindley did nothing but laugh over it. Still, he never gave a hint that Sophie and Miss Sands were hiding in this very room. In fact, his good-natured insistence that he and Fitzgelder go trolling for entertainment and pleasure elsewhere must have successfully swayed Fitzgelder into agreement.

"Hell, I deserve a night out after all this," Fitzgelder remarked.

"Indeed you do," Lindley encouraged. "As I always say, when the time is right, one must disappear into the night."

"You always say that, do you?"

"Oh, yes. Quite frequently."

"Well, I've never heard you say it."

"There are a great many things you've not heard from me, my friend," Lindley remarked. "Perhaps someday you will."

With that Fitzgelder grunted but allowed that a night out was in order. Nonchalant and as innocent as babes, the two men seemed in high spirits as they set off. It was not at all as if one had just boasted of rape and the other plotted murder only moments ago. *Vile, terrible creatures.* Sophie did not even want to know where they were going, just that they were gone.

What on earth had Mr. Fitzgelder been saying about some jewelry? He claimed she had stolen it from him? Why, that was ludicrous. She'd never stolen in her life, and certainly not from an ogre like Fitzgelder. Why, he'd likely kill anyone who stole from him! Heavens, did he truly believe she had? This was dreadful.

The women huddled silently until the last footstep faded away. Were the men gone? Sophie listened. The house was quiet around them.

"I can't let it happen," Miss Sands whispered softly.

"Can't let what happen?" Sophie barely breathed in question.

"Rastmoor," the actress said quickly, creeping out from behind the cabinet. "I've got to go warn him."

"Who on earth is Rastmoor?"

"Fitzgelder's cousin; the man he plans to have murdered!"

"Oh, but Miss Sands! You certainly can't mean to involve yourself in this business!"

"I've been involved for years. Now come out. Your friend Lindley was right; this is the perfect opportunity to disappear into the night."

Sophie frowned. What on earth was Miss Sands getting them into? The woman would be dead wrong if she thought she could prevent what Mr. Fitzgelder had planned. And indeed, she was wrong about Lord Lindley, too.

True, the time could very well be right to disappear into the night, but Sophie would *never* think of that man as her friend. All he would ever be to her was a liar and a very poor poet. And the man who likely stole her most expensive pantalets.

DAMN, BUT HE WISHED FITZGELDER WAS DRUNK. THE man was so much easier to control when he was well into his cups. For now though, at least, he had him out of the house. With luck, Miss Darshaw would heed his warning and take herself away from there while she had the chance. With even more luck, she wouldn't entirely disappear. He should very much like to find her again, for various reasons.

Just now, though, Lindley had his hands full enough. He led Fitzgelder to the carriage he'd arranged for him. Pray to God Eudora was holding up her end of things and was already inside it.

She was. The still-stunning Madame smiled coyly when Lindley pulled open the door and peered inside. Even in the dark of night her creamy complexion and dazzling teeth glowed. The evocative scent of exotic perfume tinted the air around her. It was a temptation Fitzgelder surely could not resist.

"I say, Fitz! Look who's come 'round to visit," Lindley said, as if surprised at finding her there.

"I heard things were getting a bit dull for our lively Mr. Fitzgelder," she cooed in that warm, sultry voice she'd long ago perfected. "I was hoping I could help out."

Fitzgelder's shameless gawking and the leering anticipation in his eyes announced plainly that he was convinced she might be able to do just that. "I do believe this night might not prove a total waste, after all. Good evening to you, Eudora."

He climbed into the carriage and situated himself beside the alluring woman. Then he motioned for Lindley to join them on the bench opposite.

"Come, Lindley. Madame can surely make room for both of us." Then he laughed at what, apparently, he thought was a most humorous double entendre. "Though not at the same time, I daresay! Although I bargain we could both work at parts of her together. What do you say? The three of us, old man?"

Never in a million years! "Not tonight, I'm afraid. I'll meet you at the house."

Fitzgelder laughed again. "Need time to recuperate from that little seamstress, I take it?"

Lindley cringed. Eudora's eyes went just the slightest bit rounder. "Seamstress?"

"That little doxy I took from your place," Fitzgelder explained. *Damn him.* "She's been running me a merry chase, too. Somehow Lindley got her alone tonight. Bloodied my lip, the bitch did, but it would seem Lindley's got a better way with females like that."

"Yes, I've noticed he does have an eye for seamstresses," Eudora said.

"My carriage is waiting," Lindley said, ignoring Madame's comment. "I'm sure you won't miss my company at all."

Fitzgelder laughed. This was all just a game for him, wasn't it? Others might suffer—hell, he'd pegged his own cousin for murder—but yet Fitzgelder could laugh. No vengeance could come swift enough, as far as Lindley was concerned.

Still, he had to be patient. Eudora would help. She knew how to keep the man occupied tonight, although it pained Lindley to think to what ends she might have to go. Best not to think of that, he decided. Besides, no one forced Eudora to do what she did not wish—though it did seem the woman wished quite a bit.

Lindley, however, did not. Justice would be the only thing on his mind when he made his appearance at the house where Fitzgelder's revels would continue tonight. And no one would even notice that Lindley chose not to participate in the sordid events in Madame's exclusive rooms. He would have ample time to arrange things as needed to suit his own purposes.

Wishing Fitzgelder had at least waited for Lindley to shut the carriage door before he pounced on Eudora, the earl was finally rid of the man. The carriage clattered off and Lindley made his way back to his own carriage that waited nearby. His man Feasel stood beside it.

"Do we follow, milord?"

"No. I've got something else for you, Feasel."

"Anything."

"A young couple should be coming from the house at any moment. They will be trying not to be seen. I need you to follow the girl—the one in the dress, that is—at all costs. You'll recognize her. It's Miss Darshaw."

His man nodded. "Ah, so she's finally leaving this place, is she?"

"Yes. Report back where she goes, who she meets."

"And the young man?"

Feasel didn't even bat an eye when Lindley explained.

"The man is a woman; an actress. Any information on her would be helpful, as well."

"Mind if I take Tom?"

"By all means. Whatever you need," Lindley replied, then made sure to meet his servant's eye. "This one's important, Feasel."

"They all are, sir."

"Yes, but this is more so. If Miss Darshaw does not come out of this house, find some excuse to get her out. She cannot be here when Fitzgelder returns. Things have gotten too risky."

"I'll take care of it, sir."

That was enough. He knew his man wouldn't let him down. Lindley nodded and climbed up inside his phaeton. He heard Feasel give one sharp call and Tom hopped off his post on the back of the carriage. The boy was a good help. It had not been easy finding servants he could trust to carry out his clandestine efforts, but Feasel and his son, Tom, had proven invaluable. They'd follow Miss Darshaw. She might think she was disappearing into the night, but Feasel would find her.

And then he would report to Lindley what she was about. She'd not seen the last of him, no indeed. Lindley would find Miss Darshaw at some point and the girl would tell him all and would enjoy doing it, too. He knew ways to make women talk. Rather pleasant ways. And despite the lies he'd told Fitzgelder just moments ago, Lindley suspected she'd be more than competent.

But first things first. Not only did he have the rest of tonight to endure, he had a wedding in Warwick to attend. He'd best leave first thing in the morning for that. Fitzgelder's men were already on their way to lay the trap. In less than two days' time Rastmoor would be returning on the very road where those killers awaited him. Lindley would have to get there first and convince Rastmoor that London could wait. It could be the only way to prevent Lord Anthony Rastmoor from being murdered by his own cousin.

Lindley's anticipated meeting with Miss Darshaw would simply have to wait. He could certainly use his time to plan an attack, however. Indeed, he would contemplate long and hard the many things he might do to encourage the girl to talk. Among other things.

Chapter Four

Sophie was too tired to even speak. They'd managed to get away from Mr. Fitzgelder's house, but the night had been long and nerve-wracking. Sophie simply could not get over the feeling someone was following them, lurking in every shadow around them, though of course it could not be. Miss Sands promised her they were quite safe, taking refuge in the storeroom of a shop belonging to a couple who she claimed were friends of the family.

Unfortunately, these friends had gone home for the night. Miss Sands and Sophie were trespassing. It was a most dreadful, anxious feeling.

But even worse was the feeling Sophie had when she pulled her aching foot up onto her lap to rub it. Something fell from the pocket of her apron. Something metal. Something shiny. Something very much like the locket she had seen Mr. Fitzgelder holding when she mistakenly walked in on him in the linen cupboard that evening.

"What's that?" Miss Sands asked, seated on a box of potatoes and trying in vain to yank off her left boot.

"Mr. Fitzgelder's locket!"

"What? His locket? By heavens, you *did* steal jewelry from him!"

Sophie grabbed up the glinting object and balled it into her fist. "No! I swear, Miss Sands, I don't know how it came to be here."

Her companion merely laughed at her panic. "I'm not condemning you, Sophie. I think it's marvelous, actually. Serves the ogre right."

"But it's true, on my mother's grave! I didn't take it. It must have fallen into my apron on accident when he . . . when we had a disagreement."

"When the rutting brute blackened your eye, you mean."

Sophie couldn't help but put her hand to the place. It was still tender. "I must look a sight."

"It's fading," Miss Sands assured her. "Clearly he's inept even at abusing women. But now that you've taken his locket—"

"I didn't take it!"

"Now that you've *ended up* with his locket," Miss Sands corrected, "you'd best be extra careful that he doesn't find you. I doubt he'll be so understanding."

Sophie shuddered. "Locket or no, I have little intention of letting him find me. He's a murderer!"

Miss Sands scowled, her boot finally sliding off her foot. "Not yet, let us hope."

"You truly believe we can get there in time to warn your friend, this Mr. Rastmoor?"

Miss Sands rather grunted. "He's hardly my friend, nor is he a mister. He's a highborn lord."

"Oh! Heavens, do you think he knows Lord Lindley?"

"Likely. They do seem to run in packs, these worthless noblemen."

"Still, you don't want Lord Rastmoor to die."

Now Miss Sands sighed. "No, I don't."

"And you are certain you know where he is? Where this wedding is being held?"

Miss Sands nodded. "Yes, I'm quite certain. He has a close friend just north of Warwick, and I read that gentleman is about to be married. Rastmoor will be there."

"I hope you're right, and that we get there in time."

"You mean you hope that *I'll* get there in time."

"No, I'm going with you."

"I can't ask you to do that, Sophie."

"You've made that very clear, Miss Sands. But you helped me escape Mr. Fitzgelder. I owe you what little assistance I can give. Besides, you offered me a position with your father's troupe. If I let you go on and get yourself killed, how will I ever locate your father again? I'll starve with no honest living."

She hoped Miss Sands would not take offense, and she didn't. She smiled.

"Well, then, I suggest you find someplace to curl up and get a couple hours of sleep. Lord knows we must have walked clear across town tonight, and we'll undoubtedly have a goodly walk tomorrow to catch the mail coach. I hope Mr. Fitzgelder isn't hunting for us in this neighborhood. I hope he will assume we've gone to the theater district."

"Even *I* don't know precisely where we've gone," Sophie admitted, stifling a yawn.

"Good. Perhaps Fitzgelder doesn't either."

It was very late, indeed, and her whole body ached from nerves and more than an hour of walking, on alert at every step to avoid anyone. Every approaching carriage could have carried one of Mr. Fitzgelder's men. Every creaking door or skittering rat could mean the approach of danger. Sophie was simply worn-out. It would be heavenly to curl up and rest, as Miss Sands suggested.

She found a clear spot in a corner and pulled up a rug to lay out on the hard floor. It wasn't comfortable, exactly, but as tired as she was, it would do. Miss Sands seemed to be quite content with the spot she had made for herself on those potatoes. Not Sophie's first choice, but each to her own, she decided.

"I'll stay awake and watch for any sign of trouble," her friend announced.

"But you must be every bit as worn-out as I am!"

The woman shook her chestnut head. "No, I haven't been working as a housemaid for a monster. There is no question you must be the exhausted one."

"Seamstress," Sophie said against another yawn.

"What?"

"I'm actually a seamstress. I only worked for Mr. Fitzgelder because his house is on such a fine street. I hoped I might meet the sorts of respectable people who could help me work my way into a proper shop, or something."

Miss Sands nearly snorted. It seemed ridiculous to Sophie now, too. She'd gone to Mr. Fitzgelder in hopes of meeting respectable people? How foolish.

"Well, Papa and I may not be the upper ten thousand, but we'll treat you a damn sight better than Fitzgelder has. Here. You can use this."

Sophie caught the blanket Miss Sands tossed to her. It was rough, but it was warm and showed no signs of vermin.

"What will you use?"

Miss Sands simply leaned against her potato box and pulled up the bolt of burlap that had been lying at her feet. "See? We'll both be snug and warm."

"All right. I'll keep the blanket then."

"Good. Now get some rest so you're not cranky in the morning."

Sophie did her best to get comfortable on her rug with her rough blanket. "I will. And thank you, Miss Sands."

The dark storeroom was quiet. The sounds of the town around them were distant, muffled. The occasional dog barked here or there, and somewhere on the next street a carriage clattered slowly along. For the first time all night Sophie thought perhaps Miss Sands was right. They might possibly be safe here.

"No, not Sands," the young woman spoke, interrupting the silence.

Sophie started. "What?"

"My name isn't Sands."

"It isn't?"

"No. I've been using that name for a while now, avoiding Fitzgelder."

"Oh. What is your name?"

There was a pause before she answered. "Julia St. Clement."

"That's very pretty."

"I miss it. But, I'd miss a whole lot more if Fitzgelder ever found us out. So, Papa and I use assumed names and try to avoid London. It was just by chance we were passing through this week. We shouldn't have."

"Yes, but I'm rather glad you did. And I'm sure your friend will be, too, once you've saved his life and everything."

Miss Sands . . . er, rather . . . Miss St. Clement actually laughed out loud for that. "Well, I suppose we'll see about that, won't we?"

Sophie recognized that as rhetorical, so she didn't bother with a response. Yawning was just about all she could do at this point, anyway.

"Thank you for telling me your real name, Miss St. Clement," she said as her eyelids drooped.

"Yes, but we need to remember it's Clemmons now. We'll be traveling under that name, both of us. You can still be Sophie, but I'll be Alexander."

Sophie shifted to lie on her side and tucked her hands up under her cheek. She realized she still clutched the troublesome locket. Bother, what a mess things had become.

"So much fuss and fabrication," she said with a weary sigh. "I wonder how you can keep it all straight, Miss St. Clement."

"One learns, Sophie. You will, too."

Sophie had energy for just one more yawn. She hoped Miss St. Clement was right. About everything.

"THEY'RE STILL IN TOWN, MILORD," FEASEL SAID AS Lindley battled an unruly cravat and a heaviness from lack of sleep. "We kept an eye on them all night."

"And Fitzgelder's men?"

"Still sniffing around, but that chit in the trousers is a wily one. She outfoxed them, taking your Miss Darshaw off clear to the other side of town."

"And you're sure they weren't followed?"

Feasel grinned over the shaving basin. "'Course they was followed. By *us*. I left Tom there to make certain they didn't run out. Spent the night in the back room of some little shop, they did."

Lindley contemplated this. It would seem Miss Darshaw intended to remain in company with the costumed actress. Well, he wasn't sure he could commend her for taking up with these shifty theater persons, but it did appear that the actress had been wise in assuming a masculine disguise. So long as she could carry it out for a prolonged time. Two women traveling alone would certainly garner some measure of unwanted attention, but a woman traveling with a woman dressed obviously in men's clothing would make them an absolute spectacle. That, indeed, would not go well.

"I'm not entirely certain this actress person is to be trusted. What did you find out about her?"

Feasel shrugged. "Not a great deal, I'm afraid. No one seems to know any actress named Sands. I can't find anyone who's seen or heard of her here in London."

"Then perhaps she's not generally from London," Lindley suggested, ripping his cravat apart and starting over. "Question some of the servants at Fitzgelder's house. If we're in luck, one of them might know how he came to be in contact with the troupe. It was very plain last night that he was expecting this Sands woman."

"I've already got someone over there. We'll see what she finds out."

"She?"

"My sister's oldest girl. She's a sweet-faced young thing. She'll get herself well into the good graces of some of the staff there. If there's anything to be found out, she'll find it, sir."

"Your niece, Feasel? Are you certain you wish her to be in that man's house?"

Feasel snuffed as if offended. "There's not a one of my kin that can't handle himself—or *herself*—when backed into a corner, milord. Sally's a good girl. She'll manage, all right."

"I suppose you know best. But let's hope she can learn something soon. The quicker we discover where Miss Sands comes from, the quicker we get an idea where she might be going."

"Already know that, sir," Feasel said, casually reaching to dust a speck of lint off his master's coat.

"Well, where is it, man? How did you find out?"

"We heard them talking last night, sir. They're planning to catch the mail coach this morning."

"Good work, Feasel. So where are they headed from there?"

"You likely won't approve, sir."

"I don't approve of you being so cagey. Where are they bound?"

"To Warwick, sir."

"Warwick?"

"To try and warn Lord Rastmoor before Fitzgelder's mongrels sink their fangs into him. I heard the one girl make mention of it."

Lindley ripped at the cravat again. "Oh, hell. Bloody hell."

Just how was he supposed to go about looking after Miss Darshaw and her foolhardy actress friend if they didn't have the sense to run the other way from murder? *Bloody hell* was right.

"Don't worry, sir—" Feasel began, but he was cut off by a knock at the dressing room door.

It was the butler, bearing a note. Apparently the man thought it was important enough to carry it himself. Lindley sighed. He supposed he ought to take a moment or two to see what this was.

He needed even less than that. He knew the handwriting immediately. *Eudora.* Blast, but what did she need? It could only be trouble if the woman was up writing notes already after the late night she'd spent pretending to enjoy Fitzgelder's, er, company.

It took but a moment to identify the purpose of the note, but frustratingly there was no clue as to its reason. Eudora was quite abrupt, as a matter of fact. She declared that she simply had to see Lindley before he did anything today. Period.

Now she was the one to order him about, was she? Well, he supposed she had her right. Whatever this was, it must be important. He'd stop for a visit before leaving town.

If, that was, he didn't strangle himself with this bloody cravat first. He growled as his latest attempt resulted in dismal failure. Feasel sighed and stepped forward to rescue the proceedings. Lord, but once this whole business with Fitzgelder and the rest was finished, Lindley had half a mind to retire to his country home and never so much as look at a starched cravat again.

"I SAW HIM AGAIN," SOPHIE WHISPERED AS SHE AND Julia made their way along the streets, blending in as best they could with the locals who bustled about their business so early in the morning.

"Are you certain?" Miss St. Clement asked.

"Yes. It was the same boy I saw on the last street. Now why would he be here?"

"Perhaps he's simply going in the same direction we are."

Sophie wasn't convinced. "I believe he's following us."

"Well, there's one way to find out."

Miss St. Clement took Sophie's arm and suddenly ducked into an alley. They were certainly not in the best part of town, and Sophie shuddered at the thought of what—or who—might be in the alley, but she had to admit it would indeed be a fair test of whether or not that boy was following them. Except that she really did not need to test her theory. She knew in her heart it was no coincidence she kept seeing him. He was following them, and had been since last night.

"I saw him last night, too," she whispered.

"What?" Miss St. Clement said, pulling her to a complete halt in the middle of the grimy alleyway. "You saw him following us last night?"

"I saw him last night, but I didn't know he was following us. I noticed him on the street near Mr. Fitzgelder's house, but I assumed he was there looking for Lord Lindley."

"Lindley was gone by the time we left there last night."

"I know, so I assumed his boy would go find him elsewhere."

Miss St. Clement frowned. "How do you know he's Lindley's boy?"

"He's wearing the livery," Sophie explained. "At least, I'm fairly certain that's Lord Lindley's livery."

"And you recognize that because . . . ?"

"Because messages would be brought to and from the house where I used to work. Lord Lindley was rather, er, intimate with the mistress of that house."

Miss St. Clement rolled her eyes, smoothed her mustache, and adjusted her hat. "Men."

"But what do we do, Miss St. Clement?" Sophie questioned. "What if he follows us all the way to the coaching house? He'll see what direction we are taking and he'll report to his master. Lindley knows we overheard Mr. Fitzgelder's plan! He'll realize where we are going."

"And he'll tell Fitzgelder all about it, too. He'll have another band of cutthroats sent out after us. Damn."

"Yes," Sophie agreed. "Damn."

Miss St. Clement chuckled at her. "You shouldn't swear, Sophie. It really doesn't suit you."

"But you swear, Miss St. Clement!"

"I'm an actress."

Actresses weren't known for being, er, entirely proper. Well, then again, neither were seamstresses who had spent four years living in a brothel.

"And I'm hardly a lady, Miss St. Clement," Sophie declared. "So I'll damn things if I like."

Now the actress actually laughed. But it was not at her, so Sophie decided to be rather flattered that her worldly companion found her so amusing. She was quite certain if they didn't end up killed by Fitzgelder's men, they could quickly become close friends. That would be nice. Sophie had left all her friends behind at Madame Eudora's when she went to work for Mr. Fitzgelder. Aside from one dear cousin she hadn't seen in nearly seven years, Sophie was sadly bereft of friends.

But she supposed she'd be even more sadly bereft of her life if she and Miss St. Clement didn't find a way out of this narrow alley. Where did it lead? She peered down it, the long length of slick, cobbled roadway smeared liberally with all manner of filth. At the far, distant end, the hum and bustle of traffic assured her they were not precisely trapped, yet she really could not wish to wander any further into the depths. This alleyway was little more than a stinking crevice between two ramshackle buildings. In this part of town, there was no telling what might be waiting for them, watching from the smutty windows and dim, recessed doorways.

Yet she already knew what was waiting for them at the other end. That boy in Lindley's livery, the messenger who would carry news of them to his master, or worse, to the homicidal Fitzgelder. It seemed their only hope of getting to the coaching house unseen was to run this gauntlet. By the time their stalker realized what they were up to, they would be at the far end, hiding among the crowd. Then they could double back around the block and make it to their destination. How wonderful it would be to finally put London behind them!

And Warwick . . . Well, Warwick was very special to her. Some of Sophie's happiest days had been spent not far from there. How lovely it would be to see the river and smell the country air again. Yes, it would be worth it to risk this dank alley.

"If we want to make it to the coach house on time, we'd best hurry," Miss St. Clement said.

"Perhaps a run?" Sophie suggested, recognizing the same trepidation on her friend's face that she felt in her own soul.

"Indeed. We should run."

And so they did. Sophie was actually quite surprised at how quickly they passed those dirty, faceless windows and the dark, shadow-filled doorways. No one appeared. It seemed traversing this alley was as harmless as a stroll through Hyde Park at the height of the Season. If not for the smell of refuse and decay, she could have actually called their way almost pleasant.

Until something large shadowed the way ahead of them.

Sophie gasped and Miss St. Clement grasped her hand, pulling her to a stop and yanking her into one of those fearsome doorways. The women plastered themselves against the weathered door, scarcely breathing. Sophie gave her companion a worried look, and Miss St. Clement pressed one slender finger to her lips. They listened.

Their way had been blocked by a wagon. A large, sturdy wagon pulled by one huge horse was slowly being backed into the alley. The voices of two men called out, urging the horse and directing each other.

"All right, lock it there," one voice called in a thick rural accent. "Let's hope they got someone in there what can help us haul the bloody thing."

Now there were sounds of footsteps, and a door nearby creaked open. A shrill female voice joined the others, apparently criticizing the looks of the wagon. The men assured her it was good enough for the job and reminded her about their pay.

"My mistress will see you paid; she's not some good-for-nothing. But keep in mind this is a fine piece of furniture, this is. She won't want the likes of you banging it around and jostling it to pieces in that rattletrap cart you brought," the woman said.

The men grumbled that they'd moved furniture from better houses than this and pronounced their wagon worthy for the task. The woman finally agreed, inviting the men indoors. It all seemed very commonplace, and Sophie sighed in relief.

These men were simply here to haul something, not to commit murder. The wagon blocked their way and was an inconvenience, for sure, but it was not life threatening. They would easily be around it.

The voices faded and the footsteps tramped on the stoop into the building. The men had followed the woman inside, presumably to get whatever it was they were going to haul. Sophie chanced to speak.

"Do we dare try to go around it?"

The women peeked out from their hiding place. It was a tight fit—the wagon very thoroughly blocked the opening.

"We can make it," Miss St. Clement said, and she was just shifting to move out from where they hid when the shrill woman's voice was heard again.

"It took three hired boys to bring it down from the boudoir. Are you certain the two of you can manage it out the door and into your wagon?"

"Of course we can manage," one of the men grumbled back at her. "Now step aside so we can get it up in the cart."

At every *bang* and *clunk* the woman shrieked out cautions and directives, yet none of it seemed to have any effect on the men. They were silent, from what Sophie could tell. Probably just eager to get their item loaded and be away from this screeching taskmistress.

At length the sounds led Sophie to imagine the item—large, whatever it was—being shoved into the wagon and the boards slid into place at the rear to hold it there. Yes, finally the task was done and the men would be moving the wagon. There was hope the young women might still get to the mail coach on time.

"There, now that's a job well done," the woman said with grudging finality. "But just see you get it to Oxford in good condition. And be glad my mistress ain't sending it off all loaded up and heavy. This is going to be a birthday gift for her sister what's got five brats and no place to never put nothing. So keep it tidy."

"Never you mind, woman. We'll get it there in one good piece, we will. Now your mistress will be giving us a tidy little something for coming all the way to Town just to get this thing."

"Yes, yes. She's got your fee. Told me to take you down to cook to get you something for your afternoon meal, too. Come inside. I'll send a boy out front to stand with the horse."

The men were all in favor of this idea and quickly let the woman lead them back into the house. So they wouldn't be moving that wagon out of the way just yet. Drat, but this would certainly slow things down.

"We'd better hurry," Miss St. Clement said. "She said she'd send a boy out to watch the horse. If she does, there's a chance that he'll see us leaving the alley. Then when our friend waiting for us at the other end comes down here hunting us, this boy will be able to tell that boy where we've gone."

Sophie peered out into the alley. Fortunately there was no sign of any boys at either end. Yet.

"Let's go!"

They darted out, moving quickly toward the wagon. They'd squeeze by and be on their way in no time. Things were going to work out, after all.

"It's a good thing Lord Lindley didn't tell Mr. Fitzgelder we were hiding in that room last night," Sophie said. "Else Mr. Fitzgelder might guess we were headed for Warwick to warn your friend and not even need one of these boys to tattle on us."

It sounded foolish the moment she heard herself speak it. Miss St. Clement must have thought the same thing. She stopped in her tracks, wedged between the wagon and the cold brick of the nearest building. Sophie plowed into her, but the woman didn't even have to open her mouth for Sophie to know what she must be thinking.

"Then just why *did* Lindley send that boy after us?"

Sophie gulped. Indeed, that was a fair question. It was more than a fair question—it was the *only* question. If Lord Lindley had sent someone to follow them this far, then he would know they weren't simply running back to the theater district and whatever friends Miss St. Clement must have there. The logical assumption, then, would be that they were leaving town. And everyone knew the logical way to leave London—for anyone who did not have a carriage at their disposal, at least—was to pay passage on the mail coach.

That boy had trailed them this far; he likely could guess their destination. If he lost sight of them on the street, no doubt he'd simply go on ahead. He'd be waiting for them at the coaching house! Or worse, it wouldn't be merely a boy in Lindley's livery waiting there. She and Miss St. Clement might show up to find some of those grown men Mr. Fitzgelder seemed to favor for committing unthinkable acts of violence.

"Lindley must already have an idea where we're going," Miss St. Clement said, confirming Sophie's fears.

"And he likely knows how we're planning to get there. They'll be expecting us."

Miss St. Clement nodded, tapping her finger on her chin as she thought. It would seem that their valiant effort to save this Lord Rastmoor was thwarted before it even began. What were they to do?

What a pity they weren't wealthy like Lord Lindley; then they would have funds to hire a private carriage, one none of their pursuers might recognize. They could travel in comfort and happy anonymity.

And then she realized what she was gazing at.

"Miss St. Clement . . ."

"I'm trying to think of a way out of this, Sophie."

"Yes, I know, but—"

"We simply must get to Warwick in time to warn Anthony!"

"Yes, I know, and I think—"

"If we only had another way out of town."

"Miss St. Clement, I think I found us one."

A simple nod of her head toward the wagon caught the young woman's attention. There, in the back of the wagon, was a huge clothespress lying on its back. From what the woman had said a few moments ago, they could expect to find it empty.

"Let's see if we'd fit!" Miss St. Clement said, moving back around to the rear of the wagon and hoisting herself up.

Sophie did her best to follow, but she was not as appropriately dressed for climbing as Miss St. Clement was. It hardly mattered. In a moment's time Miss St. Clement had hopped up and yanked open one of the heavy wooden doors on the cabinet. It was, sure enough, empty. There was more than enough space for two female stowaways.

Miss St. Clement smiled down at her and reached a hand to help her up.

"You're a genius, Miss Sophie," she said. "Now hurry before anyone sees us."

HE HARDLY HAD TIME FOR IT, BUT LINDLEY OBLIGED Eudora's note and was now seated in the woman's cloyingly perfumed sitting room. She kept him waiting a good ten minutes, and by the time she swept in, dressing gown floating and hair perfectly coiffed, his fingers hurt from drumming them on her center table.

"I'm really in quite a hurry, Eudora. What on earth is so pressing that you summoned me over here only to keep me cooling my heels so long?"

She was obviously unconcerned about his impatience. "Lindley in a hurry? That is rare indeed. Off to Fitzgelder's to visit a certain seamstress again?"

Oh, hell. She couldn't have called him here just to discuss that, could she? Surely she knew him well enough to realize Fitzgelder had been misinformed when he brashly announced Lindley had been shagging Miss Darshaw.

"Eudora, I understand you have a certain fondness for the girl, but do you really suppose I would be so careless as all that? You know where my interests in Miss Darshaw lie."

But Eudora simply smiled and glided into the seat across

from him. He'd stood when she entered, so now he sat again. Bother, he really did not have the time for this foolishness.

"I've seen for some time now where your interests in Miss Darshaw lie. But I didn't expect you would stoop to forcing yourself on her."

"What? I never!"

"Ah, so it's like that, is it? She was ever appalled when I suggested the notion of furthering acquaintances with any of my generous clients, but I always wondered if perhaps her mind could have been changed were you to ever enter into the discussion."

"You mean you had men asking for her? And you would have happily procured her for them? Good Lord, Eudora. I thought you told me she was not here to be used that way!"

But Eudora merely shrugged and turned coolly to the tea tray that had been set up beside her. "A woman of her stature will hardly end up being used for anything other than that, my dear Richard. I would have certainly never forced her into it, but why should I stand in the way of letting the girl profit from the good looks the Almighty himself saw fit to give her? Oh, don't glare at me that way. I was not the one making use of her at Fitzgelder's house last night."

"Nor was I, let me assure you."

She allowed him a sideways glance, that familiar smirk on her beautiful face. "That's not what Fitzgelder seemed to believe."

"He was misinformed. Purposely."

Now she raised an eyebrow to go with that dubious glance. "Oh? If you thought claiming you'd marked the girl as your own would somehow discourage his attentions toward her, I daresay you only succeeded in the opposite. Even when quite swimming in his cups last night the man seemed fully intent on seeking her out the very moment he returned home."

"Well then, he must have been sorely disappointed. She was long gone by the time he returned."

This actually produced something other than the coy expression that generally graced Eudora's face. "Oh? Gone where?"

"I don't know." And it was true, at the moment, at least. Surely by now Miss Darshaw and her companion were on the mail coach and traveling north. Somewhere. "She was planning to leave town."

This left Eudora looking positively surprised. "Leave town? How? The girl has barely a penny to her name. And she certainly won't get far traveling alone, not with her pretty face and hopelessly naive disposition."

"She wasn't alone," he was most happy to inform her. "She has a husband now."

If Eudora seemed surprised before, she was absolutely flabbergasted now. He supposed he ought not dangle her this way, but for some reason he didn't quite trust her with the truth where Miss Darshaw was concerned. Not now that he'd learned the older woman had tried to talk the girl into a life of depravity with the rest of the girls in her stable. Sophie Darshaw was above that. Not much, but certainly a tiny step, at least. Just as Eudora should have been.

"She and her new husband were leaving, putting the girl's past behind them and starting anew," he announced.

Eudora met his eyes with a straight, steady gaze. "Where?"

"What do you mean?"

"Where are they going?"

"How do I know that? I'm certainly not the girl's keeper. That's up to her husband now, I suppose."

"What's his name?"

He supposed he should have just dashed off the obviously false name the actress had been using, but something gave him pause. Overall, he trusted Eudora, of course, but somehow he just couldn't bring himself to divulge this. The woman was just a mite too eager for the information. Lindley hedged.

"I don't know that she mentioned it."

"She told you she married yet she didn't tell you the fellow's name?"

"I didn't ask her, I suppose. It's not as if Miss Darshaw . . . or rather, Mrs. Whoever-she-is-now . . . and I spent hours in lengthy conversation. I merely greeted her by her maiden name and she simply informed me she'd become married."

"And you didn't question her?"

"Contrary to what you apparently believe, my interest in Miss Darshaw . . . or whatever . . . is not all-consuming. I wished her well and promptly put the matter from my mind."

"Not entirely, it would seem," she drawled, coy again, "as clearly you found time to indicate to Fitzgelder that you'd been on the most friendly of terms with the newlywed. You knew he'd be ragingly jealous."

"I knew he'd be easily misled. I'd been found out exploring a room in the man's house where I had no business being. You know my suspicions of him; you know I could ill afford to have him question my presence there. So, I concocted a reasonable story."

"That you had been in that room shagging the seamstress."

"Yes."

He defied her to doubt that. After all, it was every bit the truth.

"Well, then. I suppose we should be thankful that he believed you."

"If, in fact, he did. I cannot be entirely certain with him."

She nodded, allowing agreement. "He is cagey, indeed. Yet he is a man, and men are simple creatures. Surely he'll become obsessed with the girl now that she's gone and you claimed to have succeeded with her while he was left wanting, so to speak."

"Plus the fact that he's taken the notion she absconded with something of his."

Her brow furrowed, a thing vain Madame generally would not allow to happen. "What, Sophie stole something? I cannot believe it."

"No, nor do I. But he seemed quite convinced."

Eudora actually laughed aloud at that. "And just what on earth would he say she stole from him?"

"Jewelry, he says."

"What? She would never. The girl is as honest as . . . er, what sort of jewelry?"

"What sort? I haven't the foggiest. Look, Eudora, I'm sure it's to her credit that the girl made such a favorable impression on you during her years here. I'm happy that you care so much for her well-being. But if you don't mind, I truly must be on my way. I'm late as it is."

She sighed as if he were little more than a tedious child. "And what on earth is it that cannot wait but has the great Earl of Lindley rushing off this way?"

"A wedding," he replied simply. "Out of town."

"A wedding? How quaint."

"Yes, so if you can possibly spare me for a few days, I must be on my way."

She nodded as if she were graciously dismissing him. He'd already begun to rise with or without her permission.

"Very well, Richard, but do let me know if you should happen to learn anything of our dear Miss Darshaw's whereabouts."

How on earth did she expect him to learn anything about that? He would, of course, but he truly could not see how Eudora should expect it of him.

"Of course," he said with a simple bow to her. "Good day, Eudora."

"Come see me the moment you're back from Warwick, my dear Richard."

"As you wish."

He gave a mild smile and let himself from the room. He cared a great deal for Eudora; loved her, he supposed. She was one part of his life he would never regret—he knew that for a fact. But by God, he also knew he had never told her where the wedding he was attending would be held.

Chapter Five

Sophie was only too happy to stand up straight and stretch her limbs. She wasn't at all certain which had been worse, the ride from London to Oxford in that awful, cramped cabinet or today's journey from Oxford on the overly crowded mail coach to . . . well, to wherever it was they were. She stretched her arms painfully over her head and grimaced at Miss St. Clement.

"Surely we must be near Warwick by now," she mumbled, noting the small size and shabby nature of the posting house they had stopped at.

Miss St. Clement frowned. "No, the driver claims this is some place called Geydon. Warwick is nearly an hour north of us."

Sophie managed to hold back the curses she felt creeping onto her tongue. Despite what Miss St. Clement seemed to feel, Sophie was an adult and perfectly permitted to adopt such language should she so desire. Trouble was, right now such language would draw the wrong sort of attention. For the last leg of this journey she'd been the demure Mrs. Clemmons, riding in sweet silence beside her dear husband.

"If Warwick is only an hour away, why on earth are we stopping here?" Sophie asked.

It appeared Miss St. Clement was every bit as frustrated as Sophie. "The driver claims there is something wrong with one of the horses we took on at Banbury. I, however, believe it is more likely the driver has some sort of arrangement with the owner of this dilapidated establishment. I suppose we will be prevailed upon to dine here, or perhaps even spend the night and finish the last leg of our journey tomorrow."

For shame. How unfair to take advantage of weary travelers like this, not to mention the Royal Mail that would be delayed due to such tactics. Then again, Sophie did have to admit she was a bit hungry. And certainly a night's sleep sounded like a slice of heaven to her. Miss St. Clement knew her well enough to recognize what Sophie had hoped did not show on her face.

"You wish to see about supper, don't you?"

Sophie nodded, sheepishly. "If it is only an hour or so more before we find your friend . . ."

"Very well. I daresay I could do with something to eat, as well. The driver assured us we have time."

"Of course," Sophie said, already dreaming of a plate full of something warm. "He and the innkeeper could hardly turn much of a profit if the coach was set to leave again before we all had time to purchase a meal."

"Come along, then."

Sophie followed her friend—who was still carrying on her charade as a now very rumpled young man—into the posting house. It was dim inside though the sun was just now beginning to set for the day. The sooty windows let in very little of the orange glow from what appeared to be a lovely evening. Pity they could not be spending it in activity any more pleasant than hiding from their pursuers.

Although, since climbing into that farm cart a day and a half ago they had not seen any signs of being followed. It had been a stroke of luck to find that big, empty cabinet. If Lindley's boy had come down that alley looking for them, he hadn't thought to check inside. The simple men who had been hired to haul the cabinet didn't think to look in it, either, through their daylong journey. Aside from a rather jarring, rumbling ride all the way from London to Oxford, Sophie could hardly complain about their manner of escape. It seemed most efficient.

They'd arrived in Oxford yesterday at just about this time in the evening. Hungry and exhausted from the constant worry that their drivers would notice them, they were only too eager to climb out when the wagon finally stopped. Oh, certainly the drivers had stopped several times along the way, to eat their lunch, look to their horse, and whatnot, but always it appeared they were out in the middle of nowhere. At that final stop, when Miss St. Clement pushed that heavy door up and they chanced to peek outside, they recognized the familiar safety of civilization.

As soon as the driver and his companion left the cart to go to the door of the modest home that must have been their destination, Sophie and Miss St. Clement took their chance. They clambered out of the cabinet and made a dash for the next street. She could not be sure if anyone even noticed them. They ran and ducked around corners and buildings until they were certain anyone following at that point must be lost. It was rather exhilarating, as a matter of fact. Sophie was becoming quite proud of herself.

But the inn where they had stayed last night and the cost of their coach fare today had certainly drained what little resources they had. Lunch had been a sparse, economical thing, and likely dinner would be the same. She supposed she'd do well to make the best of it. Should they encounter any trouble getting word to Miss St. Clement's friend once they arrived in Warwick, likely they'd have to choose between paying for an extra night's lodging or a seat on the coach to Gloucester to find her father.

Nodding politely to several of the other passengers who'd shared their coach, the two women made their way into the building. The unkempt proprietor was all too eager to serve them. They took seats at a table toward the rear of his dim little common room and settled in. Miss St. Clement rejected the man's suggestions of mutton or bacon but conceded that soup was just what they wanted. Sophie tried to pretend that was so. Grumbling, the innkeeper scuttled off to collect their measly—and inexpensive—soup.

And it was measly, too. The vegetables were limp, and Sophie supposed she could hunt all day and not find a morsel of meat in it. Oh well, it was the best they could do. She would not complain—much.

At least she didn't have to eat her soup through a mustache as poor Miss St. Clement had to. The woman seemed positively miserable. Well, Sophie supposed that was to be expected. They'd had an uncomfortable journey, and there was the constant concern that all of it was in vain. They had no way to know whether Fitzgelder's men had already made it to their destination and carried out their dreadful plans. The man Miss St. Clement was hoping to save might already be lost.

It was too tragic to contemplate. Sophie decided she'd do well to try and cheer her friend.

"I can't wait to see this Lord Rastmoor's face when he meets you again."

The actress cringed. "Hopefully that will never happen. With luck we'll find he's safely at his friend's home and I can simply send a warning message. He'll find out what Fitzgelder is about, and you and I can be off to meet Papa."

"You don't want to see him again?"

"Heavens no!"

"We've come all this way and you're not even going to see the man?"

"Exactly."

Sophie could hardly believe she'd heard right. After all this, Miss St. Clement did not even wish to so much as see him? But surely that couldn't be. It was obvious to anyone that Miss St. Clement had more than a friendly interest in this Rastmoor. It just couldn't end without them meeting again!

"That's so sad. I was hoping the two of you might . . ."

"Sorry, Sophie. That only happens in novels."

She changed the subject by launching into a discussion of their plans. She expected to simply leave a message in Warwick to be delivered to her friend and then be off directly to Gloucester. Indeed, she sounded quite determined there would be nothing more to it. The excitement she feigned at the prospect of Sophie joining their troupe and perhaps even laying down her needle in favor of actually treading the boards with them was almost convincing.

"Acting?" Sophie nearly laughed aloud. The idea of taking up the path that had once fully consumed her parents was more than a trifle ridiculous. Why, Mamma had been beautiful, extraordinary. She was elegant and sophisticated and charmed her audiences wherever they went—this is what Sophie recalled of actresses. She could never measure up to the likes of that.

"Oh, I'm sure I could never be so very good at that. All those lines I'd have to memorize!"

"You've been playacting the part of a blushing bride for three days now, and so far the audience seems quite enthralled," the actress said, sweeping her arm wide to indicate the patrons of the posting house.

Sophie wasn't impressed with such high praise. "I believe our audience would be no less enthralled were I simply a chicken tucked under your arm. They've hardly taken note of us at all."

"There, you see?" Miss St. Clement said with a wide smile. "You've played your part to perfection. Who's to say you might not make a memorable Juliet or Ophelia or—"

But Sophie had stopped listening. Her full attention was caught by the broad, elegant figure in the doorway. *Good heavens!* Could he possibly have found them already?

"Lord Lindley!" she gasped.

"Lord Lindley? I don't believe we have any scripts with Lor—"

By then Miss St. Clement must have seen the look on Sophie's face. Her voice trailed off. Or perhaps it was simply drowned out by the pounding of Sophie's heartbeat.

THIS WAS A BLOODY WASTE OF TIME. SOMEONE HAD tampered with Lindley's carriage and weakened the axle. Not surprisingly, it had broken.

Now he was forced to delay his return to London and stop at this godforsaken posting house and hope they had someone available who could make adequate repairs. He supposed he should be thankful no one had come along to murder them on the road, helpless as they were with a lame carriage and twilight full upon them. The only explanation he had for it was that Fitzgelder's henchmen could not have guessed precisely where that axle would have given out. If he and his companion had waited with the carriage in hopes of snagging a ride with someone, they might very well have been exactly where Fitzgelder wanted them.

But how had Fitzgelder's men gotten to his carriage? He had gone straight from London to his friend Dashford's wedding, stopping for the night and then driving all day. Nothing appeared wrong with his carriage at that point, and he arrived just in time to witness the vows.

It was a nice wedding, as far as weddings went, but he had to admit the bride held an unexpected interest for him. Her uncanny resemblance to Sophie Darshaw was most disconcerting. *Most* disconcerting.

For a frightening hour or so, he'd begun to fear he was obsessed with the London seamstress, finding her features on even strangers' faces. True, he'd long found Sophie Darshaw more than just passably attractive, but surely there was nothing more to it than that. Was there? Still, as Dashford stood at the altar to pledge himself to his blushing bride, all Lindley could see was Sophie. Truly, it was quite horrifying.

Thankfully, though, the mystery had been mercifully solved. Immediately following the ceremony, Lindley attached himself to Rastmoor. Indeed, his friend was alive and well; Fitzgelder had not yet accomplished his goal. When the unsuspecting target announced that he would be rushing back to London to deal with some family troubles, Lindley was conveniently there to offer his conveyance and companionship. He did not let Rastmoor refuse.

And this was when he happened on an interesting bit of information. Lady Dashford, it would seem, had charged Rastmoor with a task. When he returned to London, he was to locate her missing cousin, a young woman named Sophie Darshaw.

Well, this had been quite more of a coincidence than Lindley expected, but it did explain why the ladies bore such a striking resemblance to one another. Things were increasingly complex. Lindley had some knowledge of Miss Darshaw's background, but he had not realized Dashford's new wife figured into things. He would have to give thought to this and wonder what it all meant.

Eventually they left the happy couple and went on their way. For the first leg of their journey the axle gave no trouble at all. They took a break for a midday meal and got back on the road. That must have been when the criminals took their opportunity to tamper. They would have known a damaged axle would surely break on these roads, still heavily rutted from an unusually wet spring.

So here they were, two gentlemen with deadly enemies, stranded at a posting house in some unknown place called Geydon; victims despite all his care and planning. Clearly he'd let his guard down or allowed himself to become somehow distracted. He would not let it happen again.

Lindley stabled his horses and arranged for his carriage to be hauled in and repaired. Like it or not, they'd be spending the night here. He wasn't hungry, but it would draw suspicion if he did not act like the dandy he'd become accustomed to portraying. He declared himself ravenous and flirted with the young serving maid who opened the door as they entered the posting house. He forgot her face the moment he walked past her.

The common room was dim, and it took a moment for his eyes to adjust. It was dusk and yet the lamps had not been lit inside. He led Rastmoor in and was scanning for a table where they might be alone and yet not too far from the doorway should a hasty exit be required.

Instead of an empty table his eyes fell on one occupied by a young couple. A young couple he recognized. *Miss Darshaw and her female husband.*

She appeared to see him at the same moment he noticed her. The girl's eyes grew huge and terrified. He watched as her lips formed his name. The actress with her turned suddenly, and her expression changed from mere surprise to absolute horror.

Lindley stepped farther into the room, allowing Rastmoor to get a full view of the couple. He noticed Miss Darshaw immediately, as Lindley had no doubt any man in the room would have done. Despite her travel-worn apparel and the weariness in her eyes, she was lovely. And so far, she was safe from Fitzgelder. Even her bruises were gone.

But now her glance moved from him and shifted to Rastmoor. She glanced back and forth between him and her pretend husband. Why on earth did that actress seem so pale and alarmed? And what was this little smile that crept over Miss Darshaw's pretty face? Did she actually smile at Rastmoor? No, she was simply nervous at the way he stared.

And he was staring. Indeed, why the devil did the blackguard feel the need to stare at her this way? It was positively uncalled for, blast him.

Lindley decided he'd best put a quick end to any of Rastmoor's idle fantasies.

"Why, Mr. and Mrs. Clemmons," Lindley said, making it clear to whom he was speaking and moving toward them. "How odd to run into you here. I had no idea you were traveling this way else I would have invited you to share my carriage."

Both women seemed at a loss. Miss Darshaw was first to find her voice. "We had a rather sudden change of plan. Didn't we, Mr. Clemmons?"

"Er, yes," the actress said, careful to keep her wavering voice as low and masculine as possible. She was a fair actress, and Lindley could see Rastmoor had not the least suspicion. After all, he was too busy gazing at Miss Darshaw. *Damn his eyes.*

"Forgive me," Lindley said, determined to curb the staring. Besides, just in case Rastmoor hadn't noticed the striking resemblance between Miss Darshaw and Lady Dashford, Lindley needed to inform him. "Everyone has not been introduced. Lord Rastmoor, this is Mr. Alexander Clemmons and his lovely wife, Mrs. Sophie Clemmons. We met a few days ago in London."

He took extra care to emphasize Mrs. Clemmons's first name. Rastmoor nodded. Yes, he understood. He smiled and gave the couple a polite bow.

They made small talk, asking the couple whether or not they planned to spend the night there. It appeared they were undecided. At least, the actress was undecided. Miss Darshaw seemed quite eager to stay. She also seemed unaccountably interested in Rastmoor. Whyever could that be? Surely she wasn't drawn in by his too obvious staring. Was she?

Hell, but she certainly did appear friendly, smiling for Rastmoor and chattering pleasantly. "The roads have been so very difficult," she sighed and pouted. "I do truly dread getting back in that coach to be jostled along to the next posting house. Perhaps if Mr. Clemmons knew some of his gentlemen friends were to be staying here tonight I could stand a better chance of convincing him."

Even "Mr. Clemmons" seemed appalled at her amiability. Whatever was the girl up to? Well, this would work to his advantage, whatever her game. Lindley certainly was happy enough to have all of his charges neatly under one convenient roof. Likely this meant Feasel was somewhere nearby, too. He'd been assigned to trail the women. This should make keeping everyone alive just that much simpler.

"Shame on you, Mr. Clemmons, forcing your young bride to travel under these conditions," he said, content to play along for the moment. "Rest assured, Mrs. Clemmons, if it will gain you a few hours' respite from the torment of travel, Rastmoor and I will do our best to persuade your husband to obtain a room for the night. In fact, I'll go see to making arrangements with the proprietor." He glanced at Rastmoor to see if the man was in agreement. "Don't worry, Clemmons, tonight will be at my expense."

Rastmoor was only too happy to be left alone to speak with the nervous couple. Lindley found it perversely amusing. Curious about Lady Dashford's unexpected relationship to Miss Darshaw, Lindley had thought to gauge her reaction by telling her about Sophie's supposed marriage. It did seem to come as a complete—and welcome—shock to the lady, which led Lindley to believe she was no part of the intrigue. It did, however, cause Rastmoor some concern. During their ride from Warwick, Rastmoor had discussed his concerns about this Sophie Darshaw and her too-convenient new husband.

It seemed Rastmoor worried Mr. Clemmons was in some way plotting to take advantage of Sophie's connection to the Dashford name. He feared the man may have married Sophie simply to use blackmail or extortion to keep Lady Dashford's connection to them from coming to public light. Lindley did not know what to think of this development and was happy to let Rastmoor learn what he could about this so-called blackmail scheme.

He doubted, however, Rastmoor would learn much. If Sophie were using this false marriage to gain some profit from her newlywed cousin, she'd certainly gone about it all wrong. And if Lady Dashford were so dreadfully ashamed of Sophie, why commission Rastmoor to find her? Things did not add up. Besides, Rastmoor was basing his concerns on the mistaken belief that this actress was truly Miss Darshaw's husband. Lindley was more convinced than ever—given the way the actress could not seem to take her eyes off Rastmoor—she was completely female.

But so far Rastmoor was still seething with the wrong sorts of suspicion. "See about getting us a private dining room," he instructed Lindley. "I'm sure the Clemmonses will wish to join us in a quiet supper."

Lindley agreed and headed off to find the proprietor. He doubted the Clemmonses wished to join them, nor did he expect the supper to be quiet. It would, however, promise to be interesting.

SHE'D GUESSED RIGHT—THE HANDSOME, RUDDY-haired man with Lord Lindley *was* Miss St. Clement's friend, Rastmoor. Sophie had known it the minute she saw the actress's face when the man walked into the room. And she'd been right about her other suspicions, as well. There clearly *was* something unfinished between Miss St. Clement and her ill-fated Rastmoor. No wonder the woman had been so determined not to let Fitzgelder's plan succeed.

Despite what she may have said, Sophie had no doubt Miss St. Clement still harbored special feelings for the man. It was written plainly in her pained expression, though of course the actress tried to hide it. She cared very much for this unobservant gentleman.

Therefore, Sophie felt it was her duty as a friend to keep the pair together as long as possible. Surely at some point clarity would strike inside Rastmoor's ginger head and he'd recognize Miss St. Clement. Then perhaps they would put their differences—whatever they were—behind them and acknowledge their true feelings. It was a beautiful sentiment.

Although in vain, Sophie soon realized once they'd been ushered into a private dining room with the two dashing gentlemen. Lord Rastmoor had hardly spared a glance at Miss St.

Clement. She, for her part, was doing nothing to draw attention or give away her deception. It appeared the couple were never to be reunited, if Sophie were to judge by the way Rastmoor continued to stare at her and ignore Miss St. Clement. Perhaps at first it had been just the tiniest bit flattering, but now, as they all sat down together and waited for the innkeeper's wife to bring the promised stew, Sophie could safely say she was not at all flattered by the gentleman's attention. Unnerved, but most certainly not flattered.

It appeared Miss St. Clement did not much appreciate it, either. Her eyes flashed, and Sophie wondered if perhaps there'd be no need for Fitzgelder's men to follow through on their plan. Miss St. Clement would do it for them.

Lord Lindley, however, seemed blindly unaware of the emotional undercurrents swirling around him.

"So, Clemmons, what brings you out here to Warwickshire?" he asked cheerfully.

It was uncanny how Miss St. Clement had managed to fool these gentlemen. Not that Sophie didn't think her a fine enough actress, but still—one would think men might be more observant about their own kind. How could they not recognize the way Miss St. Clement's mustache kept sagging at one side or the way she periodically batted her very feminine eyelashes in an attempt to keep her emotions from showing on her face? But apparently these men were easily misled.

"Nothing, really, sir," Miss St. Clement replied to the question. "We're simply passing through."

"Oh? You're not on your way to pay a call on Mrs. Clemmons's family?" Rastmoor asked.

What was that? Sophie wasn't altogether certain she'd heard him correctly. Had he asked about her *family*? Good heavens, what did Lord Rastmoor know of her family? Surely this man had no reason to know anything about Grandmamma or any of Sophie's unmentionable connections. He couldn't, could he?

"I wasn't aware Mrs. Clemmons had family in Warwickshire," Miss St. Clement said quickly.

"I don't," Sophie replied. "My grandmother used to live not a great distance from here, but she passed away. I've no more family anywhere."

"Your grandmother?" Miss St. Clement asked. "I'm sorry. I didn't realize that."

"It's all right," Sophie replied. "You couldn't have known."

Rastmoor bullied on, not seeming to care that the passing of one's dear grandmother might be a sensitive subject for most people. "And just where have you been living, Mrs. Clemmons, in the years since your grandmother passed away?"

Sophie wasn't certain what he meant by that. Was he truly just making idle chatter or did he know? She took a deep breath and tried to decide how to answer. Just what had Lord Lindley told his friend about her and her previous living arrangements?

Rastmoor didn't wait for her to respond. He went on as if this were the most ordinary conversation. "Were you at Madame Eudora's brothel for the entire past four years, or did you find work elsewhere, too?"

Oh, but the way he said it made it sound so foul, so dirty! Indeed, she supposed it was, but then she'd rather gotten used to her life there. She had friends and Madame cared for her. True, Madame had made it no secret she'd love to see Sophie take a more active role in the business, but she knew that was not meant as insult. Madame thought Sophie could do quite well for herself, and there was something heartwarming in that.

But what must this Rastmoor think of her if Lindley had been so quick to tell him of her past? Worse, what might he expect of her? And Lindley, too; did he have expectations? After all, he could have told Fitzgelder they'd been hiding and overheard his scheme. What if he intended to exact some form of payment for his benevolent silence?

And of course anyone could guess what payment would be expected from a woman who'd spent several years living in a brothel.

"A *brothel*?" Miss St. Clement sputtered.

The gleam in Lord Rastmoor's eye was positively malicious. Sophie glanced from him to Lindley. Had she been hoping to find something of comfort in Lindley's face? Well, she did not find it. He seemed little more than amused—entertained, perhaps—by his friend's most inappropriate conversation. Almost imperceptibly, he raised one eyebrow and smiled at her. Good heavens, these men were very nearly propositioning her right here, under the very nose of the person they believed to be her husband!

Furious, she jumped to her feet. By God, she was not about to become their little plaything.

"That's none of your business!" she announced. "I'm not there anymore, and I won't go with you . . . either of you!"

Miss St. Clement seemed every bit as offended by all of this as Sophie felt. She leapt to her feet and stormed at them. "Leave her alone! Hasn't she been through enough with the likes of you? Take your filthy minds and your petty accusations out of here this instant!"

Lord Rastmoor seemed to have been about to speak, but Miss St. Clement did not allow him. She lunged and swung her fist at him. Sophie was every bit as surprised by this sudden violence as their companions. Lord Rastmoor staggered back, plowing into Lord Lindley and throwing him off balance, too. Both gentlemen toppled over, crashing into chairs, and boots thudded loudly on the wooden floor. Sophie cringed back into the corner, just hoping to stay out of the mess.

What on earth would possess Miss St. Clement to do such a thing? Heavens, did she forget she was hopelessly outmatched by these two strapping men? Yet, it seemed that her action had accomplished what she intended. The men were temporarily distracted and the way to the door was now free.

"Come, Sophie," the actress said, grabbing up Sophie's hand. "The mail coach is still in the yard. Let's get out of here."

But before anyone could make any further move, a loud crack split the air and glass from the window shattered around them. Sophie let out a shriek, and she was fairly certain Miss St. Clement did, too. The chair between Rastmoor and Lindley sent a shower of oak splinters flying everywhere.

Good Lord, had that been gunfire? Someone was shooting at them!

"Get down!" Lindley yelled, shoving the table over on its side to provide some measure of protection should more bullets come hailing through the only window in the small room.

Sophie was more than happy to make use of his quickly constructed barricade and dropped down to cower behind it, instinctively pulling a chair over her, as well. Miss St. Clement was beside her, but she could not catch her friend's eye. The actress seemed to be far more concerned for Lord Rastmoor's well-being than her own.

The gentlemen did not waste time. When no immediate repeat of the gunfire hailed through the shattered window, they were swiftly on their feet. Ordering the women to stay down, Lindley directed Rastmoor to rush to the back of the inn while he himself would go check the front. Sophie grimaced at the thought. What if the shooter expected such? What if someone waited out there, biding his time for their target to poke his head out? Heavens, surely anyone who would be willing to murder Lord Rastmoor would never hesitate to provide the same fate for Lord Lindley!

Or a couple of incognito females, for that matter.

The men raced out of the room. Sophie held her breath, wondering if more gunshots would be the next sound she heard.

Oddly enough, it was not. It was Miss St. Clement clambering to her feet.

"Wait here," she called to Sophie as she dashed out after the men, her footsteps indicating she was trailing Rastmoor.

Well, if that wasn't the most idiotic thing! What on earth did Miss St. Clement think she might do to rescue her Rastmoor in the face of an unknown assailant with a gun? No, indeed, Sophie could not imagine how the actress could possibly be a help in this situation. By God, Sophie was going to stay right here, safely behind this table. She grabbed the leg of yet another chair and pulled it over to hide under it, as well.

How could Miss St. Clement be so foolish to rush out there as she had? Was her concern for Lord Rastmoor so great that she'd rather die with him than stay back here and live? The woman was mentally unstable.

Still, Sophie knew women often did foolish things when they let their hearts become captive by some man. Madame had warned her of such things. She'd seen it for herself during her years at the brothel. Indeed, her friend Annie was a perfect example.

Poor Annie, such a sweet girl from such a tragic background. Annie had done what she could to help her impoverished family feed ten hungry children, but it was never enough. Somehow she'd ended up working for Madame Eudora. She was pretty and had learned her manners well enough that she'd caught the eye of gentlemen and was doing quite well, earning a fair amount and able to pay her keep with Madame and still have some to send home to her family. She and Sophie had become fast friends.

But then Annie fell in love. She lost her heart to one of her usual callers and began to beg and plead for Madame not to ask her to see any others. Well, Madame could hardly agree to that, could she? Everyone in her household simply had to earn their keep. Unfortunately, Annie had no special skill with a needle as Sophie had. If Annie's favored gentleman had not been willing to pay an exorbitant amount to keep Annie all for himself, Madame would have forced her to continue her usual labors.

But Annie's lover managed to scrape up enough to keep her. Madame moved her to share a room with Sophie to make room for another girl and to keep things as economical as possible while allowing the man to be Annie's only visitor. He was always very discreet, Sophie never so much as laying eyes on him.

But before long, Annie announced she was with child.

Madame raged that this was the penultimate foolishness. Annie could have had a promising career, could have found a protector with deep pockets and one day have gotten a house of her own and fine clothes. With her pretty face and innate elegance, she could have been a great courtesan. To give all that up for love was more than unimaginable, as far as Madame was concerned.

Sophie was tempted to agree. What sort of life could Annie give her child, relying solely on the good grace of some randy, never-present gentleman? It was no life Sophie envied, that was for certain. In fact, it was then Sophie realized she must do more to take charge of her own life. So she left.

And look where that had gotten her—mauled by Fitzgelder, running for her life, and now hiding under a chair. Two chairs and a table, actually. *What a coward.*

Cautiously, she pulled herself out from under the chairs and rose up onto her knees. The posting house had gone silent.

Everyone seemed to have rushed outside after the commotion, either to escape or to find out what was going on, she supposed. She glanced around and saw nothing.

She did hear something, though. Rising and creeping slowly to the door, she peeked out into the hallway. It was very dim, the nearby stairway blocking the lamplight from the common room. What had she heard? A floorboard creak? Someone on the steps? She moved forward to get a better view.

A man's hand was suddenly covering her mouth, and she was pulled roughly into his embrace. She was too shocked to scream—couldn't have, anyway, from the tight hold he had on her—but managed to wriggle and kick against him. Why oh why didn't she stay under that chair?

Her first thought was perhaps Lindley had come back, yet it was not him. Every one of her senses screamed that loudly. Lindley was not here—he was nowhere around to either save her or be a part of whatever plan this new stranger had for her. No one was here. She was on her own again.

Yet, as she struggled against him, the man whispered in her ear.

"Chut, ma Fifi. *Calme-toi. Calme-toi. C'est moi."*

She froze. She knew the voice. She knew the words. She knew the private name he called her. She knew this man.

Yet it could not be him. *He was dead.*

"Papa?" she mumbled the word beneath his grimy hand.

Slowly his grip released. *"Oui,* Fifi. *C'est moi."*

She didn't move, so he turned her to face him. It took a moment before she could make herself look up into his face. *Papa. It truly is him.*

"But it cannot . . . You can't . . . You were . . ."

He shushed her again. "There will be time enough for explanation. We must hurry now; leave this place."

"But Lord Lindley . . ."

Now Papa grabbed her shoulders again. "What did he do to you, *ma fille*?"

"Nothing! Nothing, Papa, but someone shot at us and Miss—"

"Yes, thank heavens they missed," he interrupted before she'd been able to mention her traveling companion. "That damn Clemmons fellow you are traveling with is no good for you, Fifi. You must trust me on this! He has brought you here where Lindley could find you."

"But Papa, he's not—"

"Listen to me," he said, forcing her to meet his gaze. His eyes were the same silvery gray she always remembered, but they looked older, more tired now. "Lindley is a dangerous man. You can never trust him, Fifi."

"But Papa—"

"And I know you are not truly wedded to Clemmons, either. Now you must come with me right away or become trapped in their web."

"Trapped in their—"

"Shh, they are coming back. We must hurry!"

He took her elbow and began leading her up the stairway. It appeared he had just come down that way. What on earth was Papa doing upstairs at this posting house? Her emotions were a jumble and she feared she could not think straight.

Heavens, but Papa was alive! Over four years now she'd thought he was dead, leaving her and Mamma alone to fend for themselves. Where had he been? What could have kept him away for so long, even after Mamma died? She was overjoyed and furious at the same time.

He took her up to a room and quietly ushered her in. She hoped he might pause now to give her some idea what was going on, calm her rattled nerves with some explanation. He didn't, though. Instead he merely went straight to the window that hung open.

"Come, quickly," he said, stepping outside.

She cried out but then realized the window opened onto the roof of a lower part of the building. Papa was leading her out there. Should she follow? What of Miss St. Clement and the others? But then again, this was her father, who she'd mourned for so many long, lonely years! How could she not follow him?

She did, her dress catching but slightly on the sill. She managed to loosen it, and in no time she was trailing after him, up to the crest of the roof, carefully around the chimney, and then over to the other side. Thankfully, the pitch was not too steep and she had no trouble following him. They must have been over the kitchens, and directly next to the roof was a high stone wall that surrounded the tiny garden where vegetables and herbs were growing.

Papa climbed off the roof and walked carefully along the wall, glancing back with a look to tell her she was expected to do the same. Well, he seemed to know what he was doing, so she followed. The stone wall was sturdier than it appeared, she was glad to find. She tiptoed along it like a circus performer until they came to a smaller building.

Papa turned and took her hand, helping her up onto the roof of the building, where she was surprised to find a gable with an opening. Without so much as a pause, they were able to step right into the loft of what turned out to be a laundry house. The smell of lye was strong, but not overwhelming. With evening heavy on them, the little building was empty of people. She and Papa had the whole place to themselves.

Except for the horse happily munching on a shirt down below them on the ground floor.

Papa smiled at her unspoken question. "Yes, *ma chérie*, that is my horse. I hid it here. Now come, as soon as things are clear, we must be off. I have my gig hidden nearby, and you will be safe."

"Papa, truly, you must imagine how confused I am, and . . ."

He put his fingers to her lips and shushed her again, but so gently she could not complain.

"*Sans bruit, ma belle*," he whispered. "Keep silent until we are gone."

"But Papa, I . . ."

"You must trust me, Fifi. I know I have little right to ask it after all these years, but for your own sake, please trust me just now."

He was so earnest, so desperate looking, so wonderfully alive that she could do nothing but comply. None of it made sense, but she did trust him. She hoped to God it was the right thing to do.

Chapter Six

The shooter was gone. Lindley had found a pair of grooms who'd been working in front of the house, preparing the coach for departure. They'd heard the gunfire, sure enough, then noticed a lone man ride off, heading south. Clearly he'd made no attempt not to be seen. Lindley felt he could assume, then, that he was supposed to follow. It was a trap, most likely. Well, no other way to get to the bottom of this.

He took a groom with him, then went around the back of the posting house. He found Rastmoor and told him what the men had seen.

"No one they recognized, I suppose?" Rastmoor asked.

"Sorry, milord," the groom said. "I didn't get a good enough look. And anyway, lots of folk were here just then, drinking and such. They mostly all took off when they heard the shooting. The gent I saw might have just been one of those. You might do better to ask the folks inside what they saw."

Lindley knew they'd not get any information that way, but he thanked the groom for his trouble and handed him a few coins just the same. The mail coach was eager to get back on the road, and it would accomplish nothing to delay it by further questions. The groom trotted off back to his work, and Lindley contemplated what to do next.

"You don't by any chance know who was supposed to get shot tonight, do you?" Rastmoor asked, rather unexpectedly.

"To tell the truth, no," Lindley replied, deciding that was a deuced perceptive question from the man. "But I do know it's not safe around here for you, Rastmoor, with Fitzgelder stirring up trouble, and all."

"That's why I'm on my way back to London now to deal with it."

"Might be better to wait, all things considered," Lindley cautioned.

"*All things?* And what would those things be?"

Hellfire, where did the man get his sudden suspicions? Obviously Rastmoor needed something to distract him from worry. "Look, you shouldn't stay here tonight; it's too dangerous. Why not head back out to Dashford's and take our long-lost Sophie with you?"

"And you?"

"I'll head after that man the groom saw."

"He said he wasn't sure that was our shooter."

"Who else would it be? You just get yourself to Dashford's."

Rastmoor nodded. "And take Mr. and Mrs. Clemmons with me."

"Right. And if there's any chance of losing the mister along the way, that's what I'd propose."

That actress was not to be trusted. Lindley would love to stay here and unravel this masquerade, for Miss Darshaw's sake, but he could only handle one deadly near miss at a time. Right now finding that shooter was his first priority. He'd just have to trust that Rastmoor would look after the girl. But not *too* well.

His friend contemplated Lindley's suggestion, then agreed. "Fine. That's what I'll do."

"Good. You go collect the Clemmonses and I'll see if I can get myself a fast horse."

"You'll go off on your own, Lindley? Isn't it a bit dangerous?"

"Don't worry. I can handle it."

Rastmoor seemed to think that a bit doubtful, but he gave a shrug and didn't question Lindley any further. Just as well, since Lindley had no intention of giving him any answers. The man did not need to know the axle had been tampered with or that the shooter could have just as easily been after Lindley as after Rastmoor. Fitzgelder might be focusing his malicious intent on Rastmoor just now, but were he to learn a few things about Lindley there was no doubt the man would just as soon see his friend murdered as his cousin. Perhaps more so, since Lindley was close to possessing information that could utterly destroy Fitzgelder.

With luck, though, Fitzgelder would remain clueless, and Lindley would finally have the names they needed to see the man hang. Justice would be served. True, a swifter vengeance might be more satisfying, but he'd promised to work within the law. For now, at least.

His boots crunched on the ground as he left Rastmoor and headed to the stable behind the posting house. The buildings were old, thick with plantings, but served their purpose. The dampness of evening was setting in, and night birds gave up their lonely calls. Things were settling down after the excitement.

Lindley grabbed the first groom he found and ordered a horse be saddled immediately. If that truly had been their shooter the grooms had seen fleeing in such an obvious way—and he suspected it was—he'd best not dawdle. That man was probably on his way now to contact his employer. Lindley was determined to find out just who that might be.

The groom bustled about his business, and Lindley tapped his foot impatiently. It was not his foot taps he heard out in the yard, though, so he peered out the doorway. By God, what was this? From somewhere a horse appeared behind the posting house. Some unidentified rider spurred the horse away and it took off on a hearty canter, clods of dirt flying up at its hooves.

But the damaged landscape was not the main reason Lindley stared. His eyes were pinned on the rider. More accurately, his eyes were pinned on the young woman propped tenuously in the lap of the unknown rider. Lindley swore beneath his breath. He did not get a close look at the man, but he certainly recognized that woman.

Sophie.

And she was most noticeably not calling out for help or struggling to escape as the man guided their horse out of the yard and onto the road. Going north. Lindley's plans changed right there and then.

To hell with the shooter who rode off to the south—Feasel was nearby. He could handle that. If Sophie Darshaw was riding north with some man, then Lindley was, too.

PAPA HAD BEEN RIGHT. HIS GIG HAD BEEN CONCEALED in a thicket not half a mile from the inn. They'd ridden there and Papa hastily harnessed the horse and got them back on the road. His patient nag seemed to care little whether she was bearing riders or pulling a gig, and Papa's gentle way with her was strangely comforting.

Perhaps she had done right by coming with him like this. The Papa she recalled was a kind man, and so far this stranger gave no indication that aspect of him had changed. If only she could be so convinced he was honest.

"Do you suppose anyone saw us?" Sophie asked, forcing herself to relax into the worn upholstery of Papa's creaking gig.

"I didn't notice anyone. I think we are safe now, Fifi. I'll look after you."

It was an absurd thing for him to say after all these years. He would look after her? Where had he been when she and Mamma had been forced to give up their modest house and go to live in a brothel? Where had he been when she was fending off Mr. Fitzgelder's pawing attentions for the past weeks? How on earth could she possibly expect him to look after her now when he'd so clearly avoided doing just that for so long?

But she couldn't bring herself to ask. There were simply too many questions, too much to say. In truth, she hardly knew this man, and certainly he could not know her. She was barely more than a child when he left, when they'd been told he died. Indeed, he was a stranger, and here she was entrusting her life to him.

"You are so quiet, my dear," he said softly.

"What would you have me talk about?" she asked.

"Well, it's been a long time since we've spoken," he said with annoying cheerfulness. "Perhaps you could tell me some of what I've missed."

"Let's see," she began, matching his cheerfulness with an angry intent. "The puppy you gave me ran away because I couldn't feed it, we lost our home and were forced to live in a brothel, and . . . oh yes, Mamma died."

"*Oui.* I know," he replied, the cheerfulness gone. Perhaps his had been as much a sham as hers. "Life has not been very easy."

"No, it has not. I wonder why you did nothing to make it any better for us?"

"Sophie, please . . . there are things you know nothing about."

"I know about Mamma's suffering. Her heart was broken and then the rest of her failed, too. Still, she worshipped you to the very end."

He was silent. Was she hurting him with her words? She hoped so. Somehow it was simply not fair that he was alive now while Mamma was gone.

"We buried her in the rain. It was a Monday."

"I know. You were very brave and did not cry."

"You were there?"

"I was, Fifi."

It was too much to accept. "I didn't see you."

"You weren't meant to."

Now just what did the man mean by that? Honestly, how could she be expected to believe it? And truly, if he had been at Mamma's funeral, how could he have not let her know? How could he have seen such sorrow and not offered any shred of comfort? Moreover, how could she possibly be expected to forgive him?

"Then you knew we were living in a brothel, didn't you?"

"I did. I was sad to see you there, but Eudora was good to you. She did not force you into her trade. You and your dear *maman* were safe."

"You know Madame Eudora?" This gig was getting even smaller and less comfortable. If Papa knew so much of her life, how could he have possibly kept himself from her all these years?

"But of course I know her," he replied and even smiled. "We are . . . friends."

Sophie shuddered to think what Papa might be implying by that. She knew what sort of "friends" Madame kept. He knew where she and Mamma were forced to live and had not done anything about it? Poor Mamma had suffered so when they'd been told he was killed in that accident. Through all this time, how could he have possibly stayed away? They'd needed him desperately. Why had he abandoned his wife and child?

Unless Madame was the reason.

"You and Madame Eudora were . . . close friends?"

He grunted—or perhaps it was a laugh. "No, Fifi. There was nothing like that. I did not leave your precious *maman* for another woman. No, it was much more than that. Someday I will tell you."

Someday. Why not now? What was he concealing from her? Should she ask? No, probably not. She wasn't certain she was ready for whatever his answer might be. These last few days had held far too many unexpected revelations for her already.

She shifted uncomfortably in her seat. Papa noticed.

"Not far, I promise," he said. "Soon you will ride in high style. Eudora has brought her carriage. We will meet her."

Again, another surprise. "Madame is out here? She has left London?"

"She knows you are in danger. She said we should find her waiting in Warwick."

"She's waiting for us?"

"*Oui*, Fifi," Papa said with a paternal chuckle. "She has missed you so much."

"And I've missed her, and the other girls," she had to admit.

"You wish to go back with her?"

She felt her soul cringe inside but was careful not to let it show. She hated that life, stitching for Madame all day long, sleeping alone at night in her cot while she knew one floor below her friends were doing all manner of sordid things with Madame's clients. No, she did not want to go back to that. Yet she couldn't very well go back to Fitzgelder and the abuse she was living with there, either.

"It's not as if I have any other home," she replied, happy to realize the harsh words must implicate him.

"No, Fifi, you have me now," he replied.

"Somehow, Papa, I cannot see how that truly helps me at this point."

He was silent, contemplating his sins, she hoped. She felt the slightest twinge of guilt for cruelly enjoying his discomfort, but so many years of fending for herself managed to assuage most of it. If Papa did not die those years ago, he should have helped her then. She really doubted he could help her now.

IT WAS WELL AFTER DARK, BUT WARWICK WAS STILL awake. Two inns faced each other across the main road, and a few people moved about. Sophie's body ached from her uncomfortable ride, though she wasn't certain her evening here would be any more pleasant. The longer she'd had to think about it, the more she'd begun to question the wisdom of running away with Papa like this.

Poor Miss St. Clement, left back there with the likes of Lindley and that Lord Rastmoor. Sophie should never have left her. True, the actress gave every impression of being a woman who could take care of herself, but she'd been a good friend. There was no telling what might happen to her now, and Sophie would be partially to blame.

Papa guided his gig toward one of the inns and brought them to a halt. Sophie should have waited for his help before getting herself down onto the ground, but she would not give him the satisfaction of allowing him to offer it now when for so long he had not. As worn and exhausted as she was, her knees very nearly gave out under her. She managed to catch herself, though. Just as she always had.

"Hmm, I was not expecting two inns like this," Papa said, dismounting to stand beside her. "I will have to find out which one Eudora is staying at."

She studied the old, whitewashed façade of the nearest building. The sign hanging above the door read "Steward's

Brake." If they had clean linen and passable beds, she'd be happy enough at either of these places, whether Madame was here or not. Perhaps a good rest would help to clear her mind and give her some idea what she should do tomorrow—go back to find Miss St. Clement or trust Papa?

"Where the devil is a groom?" Papa grumbled, glancing around and finding no one to look after their horse.

Sophie stretched her limbs and regained her balance. "Here, I'll hold the horse. You go make sure this is the right place."

He hesitated just long enough to make her wonder if he knew he had good reason to worry she might not be here when he came back. That seemed proof of a guilty conscience as far as Sophie was concerned. But she reassured him anyway.

"I'll stay here." She sighed. "I'm too tired to leave. Besides, my backside is appalled at the idea of getting back into this sad conveyance and riding for even another five minutes tonight."

"Good girl," he said, apparently relieved by her suffering.

Leaving her to watch over their gig, he gave one last glance around before he went inside. The horse watched him go, then immediately plodded away from her new keeper to go rip a branch off the rose trellis nearby. Sophie grumbled.

"Come on," she said, grabbing the halter and dragging the animal—and its trailing gig—away from the plantings. She had no idea what sort of money her father carried on him these days, but she was certain he would not wish to waste it all paying for damage to the local matron's favorite posies.

There was a patch of grass nearby, in an open space between the buildings. A leafy oak spread out overhead, and Sophie decided this might be a better place to wait for Papa. The horse followed her willingly, and she let the reins sag as the animal munched. Sophie leaned her aching body against the solid tree trunk. Yes, despite her prickling conscience, a bed safely away from Fitzgelder and the stink of London certainly would be welcome tonight.

She was midway through a well-needed yawn when she heard a sound. It came from behind and was probably nothing out of the ordinary. A rat, perhaps. But the horse's ears flicked and the animal stopped happily ripping tufts of grass. Its huge round eyes caught on something and the large head came up. Sophie leaned forward to peer around the tree.

She didn't see much, though. From the darkness, arms reached for her, pulling her into a tight hold against a body every bit as solid as the oak trunk but far warmer and entirely masculine. A hand clamped over her mouth, preventing any sound she might have been about to make. Her cheek was pressed against a soft woolen coat that smelled distinctly of Lindley.

Lindley!

"Your protector is hardly doing his job, leaving you alone out here in the dark," he said, a low growl in the stillness around them.

She struggled to pull away from him, terrified to realize she felt far more secure tucked up against him than she had the whole time she'd been traveling here with her father. Lord Lindley was a dangerous man. She feared her involuntary attraction for him might prove to be even more so.

He allowed her to push away from him, yet he did not release her. His fingers dug into her shoulders as he held her there, inches from him, as his eyes locked onto hers with a force she could not break.

"Do you need my help, Miss Darshaw?" he asked. "Or did you come here of your own accord?"

For one disturbing heartbeat she thought about lying. Oh, but she might indeed enjoy whatever help this man had in mind. Then, of course, she reined in those wayward thoughts. She did not need Lord Lindley's help, nor would she allow herself to succumb to it. Papa may have been thoughtlessly absent for the past several years, but she was far better off with him than the likes of Lindley, despite how her knees went weak the longer he gazed at her. Or perhaps, specifically *because* of how her knees went weak.

"No . . . I'm fine."

But he did not release her, not from his secure grip nor from his untiring gaze. "You don't appear fine. Who brought you here?"

"My father," she managed to say after just the slightest hesitation.

Lindley's eyes went stormy and his left eyebrow rose slightly. "Your *father*?"

She broke free of his gaze and stared intently at the tree trunk beside her. "Apparently he's not quite as deceased as I've thought him these past years."

Lindley's right eyebrow rose up to join the other. Was he surprised to find the man alive, or to learn she had believed him dead? Then again, why would she suppose he had any knowledge whatsoever that she even had a father? Of course, there would have been very little reason for Madame to mention anything about her sad past to this fine gentleman. Sophie was silly to have hoped perhaps he might have asked after her at some point. Just as she was silly now for being happy to see him.

"He has gone in to secure us a room for the night," she explained. "But whyever are you here, Lord Lindley?"

The eyebrows came back down and he gave half a sly smile. "I followed you, of course, Miss Darshaw. I saw you leave with a strange man and thought perhaps you needed assistance."

"As you can see, I do not."

"Indeed. But how odd that your husband was left behind. And with someone so carelessly shooting, and all."

She glanced around. "Is . . . er . . . did you bring my husband with you?"

Now he actually laughed at her. "No, Miss Darshaw, I did not. I'm assuming that particular person is safely back in Geydon with my friend Rastmoor. They are probably both wondering where you've gone, though."

Well, perhaps it was for the best that Miss St. Clement and Lord Rastmoor were left alone back there. Clearly they had things to resolve between them. Wouldn't it be lovely if even through all this chaos that pair might somehow be reunited? The actress had been most strenuous in her insistence that would never happen, but Sophie could not be so sure. Miss St. Clement had been quite desperate to locate the gentleman again.

"Come," Lindley prodded, still holding her with his gaze and looming far too close. "Tell me why you are here. Is this really your father you have traveled with, or is that merely the story he's inside telling the innkeeper?"

"He *is* my father!" she insisted, not at all appreciating what the man insinuated.

Just at that moment Papa proved her words by appearing at the corner of the inn and calling for her. She jolted, and Lindley's fingers dug more firmly than ever into her shoulders. She winced.

"Let me go. Please," she whispered. "He must not see you here."

Thankfully the horse and the gig and the tree and the darkness were concealing Lindley's presence. From what Papa had said of him earlier, she doubted things would go well if Papa found him with her now. Lindley seemed to concur.

He dropped his arms to his sides and took a silent step back from her. Oddly enough, she nearly staggered under the reality of having to solely support herself again. Surely it was just exhaustion that made her feel this way. Never before had she so wanted to cast herself into a gentleman's arms and beg him to carry her off. Thank heavens she was too smart for that—or too frightened, at least.

She hurried away from him, moving around the horse while it happily ignored her in favor of the grass. She caught one last look at Lindley but said nothing more to him. Whatever was going on, she wished to heaven he had not been involved. It had been so lovely to watch him from afar at Madame's, to admire him and tease herself with fantasies that this was the sort of man a woman could look up to, could trust. Obviously such men did not exist—even Papa had shown her that.

It would be best if she forgot all about Lord Lindley and concentrated on making a new life for herself. If Papa might be of help, how wonderful. If not, then she was no worse off than before. She met Papa in the yard.

"Here I am, Papa. Your stubborn horse was trying to eat the roses."

Papa glanced toward the creature, and for a heartbeat Sophie feared he might detect Lindley there, still hiding in shadow. But Lindley must have gone, for Papa merely smiled fondly at his lazy nag. "She does like her roses. Perhaps when we get where we are going there will be a whole bush of them for her."

"And just where are we going, Papa? Did you find—"

"*Chut, chut,* Fifi. Our friends are not here, so I have sent a boy across the way to inquire at the other inn. Ah, see? Here he comes with news for us."

The boy trotted across the empty street and eagerly accepted the promised coin from Papa. He informed them there was no word of Madame's arrival at the other inn, either. Papa frowned.

"Well, we will simply take a room and wait," he decided. "Tomorrow I will take you back where you belong. You will see, Fifi, all this has not been in vain."

Papa was as dramatic as ever. He seemed to truly believe he could make all of this right. Handing the boy another coin and instructing him to run to the stable and secure a place for the horse, Papa laid his cool hand on Sophie's shoulder. She felt the urge to cringe, though Papa was far more gentle than Lord Lindley had been. Most disturbing.

"Come, Fifi, your cheeks are flushed and you seem none too steady on your feet," Papa said, taking her elbow. "Let's get you into bed."

She let him lead her into the inn. Thank heavens it was Papa who spoke this way now. She feared if those words had come from Lindley she'd be following him just as easily.

LINDLEY STOOD SILENTLY IN THE SHADOWS AND watched. Sophie had been truthful with him—the man was indeed her father. Yes, he could get a good look at him now and recognized him easily. Philip Darshaw—or more correctly, Philippe D'Archaud, as he was truly named—was not a striking man. He was a bit on the small side, although by no means delicate. He carried himself with a confident air, however, and although the man had been in England for years, he'd never fully lost his continental swagger. Lindley could quite see how the fellow had built himself a successful career on the stage.

Plus, Lindley had heard stories of the great beauty that had been this man's wife. Indeed, if Sophie was anything at all like her mother, the stories had obviously been accurate. Clearly, Sophie's attractive features and eye-catching figure were not gifts from her father. It seemed all she had inherited from him was a legacy of shame and hardship.

Lindley knew a bit about D'Archaud. He'd run across the bastard a time or two, been able to determine he was—or had been—closely connected with the very people Lindley was stalking all this time. Oh yes, Lindley had been eager to meet up with Philippe D'Archaud, and he had no doubt this was the man.

At last, he was close to getting what he wanted. But there would be no sense in acting irrationally. He would wait, plan his course of action, and make certain D'Archaud would not get away. Lindley strained his ears to listen as the man spoke to his daughter.

It appeared he and Sophie would be spending the night at this place. If D'Archaud had been involved in the shooting attempt at the posting house, he had given up hope of success. At least for now. Tonight, it appeared, he and Sophie were done running.

But had D'Archaud acted alone? Who was that lone rider who'd been seen leaving the posting house in the other direction? Perhaps D'Archaud had a partner out there who had not cut his losses and run this way. He would no doubt be pursuing his goal all this while. Lindley should have ignored these two and gone after that one. It had been more than foolish to come chasing after Miss Darshaw like this.

What had he been thinking? *Rescue?* It was ridiculous. Did he truly believe the girl was innocent in all this deception and scheming? What would it matter if she was? His responsibility was to justice. Miss Darshaw was not the only innocent person caught up in this mess, but she was lucky enough to be surviving it. Others were not so lucky. It was to *those* persons Lindley held a responsibility, not to some pretty face he'd met in a brothel.

Damn, he was a fool. As soon as things were clear, he ought to go retrieve his mount where he'd left it and tear off in the other direction. Feasel would no doubt be looking for him, possibly with further news on Fitzgelder and his particular business. That is what Lindley ought to keep his mind on, not this slip of a criminal's daughter. He should go right away and forget all about Sophie Darshaw.

But something the girl's father said to her continued to repeat itself in Lindley's head. *Tomorrow I will take you back where you belong.* What could the man mean by it? Where, after all, did Sophie belong? Surely not in a brothel. What father would knowingly drag his child back to a place like that?

Yet she had no other home, not that Lindley knew of. Unless one wanted to count Fitzgelder's servants' quarters, and Lindley did not. But could that be what D'Archaud had meant? He was in league with the man, or had been at one time; Lindley knew that for a fact. Could D'Archaud be planning to take Sophie back to Fitzgelder, to have her installed there again for some purpose?

It was unthinkable, yet then again, Lindley had been forced to face several unthinkable things over the past few years. In some sick, disgusting way it made perfect sense that D'Archaud might have been instrumental in placing his daughter in Fitzgelder's home for his own personal benefit. Now it was just as logical that he might be taking her back there.

Damn him! The poor girl did not deserve that. Lindley acknowledged that he was not entirely thinking straight when he left the lonely shadows behind the inn and stalked around to the door D'Archaud and his daughter had just entered.

He strode in, easily finding D'Archaud in discussion with the proprietor, engaging them a room for the night. Sophie seemed particularly small and exhausted as she stood quietly next to her father. The father who had done nothing to keep her out of that brothel and who very likely was eager to send her back to Fitzgelder. Lindley couldn't stomach it.

"D'Archaud," he said, stopping mere feet from the man.

Sophie sucked in a startled breath, and D'Archaud whirled on him.

"Lindley. What the hell do you want?"

The men eyed each other.

"I've got a laundry list of things I want," Lindley replied. "To start with, I want you to tell me what the hell you're doing here."

D'Archaud stepped in front of Sophie. "I'm trying to keep my daughter away from the likes of you, that's what I'm doing here."

"Why, so you can drag her back to Fitzgelder's employ?"

"You've been keeping tabs on her, I see," D'Archaud sneered. "I ought to—"

The older man moved quickly, fists raised. Lindley instinctively ducked, just in time. He wished he hadn't, though. If he'd let the blackguard hit him, killing him would be that much more justified.

Lindley allowed himself the decadent luxury of giving in to his anger. He lunged at the older man. D'Archaud still had some speed left in him, though, and managed to avoid taking the full force of Lindley's well-aimed facer. The earl only succeeded in a glancing blow to D'Archaud's jaw.

But it was enough to set the man off balance. Sophie squealed and rushed toward her father while the man staggered back, grasping at a chair to try to keep to his feet. She glared at Lindley. Her cold, frightened eyes stopped him in his tracks. Whatever else D'Archaud was, Sophie still looked at the man as a child would. He was still her father, and she was ready to defend him, despite his negligent care for her all these years.

Lindley supposed he could understand this. He'd had a father, too, and despite the old man's lifestyle of waste and carelessness, Lindley had still fairly worshipped him. True, it would have been nice if his father had not left him with an estate full of debt and a string of greedy creditors camped at the door. He supposed he could empathize with Sophie's concern and natural devotion.

He stepped back, giving D'Archaud time to compose himself. The proprietor hurried out from behind his desk to beg the men to be calm. Lindley doubted that would happen.

Sophie turned her back on Lindley and focused on helping her father. He tried to take a step forward, but his leg seemed to crumble underneath him. He fell back into the chair and moaned, clutching his knee. Somehow in their brief struggle the man had been injured. How, Lindley could not entirely be certain.

Something clattered to the floor. Lindley glanced down to discover a knife. He looked back up to discover an ugly red stain appearing between D'Archaud's fingers, just above the boot. The man was bleeding. Profusely.

"Good heavens!" the proprietor called out.

"You cut him!" Sophie yelled, hovering over her father and giving Lindley a glare that was no less lethal than the knife lying at his feet.

"I did no such thing," Lindley informed her, still grappling with the details of the situation. "He must have been extricating it from his boot to use the bloody thing on *me*."

For a moment the hatred in Sophie's eyes faded and she turned her face toward her father's. "Papa?"

"I can't let him go on using you, Fifi," D'Archaud growled. "His promises are all lies—whatever he's told you, it's a lie. You've got to trust me!"

She seemed confused, but certainly no more than Lindley felt. Just what was D'Archaud rattling on about? What on earth did he think Lindley had been doing with his daughter? He was more than happy to find Sophie was eager to clear things up.

"Papa, Lord Lindley has only ever been kind to me," she explained.

The way D'Archaud rolled his eyes indicated he might not fully believe her. And rightly so, Lindley supposed. He had to acknowledge the girl was giving him more credit than he deserved, considering some of the things he'd said to her these last couple of days. Likely, though, her praise was due more to her wish to calm her father than to any real kindness she'd perceived within Lindley. *Pity, that.* He was sure he might still be quite a kindly soul if his life hadn't been wholly consumed by this hunt for justice these last few years. Besides, there was some sort of pleasurable sensation at the thought of Miss Darshaw viewing him in a positive light.

"He doesn't know the meaning of kindness," D'Archaud snarled. "I could have cut out the man's heart and he'd barely notice."

"Really, Papa!" Miss Darshaw exclaimed. "Lord Lindley is a titled gentleman. You cannot go around insulting him like this and . . . and pulling knives on him!"

D'Archaud gave a disgusted grunt. "I assure you, Fifi, it was no less than he had planned for me."

"I had no intention of resorting to violence," Lindley announced, "until you decided to drag your daughter into all of this. How deeply have you pulled her in? Is her very life forfeit for the sake of assisting you in your crimes?"

D'Archaud tried to rise up from his seat, but the blood was flowing freely from his leg and it almost seemed the man would topple over. Sophie must have recognized the situation. She grasped helplessly at her father's arm, urging him to be still, to let her tend his wound. He pushed her away.

"Sophie knows nothing of my life," D'Archaud said. "I have had no contact with her . . . not until now, when she's gotten herself mixed up with you and that, that Clemmons bastard."

"Papa!" the girl exclaimed, sounding every bit the proper, missish lady.

Lindley couldn't help but chuckle at the irony. She was scolding the man for his crude conversation when he was the very one who left her in a brothel all these years, on her own against a world full of Fitzgelders and worse. Clearly somewhere along the way Miss Darshaw had been raised in propriety and advantage. Such a shame she had fallen to this state now.

Then the full meaning of D'Archaud's words sank in, and Lindley cocked his head in curiosity. D'Archaud had mentioned Clemmons. Could it be the man did not know the truth about Clemmons? Was he truly under the impression his daughter had been chasing the countryside with a *man*? And Sophie had not set him straight? Indeed, it appeared D'Archaud was not the only one keeping secrets from his loved ones.

In some convoluted way, this seemed in Sophie's favor.

"Are you implying your daughter has no knowledge of the despicable ways you've supported yourself over the years, D'Archaud?"

"I'm informing you flat out, sir, that Sophie is innocent."

"Well, that still remains to be seen, doesn't it?"

D'Archaud snarled at him. "She has no knowledge of anything you are interested in, Lindley. If you think there is business between us, leave her out of it. I'll go with you, but Sophie remains here, unharmed."

So D'Archaud had eluded him all this time, only to go peacefully now? Lindley doubted it. Still, the man's concern for his daughter seemed genuine. Perhaps this could be useful.

"If she's connected to you, D'Archaud, she's guilty as sin. I'm taking you both. Justice will determine your fate."

Lindley wasn't quite sure how he would follow through on

that threat, considering it was late at night, he didn't know a soul in this town, and he'd arrived here on a rented hack. Still, where his daughter was concerned D'Archaud appeared to be unwilling to take chances.

The man forced himself up onto his feet—despite his daughter's protests—and he met Lindley's eyes dead-on. "I will go with you, but not Sophie. No, listen to me, damn it. I know what you're after, Lindley, and you'll never find it on your own. Take me now and I'll lead you there. But Sophie stays."

So she could meet up with D'Archaud's contact and he could send warning that Lindley was on the way? No, he was not about to fall into that trap. Sophie may not know exactly what her father was up to, but she still cared for him and would surely do whatever she could to protect him. Even now, he could see it in her eyes. She was trying to make sense of all this and decide what she could do about it.

But if Lindley could ferret out that contact person—and he had no doubt there was one—then he'd be one step ahead of things. He knew, of course, that D'Archaud had no intentions of actually leading him to the men he was after. That was simply a ruse to get Lindley away from Sophie, and of course no father could be blamed for attempting it. But if Lindley were to pretend to believe the man and go along with his suggestion, he could lull Sophie into making that contact. All Lindley would have to do after that was watch, follow, and wait.

But what to do with D'Archaud in the meanwhile? Sophie must believe they were gone and that her father was in danger. Well, that ought to be easy enough to manage.

He smiled at her and set his plan in motion.

Chapter Seven

Lindley was going to take Papa away! No, not after she'd just found him again after all these years. How could she let it happen? And the poor man was injured, his lifeblood rushing out of his body with nothing to check it. She still could not be sure who inflicted that wound, although she tried and tried to wish it were Lindley. That would make it so much easier to hate him. However, common sense told her that was not likely the case.

She had not seen Lindley with a knife, and, after all, Papa was a criminal. That seemed nearly undeniable. Why else would he have let her—and everyone else—think him dead all this time? Now that Lindley had found him, he would certainly have resorted to violence to save himself. Even if it meant attacking an earl. Lindley's story was too easy to accept.

But was it the truth? She honestly couldn't know. Lindley was a gentleman, true, but she'd certainly seen enough gentlemen come through the doors at Madame's brothel and heard the whispers of how they'd behaved in the privacy of their hostesses' rooms to know not every gentleman was, indeed, a gentleman.

Yet Lindley spoke of justice. He seemed rock-solid in his

conviction that Papa had done some terrible wrong and needed to pay for it. Of course it was true.

Papa, however, spoke of trust. He claimed Lindley was a liar and none of his words could be believed. All he asked was for Sophie to trust him. Yet, how could she?

She watched—helpless—as the handkerchief she'd held against his wounded leg began to drip blood. Right now none of it mattered; not justice, not trust, and not discovering the truth. All that mattered was saving Papa's life.

"Very well," Lindley said, interrupting her before she had the chance to beg. "I will take you, Darshaw, and leave your daughter here. I suppose the girl has been well educated in fending for herself. I doubt she's privy to much useful information, anyway."

"Thank you," Papa said, his voice sounding weak.

"Stay here," Lindley went on. "I'll go arrange a conveyance. We'll leave within ten minutes. Say your good-byes and don't force me to get ugly about this."

What, it wasn't ugly already? Oh, but this was dreadful! Papa was in the process of bleeding to death, yet he would simply agree to go with the man? He'd leave her again? Indeed, this was ugly enough for her.

"Wait!" she called before Lindley walked back out the door he'd just come in. "You can't mean to take him like this! He'll never make it. He needs a doctor!"

"He'll see the hangman soon enough."

She could scarcely believe her ears. Lord Lindley was so cold as to drag her father away, knowing he'd likely bleed to death long before they ever reached any magistrate or court of law? But that was inhumane! What on earth could Papa have done to make the man hate him so?

There was nothing she could do but watch Lindley's tall, elegant form as he strode out the door and into the darkness. By God, whatever Papa may or may not have done hardly counted for anything just now. The only thing that could make any difference was what she herself might do about it.

And she knew what to do. She'd lived long enough under Madame's roof and seen the fire in Lindley's eye. Indeed, she knew exactly what to do. She'd do it, too, by God, if it might save Papa's life.

"Hold on, Papa," she said, and she glanced up at the gaping proprietor, whose wife must have heard the commotion and appeared at his side. "Quickly! Find him bandages."

Then she kissed Papa's clammy cheek and gave him a reassuring smile just before she hurried out the door after Lindley. Papa said nothing, but she could feel his eyes follow her. She prayed he might not guess her intentions.

LINDLEY MOVED OUT INTO THE DARKNESS, AWAY FROM the doorway to the inn and the glowing lamp that had been hung there. He would not need a conveyance, but his brief absence would allow D'Archaud to give his daughter instruction. Whether she was a party to his criminal actions or not, Lindley had seen the desperation displayed clearly on her face. She would do whatever the older man asked of her, and Lindley did not doubt he would ask her to contact his friends.

He couldn't help but smile. Finally, he was this close to finding what he'd been after all this time. He would be able to go to Warren with names, details, proof that would condemn the monsters who had gotten away with murder and treason. Well, they'd not get away with it much longer. Lindley would finally be able to sleep at night.

Provided, of course, his conscience could allow him that. By baiting D'Archaud into sending his daughter to deliver word to his cronies, Lindley was thoroughly implicating the girl in her father's crimes. She may be innocent now, but once she stood in the way of justice and took warning to the enemy, she was guilty and would bear the consequences. And Lindley's conscience would bear the consequences of *that*.

He was almost relieved when he heard her footsteps behind him.

"Lord Lindley, please," she began, trotting toward him, then stopping just out of arm's reach. "You cannot take Papa. Not now."

"You don't know what he's done, Miss Darshaw."

"But I know what will happen if he does not see a doctor right away."

"He's wounded; nothing more. He'll survive."

"But the blood . . . Please, have some compassion."

She was so earnest it was all he could do to deny her. Her helpless, desperate eyes searched his. His resolve returned, however, as soon as he recalled another pair of helpless, desperate eyes that had begged him for rescue. Rescue he could not give. Those eyes had shut and never opened again. D'Archaud carried the guilt for that. Damn it, but Lindley couldn't let himself be weak now. Four souls left in the cold ground of his family plot needed justice. They would get it.

"My compassion is buried with my family, back in Kent," he informed her.

She must have recognized the icy reality of this on his face. She took a step backward, away from him. The glow from the lamp hanging near the doorway spilled out into the yard where they stood. The warm light played against the heavy shadows, making her eyes seem endlessly deep and her skin soft as rose petals. Emotion only allowed her to draw short, halting breaths. Her worn gown pulled against those unignorable curves. Damn it, why couldn't he forget just for these moments how beautiful the girl was?

"Maybe you can't feel compassion, but surely you can feel something," she said, then swallowed and gave the tiniest hint of a smile. "You are, after all, a man."

Oh, he felt something, indeed. He just did not wish to discuss it at present. "My feelings are hardly your concern, Miss Darshaw. Go back to your father and say farewell."

Now she regained that hesitant step she'd taken away. "Please, I'll do anything."

She let that phrase hang in the air. He knew exactly what it meant. Holy hell, could he actually be tempted?

"*Anything*, my lord," she repeated with another halting step closer.

By God, he had to admit *anything* sounded remarkably enticing. She was barely a hand's span away. Every soft curve of her body and every slight tremor in her lip lured him. She offered herself for the sake of her treacherous father, and Lindley wished to heaven he had the resolve to refuse.

He did not. Reacting before his better judgment could intervene, he pulled her into his arms. She was either eagerly willing or too shocked to protest; he really did not care one way or the other. All that mattered was that her face tipped up toward his and he was finally able to capture those tremulous lips with his own. She was as soft and delectable as he'd often imagined.

He pressed her for a response and was pleased to find one. Her fingers dug into his coat, clinging to him as if she were as desperate for his touch as she was to rescue her father. He explored her mouth with his own, willing her to forget everything but this moment. Damn, but it would have been easy enough for him to put all his many worries aside and simply enjoy the feel of her, the taste of her.

Of course he could not afford it, though. There must be purpose to this madness. He might allow her to crumble into mindless desire, but he would have to remain in control. He must use her for his objective and never forget what that was.

God, he wished he could, though. Holding Sophie, hearing her muffled moan and feeling the heat that flowed between them, Lindley would have given nearly everything to believe this was real. Yet of course he'd already given everything, and he knew for a fact Miss Darshaw was not what she seemed.

Her halting breath was what he might have found in any woman. Her timid, tentative exploration of his mouth as his own ransacked hers was not to be mistaken for innocence. Her willing response to him could easily be nothing more than a manufactured ploy to distract. He would not fall into the trap of imagining she'd refrained from offering herself to any number of others for far less noble purposes over her years at Eudora's.

Despite what he felt as his hands roamed over her back and silked through her loosened hair, Lindley was fully aware of who she was and what part she must play in what would follow. He could not give in to his wants. He needed her to lead him to her father's collaborators.

With an effort nearly beyond his capacity, he pushed her away.

"You are almost tempting, Miss Darshaw," he said with a smile meant to insult her. "Come back to me when you are a grown woman and we'll see what might happen then. For now, though, go give your good-byes to your father."

She appeared stunned. Probably amazed that her kiss should have so little effect on him. Well, he would be certain to allow her to continue thinking that way. Inside he might be shaken to the core, but on the surface he would force himself to be controlled. Desire would fade. Justice was permanent.

She glared at him, and a sheen of pure hatred stole over her expression. "I was wrong," she hissed. "You are *not* a man. You're a monster."

Then she turned and ran back around toward the front of the building.

That scoundrel . . . that devil!

How could she let him do that to her? He lured her into compromise and then laughed in her face. *Abominable man.* He would treat her this way and then haul Papa off to the hangman, would he? Not over her dead body!

And not over Papa's, either. Somehow they had to escape, to get out of here before Lindley came back in to collect his prey. Sophie would see to it that beast never got his hands on Papa. They had to leave—now. If Papa couldn't walk, she would drag him, if she had to.

And it appeared that would be exactly what she'd need to do.

"Papa!"

He was crumpled on the ground, lying in a heap just at the corner of the inn. It appeared as if he'd been trying to follow her—probably to stop her from throwing herself at Lindley as she had planned. Well, he needn't have bothered. The grand Lord Lindley was far above wasting his time with the likes of her, even if she had made it very clear she'd do anything to spare her father the fate Lindley had planned.

But now it seemed her offer of sacrifice had been unnecessary. Papa lay unmoving. She dropped to her knees beside him and pulled his head into her lap.

Thank God, she was not too late. Papa's weary eyes slitted open. She could see he would speak, but she tried to soothe him, to keep him still. His leg had bled profusely, though someone indoors must have offered him a bandage before he left. A linen strip was wrapped over his wound but had not been tied tightly. She quickly set to adjusting it.

"Here, Papa, let me tie this. It needs to be tighter to stop the blood," she said, moving as fast as she dared without aggravating the wound. "Hush now, and let me tend this."

But her father would not be calm. He struggled to sit, craning his neck to see around the corner of the building. "I'll kill him. By God, I'll kill him!" he muttered, repeating himself a few more times in French, adding some rather unpleasant words here and there.

"No, Papa, you must be still. I need to remove your boot."

"He put his hands on you, Sophie! Yes, I will kill him. I'll take him by the throat and I'll . . ."

"Papa, be still! You may not kill Lord Lindley."

"But he touched you!"

"No, he—"

"I saw him. He was manhandling you as if he owned you! I'll kill him."

"Papa—"

"Eudora swore to me you were safe, that none of those filthy devils were allowed near you."

"Papa, you must settle down. We've got to take care of this and find you a doctor."

Suddenly Papa's struggles became more intense. He tried to shove Sophie away, but she held her ground, keeping a firm hold on the newly tied bandage. The cause of Papa's agitation was soon evident: Lindley. The worthless nobleman was at the corner of the building, watching them. Sophie felt her breath catch.

"I'll kill you, Lindley," Papa said, his voice a tired growl that still harbored enough threat to worry her.

Apparently not Lindley, though. "So I've heard," he replied with a cool drawl. "It appears your daughter, however, would have you abandon that plan."

"My daughter is none of your business, Lindley!" Papa said, pulling himself upright and grabbing the wall beside him as he tried to stand, despite Sophie's best efforts to keep him calm and still. "I said I'd go with you, but by God, you'll leave her out of this!"

The exertion appeared too much. Papa sagged, falling against the wall. Sophie cried out and dove to catch him, to save him from collapse. She managed to prop him against the building, but his face was pale and his eyes had lost their spark. Oh Lord, but she was losing him! All his struggles were draining him right before her eyes.

"Papa . . . please, we've got to stop the bleeding."

Lindley must have recognized his chance. He was there, pushing her to the side and hoisting Papa's arm over his shoulder. How dare he! She slapped at him and tried to pry him away. He pushed her hands aside as if she were nothing more than a big, annoying gnat.

"Are you going to help me, or not?" he said finally, meeting her eyes. "Your father needs medical attention."

She paused flailing at him just long enough for the words to sink in. "What?"

"Help me get him into your carriage. There must be a surgeon somewhere in this town."

"You'll take Papa there?"

"Not if I have to carry him the whole way. Help me now."

She did without hesitation. Perhaps Lindley had some shred of humanity in him, after all. Or perhaps it was a ruse simply to get Papa away from her. Well, either way, getting Papa into the gig was a good idea. If she had to, she'd get rid of Lindley somehow and then take Papa on her own. At least then he'd have a chance at survival.

Papa demanded weakly to know what they were doing, and Sophie soothed him as best she could. "We're taking you to the doctor, Papa. He'll tend your leg and stop that bleeding."

"You leave my daughter out of this, Lindley!"

"No, Papa, I'm not leaving you!"

He struggled a bit, but it took only a few moments for Lindley to get Papa up into their carriage. The horse watched them nervously, and Sophie was glad the stable hands had been slow in their labor. In fact, this could work very well for her.

As Lindley carefully positioned Papa in the seat, Sophie stole around the back of the gig and hopped into it from the other side. She took up the reins where Papa had secured them and quickly slapped the horse into movement. The little mare gave her a look of pure insult but danced into motion. The gig jolted.

Papa groaned.

"Hold on, Papa," Sophie said. "We're leaving."

But the yard beside the inn was small and the horse had to be turned around. It had been years since Papa had let Sophie drive, and she was clumsy at directing the confused mare. True, Lindley had been thrown back from the gig when first it jerked into action, but he was still quite capable of interfering with her brilliant escape plan.

He simply waited for the gig to be turned, then jogged up to the mare and took her halter. She cooperated beautifully for him and the gig came to a standstill. Sophie folded her arms across her chest and glared.

"Move over," Lindley said. It was obvious he had no intention of waiting for her to comply before climbing in, so she had no choice but to move closer to Papa or let herself be sat upon.

Papa groaned again when she pressed against his injured knee.

"I'm sorry," she said to him, but she spared a murderous glare for Lindley.

"Sophie stays here!" Papa insisted, wincing as the gig hit a bump.

Sophie laid her hand on his arm. "No, Papa. I go where you go."

"For now we are all going to the doctor," Lindley replied and gave Papa a quick surveying glance. "You're no use to me dead."

"But you don't need her!" Papa protested. "Leave her behind."

Lindley didn't bother with a glance for her. He shook his head. "No. I'm thinking you're not so likely to go ahead and die if she's here with you. Sophie stays."

And so she did. She took Papa's cool hand in hers as their crowded little gig rolled into the darkness between the buildings that lined the narrow streets of Warwick. She tried to ignore Lindley's warm, solid form pressed next to hers. The muscles in his arms loosed and tensed as he guided the mare. It was quite distracting to be so close to him after . . . well, it was distracting.

But all that mattered now was getting Papa the help he needed. She would concentrate on that. Lindley's motives for saving Papa might be self-serving, and she was certain he had every intention of taking Papa to the authorities soon enough, but for now he was doing the right thing and she was grateful for it.

"Thank you," she whispered.

He said nothing. Her words hung in the air and mocked her. This man did not need her thanks. He probably did not want them, just as he did not want anything else she may have offered. Papa's reprieve was only momentary, and she was an idiot for feeling any sort of gratitude. Lindley must think her a fool.

Finally he spoke, words muttered so low she could barely hear them. "I'm not a monster."

THE SURGEON WAS AN AMIABLE SORT WHO SEEMED honestly not to mind being awakened in the night to tend a suspicious wound. It appeared Papa would live, after all. At least for a while.

"Is the pain very horrible, Papa?" she asked, fluffing his pillow and making sure the blanket didn't lay too heavily on his wound.

The surgeon's house was neat and clean, but small. He agreed that Papa should remain here for the night, and Sophie was glad for that. However, her eyes were heavy and she wished Papa did not occupy the only spare bed in the house. The lone chair in the corner she had claimed would be sadly uncomfortable for passing the rest of the night.

And she was certainly not about to take up Lord Lindley on his offer to return to the inn with him. Unfortunately, that meant he was going to be staying here, too. Apparently he did not trust her, and for good reason, she had to admit. As soon as Papa was well enough, she planned to take any opportunity to escape with him. That would be a bit more risky with Lindley hovering over.

"You should go, Sophie," Papa said, his voice groggy from the medicine he'd been given. "Lindley will not follow you. It is me he's after."

"I won't leave you, Papa," she said, having just told him the same thing not two minutes ago. "We'll find a way out of this together."

But Papa shook his head. He looked so weary, so sad. "No, Fifi. Lindley has me, and the law is on his side. He may have let you believe your charms hold some sway over him, but truly, he is only using you."

She felt her face go warm. "Really, Papa. You are mistaken if you think anything has passed between me and Lord Lindley."

"I saw you, *chou-chou*. You went to his arms, hoping he might care enough about you to spare me."

Now her face burned from the shame of what she had attempted as well as from the humiliation of having failed. "I had to try, Papa."

"And now here we are at the surgeon's," he said, patting her hand gently where she laid it on the cover beside him. "But do not let this mislead you, Fifi. Lindley's passion is not for you. No, he craves only vengeance. Don't give him any more of yourself than you already have, my dear."

"I've given him nothing, Papa. You must rest, now. You need to sleep. I will stay nearby."

"As will Lindley, no doubt."

"Yes. And the surgeon, should you need anything."

"To hell with the surgeon. It's Lindley I worry about . . . for your sake, Fifi. You should go. The minute you can, leave this place and get to safety."

She had to laugh at that notion. "And where is that, Papa? Back to the inn, where Lindley would surely find me? Should I walk all night back to Geydon where we were shot at?"

"London. You can go back to London."

"And live in the brothel again? No, Papa. I can't do that. I want better for my life."

"And what of your position in Fitzgelder's house? I wasn't overly fond of the idea, but Eudora assured me the housekeeper was a decent sort and would look after you."

Madame had told Papa she'd be looked after? That Mrs. Harwell was a decent sort? Heavens, but she'd never known Madame to be such a poor judge of people. *Decent* was not quite the word Sophie would have used to describe the shrewish housekeeper. The only sort of looking after Sophie had received in that house was exactly the sort to make Papa roll over in his grave. Except that he hadn't actually been *in* his grave, but still . . . he wouldn't have liked it. No, she could hardly go back there.

"I'm sorry, Papa. You must know I can't go back there."

"No, of course you can't. Damn that Lindley. Why did he have to find us?"

He tried to sit, and she could see the frustration and anger rising in him. Lord, but he was going to irritate his wound and start the bleeding again. She shushed him as best she could, for all the good it seemed to be doing.

"Papa, please be still."

"It's not enough he must destroy me, but now he's set his sights on you, *ma petite*. And to think, I was more concerned about what Fitzgelder might do to you. It would seem he's been the least of my worries all along."

"Actually, Papa, I'm afraid we still need to worry about Mr. Fitzgelder. It seems that . . . well, I'm afraid he believes I've stolen something from him."

"Stolen? But Fifi, you are no thief."

"Of course not, Papa. But Mr. Fitzgelder lost his locket and assumed that I—"

"His locket?"

"A piece of jewelry, but nothing that appears to be very valuable."

"You've seen it?"

Er, she hadn't quite meant to implicate herself. "I, that is, I saw him with it. The day I left."

"What did it look like?"

"What? Oh, well it was gold, and heart-shaped."

"Did it open?"

"Open? I don't know. I would assume so, but I did not see him open it."

"Were there designs engraved on it?"

Heavens, did Papa suspect her so much that he must needle her this way? Well, she did *not* steal that locket. True, it may have fallen into her possession, but she had *not* stolen it. Not intentionally, anyway, and she'd not admit to it now, especially not to her poor father. The man was overly anxious, and perhaps the medicine was making him imagine things. He needed to sleep, and she needed to get his mind off his many worries.

"There may have been engravings on it, Papa, but I did not look at it closely," she said simply. "I did *not* steal it. Mr. Fitzgelder simply lost it and then found it convenient to blame me. Now, go to sleep. You need the rest."

"And you?"

"I'll be right here in this chair beside your bed."

"And where will Lindley be?"

"Not in here with us, I assure you. Now please, sleep, Papa."

She adjusted the blankets again and was relieved when his body seemed to relax and his head sank into his pillow. Tomorrow they would find their way out of this, but for now he needed to rest and let that leg begin to heal. The doctor was confident that once the bleeding was stopped Papa would be fine in no time. She could only hope this would prove true. Time was something they had precious little of.

"And you're certain you know nothing more about that locket, Fifi?" Papa asked after a quiet pause while Sophie curled up in her chair.

"What? No, of course not."

"Too bad."

"Why?"

"Then perhaps you *would* have stolen it and things would not look so dire for us now."

What on earth did that mean? He *wanted* her to have stolen it? The poor man must be talking out of his head. "Papa, I . . ."

"*Chut, chut,* Fifi. Let us speak no more of it. It is in the past now. *C'est la vie.*"

Indeed, that was true. However she'd gotten the locket didn't matter. What mattered was that she *did* have it, and apparently Papa thought this might work in their favor. Well, best not to bring that up now. It would only agitate him when he needed rest. Tomorrow morning she could tell him the truth, perhaps show him the locket.

Did Papa think it sounded valuable? Could they perhaps use it to bargain with Lindley? She couldn't imagine how a man like Lindley might be swayed by a simple piece of jewelry, but perhaps it was possible. He certainly hadn't been swayed by anything she'd offered him thus far. Maybe a golden locket would have better luck.

"Good night, Papa. I'll be here if you need me."

She shuttered the lamp and the room fell to darkness. It was a good thing, too, for she would have hated to explain to Papa if he had seen her smiling at the bitter irony of her words. All those years she had missed him and longed for him to be there because she needed him; now here they were and he was alive, yet it was she who promised to be nearby for him. Life was unfair.

In silence she slid her hand into her pocket to touch the warm gold locket there. Unfair, yes, but perhaps occasionally that was a benefit. She would have never willfully stolen something like this, yet here it was. Unfair to Mr. Fitzgelder, but perhaps a godsend for them. In the morning they would find out if Lord Lindley might be interested in the small, golden heart.

It seemed he was in want of one, golden or otherwise.

THE LOCKET. LINDLEY STOOD OUTSIDE THE DOOR AND heard D'Archaud asking after it. Yes, it must be the same one—Fitzgelder must have gotten his hands on it, and Sophie stole it away from him. It simply would have been too much a coincidence not to be the case. Although, why would she deny that to her own father? If she had stolen it, wouldn't it have been at her father's request? Why keep it from him now?

It didn't make sense. Unless . . . could she be telling the truth? Perhaps she did not have the locket. Yet why would Fitzgelder have accused her, then? Someone else must have stolen it. Yes, that had to be it. Someone else knew about the secret it contained. Someone who could profit from it.

That meant things were about to get complicated.

That idea was laughable. Things weren't already complicated enough? D'Archaud only held value as long as he could give the names and locations of all the players in this game. If other parties were involved, D'Archaud's information might become obsolete too quickly. Lindley had come so close to finding his goal only to feel it slipping through his fingers. With that locket and its hidden secrets circulating out there, anyone who knew of it might find himself—or herself—suddenly become a liability.

Lindley mentally calculated how much money he still had on his person after paying for last night's lodging and then the doctor's fee tonight. This surgeon seemed a decent fellow. He wondered how much it would take to ensure the man's silence? Surely their visit here could be well hidden for a few days, at least. If not, Miss Darshaw and her father were in grave danger.

As for Lindley, his life felt secure for the moment. Danger for him lay in other areas, he was afraid. Areas that included ocean blue eyes and warm, willing lips he should never have allowed himself to sample.

Chapter Eight

Miss Darshaw looked as lovely in the daytime as she had in the moonlight. Better, in fact, Lindley realized, because now she was not so weary and worried. Her eyes were brighter and sleep had done her well. Her perfect skin was even more perfect with noonday sun streaming through the doctor's clean-washed windows. Her blond hair was freshly piled into a careless knot, and the wrinkled gown she wore hugged her shape in ways Lindley found he could not quite ignore.

Thank God she was glaring hatred toward him. He doubted he could withstand a smile.

"So you've come to check on the prisoners at last," she said sharply as he entered the room where her father still lay on the bed, a bowl of broth in his steady hands.

"You are not prisoners," Lindley replied. "Your father is recovering from his injury."

"And then what?" she asked, her angry lips forming words Lindley could barely comprehend due to some damned distracting memories of how those lips had felt against his last night. "You'll drag us off to the tower, no doubt."

"Newgate, more likely."

"Get out of here!"

"I'd like to," he said, and he dragged his eyes from her to study her father. "How about you, D'Archaud? Are you up for travel yet?"

"No, he's not," Sophie replied for him, toying with the food on the plate she held in her lap where she sat beside the bed.

"I was asking your father," Lindley said. "So, D'Archaud, how are you?"

Sophie frowned. From her expression, Lindley could tell it pained her to hear her father called by that name. Clearly she was familiar with it, with the lie of her father's life. So just how much else of D'Archaud's sordid past did she know?

"He's very weak today," she answered, again in her father's place. "The doctor says it may take some time for his strength to return."

"Yes, that was quite a gash he cut in his leg there. Rather clumsy of you, D'Archaud."

If he hoped to get a reaction from the man, he was disappointed. Sophie, however, was quite happy to respond.

"It's a wonder you did not outright kill him, my lord, the way you attacked him last night," she snapped.

Lindley chose to ignore her—or at least give that appearance—and simply turned back to her father. "Does she always do this? Are you ever allowed to get a word in? No wonder you let her think you were dead all those years."

A piece of bread came flying at his head. Lindley caught it and smiled over at the thrower. She glared at him and stabbed her fork into a piece of meat—a sausage. He winced.

Damn, but he needed to get control of himself. How could he possibly find the snarling woman so deuced irresistible? She was just as attractive when she was being belligerent as she had been last night when she'd obediently melted into his arms. *Hellfire.* The quicker he got himself away from her the better.

"Sophie," the older man said, setting his spoon aside for a moment. "We are in his lordship's debt for bringing me here and covering the bill. I'm sure he would appreciate it if you'd not throw food at him."

"On the contrary," Lindley said, biting into the bread. "I'm still a bit hungry."

"I'd have thrown a rock at you if I'd had it," Sophie mumbled. "A big one."

He had no doubt she would have, too. Sophie Darshaw could look after herself, had done so quite well for several years. Lindley would do well to keep that in mind and not underestimate her. Or let himself get distracted. He'd best get back to business and see what use D'Archaud might still be to him.

"We need to be getting on our way," Lindley began. "I've sent word to have my carriage brought up from where it is being repaired in Geydon, and I expect it to arrive at the Steward's Brake very shortly. We should go there and wait while . . ."

The sound of rapping at the front door below them interrupted. Sophie frowned, and Lindley strode past her to the window to look out. He could not see down to the doorstep, as it was directly beneath their window, but he could certainly listen. The window was open just enough that if he stooped slightly the sound of voices carried fairly well.

Rastmoor. It was Rastmoor come to pay a call on the surgeon. *How odd.* He motioned for the Darshaws to be silent and strained to hear what passed below.

Rastmoor was here—alone, it appeared—and was asking after an injured man. So, he'd somehow learned that Sophie's father had been injured last night and he assumed the man might have come here. *Unexpected.* Lindley listened for more. Would the good doctor be true to his word and deny their presence?

He did. Rastmoor went on to ask after any possible information on Sophie, but the doctor denied having seen any such person. Apparently he was convincing, too, as Rastmoor's final question was to inquire if there were other surgeons in the area. Told there were none, the man simply then went on his way, presumably unenlightened. Lindley stepped back to avoid being seen should Rastmoor chance to glance upward, but he kept his eye securely on his friend.

Rastmoor crossed the street and spoke to a woman sweeping a stairway, then questioned a man pulling a small cart. In each case he pointed back toward the doctor's house and appeared to be asking if the person had seen anyone of D'Archaud's or Sophie's description. No one had, apparently, and they each merely shrugged, then went on their way, leaving Rastmoor to continue his search in another direction.

So, Rastmoor was hunting D'Archaud now, too, was he? Well, certainly that made sense. From what Lindley had learned, that locket could be very damaging to Rastmoor were its information to become public. Last he heard, actually, Rastmoor's father had been the one to possess it and Rastmoor had inherited. Apparently Fitzgelder had altered that, and now Rastmoor would want it back.

He was unlikely to kill for it, though. Lindley had known the man a number of years and could never see him as a murderer. Oh, he'd want to find the locket and protect his family honor, of course, but not at that price. He would pay a hefty sum to get that locket back and destroy whatever was inside it, but he'd not kill.

At least Lindley hoped not. He sent a quick glance in Sophie's direction. Would Rastmoor keep in mind that she was his dearest friend's cousin? *Probably.* And it was in her best interest to keep the locket secret, just as it was for Rastmoor. He could have little to fear that she would use it against him. Still, Rastmoor would be highly motivated to get it back.

In fact, due to all of these circumstances, he might be of use to Lindley.

He moved away from the window. "I'm going out for a while."

"What?" Sophie said, pushing her plate onto the nearest table and rising. "Where are you going? Who was that at the door?"

"It was Rastmoor," Lindley replied. "I'm going to follow him."

D'Archaud simply eyed him with suspicion, but Sophie trailed him as he moved to the door. "Why? What was he doing here?"

"Looking for you, of course."

"He followed us here? But why?" Sophie asked.

"That's what I'm going to find out."

Yes, he'd been right. Things were definitely getting more complicated. And the way Miss Darshaw chewed on her plump little lower lip as she contemplated her next move added an extra level of complication that was going to make walking difficult for a few minutes. *Damn.* He hoped Rastmoor wasn't moving too fast out there.

LINDLEY WAS GONE. IT HARDLY MADE SENSE, BUT HE'D left to go trail after Rastmoor. The doctor was downstairs, and Sophie was alone with her father. Whatever Lord Rastmoor had said seemed to have had quite an effect on Lindley. He'd offered little explanation and gone off after the man. Sophie could not understand it, but she didn't need to. All she needed to know was that now was their chance.

"He's gone, Papa," she said, watching out the window as Lindley's tall, elegant form sauntered off up the street. "Hurry, we can leave now."

Papa was not hurrying, though. He was slowly stretching his limbs and yawning. The poor man seemed thoroughly exhausted. She could well understand the feeling; she'd slept fitfully at best in that uncomfortable chair. Yet they could not dawdle. They would have plenty of time to rest once they were away from here, away from Lindley.

There was a knock at the door, and the doctor's housekeeper poked her head in. "Your friend said to tell you he'd be back soon and you're both to wait here for him."

"Yes, I'm sure he'd like that," Sophie grumbled.

"Here's some tea for you, miss," the housekeeper went on, pushing the door open and backing in with a tray. "And for you, sir, a draught to help you sleep. The doctor would like you to drink this."

"Thank you, Mrs. Nally," Papa said, accepting the tray as she put it down for him and examining the little bottle she held out. "A sleeping potion?"

"It's very mild, but you'll rest like an infant."

Papa held the bottle and gave the woman a weary smile. "Tell the kind doctor we appreciate all his efforts on my behalf."

"Just be sure to do as he says and you'll be right in no time," the housekeeper replied as she circled the room, collecting their lunch dishes. "Now, if there's anything else?"

"No, thank you," Sophie said, dismissing her. "We're just fine."

"Very well, then." Mrs. Nally bobbed a curtsy and headed for the door. "Once your friend returns the doctor will probably want to leech you again, sir, but for now, just rest."

"Yes, I will. Thank you."

Papa was too kind by far. Thank heavens they'd be gone long before those horrible leeches came out again. How Papa could possibly benefit from having yet more blood sucked out of him after the way he nearly bled to death last night, she could not guess. Probably it was Lindley's sadistic idea. Sophie closed the door behind the housekeeper and made her way back over to the window to keep watch.

"Come, Fifi, take some tea."

"I don't care for tea, Papa. Who knows how long Lord Lindley will be gone? We need to get away while we can!"

"Yes, but why not do it after tea? Come, it will help settle your lunch and calm your nerves."

"My nerves don't want to be calm, Papa. They want to be gone."

But he was proceeding with the tea, stirring sugar into hers just the way she liked it. "Tea will help. Come, sit with me."

She sighed but gave in. He offered a cup and she accepted, plopping herself into the chair she'd slept in last night. Very well, she would drink tea with Papa, then they would be off. They would leave this house, leave Warwick, and leave Lindley wondering where they had gone. She drank the tea down quickly. Papa chuckled as he watched her.

"I see you are in a hurry."

"We haven't got much time," she reminded him. "Do you think you can you walk? I suppose you can lean on me, but that staircase will be a bit tricky . . ."

Papa shushed her. "*Calme-toi*, Fifi. I'm not in my grave quite yet, am I? You just relax."

He sat up and slid his legs over the side of the bed. Reaching for his boots, he began to pull them on. His actions were a bit rough for her tastes.

"Careful!" she warned him. "Watch the bandages."

"*C'est bien, chou-chou*. Now you just relax yourself. Wait

here while I go make sure the way is clear so we can leave undetected."

"We should go together!"

"No, you must stay here. What if the housekeeper returns? You must be here to answer the door and tell her I am asleep. *Chut*, Fifi. Stay in your comfortable chair and finish your tea. All will be well. You shall see."

He gave her a smile that hardly looked like that of a man who had been at death's door last night. For that matter, he'd seemed weary and faint not just ten minutes ago. One cup of tea could not have restored him so quickly. He must have been pretending such fatigue for Lindley's sake.

Smart man. Papa's pretense would have set Lindley off his guard. Sophie was amazed she had not thought of it until now—yes, Papa playing the part of the incapacitated victim was quite brilliant. Lindley was gone and expected Papa to be too weak for escape. Well, he would soon see he'd been played a fool.

Good thing Papa was too clever to have taken the doctor's prescribed sleeping draught. She glanced over at the discarded tea tray. There was the bottle lying next to Papa's untouched tea. Yes, it was a very good thing Papa had not done as the doctor suggested. She'd have the devil of a time dragging his sleeping form out of here before Lindley returned.

But all was well now. Papa was feeling better, he was alert, and he'd gone to get their gig ready for departure. All she had to do was sit here and wait.

She didn't mind waiting, not really. In fact, it seemed rather a good idea, now that she considered it. This chair was not nearly as uncomfortable as she'd thought during the night. It was actually inviting. She nestled back into it and leaned her head against the soft upholstery. Yes indeed, quite a comfortable spot to wait for Papa's return. She could wait all afternoon for him in this comfortable chair, as a matter of fact . . .

RASTMOOR WAS STAYING AT THE STEWARD'S BRAKE. Lindley had not wanted to be too obvious about his inquiries after the man, but he'd learned Rastmoor had arrived around lunchtime and had been traveling with a young man. Lindley saw no sign of this young man, but if he had to hazard a guess he would have said Clemmons, that imposter posing as Sophie's husband. Well, wouldn't Rastmoor be in for a surprise.

Lindley's carriage had still not arrived from Geydon, and he grumbled about that. What in heaven's name could they be doing to it down there that might take so long? Was a broken axle such an impossible thing to fix? He needed that carriage now.

Securing two rooms at the Steward's Brake, careful not to let Rastmoor know he was about or had been asking after him, he went back to the surgeon. He'd left word that D'Archaud should be given something to send him sleeping for a couple of hours. Naturally Sophie would not leave her darling father, and he doubted she was quite up to carrying his snoring body away over her delicate shoulder, so he was confident they would both be there when he returned. The old man needed the extra rest, anyway. He'd looked rather worse for the wear this morning when Lindley had checked in on him, and then again when he'd seen them at lunch.

Some people were simply not fast healers, Lindley had decided, and he was glad he'd chosen to bring the man here rather than let him bleed out on the road. True, he'd been a player in the tragedy that had marred Lindley's life those years ago, but how would justice have been served to lose the man before he'd shared what he knew? Yes, now that D'Archaud was well and rested up, Lindley would find him far more useful.

He was eager, in fact, to stalk into that room and see for himself just what Philippe D'Archaud might know about the conspiracy that had gone so horribly wrong and killed four people Lindley had loved. Indeed, this information would be most welcome. As would, he had to admit, being subjected to more of Miss Darshaw's delicious hatred.

The housekeeper let him into the house and informed him the surgeon was out making a call on one of his elderly patients. She assured him, however, that the sleeping draught had been delivered and there'd been not a peep from their guests upstairs in the hour since Lindley had left. He couldn't quite see this as a good sign. Somehow he had expected more than a peep from Miss Darshaw.

Trying not to appear alarmed, he hurried up the stairs to the room they'd been given. The door was not locked, and he threw it open without so much as a knock. As he feared, the bed was empty. D'Archaud, it seemed, was gone.

"Damn it," he muttered, then noticed Miss Darshaw.

She was curled up in the same chair she'd been forced to sleep in last night. Her cheeks were rosy, her expression was peaceful, and she could have been an innocent child slumbering there if not for the eye-catching swell of breast and the enticing curve of her hip.

Lindley decided he'd better rouse her immediately, for several reasons.

But she would not waken, not when he squeezed her hand, not when he brushed her cheek, and not when he traced his finger across her fresh, pink lip. She did, however, moan at that. Sadly, moaning was not what he should be after just now, he reminded himself, so he went back to rubbing her hand.

The girl was beyond his reach, though. A glance over to the tea tray with its empty draught bottle and then a quick look at the drops of tea in the bottom of the cup beside Miss Darshaw informed him what had happened. Damn that D'Archaud! He'd drugged his own daughter to make his escape. What a bastard!

Damn the man to hell. He would abandon her here—with the very man they called enemy—for the sake of his own worthless hide? Maybe leaving him to bleed out on the road would not have been such a bad idea, after all. What sort of father did this to his own child? Had he not seen the way she fairly worshipped him? Would have gladly sacrificed herself for him?

She deserved so much better than a parent like that and the life that came with him. By God, Lindley would see him pay . . . for this and for all his other crimes. Lindley touched one of Miss Darshaw's soft blond curls. Perhaps someday she would not hate him for it.

He leaned in and kissed her forehead. It was a gesture he would never have admitted to, but it was rewarded by another soft moan from the recipient. What a shame their lives had not been different.

Carefully he slid his arms under her body. She was dead to

the world, and he was careful to mind his manners as he gently scooped her up and carried her to the bed. That draught would likely not wear off for several hours. Her father hadn't seemed to care much for her welfare, so the least Lindley could do was see the girl did not get a stiff neck. That chair looked damned uncomfortable.

With Miss Darshaw neatly tucked in, Lindley closed the door behind him. *Damn that D'Archaud.* And damn that if he ever saw Miss Darshaw again, she would probably be looking at him as the man who'd led her father to the gallows.

THE WORLD SLOWLY BECAME REAL AROUND SOPHIE, as if she were waking from a long sleep. Wait a moment, she *was* waking from a long sleep. And how the devil did she get into this bed?

This was Papa's bed! But where was Papa?

And then she remembered. Papa had gone to get things ready for their departure. She glanced at the window. The shadows were long—it was well into evening. Good heavens, how on earth had she slept this long?

The tea . . . the bottle on Papa's tray . . . Merciful Lord, Papa had given her the sleeping draught! She'd fallen asleep in that damned uncomfortable chair. But then how had she ended up in the bed?

Lord Lindley. She'd thought she'd dreamed that, his presence here, his gentle touch as he lifted her into the bed, the way he'd removed her gown . . . Wait, she *had* dreamed that part, hadn't she? A quick check of her attire assured her that at least most of what she vaguely recalled had been a dream. Her cheeks burned hot. Heavens, what could have been in that sleeping draught to give her such fanciful dreams? Truly, she had no idea her mind could even think such things up!

She jumped to her feet and then waited half a moment for the room to stop spinning. As soon as it did, she rushed out into the hall and ran down the stairs. She found the housekeeper setting out the supper things.

"Ah, there you are miss. You were sleeping so soundly I was afraid you'd miss your meal. The doctor's been out on calls, but he should be in any time now and—"

"My father! Where is my father?"

The housekeeper clucked her tongue. "Gone out, I'm afraid. It's hard when they get feebleminded."

"Feebleminded?"

"They do wander, don't they? That nice gentleman told me how you'd be so worried for your poor, aging Papa when you woke up from your nap. But fear not, dearie. Your gentleman was so concerned, he took right off after him. Don't you worry, he'll have him soon, I don't doubt."

Nor did Sophie. Lindley would be furious. Well, so was she. *Feebleminded?* How dare he make up a story like that about Papa! Papa was no more feebleminded than Lindley. Hadn't he managed to outsmart the cagey nobleman? Yes, he had. *Feebleminded indeed.*

She glanced at the clock on the mantel. Was it really so late? Papa had been gone for hours. With luck that would put him far ahead of Lindley.

"So, Lindley was here?" Sophie asked, trying to keep her tone calm while inside she was a rush of emotion.

"He was, dearie. Stopped upstairs to see you, but you were asleep."

"And how long ago was that?"

"Oh, a couple hours, at least. He only stayed for a moment or two."

So he had been here, but only for a moment. Then obviously those shocking images in her mind had been only a dream. *Drat.*

Rather, *good*! She meant *good*. Yes, it was a very *good* thing it had only been a dream. *Good, good, good.* Yes, she was quite relieved.

"Er, did he happen to say where he was going? Where he thought he might find my father?"

The housekeeper went back to her duties and shrugged her shoulders. "No, don't recall that he did. I'm sure once he finds your father he'll bring him back for you. Don't you worry, miss. You're a lucky girl to have such a fine gentleman to look after you and your poor, feebleminded father."

"Yes, aren't I," Sophie mumbled.

She left the housekeeper to continue her duties and then sauntered back up to her room. Papa was gone, and there was nothing here to say he'd any intention of returning. She knew he did not. He probably assumed she'd be better off without him. Perhaps he was right. Still, though, she couldn't help but worry.

He was her father, after all, and she loved him. She'd only just gotten him back and had no wish to lose him again. Not like this, not when she could help him. But where could he be?

Surely not in Warwick, although he'd been hoping to meet with Madame at that inn where they'd stopped. Perhaps Madame had arrived and was waiting there. Ah, and Lindley didn't know about that, did he? He might have expected Papa to get as far away from Warwick as possible. The inn would be too obvious a place for a man on the run to hide. Lindley would assume Papa was too smart for that. He'd probably gone right past there on his way out of town, hunting elsewhere for his missing prey.

It made sense, then, for Sophie to hurry herself on over to the inn. Even if Papa wasn't there, perhaps Madame was. Sophie could go to her for help. Madame would help her, she knew it.

Grabbing up her bundle of things, she left the room and tiptoed quietly downstairs. She hoped Lord Lindley had already settled their bill with the doctor, but if he hadn't, she certainly didn't want to be the one caught leaving unexpectedly. The housekeeper was humming off-key to herself in some back room as Sophie let herself silently out the front door.

Chapter Nine

Lindley didn't learn much by following Rastmoor. It seemed the man really had no idea what he was doing, wandering around town questioning random passersby, hoping to find someone with any hint of a clue as to Sophie's whereabouts. He hardly seemed to care about D'Archaud, which didn't help settle Lindley's nerves.

Why was Rastmoor so obsessed with finding Sophie? Was it just because he'd promised his friend he'd search for Lady Dashford's long-lost cousin? Or was it the locket that motivated him? The latter made more sense but did not bode well for Miss Darshaw. Concerned, Lindley trailed after Rastmoor until the man finally tired and made his way back to the Steward's Brake. It appeared his only goal at that point was to get drunk.

Well, so much for Rastmoor giving him any information. Lindley might have done better to ignore the man and toss a coin to decide which direction to go hunt for D'Archaud. Of course, he would have to have done that without his phaeton. Damn those stable hands down in Geydon, but how many years was it going to take to get that thing brought up here? The men at the Steward's Brake assured him they'd sent someone over there first thing, yet here it was evening and still he had no word on it. D'Archaud was probably miles and miles from here by now. Most frustrating.

He'd best head back to the Steward's Brake where he'd taken a room for himself. He wanted to be easy to find if, by some miracle, his phaeton ever did arrive. It would also be easier to keep an eye on Rastmoor just in case the man did get some notion of where to find Sophie or her father and set out to make trouble for them.

Plus it would be far safer for him to sleep here rather than risk going back to the surgeon and being under the same roof as Sophie Darshaw—for several reasons.

He'd sent word for Feasel to meet him here. He really had no idea where the man was, but someone back in London would know. Somehow Feasel always kept in touch with his people. Trouble was, with all the chasing around they'd both been doing, there was no telling when his message might meet up with the man or how long it would take him to arrive here. With luck Lindley would have turned up some sort of lead on D'Archaud and already be on his way by that point. Then Feasel would be stuck waiting here until further word arrived.

But what to do until then? He wondered if he ought to take the chance of seeking out a report on Miss Darshaw's well-being at this point. Surely she'd come out from the effects of that draught by now. Likely she'd be furious with her father for leaving her. He could hardly blame her for that—he was furious with D'Archaud, as well. It was probably fortunate for the old man, as well as for the sake of justice, that Lindley hadn't found him yet.

But what of Miss Darshaw? She might know where to find him, mightn't she? He was, after all, her father. Surely he would have told her where . . .

No, that was unlikely. D'Archaud had probably told her nothing, else he would not have drugged her like that. He was, after all, willing to let the poor girl think him dead for the past four years. Why should she have any more notion today where the man might run off to than Lindley had? In fact, Lindley probably knew more about the man than his own daughter did. No, he could not use this as an excuse to go visit her.

Damn, but he needed to get her out of his head. What was

wrong with him that he could be so all-consumed by such a silly thing as a female? A female who left a brothel to go reside in Fitzgelder's home, no less? By God, he was addled like a schoolboy. He simply had to get control over himself.

Perhaps he should not repair to his room but head for the mews to recheck the status of his carriage. That would at least distract him from this infernal waiting and those unwelcome thoughts of Miss Darshaw and what she must be doing right now. But what *was* she doing right now?

Damn it. He should have left some money for her. No telling how she would be forced to make her way alone now. Maybe he ought to go and . . .

No, he was being a fool. Miss Darshaw was none of his concern, and he'd do well to forget about her. Perhaps the surgeon would take pity on her and let her stay on until she could find respectable work. Or perhaps the surgeon was not a blind idiot and could see for himself just what sort of work a woman like Miss Darshaw was best suited for. He'd certainly keep her around then.

Hell, but that did not sit well with Lindley.

Very well. He would re-ascertain the situation regarding his missing phaeton and then he would go back to the surgeon's house. Simply to ease his own conscience and nothing more. What became of Miss Darshaw was no concern of his.

He repeated this phrase several times as he marched around the corner to the mews behind the Steward's Brake.

IT WAS A PLEASANT EVENING, ALL THINGS CONSIDERED. Sophie was glad to be out walking in it, clearing her head from the remnants of that awful draught Papa gave her. Honestly, what sort of father would do that to his own child? Lying to her, then abandoning her like that.

Yes, he would probably say he did it for her own good. And he might even be in earnest, thinking this the best course. But what did he think she would do now? Well, she could only hope Madame had arrived and would welcome her back.

She readjusted the little pack of belongings she'd tucked under her arm and tried to remember her way from the surgeon's house back to the Steward's Brake. She wasn't perfectly certain she'd made the right turn. The streets were somewhat narrower now than she recalled, and though Warwick had not appeared a thriving metropolis, she had to admit it was just large enough for her to possibly be a little bit lost. *Drat.*

Most people must have been indoors, sitting down to an evening meal, as the streets seemed somewhat empty. She'd passed a few pedestrians but hadn't thought to ask directions. One lone carriage—a nice one, too—sat at the side of the street just up ahead of her. There seemed to be a surplus of nice carriages in Warwick, as she was positive she'd seen one quite similar in front of the surgeon's house. Or had it been the same one?

Well, that hardly mattered. Perhaps as she walked on she would encounter someone else to ask whether or not she was headed the right way. Ah, there was someone now. A man stepped out of a recessed doorway just ahead of her. He had his head down and had not seen her yet, so she walked steadily toward him.

It was a bad idea, though. No sooner had she come within greeting distance than the man's head popped up, his eyes focused directly on her with an unpleasant smile oozing over his lips. She'd never seen this particular man before in her life, yet it was almost as if he'd expected to find her here and was quite glad he did. She stepped back.

He stepped forward, his hand shooting out to grab her at the throat. He shoved her around a corner, into the dark gap between two buildings. The pack tumbled out of her arms, and she was helpless against his unexpected actions. Good heavens, she couldn't let him do this! She fought back as best she could.

But the suddenness of his attack had her off balance, while his grip on her throat kept her from screaming. It was a nightmare. She struggled and kicked, but he was just out of her reach.

His hand was still at her throat, and he used his body to pin her against the wall. His other hand came up to her neck. Was he going to choke the life out of her? Not if she could help it! She fought all the harder against him.

But his hands circled her neck, feeling their way as if searching for something. The best way to completely obliterate her windpipe, probably. But her struggles still accomplished nothing.

"Where is it?" he growled at her.

"Where is what?" she gurgled back.

He paused slightly before answering. "Jewelry! Ain't ye got no jewelry on ye?"

Did she look like someone who wandered strange parts wearing a lot of jewelry? If she wasn't so horribly terrified she might actually laugh. If she had any air left in her lungs, that is. As it was she was doing well to remain conscious and gasp out any sort of short reply.

"No jewelry . . . sorry."

She didn't want to think what he might then try to take in return.

He fumbled at her clothes, letting just enough pressure off her throat that she thought maybe she might be able to call out for help. She cried out in pain instead when he was suddenly dragging her down toward the ground. But his hands released her at the last minute and she regained her balance, jumping away from him and plastering herself against the heavy beams of the wall beside her.

He didn't come after her. Instead, she glanced back to find her assailant sprawled on the ground, thrown there by the tall man who stood over him.

Lindley.

What on earth was he doing here? Was he in league with this scoundrel who'd attacked her? No, it didn't appear so. Lindley kicked the fellow so hard he yelped like a scared dog and curled into a ball. Sophie did not get the idea they were at all friendly.

Still, Lindley was not exactly smiling when he turned to her.

"What the hell are you doing, striking up conversation with strange men on the street?"

"I was not conversing with him!"

"You certainly were going to. What, did you think you could try some of those tricks you learned at Eudora's and convince him to part with some coin before you gave up your goods? Not too clever, Miss Darshaw."

"I most certainly was not going to . . . How dare you accuse me of something like that!"

"Then what did you have in mind, walking right up to him on a public street like some brazen hussy?"

The man tried to scramble up to his feet, but Lindley kicked him again. Wisely, the assailant collapsed once more. Lindley hardly seemed to notice, his eyes remaining pinned on Sophie.

"I was merely going to ask him directions," she replied.

"And I'm certain he'd have been most happy to give them to you," Lindley said, taking a worrisome step toward her. "Directions on how to do what, precisely? Maybe I can be of some help."

"I was looking for the way to that inn where you nearly killed my father last night," she said, hoping he might not remember what else transpired at that inn.

"Following me, were you?"

"No. I thought perhaps . . ."

She didn't want to finish that thought. There was no need to let Lindley know she thought perhaps her father might still be there or that Madame was expected. Fortunately, movement caught her attention and she was able to shift the topic.

"Your man is escaping," she announced as her attacker silently made it up onto all fours and began crawling out toward the street where they had come from.

Lindley did nothing but shrug as the man scrambled to his feet and ran away. "Let him go. It appears he did not get what he was after."

The long, bold look he ran over Sophie's disheveled person told her he had little doubt what the man had been trying to do here in the shadows of this unpopulated street. She figured she ought to be quick to redirect her savior's way of thinking. Again.

"He wanted my jewelry."

Lindley's frown told her this was, indeed, not the way he'd been thinking. "Your jewelry? Really now, Miss Darshaw, but you purport to believe that street rat attacked you because he expected to find jewelry? Surely neither of us is so naive as to believe this."

"It's what he said!" she defended, though truly this was none of his business. "He expected I should have some jewelry."

"You're an unwashed little housemaid who ran away three days ago. You've slept in your clothes and your hair is uncombed. How could he possibly expect *you* to have jewelry?"

Well, despite the fact that it was all true and she really could not have cared less about the man's opinion of her, this was by far the cruelest thing he could have possibly said. The thought that he should see her this way . . . that she might actually *be* this way . . . drove a spike right into her soul. Lord, but how she hated him. He made her feel dirty and unimportant. No man should ever have the right to make anyone feel such a thing.

"You know nothing about me," she said and shoved her way past him.

Her packet of things was lying nearby. The ruffian who attacked her could have grabbed it easily, but apparently he was more interested in escaping Lindley's boot than filling his pocket. Sophie was glad for that. Those scissors she'd stowed in there had cost her a pretty penny and she would hate to lose them.

Scooping her things from the dirt where they lay, she realized she was swallowing back the stinging onslaught of tears. Drat, but she could not let herself become emotional now. She had to get away, to put Lindley from her mind and find Papa. Nothing else could matter to her.

Somehow she would survive this. She'd get away from Lindley and all would be well. Papa would be well. She'd do what she had to do for things to be well. She'd find Madame.

She'd been a fool to think she could have ever made anything of herself outside her life at Madame's. It was pure folly to believe she could find a respectable situation. All her life she would be nothing more than what Lindley thought her, a dirty little bit of trash from Madame's brothel.

Even her own father had seen no need to stay and protect her. He'd left . . . twice. Only a daydreaming little twit would pretend things were not the way they were. It was stupid to ignore the opportunities Madame had tried to offer her. By God, she'd go back there now and make up for it. She'd take whatever money was offered her and never, ever let herself foolishly rely on kindness from the likes of Lindley and his condescending smugness again.

Apparently, though, her eyes were determined to have a good cry first. She could not see to walk away and had to pause in her grand exit to swipe at the tears with the back of her hand. *Drat it all.*

Lindley muttered something—profanity, she thought—behind her. Then he came closer and actually touched her. His large hands were warm on her shoulders, and she really, truly wished she did not enjoy the feel of his body brushing against hers as much as she did.

"Don't cry," he said softly.

"I'm not crying."

"You are." He reached in front of her to offer a handkerchief. It seemed impossibly clean here in this dirty, forgotten alleyway.

"Well, I don't wish to."

"I know. You wish to leave and find your father."

"Yes. You wouldn't happen to know where he is, would you?"

"No, I was rather hoping you could help me there. I take it you cannot?"

"Sorry."

"And why were you on your way to the inn?"

She decided not to answer that, so he turned her around. Of course she wouldn't look up at him, so he put his fingers to her chin and turned her face up toward his. *Drat again.* He was a horrid, horrid, evil man and she was ready to melt into his arms just as easily as she had last night. What a sap-headed idiot she was!

"I . . . er, I was hoping to find a way back to London." That was a sensible answer that made no mention of Madame or her hope that Papa might be still hiding there.

"And just how were you planning to pay for this way back to London?" he asked.

Oh, so he doubted her ability, did he? Well, she'd show him.

"Despite your conviction to the contrary, I could earn that fare with ease."

He just smiled at her declaration and reached his hand up to touch her hair. Her stupid body seemed to have no will of its own, and she leaned into him. It was most frustrating.

"When your eyes get bright and ferocious like that, Miss Darshaw, I daresay you could lure any man to take you wherever you might ask him."

She pulled away and forced her lungs to begin working properly. "Don't think for one minute I have any intention of luring you, my lord. There are plenty of others who would be more than happy to help."

"Oh, indeed," he said. "But don't you think for one minute that I'll let any of them get within twenty feet of you. So just how will you pay that fare?"

"I'll find a way."

"Oh? You have money? I was assuming you did not."

He'd assumed right. Still, she had that one item that Papa seemed to think might be of some use. She still had that damned locket. It was not a tiny object, and obviously Fitzgelder valued it. Perhaps Lindley did, too. And if not him, then surely she could find someone to give a decent price.

"It turns out that thief you just sent on his way was correct after all," she announced. "I do have jewelry."

Lindley looked doubtful. "Then you are doubly foolish for walking up to strangers on the street. Miss Darshaw, you cannot just . . . wait a moment. Fitzgelder said . . ." His words faded into a knowing smile.

Oh yes, she'd forgotten about that. Mr. Fitzgelder had told Lindley about his suspicion that she'd stolen his locket! Drat, but this was not good. It suddenly seemed as if she'd not thought this through fully.

If she admitted now that she had the locket, what was to stop Lindley from simply taking it and having her jailed for thievery? Oh, but she should not have said anything! What an idiot. Perhaps if Papa had not drugged her earlier, her mind would have been clearer and she would have realized not to make mention of it. Now it was too late.

"You've got his locket, don't you?" he asked.

"Er, no."

"Yes, you do. The bastard was right; you did steal it from him!"

"I did not steal it! The man attacked me, and in my struggles it must have fallen into my apron. I didn't even know about it until much later."

"But you do have it."

"Good-bye, my lord."

This would have been a most excellent time to walk away. Unfortunately, Lindley grabbed her elbow.

"Let me see it," he said.

"No."

"Really, Miss Darshaw, do you think you can keep it from me? Now let's take a look at it."

"And now who's being foolish? I've already been accosted by one thug on this street. You suggest I should start waving a gold locket around here?"

"Excellent point. We'll continue this discussion at the inn."

Before she could protest he had her hand tucked neatly in the crook of his elbow and was leading her politely along the street. He kept his hand firmly on hers, and they must have looked to anyone they met to be a very willing couple. She supposed she could have fought him, but one word of *pick-pocket* from him would certainly bring a world of trouble for her. Who would take the word of an unwashed housemaid over that of an elegant gentleman? She would have little choice but to walk along meekly at his side.

One good thing, though. She would find the way to the inn and not have to worry about stumbling into danger again. No, as far as danger went, she was walking hand in hand with it already. Little chance of stumbling into it.

SOMEONE KNEW ABOUT THE LOCKET. THAT WAS THE only explanation Lindley could think of. That petty criminal who'd crawled away from them could have never mistaken Sophie for a woman of means. If he'd specifically asked her for jewelry, then he must have known there was more than met the eye.

Hell, if the man had let his eye decide what goods to take from her, no doubt jewelry would have never entered into the conversation. The fact that the young man even bothered with conversation at all was every bit the proof Lindley needed to formulate an opinion that this had been more than a chance robbery. A true criminal would have dragged a woman like Sophie off alone, taken what was convenient, and searched her person for any valuables after the fact. At least, Lindley supposed that's what would have happened.

Those sorts of goings-on were not exactly his area of expertise, thankfully.

They arrived at the inn, and he was happy to see the proprietor busy in the yard with an overly fine carriage. He was either just receiving guests or seeing them off, but either way it was clear the man wanted to be on hand to help them lighten their heavy pockets. Fine with Lindley. He was not looking forward to explaining the sudden appearance of Miss Darshaw. They slipped indoors, and he escorted her directly to the room he had taken for himself earlier.

"You can't keep me here, you know," she said with a fiery glare as he locked the door behind them.

"It's for your own safety," he said. "Don't worry, Miss Darshaw, I'm not interested in acting the part of your prison warden."

She eyed him with such ferocious distrust that he couldn't help but continue.

"Unless, of course, you'd like me to."

"No. Thank you. What I want is to find my father. Do you know he was so desperate to get away from you that he had to resort to drugging me?"

"Yes, I saw that."

She must not have cared much for the idea of him spying on her while she was incoherent. A flaming blush crept over her complexion, and she twisted her fingers nervously. Could she have been aware that he visited the surgeon's house and took the liberty of tucking her into bed? He rather hoped not. It would not do for her to realize just what hold she had over him, bringing out these unwanted feelings of protective tenderness he so wished he could deny.

"Your father was a coward to abandon you like that, Miss Darshaw," he said, keeping himself safely across the room and staring absently out the window to avoid meeting her gaze. "Are you still so eager to defend him?"

Of course she was. He knew before she even answered.

"He's my *father*."

Yes, she was right. Blackguard though he might be, D'Archaud was the only father she'd ever had, and as far as she was concerned, he'd just returned from the dead. She had no one else; it would be only natural for her to defend the man, criminal or not. Given the least opportunity, she would do whatever she could to protect him. Lindley would be wrong to expect her to do anything else.

At the same time, Miss Darshaw would be wrong to expect Lindley to allow her an opportunity. He would do whatever he could to keep her from helping the man who had played such a role in destroying innocent lives. Indeed, Lindley held the cards here. He would decide whether or not this tempting young miss followed after her scapegrace father or whether she remained here. Safe.

"Show me the locket," he ordered.

She did not comply. He moved a few menacing steps closer to her.

"I will have it, Miss Darshaw," he said. "Unless perhaps there is something else you might wish to offer me?"

"I thought you made it clear I have nothing else you want, my lord."

She faced him squarely. Her jaw trembled just slightly, but she kept a bold front. He had to admire that. Still, did she honestly think he couldn't just take the item from her? Was she willing to consider toying with him in a vain effort to keep it from him? By God, he almost believed she would. Well, then. He'd best take care not to allow her to call his bluff.

"Then you are a foolish girl to waste my time with games."

"I do not play games, sir," she said. "My father indicated this locket has some sort of value. It appears he was right. I truly would be a fool just to hand it over to you without a fight."

"A fight, Miss Darshaw? You think I need to resort to *fighting* to get that locket?"

Her steady gaze held his. "I assumed, since you've made it clear I'm just a dirty little nobody with nothing else to interest you."

Botheration, but she had plenty to interest him. Had she at last figured that out, read the way his eyes couldn't help but stray over her body as they'd been having this discussion? Did she realize how difficult it was for him to keep himself focused on what he *should* be doing rather than what he'd prefer to be doing?

"Where is your father, Miss Darshaw?" he asked, unhappy with the strain he could hear in his own voice.

"I don't know. He's managed to escape both of us, my lord."

"Then let me see that locket. Perhaps it holds the key to where he might be going."

"That's ridiculous. How could Mr. Fitzgelder's locket—"

He didn't let her finish the question. Obviously her father had not given her any information about that locket, yet he'd allowed her to keep it. That had to mean it contained just what Lindley had long suspected: the list of French sympathizers who D'Archaud could run to for help. He would want Sophie to have that, to use it to find him. Yet if someone knew she possessed it . . .

He took her by the shoulders. "As long as you have that locket, your life is in grave danger, Sophie."

She stared up at him, not seeming to grasp the full force of his meaning. Indeed, it would appear she completely misunderstood it altogether.

"You would kill me for the locket, my lord?" she asked at last.

Fear radiated from her, yet she stood her ground. Her chest was heaving, and he couldn't help but glance down at it. The fabric of her faded gown pulled tight and made it easy to see the outline of a chain hanging there. Something heavy weighed it down and disappeared into the cleft between her fresh, round bosoms. He hated to think what would have happened if the man in the alley had discovered it.

The locket. She was wearing it. *Beneath her clothes.* Damn, but that thought should not drive him wild the way it did.

"No, Sophie," he said, touching her cheek with the gentlest brush of a fingertip. "You have nothing to fear from me."

Of course that was a lie. It was, however, an excellent start in his campaign to get his hands on that locket. He slipped his arms around her and pulled her close, finding those pink, quivering lips every bit as sweet and inviting as they had been last night.

HE DID WANT HER. THE WORDS FAIRLY SANG THROUGH her brain as she let herself melt into Lindley's kiss. He was strong and forceful, and she responded in kind. How could she not?

Of course she knew he was just using this to distract her. Lord, yes, she was distracted! His lips were demanding, and she could not help herself but to give in. Lindley's hands slid over her back, holding her, caressing her. He toyed with the strings that the surgeon's capable housekeeper had tied for her this morning. She was torn between hoping the woman had done an adequate job and hoping she'd failed miserably.

Then again, the longer Lindley could be kept on task the better. Sophie was rather coming to enjoy the bolts of unexplainable electricity that shot through all parts of her as his lordship continued his marvelous exploration of her mouth and the oh-so-pleasant caressing of her other parts. She knew it would all come to an unwelcome halt should Lindley manage to get those dratted strings loose and slide her dress from her body.

He would get the locket then and be done with her. She knew that was all he truly wanted. *Pity.*

"Why do you want it so badly, my lord?" she asked when his lips moved to trail kisses across her jawline and down her neck.

"I've been asking myself the same thing," he murmured. "Perhaps it is because of the way you . . ." He paused, stopping himself midsentence. His head rose up from his efforts to very nearly inhale her and he frowned. "What do you mean?"

"I meant the locket, my lord," she said, and she couldn't quite hide the little smile that took hold at the corner of her lips. "What did you think I meant?"

"I rather hoped you had somewhat forgotten the locket for a moment or two."

"So you could more easily relieve me of it, of course."

"Well, I did tell you that was my intent."

"And I suppose I should be grateful you decided to use kisses as your weapon rather than something a bit more deadly."

He let her go and stepped back, rubbing his neck as if seducing her had been a very great effort on his part. "Yes, it does seem my weapon of choice turned out to be rather ineffective."

"Then will you resort to violence?"

"No, Miss Darshaw, I've no desire to see you harmed."

"But you do wish to see my father hanged."

"Your father must be brought to justice."

"And this locket will direct you to him?"

"Possibly. Have you not opened it?"

"I've been running in fear of my life. When have I had time to play with some stupid locket Mr. Fitzgelder carelessly dropped into my apron?"

"So you don't know the contents?"

"Do you?"

He cocked his head and contemplated her a moment before answering. "I believe it contains a list of men who have been sympathetic toward your father and support his criminal activities."

"Ah. No wonder you want it."

"Yes. I do."

"And what of Mr. Fitzgelder? What was he doing with it?"

"I believe he received it from the previous owner."

"My father?"

"No."

He did not elaborate. She waited, but he did not continue. Clearly if he had any intentions of giving further details he would have. She wasn't sure how to go about dragging them out of him.

"So . . . Mr. Fitzgelder would use that against my father?" she asked.

"Mr. Fitzgelder is in league with your father."

"What? My father would never partner with someone like that!"

"Oh? Then why did he allow you to live in the man's house?"

"Because he was dead and he didn't know about it!"

"He's not dead, and he *did* know about it."

He had a point there. Indeed, Papa had not been dead. He claimed to have known all about her living arrangement with Madame and of course he knew when she left there to go to Fitzgelder. Indeed, why had Papa allowed her to stay in that house with that horrible man?

Lindley snorted and stomped back toward the window. "I know he's your father and you feel some natural loyalty toward him, but Philippe D'Archaud is not a good man, Miss Darshaw. You're better off rid of him."

"Am I? I'm better off stranded here in some strange town where it's not even safe for a girl to walk along the street in broad daylight?"

"It's evening time, Miss Darshaw. And I tell you, that man who attacked you knew who you were and was after the locket."

"All the more reason for me to wish my father back."

"And wish me to hell, right?"

"Or at least somewhere that isn't here."

Oh, but what a liar she was! She found herself aching to end up in his arms again. Heavens, she truly didn't want the man anywhere *but* here right now.

"I'm not leaving you, Miss Darshaw."

"Of course you are. You're just waiting to take the locket, then you'll go find my father. That's what you'll do."

"Yes, eventually, but only after I've seen to arrangements for you."

"Arrangements? What is that supposed to mean? Am I a pot of flowers that you can simply *arrange* me?"

"You know what I mean. I'm not an ogre, Miss Darshaw, to drag your father off in chains while you are left behind to starve. I'll set you up somewhere."

As his mistress? Oh, but that would be wonderful! Er, no, that wasn't what she meant. It would be dreadful, awful, horrible. Yes, it would be very bad. She would not like that at all.

"I do not wish to be set up somewhere, my lord," she said, lying again. "I want to find respectable employment and support myself."

Lord, but that sounded so dreary just now.

"Then that is what I'll do," he replied.

"You'll find me employment?"

"If that is what you wish."

"And if it isn't?"

"But you just said . . ."

"I mean, I would be particular about my employment."

"Of course. I'll arrange something suitable."

"You wouldn't send me back to Mr. Fitzgelder, would you?"

"Damn it, I wouldn't send a dog back to Fitzgelder."

She wasn't entirely certain that was good news for her. "I'm glad to hear I rank at least as high as a dog. Thank you for that, my lord."

"Now you're just being petulant. Give me that locket, Miss Darshaw."

"No," she said and held her arms tight around her as if she feared her dress might fly off on its own, exposing the locket for Lindley's easy harvest. "If you're not going to take it from me by force, then I'd like to know what you intend to give me in return."

"So it's for sale, is it?"

"Perhaps."

He smiled at her. "I'm not certain you'd appreciate my terms."

"I'm not certain that you actually have any terms, my lord."

"Oh, I have terms, Miss Darshaw. I most certainly have terms."

He moved toward her again, and she instinctively stepped backward. This just made him smile even more broadly. *Drat.* He recognized her fear.

"So you are ready to hand me that locket?"

And then he would go hunt down Papa. She couldn't have that.

"You've not heard my price yet."

Did he just roll his eyes at her? Yes, by heavens, she believed he did. So she was nothing more than a petulant child to him, was she? And probably an unwashed one, at that. Well, she'd best rid him of that notion right away.

"One night," she said in a tone he could surely not misunderstand.

"What?"

Apparently she'd not been quite so clear as she'd hoped. "One night. You remain here for one night, giving my father time to gain that much more lead, and I'll give you the locket."

"I thought we'd already established that I could simply take the locket."

"Then why are we still having this conversation? You could have had the locket the minute you realized I was carrying it."

"Wearing it. You're wearing it around your neck."

"What? How do you know that?"

"I'm a man, Miss Darshaw. I'm quite versed in detecting what women are wearing—over *and* under."

"Well, then you've certainly wasted a lot of time, my lord. I would have thought such a well-versed man would have had me out of this dress and gotten that locket into his possession by now."

"I had thought you might appreciate if I took my time, Miss Darshaw," he said, stalking her like a wolf and closing the distance between them. "However, I'm quite content to move as quickly as you like."

He proved his words when he caught her in his arms again. She felt herself very nearly jerked off her feet as he pulled her into a crushing embrace. Yet he did not kiss her, though she was ashamed to realize she heartily wished he would. Instead, he stared at her, angry eyes boring into her.

"It's a dangerous thing to toy with me, Miss Darshaw. You have no idea how far I'll go to accomplish my goal."

"Will you promise one night?"

He was careful in his reply. "You will give me the locket if I spend the night here? And where will you be during this time? Off to warn your father, no doubt."

"Where would you have me, my lord?"

"Here, of course."

"Then here I'll be."

"I'd hardly be a gentleman if I did not inform you this deal would seem to be heavily in my favor, Miss Darshaw."

"I'm flattered you see it this way, my lord, but you must fail to realize how valuable my father's freedom is to me. I assure you, I'll get far more enjoyment from the knowledge I've helped save him from you than you will certainly get from . . . well, from me."

His amusement was obvious. "Oh, but there you are very, very wrong, my dear."

Finally he brought his face down and kissed her. Ah, but she really could grow accustomed to this. Well-versed, indeed—the man was a veritable expert. She gave herself up fully to the pleasure of his touch and slipped her arms timidly around him.

By God, if submitting herself to this delicious torment was

something she had to do to save Papa, she would certainly go at it with all her might. She could only hope Lindley might do the same. From what some of the girls said back at Madame's, it was not uncommon for some men to finish things rather quickly. She was not at all interested in that tonight.

Indeed, tonight things simply must go on and on and on. For Papa's sake, of course. Every minute that passed meant he was getting farther and farther away from Lindley's grasp. And she was being drawn closer and closer into it.

She forced back the waves of missish terror that threatened to denounce her bold behavior. No doubt she would harbor heavy regrets after this, but for now she was determined to forget anything but her immediate goals. Thankfully, the way Lindley guided her tongue with his and stroked one competent hand along her spine and down to massage her backside did much to help her accomplish this. Yes, it was most helpful indeed.

Oh, but she was such a dutiful daughter to wish for hours and hours of this.

Chapter Ten

She was teasing him, distracting him, using his own desire against him. Lindley wasn't a fool; of course he recognized what the girl was up to. He simply didn't care.

If she was so determined to keep him from going after her father, then who was he to argue? Hell, arguing was about the last thing on his mind. Right now all he could think about was how damn good Miss Darshaw tasted.

Felt good, too. Her backside was firm and round under his hand, just the way it ought to be. She was soft and pliant for him, pressing against him almost as if she were enjoying him. Perhaps she was. He certainly was going to do everything in his power to make it that way. This might be just a part of the game for both of them, but he'd be damned if she'd wake up tomorrow regretting it.

But of course she would regret it. If she were the sort to give her favors easily she would never have battled Fitzgelder with such fury that day in his linen cupboard. She would never have left Eudora's in the first place, for that matter. The very fact that she was not struggling against Lindley now was more a credit to her affection for her father than to any eagerness on her part to tumble into bed.

Still, it was clear the woman was not suffering. Nor was Lindley. The night would certainly not be a hardship on either of them.

Except that he had no intention of remaining there all night. Miss Darshaw might be giving herself willingly now, but he knew she'd be cursing him soon enough. He'd love her into unconsciousness, take that damned locket, and be off to track down her black-hearted father.

Damn the man for putting them both through this.

SHE WAS WARM FROM HER HEAD TO HER TOES AND ALL parts in between. It was heavenly and made it so simple to ignore what was really going on. She pressed herself more tightly against Lindley and imagined she could feel every contour of his stone-carved body right through his elegant clothing. If she was going to ruin herself for the sake of a father who'd left her, at least she had the good sense to do it with the most beautiful and competent man in all of England.

He was so competent, in fact, that she thankfully did not have to do much of anything to be a full and smiling participant. His kiss left her pleasantly weak, and when he took a break from ranging his hands over her body it was only to scoop her into his arms and carry her toward the bed. *The bed.*

Heavens, but was she sure about this? All those years at Madame's she'd refused to even consider letting any man come near her. Now she would be submitting herself to a night in Lindley's bed? Yet how could she not? His touch sent her out of her mind with wanting, and it was the only thing she could do to help Papa . . .

No, this had far more to do with Lindley's touch than it did with helping Papa. She had to admit that to herself. She would gladly let Lindley take her to bed tonight simply because she couldn't help herself.

He wanted her and, fool that she was, she wanted him, too.

Still, she was just a wee bit nervous. When he settled her onto the lumpy, overused mattress she had to make a conscious effort not to leap off and run to the other side of the room. It did help that he was right there, his hands still roaming over her and his lips coming back down to take hers. Yes, that did much to take away her flight instinct.

But then she felt her skirt sliding up as his hand moved down to find its way beneath the fabric. Heavens, he was touching her a good six inches above her knee! No man had ever *seen* her knee, let alone touched it. Indeed, she'd admonished him about wasting time, but now she wished she hadn't. This was going far, far too fast for her already. She pushed his hand away.

He seemed to recognize her hesitation and sat up, putting wonderful air between them. She felt her head clearing immediately. This had been such a mistake! Thank heavens he was not going to force her.

At least, she hoped he would not. As she glanced up into his face she could not be entirely certain about that. There was a smoldering glow behind his eyes and a smile at his lips that did not seem to indicate a man who was quite through for the evening.

He shrugged his needlessly broad shoulders and began to remove his coat. Every muscle in Sophie's abdomen tightened as she was treated to the remarkable view of his shirt pulled taut against his chest, and an equally taut smile pulled at his lips while his eyes stayed on hers. Indeed, he was not through for the evening. Heaven help her, but it would appear he was only just starting.

"Now, since you have proclaimed yourself commander of these operations, Miss Darshaw, would you be so kind as to inform me whether you wish us to take the time to remove all our clothing at this point, or only the parts that will get in the way?"

She couldn't reply, couldn't quite comprehend, really. He was so blunt, so cold about this! Could she really follow through and match his indifference? Oh, but she was not indifferent, not at all! She was terrified to her core, yet heated and weak at the sight of him in shirtsleeves. Whatever would it do to her to have the man *naked*?

It would buy her some time, however. Perhaps she should ask him to disrobe for her. Slowly. One article of clothing at a time. He would start with his cravat, pulling it leisurely from around his neck, stretching it out longer and longer until it released its hold on him, and his shirt might gape open. What would she find there? Would he be every bit as solid as he had felt, with definition like the breastplate of a Roman warrior she'd seen in sculpture? Would he have fine wisps of dark hair that invited her touch?

Oh, but how she would love to find out! She could instruct him to remove his shirt altogether, leaving him exposed, his skin gleaming in the last glow of the setting sun that filtered through the window. She could see him quite clearly in that light, and no doubt the view would be remarkable.

Then of course he would move on to his trousers, to those last dreaded fastenings that separated him from the world, the final barrier to keep her from gazing upon . . .

No, good heavens, no! She simply could not do that. She needed to keep her head, to find a way out of this, away from him. Somehow she had the strong suspicion she would find herself not nearly as motivated to run away from a naked Lindley as she ought to be.

"We should keep as much of our clothing on as possible, my lord," she said, and her voice came out as tight and restricted as her bodice felt just now.

His smile didn't fade, and the smoldering glow behind his eyes didn't dim. "Very well, my dear. Just the basics it is."

As simple as that, his hand was back under her skirt. She squirmed, pushing herself away from him in a reflex action. Her head banged into the wall.

"What the devil was that?" he asked, momentarily distracted from whatever he was trying to do under her skirt.

"Ouch."

"Well hold still! I'm not going to bite you. Yet."

She told herself he meant that last part in jest.

His hand was sliding up her leg again, on the calf, past the knee, up the thigh . . . She squirmed a bit more carefully this time. He gave a growl that was half laugh and half animal sound. Her heart rate picked up, and she was suddenly out of breath. He leaned toward her and kissed her again. Ah, but this was not nearly so worrisome as his hand on her leg. She let herself float into the kiss.

He was pressing her into the bed, his body warming her and making her forget that breathing was an important aspect of life. Who needed air when there was Lindley to breathe? Her eyes drooped shut, and she concentrated all her senses on him: his scent, his weight, the tantalizing stubble of his cheek as he brushed against her. Oh, and those wonderful sensations as his hand continued over the inside of her thigh toward her . . .

She squirmed again, this time rather violently. Her teeth accidentally clamped down on his tongue. When he pulled away from her with a start, his chin slammed into her nose. At the same time, her legs involuntarily bent upward in an effort to protect certain delicate areas from the onslaught of his unexpected hand. Her knee contacted his . . . er, *him*. Forcefully.

"Good God, Miss Darshaw, are you trying to kill me?"

"No! Oh, I'm so sorry. Did I hurt you?"

Apparently the damage would not prove fatal, because he pushed himself up to sitting and cocked his head to one side to stare warily at her.

"I can see why Fitzgelder was so frustrated after having you in his house for a month," he said. "You're a regular artist of self-defense."

"I'm sorry, I didn't mean—"

"To kill me? No, of course not. You merely hate me and were only attempting any of this out of some misbegotten notion that it would in some way assist your father."

"Yes, but—"

"It's only natural that you would rather bloody my mouth and disable my person than share my bed, Miss Darshaw. I can hardly hold it against you."

"Still, I didn't mean to—"

He shook his head in disgust and rose, standing over her and readjusting his skewed clothing.

"Some women are not of a passionate nature," he said. "I suppose you cannot help it if you are incapable of responding as any normal female would."

Oh, so now she was abnormal along with unwashed and uninteresting? *Well!* It was not as if he bore none of the responsibility for her instinctive reactions.

"I most certainly *am* a normal female!" she declared. "If you had not been in such a heated rush to . . . to . . . well, heatedly rush into things, perhaps I would not have reacted as I did."

"So, you did not intentionally attempt to emasculate me?"

"No, of course not. You simply, er, tickled me."

And now he laughed at her. "Tickling is often thought of as a pleasurable thing, Miss Darshaw. Any normal female would have enjoyed what I was doing."

"I did enjoy it! I mean . . ."

Oh, bother. He'd tricked her into admitting it, hadn't he? Her face burned, and she knew the color must be most unbecoming. He laughed again. She wished he'd quit doing that.

"Yes, I thought you did. So why did you endeavor to bite off my tongue?"

"If I had meant to do that on purpose I quite assure you I would have succeeded."

"Yes, because you are a cold, unfeeling person who has no feminine sensibilities."

"I am not! I have all sorts of feminine sensibilities."

"And I was hoping to discover a good number of them when you particularly made it rather difficult for me to continue."

"If you've been so gravely damaged, then why on earth do you keep laughing at me?"

"Because I'm afraid if I stop laughing at you I'm likely to swoop down on you and finish where we left off."

"And you don't want that."

"On the contrary, Miss Darshaw. I want that very much, I'm afraid. You, however, do not. Am I correct?"

No, he wasn't. Her body ached to tell him so. Her mind, however, was a different story. It would not let her utter a peep.

"That's what I thought," he said after a lengthy pause that should have given her more than enough time to re-engage his attentions.

He grabbed up his coat from where he'd tossed it on the floor and proceeded to dust it off. So much for her wonderful fantasies of him enticingly stripping off his clothing. He slid his arms into his coat and was, once again, the elegant nobleman who held her father's life in his hands. At least, he would be, had he gotten the locket.

"Where are you going?" she asked, suddenly recognizing he meant to leave her.

"I'm checking on my carriage. It should have been delivered here by now."

"And then you'll leave?"

"Yes. I *will* find your father, Miss Darshaw."

She wondered if pouting or tears might have any effect on him. It didn't seem so.

"Now, now," he said, moving to the side of the bed and sitting next to her. "I promised to make arrangements for you and I will. Fear not. You'll be cared for."

Cared for. As if that would help poor Papa. So nothing had changed, even after all that. She'd subjected herself to humiliation and girlish heart palpitations all for nothing. A man like Lindley would certainly get anything he wanted, while a girl like her would lose her father. *As usual.*

"What sort of arrangements do you have in mind, my lord?" she asked as he retied his cravat.

"I told you, that's up to you to decide," he answered, rising to go to the door. He let himself into the hallway. "Wait for me here. I'll be back shortly."

Yes, of course he'd be back. He'd left the locket still hanging around her neck, safely under her dress. How pitiful. The man had probably bedded half the women in London and yet she was still so disinteresting to him he couldn't be bothered to so much as reach into her bodice to get it.

HELLFIRE. HE'D LET HIMSELF GET SO DISTRACTED BY the temptations of Miss Darshaw's soft skin and willing lips that he'd completely forgotten about the locket. What the devil was wrong with him? She was just a woman, for heaven's sake. He'd had lots of women. Granted, not recently, but still . . . he should have been able to keep focus long enough to remember what he was about, damn it.

He'd thought she'd been quite pleased with the direction things had been going, that she'd been as distracted by their actions as he'd hoped to make her, but apparently not. She'd come to her senses well before he had, as a matter of fact. *Damn it.*

And now she sat up there with the locket. He'd conveniently left her alone with plenty of time to examine it and dispose of whatever might have been contained there. *Double damn it.*

It would be useless to go back up to her at this point, so he continued on to the mews to see about the status of his carriage. At least if Miss Darshaw took advantage of his absence to leave Warwick in an attempt to track down any of the names she might find inside that locket, she was in no position to travel any faster than he could, at this point. If by some miracle his phaeton had finally arrived, he would clearly have the upper hand.

Still, he'd have to keep close watch on her in case she did decide to try and leave him behind. He had a strong suspicion he'd been underestimating her thus far—she'd been able to handle him far better than expected. Perhaps Madame had taught the girl more than he'd been led to believe.

Or perhaps he was losing his touch.

Thankfully he was distracted from having to contemplate that horrible thought in any measure of depth. He located the stable hand he'd been instructed to find and was told his carriage had indeed just arrived. His horses were even now being rubbed down and tucked away for the night. He could leave first thing in the morning.

He didn't bother to mention to the stable hand that he'd no intention of wasting another night in this place. Rushing off with no clue in which direction to proceed would certainly help no one. Besides, he had the not-entirely-small matter of Miss Darshaw to deal with.

He'd meant it when he promised to make arrangements for her. Of course, he really had no idea what those arrangements would be, but on the slight chance that the girl was not interested in chasing off on her own after some hint of her father's whereabouts, he had no intention of simply leaving her here to scrap for herself as best she could.

She deserved to be cared for. He would find her a position somewhere, or leave her with some access to funds that would see her through. Perhaps he might hire her a way back to London, although that would surely put her back in the brothel and possibly at the mercy of Fitzgelder. No, he would do well to convince her to stay here, where she was safe.

Except that she was not. That man in the street had attacked her, and Lindley was still convinced it had something to do with the locket. No, he could not be sure she was safe even this far from London.

Then he would take her with him.

No, that was ridiculous. She would surely get in his way, and even more surely she'd consciously attempt to thwart his efforts. Taking her with him to hunt for her father would be the height of stupidity. He'd just have to think of something else to do with her.

Oh, he could think of a few things he'd like to do with her, all right. But none of them would help secure her in a safe place or help him locate her blasted father. He'd best find some way to redirect his thoughts. Quickly.

The man lurking in shadow at the far corner of the building did that quite nicely. Lindley's thoughts were immediately redirected as he made his way across the open space between the mews and the inn. What the devil was that man doing, hiding there, watching him?

He scanned the area, wondering if there was any way he might leave the man's sight and then double around, hopefully to catch him unaware. But the yard was open, and by the time he would make it into the inn through a rear door, then back out the front to wrap around, he felt quite certain his shadow-man would be gone.

He was still mentally examining his options when the man suddenly moved, sliding out from his hiding spot and trotting across the yard toward him. Lindley's nerves went on high alert until suddenly he recognized the man. *Feasel.*

"Don't spy on people, then come leaping out that way, Feasel," he warned. "If I'd had a pistol I'd have likely shot at you."

"Unless you've drastically improved since that last hunting party at Durmond Park, you'd likely have missed, my lord."

"You know good and well I could have shot that ruddy fox if I'd have wanted."

"Aye, if you weren't so bloody softhearted toward the little things."

"As long as my poultryman keeps them out of my henhouse, I see no reason to randomly exterminate the local fauna."

"Softhearted. And worse, your friends all think you're a lousy shot."

"Ah, but so will my enemies. I'd rather have them learn the truth regarding my rumored incompetence the hard way."

"Yes, that's just so for enemies, but I was referring to your friends, my lord."

Lindley tried not to visibly frown. Since taking on this role of self-appointed avenger he'd not had a lot of time for friendships. He'd given up the luxury of trust, and damned if that didn't make friendships a bit obsolete. Besides, he'd been busy playing the friend to Fitzgelder and his reprobate crowd. All his decent friends had been rather eager to avoid him of late.

"How did you find me so quickly, Feasel?" he asked, happy to change the subject.

"Oh, I keep my eye on you, sir. Someone's got to."

"Well, I'm glad you do. Things have gotten a bit, er, complicated."

"Aren't they always, sir? So what is it this time, are you concerned about your friend Rastmoor drinking himself into oblivion in there?"

"You noticed him, did you?"

"Aye. Did he follow you here, you think?"

"Ostensibly, he made some kind of promise to Miss Darshaw's relatives that he'd find her, so I presume he followed *her* here. I haven't decided yet whether or not we can trust him."

"So you've got that chit with you, eh?"

"I thought it ungentlemanly to leave her on her own, yes."

Feasel laughed. "Of course, my lord. Leave her on her own and she might go back to that husband of hers."

"I told you about that husband."

He laughed again. "You did, and I'm thinking Miss Darshaw might have some competition on her hands. That 'husband' seems to have taken a fancy to your Lord Rastmoor, as a matter of fact."

"So Rastmoor's traveling companion is our roguish actress?"

"Aye, same one, and still wearing trousers, my lord."

Well, that did add another element. What was that woman's

role in all of this? Was she in this with Rastmoor, hunting Sophie for the locket? Indeed, so much cloak-and-dagger could not bode well for Miss Darshaw.

"Hell. You're going to have to help me with this, Feasel."

"Don't I always, sir?"

Now Lindley laughed. He slapped his faithful retainer on the back and nodded his head toward the side of the building where shadows were heavy and no windows looked down. He would need to fill him in on a few things, and they had little time to waste. Also, it would be best if he did not make his presence known to Rastmoor, just inside the inn. Or that strange, masculine actress. The less they knew, the better.

"Yes, my friend, you always do."

SOPHIE ADJUSTED HER LITTLE PACK, CAREFULLY MAKing sure everything was neatly stowed. There was no telling when Lindley would return or what he'd expect when he did. She had to get out of here now.

She carefully tried the door and was pleasantly surprised to find he'd not locked it. It seemed the man didn't really care whether she stayed or left at this point. Perhaps he didn't need the locket to find Papa after all. Perhaps he'd run into him here already. She should have thought of that before she let the man walk out the door.

Papa could very well be here, and Madame, too. It would all be quite ugly if Lindley found him. Before she left, she'd check with the innkeeper. He would know if a man by Papa's description had arrived or not.

Tiptoeing into the hall, she nearly ran into a maid who came scurrying up the stairway. The maid was carrying a pan of steaming water and appeared none too happy about it. In the distance Sophie could hear a baby crying.

"Excuse me, miss," the maid muttered, dodging her.

"Yes, it's fine," she said and had to step back quickly as the maid struggled to keep the towels slung over her arm from falling to the floor. In her efforts, she sloshed the hot water and very nearly gave Sophie an unexpected bath.

"Oh, bother!" the maid exclaimed. Her towels hit the floor.

"Here, let me help you," Sophie said, propping her pack

under her arm and stooping to gather the towels for the girl. "That's quite a load you've got there."

The girl held out her arm for Sophie to lay the towels back where they were, but she was far too busy grumbling to give a word or two of thanks.

"That brat's going to keep the folks here up all night. My mistress says take up a warm bath and some towels, that ought to soothe the babe. So here I am, wetting myself just so some whining brat gets a bath it probably don't really want."

"I'm told some babies enjoy the warm water," Sophie said, for lack of anything else. Besides, she knew for a fact it was true. Her friend Annie's baby adored being washed with a nice, warm cloth. It put the infant to sleep right way. At least, that's how things had been last she'd heard from her friend.

"Well, all I'm going to say is where's this Mrs. Alton's husband while she's bouncing 'round the countryside with this baby what won't stop its wailing?"

The maid did her best to carry the rest of the water past Sophie and to a door just a ways down the hallway. It did appear the sounds of the crying baby were coming from that direction. Unfortunately, the maid did not have a free hand to knock at the door. Sophie sighed and hurried over to her. Perhaps this warm water—what was left of it—would indeed soothe the poor child. Surely Sophie could spare a few moments to help get it across the threshold.

She knocked. The wailing continued, but footsteps sounded from inside the room and quickly the door was thrown open. Sophie was about to step away at that point and let the maid complete her task unassisted, but the sight of the young woman who stood just inside the room caught Sophie completely by surprise.

"Annie?"

Good heavens, it was her dearest friend! And there, just beyond Annie in the room, sat Madame herself, holding the crying child and looking a bit worse for the wear.

"Sophie!" Annie cried out, reaching to grab her and pull her into a happy embrace.

The maid with the bathing implements muttered under her breath and pushed her way past the reunited women to go deposit her items on the nearest table. The annoyed glance she spared for the infant said she might possibly not be very fond of children. Fortunately Annie appeared not to notice.

"Sophie! We've found you!"

"Yes, and I—"

Madame cut her off, however, and quickly turned her attentions on the maid. "We're glad you've arrived, Sophie. Now that these things have been brought, perhaps we can all have some peace and quiet. Thank you, that will be all."

The maid was only too happy to be dismissed. She didn't bother with a polite curtsy but simply stomped out of the room and pulled the door shut behind her.

"Surly creature," Madame said. Sophie assumed she referred to the maid, although she could not be certain. Madame had a weary, put-out expression.

Annie hurried over to take her babe from the older woman, though it did little to silence the poor child.

"She's not been traveling well, I'm afraid," Annie said, stroking her child and carrying her toward the bowl of warm water. "I'm hoping a gentle bath might help calm her."

"Is there anything I can do?"

"No, Annie will handle things," Madame replied. "We're just very happy to see you, Sophie. It means we can head back to London right away."

"Right away? Do you mean tonight?" Sophie said, not missing the worried expression on Annie's face at this suggestion. "Perhaps it would be best for us to wait until Rosie has had some rest."

Clearly Annie agreed, but she said nothing. Instead she simply worked to remove some of her child's outer clothes and made a soft pallet to lay her on the table beside the water bowl. Her actions were at least distracting to the child, who seemed to be most curious about the contents of the bowl that she awkwardly reached for. My, but the baby had grown in the weeks since Sophie had last seen her. Such a pretty little girl.

It would be wonderful to return to London with Madame and Annie. Perhaps she could learn to help care for the child and make herself useful at the brothel again. Yes, perhaps Madame would increase her pay if she could do more than simply sew. And perhaps it would help Annie, too. If the child's father was no longer interested in supporting her, she would need to return to work, if she hadn't already. Sophie had often heard it was common that men lost interest in their kept women once a child entered the picture.

"I'm sure the child would be far more comfortable back in her own home," Madame said. "We should leave as soon as possible. Quickly, Sophie, you should gather your things."

Sophie was a bit ashamed to indicate her tiny little pack. "Er, I already have, Madame."

"I see. Your father must be in a great hurry. I'm afraid, Sophie, it's not safe for him to remain in one place very long. He's made some enemies, my dear."

"So I've learned. Honestly, Madame, how long have you known my father was not dead? You should have told me."

"You know I would have told you if I could have, my dear."

"If you *could* have? What on earth prevented you? I grieved for him, Madame!"

"Shush, Sophie. You'll upset the baby again."

Indeed, she didn't want that. Sophie glanced over to the mother softly cooing to her child as she gently rubbed a dampened cloth over the tiny fingers and toes. The babe's cries had turned to happy gurgles. Sophie decided any angry questions she might still have for Madame could certainly wait for another time.

"I'm just happy your father was able to find you and was willing to wait this long for us," Madame said, taking advantage of the change in topic. "When did you arrive here, dear?"

"Last night, Madame, but—"

"You've been here since last night? But I did not see your father's name in the register book, not here and not at the inn across the street."

"That's because we did not register at an inn last night."

"Then wherever did you sleep?"

"After Papa was injured in the fight, Lord Lindley was kind enough to—"

"Injured in a fight?" Annie questioned, her attention snapping back to their conversation.

Madame was more interested in the other subject of Sophie's statement. "Lord Lindley? Was he here?"

"He went down to check on his carriage. He ordered me to remain in our room, but I decided to—"

"*Our* room?" Madame and Annie said, very much at the same time.

"You stayed here last night with Lord Lindley?" Madame continued.

"No! Of course not." Heavens, but she was quite happy to still be able to deny any accusations they might make. *Most* of their accusations, at least. "Papa was injured, so Lord Lindley took us to the surgeon. We spent the night there while the surgeon patched Papa's leg."

"Was he hurt very badly?" Annie asked.

"He was cut, but the surgeon stopped the bleeding and assured us that if he rested all would be well."

"I'm glad to hear it," Madame said. "Where is this surgeon? Give me the direction and I will send someone over to fetch your father so we may be off."

"I can't," Sophie said.

"You don't know the direction? But if you just came from there . . ."

"No, I can't have you fetch Papa."

"There, there. I'm sure he'll move very carefully and not aggravate his wound," Madame soothed. "No doubt even the surgeon would allow it."

"It wouldn't matter if he did. I'm afraid he's got no say in the matter now. Papa's gone."

"He's gone?" the women chimed together again.

"Yes, I'm afraid so."

Madame seemed doubtful. "Gone? Do you mean, he is dead?"

Sophie practically choked at the thought of it. "Oh, no, Madame! I simply mean he has left, run off."

"He's gone off and left you here alone? With *Lindley*?"

"Well, when he left it appeared Lindley had gone, as well. But then Lindley came back. It was rather a good thing, too. You have no idea what sort of footpads they have in this town! I was simply walking along, minding my own business, when suddenly a man leapt out and—"

Madame hushed her. "We have no time for stories. Your father is in grave danger and you just let him wander off from you, Sophie?"

Well, this was just a bit uncalled for. She was beginning to be a mite unhappy with the lack of concern she could feel from her former employer.

"I thought the man was dead for years, Madame. It's not as if I've much practice at being his keeper, you know. Besides, he drugged me!"

But even Annie seemed to care little for the various mishaps Sophie had endured over the past few hours. "He could be anywhere by now, Madame," she said, still daubing the baby with a now lukewarm rag. "Someone should be sent to find him!"

"I'm sure Lindley will do that soon enough," Sophie muttered. "He's got great plans to apprehend him."

"But he's done nothing wrong!" Annie protested.

Sophie was touched that her friend would be so quick to defend him, but she felt she owed it to her to admit the truth of her father's past. "I'm afraid pretending to be dead is the least of my father's sins, Annie. He and Lindley have both assured me his past holds many secrets that I may not wish to know about."

"You seem to be on quite excellent terms with Lord Lindley," Madame said. "I'm worried for you, Sophie. Lindley is not a man to be trusted—certainly not by a girl as green as yourself. I hope you've not let yourself be swayed by the man's empty words and flattery."

"I promise you, Madame, he's wasted no flattery on me," Sophie assured her. "He did take Papa to the surgeon, however, when clearly he would have rather just—"

Madame pinched her eyes shut and almost appeared as if she would break into tears. "Oh, my poor, poor child! You've succumbed to his enticement!"

"I have not!" *Not all the way, anyhow.* "I appreciate that he showed a bit of human kindness toward my father, but I was in the midst of taking advantage of his absence to leave the man. He says I hold the clue to finding where my father has possibly gone, and I intend to learn whether or not I do. Without Lindley."

Madame was not quite as happy to hear this as Sophie might have expected. In fact, the woman was quiet for a moment or two, contemplating things. "You have something that might tell us where your father is? Show me."

She held out her hand, clearly expecting Sophie to place something in it. Something about Madame's demand didn't sit right with her, though, so Sophie left the locket hanging securely around her neck. What would make the woman assume that the clue she referred to was something Sophie could just pull out and place in her hand?

"I . . . can't."

"Sophie, you can trust me. I will help you find your father."

Apparently she could not trust Madame, not after all those years she'd lived ignorantly under her roof and the woman never bothered to tell her Papa was alive.

"It's not a thing, Madame," Sophie explained. "Lord Lindley believes I must know something; perhaps I recall some person or a place my father may have talked about in the past. That would be a clue to where he's gone now."

Madame dropped her hand. "Oh. Well, do you?"

"No. At least, I can't think of any. Lord Lindley was hoping that he could encourage my memory as we traveled."

"Yes, he'd certainly like to try that with you, my dear," Madame said. "But he would not be kind to you. He would hurt you."

She was fairly certain Madame was not speaking of some abstract broken heart. Did she really believe Lindley would be cruel, might even abuse her? Heavens, and to think Sophie had been alone with the man in such an intimate setting! She was fortunate he lost interest and left her when he did. Still, he'd not shown any signs of that sort of unpleasantness. He'd been quite tender for a moment or two, in fact.

"He does not seem such an ogre, Madame."

"He's not for you, Sophie. You're better than that. Please believe me, my dear. He's the sort of man who uses women for his purposes and discards them as quickly. Truly, he will leave you worse than he found you and abandon you flat. You cannot stay with him."

"Luckily I was leaving just now."

"Smart girl."

Annie piped up with a concern, however. "I only hope when he returns from checking on his carriage that he doesn't decide to search the place for you, Sophie. If he finds us he'd certainly suspect we were aiding you."

Those words seemed especially meaningful to Madame. Her brows wrinkled and she tightened her lips. "Yes, he would search the place, wouldn't he? And if we attempt to leave now we'd surely run across him. Seems we have quite a dilemma."

"But I could hide myself and you could simply say it was all a coincidence, that you had no idea I was here and haven't seen me," Sophie suggested.

Madame shook her head. "No, of course he'd never believe that. What possible reason could Annie and I have to be traveling out here? No, he must not find us. Sophie, you will simply have to go back to him."

"What?" Now it was she and Annie who replied in unison.

"Madame," Annie began. "You cannot send her back to him, not if he's as cruel and dangerous as you say!"

"Shush," Madame replied. "He will be kind at first, to win her trust. Sophie, you must go back."

"But I can't! Madame, I need to leave, to find my father. This could be my only chance."

"Listen to me, girl," Madame said, her voice growing hard and clipped. "I will help you find your father. Yes, I may have some notion where he's gone. If you value his life, you will trust me."

"You know where to find him?"

"Perhaps, but it will do no good if Lindley finds us here. He will know we are here to help you and keep your father safe from him. You can keep him from finding out."

"What would you have me do?"

Madame's expression was very serious now. "What would *Lindley* have you do?"

"What exactly do you mean, Madame?"

"Come, come, Sophie. He is a man, after all. Surely you have some idea what he wants from you."

"I . . . I don't know," Sophie replied.

It was painfully honest, too. Clearly Madame had some notion that Lindley was interested in her, but Sophie had already learned the hard way that Lindley's interest ran little further than what she might know about her father. Aside from the locket, she truly had no idea what the man wanted.

"Of course you know what he wants," Madame said. "He's a man. You may play innocent and naive, little Sophie, but you are no fool. I've seen Lindley's eye linger on you when he'd come to call. You can't have missed it, blushing and skirting around nervously when he was there. You know what he wants, and I'm surprised you claim not to have given it to him already."

"Madame!"

"And you know what Lindley wants with your father, as well, don't you?"

Yes, indeed she did know that, only too well. She nodded.

"Then you understand how serious this is," Madame went on. "You must go back to Lindley and see that he is occupied. Let him think that with enough sweet talk and cajoling you might recall some clue to your father's whereabouts. Keep him safely in that room until he is sleeping."

"I don't know that Lindley requires sleep, Madame."

"All men require sleep, Sophie. Eventually. After certain exertion."

Annie made a little squeaking sound. "Madame, you're not suggesting that Sophie should . . ."

Madame shot her a glance across the room. "And you would rather Lindley discover us and then track down her father?"

Annie dropped her eyes, shook her head, and hugged her baby.

Sophie wanted to be quite certain she understood things. "You mean you want me to go back to the room and allow Lord Lindley to seduce me?"

"Seduce *him* if you have to," Madame said with a shrug of the shoulders. "It's not the worst thing in the world, Sophie. Of course, the first time it might be a bit uncomfortable, but Lindley knows what he's about. He'll make it endurable."

Endurable? Good heavens! Could Madame really be asking this of her? Was this truly the only way to save her father? She hoped not. If it was, then she had already failed. Lindley had flatly rejected her.

"Go, Sophie," Madame instructed. "Trust me. You won't have to work very hard. Give Lindley what he wants and let him think that after a nice rest you can lead him to your father. While he is busy with you, Annie and I can leave. We'll wait for you on the road."

"On the road?"

Madame smiled in the kind, motherly way she would sometimes. "Just south of here on the London road there is an old stone wall. At the end of it, we'll be waiting. All you need to do is get Lindley to sleep, then slip out and meet us."

"And you'll take me to my father?"

Madame nodded. "We'll find your father. Then all will be well and you will never have to face Lindley again."

It seemed too good to be true, but Madame made it sound so simple. Indeed, it *was* simple. All she needed was to distract Lindley long enough for her friends to escape undetected, then she could slip out. And judging by Lindley's recent disinterest in her, perhaps that would require less involvement on her part than Madame suspected.

Give Lindley what he wants. Indeed, all he wanted was the locket. She could certainly use that to her advantage, couldn't she?

"All right, Madame," Sophie said, drawing in a deep breath. "I'll do it."

Chapter Eleven

He'd spent more time with Feasel than expected. Lindley checked his pocket watch and frowned. *Getting late.* Did they really have that much business to attend to, or was he simply avoiding going back to face Miss Darshaw?

He decided not to answer that.

Feasel told him about an incident on the road that Rastmoor had been involved in last night, back near Geydon. Apparently Lindley had taken off after D'Archaud just in time to have missed it. He almost wished he had not.

A carriage with two innocent women and a babe was attacked on the road by highwaymen. Feasel only had his information secondhand, but he'd learned one of the attackers was killed and the one who survived gave a report that seemed of special interest to Lindley. The man claimed he and his partner had been hired by someone to waylay a carriage and that somehow they'd come upon the wrong one.

Unfortunately, Feasel had been unable to question the man directly. While waiting for the proper channels of justice to run, someone managed to do away with the fellow. *Pity.* From what Feasel had heard, the description of the carriage the man said he'd been hired to assault sounded remarkably like Lindley's carriage. The very one that had suffered a disabled axle that would have made them easy prey to any observant highwaymen, had those particular highwaymen not mistakenly attacked the wrong carriage.

Indeed, Lindley must be getting closer to his enemies if they were getting this close to him. He would do well to take more precautions from here out. For one, he instructed Feasel to hire anyone he needed to make himself safe. It would be no help at all if the one man Lindley counted on was murdered while he loitered in the shadows.

Feasel agreed to take care, admonishing his master to do the same. They agreed on a meeting place, but Feasel insisted that travel by night on the London road was too risky. Lindley would just have to wait until morning to start out after D'Archaud. He was sure Miss Darshaw would be happy to hear that. Hell, it was what he'd already promised her, wasn't it?

He left Feasel to slip back into the shadows—as the man did so very well—and made his way back into the inn. A quick glance into the common room proved that Rastmoor was still there, sitting all alone over his cups. He looked like hell, and Lindley was half tempted to go to him. But he could not. Rastmoor might be the enemy. There was too much at stake for Lindley to fall in the trap of trusting anyone. Or caring.

The stairs creaked as he made his way up toward his room. The baby that had been crying earlier when he left was quiet now. Poor thing, probably upset by its unfamiliar surroundings and upended routine. He recalled how travel could sometimes be difficult for little ones. He forced the memory back into the dark recess where it usually lingered, safely ignored.

The door to his room was toward the end of the narrow hallway, and he stalked quietly toward it. Things appeared just as he left them, and he had a brief flash of concern. Had he locked the door, or been in too much of a frustrated hurry to leave? He didn't recall locking it. He should have. What if Miss Darshaw had thought to leave? Or worse, what if someone had come in after her? He tried the handle and it opened easily for him. *Damn.* He should not have left her so unprotected.

The room was dim. A lone candle had very nearly sputtered out. His eyes adjusted to the flickering light, and at first he saw no sign of Miss Darshaw.

Damn it, he'd kept a close eye on the building, but of course he could not have seen all of it at once. She could have easily found a way out and left him by now. She would be out in the darkness, alone and unprotected, an easy victim to whomever had attacked her in that alleyway.

But then his eye caught on the bed. The shape there seemed so small he'd nearly overlooked it. She was here, curled up under the covers and fast asleep.

Thank heavens.

He pulled the door shut behind him and moved toward her. Why hadn't she left? He only now realized he'd half expected her to. It would probably be best if she had, since she'd made it clear she wanted nothing more to do with him. His body was telling him he wanted everything more to do with her.

Then he noticed her dress tossed carelessly on the floor. And there, hanging limp over the bedstead, was her shift. *Really?* She'd known he was coming back and yet she'd removed her clothing? That hardly sounded like Miss Darshaw.

Fighting a wave of worry, he carefully slid the cover back to reveal her ivory shoulder. She was bare, shoulder, arm . . . and graceful neck. Good God, her neck was bare! The locket was gone.

Someone must have come in, abused her, and taken the locket. He didn't know which was stronger, his sudden terror for her well-being or his fury at what so obviously occurred. Terror won out and he dropped to his knees beside her, scooping her into his arms and brushing back her wayward hair, silken blond strands that hid her lovely face. Was she bruised? Frightened? Traumatized? Or worse, was this the sort of sleep she might never wake from? He hated himself for leaving her alone up here.

Her silent form suddenly came to life in his arms, writhing and kicking against him. He was nearly beside himself with relief. She would survive.

He held her tighter and whispered into her ear, "You're fine. Don't worry. I'm here now."

For a moment the writhing and kicking stopped. He was

about to lay her gently back onto the pillow when it started up again. She kneed him roundly in the ribs.

"Sophie, it's me!" he protested, dropping her and leaning back so she might see him clearly.

"I know it's you! Who else would it be?" she said, scrambling to pull the thin covers back over herself.

Damn, but he'd hardly got more than a glimpse of luscious bosom and youthful flesh.

"But I . . . Are you unhurt? Did they harm you?" he asked, reaching for the covers and then thinking better of it when he caught the look of murder simmering in her eyes.

"Did who harm me?"

"Whoever came in here and, er, removed your clothing."

"*I* removed my clothing, my lord," she replied.

"*You?* So, you were not attacked?"

"Not until you came in here."

He sat back on his heels and glared up at her. "I did not attack you. I was afraid you'd been molested."

"Not yet, my lord."

"But you knew I was coming back. Why on earth would you take your clothes off and leave them scattered around the room?"

Now she lowered her eyes and a charming flush of color stole over her. He suspected she was every inch the blushing maiden. He suspected, too, that he must indeed be an absolute ogre for the way he was, even now as she was so obviously embarrassed, wishing to devour her with his eyes. And other parts as well.

"I felt sorry for the way we parted," she said, not looking at him. "I thought perhaps we could . . . er, that I could . . . that we should make friends, my lord."

"Friends?"

"Yes, or something like that."

He could make little sense of this. What on earth was the girl up to?

"Friends?"

"I thought if we had to, er, pass the night together, we might as well be friends."

She didn't speak but kept her eyes pasted on a spot at the end of the bed. So she wasn't going to explain herself? Well, someone needed to speak to distract him from following his instinct and leaping back up onto that bed with her. For both their sakes, he stayed where he was and forced himself to be annoyed.

"Yes, Miss Darshaw, clearly waiting naked in my bed is the best way to make *friends*. I'm shocked it isn't much more utilized in polite society. 'Miss Dalrymple, have you met my Great Aunt Agatha?' 'Why yes, she was waiting naked in my bed just yesterday. We're lovely friends now.' We hear that all the time, don't we, Miss Darshaw?"

"Don't mock me, sir."

"Then don't show up naked in my bed and expect me to wish for anything akin to mere friendship."

"I'm not naked in your bed, my lord," she said as prim as a schoolmistress.

"You certainly looked naked a moment ago," he growled back. "And here is your gown, and your shift, and your stockings . . . so I'd like to know just how, then, you manage to be anything other than naked in my bed."

She tipped her chin defiantly and turned her eyes away from him. "I had a few items in my pack."

"Now you have my curiosity. It was a rather small pack, Miss Darshaw."

She didn't reply, so he decided to see for himself. He reached to pull her covers back, angry that she should think to toy with him this way. Could she possibly not feel any of the same passion he felt toward her? Did she sense none of the tension that crackled through the air between them? Was she truly unaffected by . . .

Great Jupiter in the sky. The hellcat was right—she was *not* naked. Not quite.

But what the devil was it that she wore? He'd dragged the covers from her grasp and now stood in awed silence as his eyes raked over her, ravenous for the sight but not entirely sure what it was they saw.

"What is that?"

"It's what I'm wearing."

"I can see it's what you're wearing, or very nearly wearing. What is it?"

"Er, I'm not certain it has a name, sir."

He swallowed. No, he supposed a costume like this really had no use for a name. One was hardly likely to be discussing it in polite company after the fact, and right now, gazing at it, conversation was the very last thing to cross Lindley's mind.

He cleared his throat, swallowed again, and pretended he could think straight.

"So, Miss Darshaw, *this* is what you wear to sleep in?"

The article was pink. A fresh, vibrant pink that made him think of cherry pastries. Or the inviting flush on Miss Darshaw's cheeks. Or Miss Darshaw's lips. Or Miss Darshaw's, er, other lips.

And the article was silk, which glistened in the candle glow and made his hands reach out for the softness of it. Or Miss Darshaw's silky warm skin. Or her lips. Or her, er, other lips.

And the article hardly covered any of these. It was nothing more than a mesh, a woven lace of glistening silk cords, knotted artfully together around the enticing framework of stays. Stays that accentuated her curves and hoisted her delectable breasts up and held them on display, offered them up as a feast for his animal lust. He had to forcibly hold himself back from taking the woman up on that offer.

Halfway down, the silky mesh was woven into a band. It wrapped around to highlight her slender waist. The way the various cords of silk interlaced gave an effect somewhere between fishing net and Grandmamma's tatting. Never in a hundred years would he have expected either to send his blood pounding as if he'd just run a marathon.

As if he weren't affected enough, the tantalizing costume did not end at the waistband. No, cords of this vibrant pink silk ran from the band down over her thighs, knotting into a wider mesh. The taut, ivory skin of her rounded bottom pressed against the cords and puckered, like the flesh of ripened fruit. He was drooling to take a bite.

Never had he encountered such a garment. Never had he felt such powerful desire for any woman. The effect this deadly combination had on his self-control was terrifying. Damn it all, but Miss Darshaw looked like every heated fantasy he'd ever had. How on earth was he supposed to keep himself away from her tonight?

"I thought if I wore this, my lord, you might be more inclined toward, er, friendship," she said.

His addled brain struggled to make sense of her words. It was no use. There was no sense to those words.

"Look at you, Miss Darshaw," he said, half choked by his carnal hunger. "What on earth would make you think we might strike up a polite friendship after this?"

"Perhaps *friendship* is not exactly the right word for it, my lord," she said, her voice shrinking. "But I don't know quite what else to call it."

He knew what he'd call it, but he decided "plugging her like a raging beast" would probably sound like a bad thing to Miss Darshaw. It didn't sound like such a bad thing to him. No, not at all. Still, he was a gentleman. He drew a deep breath, took his eyes off of her, and stood.

"Be careful for drafts, Miss Darshaw," he said, yanking the thin coverlet and tossing it over her. Damn, but he hated to cover that view.

She clutched the blanket to her and pouted. "But don't you . . . can't we . . . wouldn't it be . . ."

"What are you trying to say, Miss Darshaw? Spit it out."

"If I knew how to say it, sir, I would! I'm trying to suggest that we should, er, well . . ."

"I think *you* should go to sleep and get some rest."

"Well!" She slapped the bed beside her, muttering under her breath. "Thickheaded, mutton-brained man . . . I can't believe I even considered it with you!"

He was beyond patience. "Considered *what*, for God's sake, Miss Darshaw?"

"Shagging, of course! Honestly, why on earth else would I be lying here shivering in this uncomfortable contrivance?"

He could scarce believe his ears. "You were waiting here for me so we could . . . ?" Hell, but he couldn't even say it.

"Start swiving. Yes, prigging and docking and pumping the well, my lord. I'd heard rumors you might be of an inclination to do such things." She glared at him as if he'd just insulted her mother. "Apparently, though, I was mistaken."

"Apparently you were . . . ? Damn it all, Miss Darshaw! A lady doesn't just strip off her clothes and fall asleep in a man's bed like this! And, good lord, a lady would never be caught dead wearing *that*!"

"Since when has anyone mistaken me for a lady?" she said with a disgruntled snort. "And I'll have you know I worked very hard creating this costume. Madame says my work is exciting and unique."

"Hellfire, Eudora encourages you to create things like this?"

"She's very proud of the work I do! But I'm sorry if I've offended you, my lord. Apparently my skills at seduction are hardly up to your standards."

She was sitting now, holding the coverlet around her. He could just make out the silhouette of her breasts, still perfectly exhibited by the provocative garment. They were firm and round and just the perfect size for . . . Hell, if her seduction skills were any more up to his "standards" he would probably explode where he stood.

"If you were waiting here to seduce me, then why did you kick me . . . again?" he asked.

She pulled the coverlet tighter and snuggled it around her body. Her lush body. Her young body. Her alluring body. Her body that he could still see vividly in his mind's eye even though the damned blanket now covered it—mostly.

"You startled me!" she replied. "I didn't expect it to take you so very long to check on your precious carriage. I suppose I fell asleep."

Even when she behaved as a petulant child he still wanted her. This was not at all a good thing. He knew, of course, she didn't want him. Not really. This seduction ruse was simply a return to her first intent, to keep him here as long as possible to give her father greater chance at escape. Apparently she was willing to go to any end for that goal, even so far as wearing this monstrosity and shagging someone she hated.

Well, then. How relieved she would be when he told her they would be staying here tonight and she need not have gone to all this trouble.

Not that he didn't appreciate it, though! On the contrary. Should things get a bit chilly later in the night, one thought of Miss Darshaw wriggling her body into—or out of—that astonishing costume, and he'd warm right up. He'd not sleep much, though, and he had to admit he was dead tired after his travels and restless night watching D'Archaud.

But what was he to do then? He didn't dare leave her alone—she'd take the locket and disappear, probably going off to get herself killed. He had to stay right here, where he could keep an eye on her. He must remember, though, that an eye was all he could keep on her, despite those alluring peaks teasing him beneath that thin cover. By hell, he supposed he'd just have to find a way to make himself comfortable in a chair and leave Miss Darshaw alone in the bed.

That, he knew, was the only way he'd ever manage to . . . well, leave her alone.

"I will sleep here and you will remain in the bed," he announced, feeling rather noble as he propped the one spindly chair they had against the door just in case she might have any notion of leaving.

"You can't sleep in a chair," she said.

"You seemed to survive it last night," he replied.

"That was a much larger chair. And it was horrible."

"You just worry about yourself. Go to sleep, Miss Darshaw."

"So you can leave?"

"No, I'm not leaving."

"Your darling carriage is still not repaired?"

"It is, and it has been returned. Finally."

"So of course you are eager to leave."

No, right now he was eager for something else. He only *wished* he could leave.

"It's too dangerous. We will stay here and leave tomorrow," he said.

"We?"

"I told you I will make some sort of arrangement for you. Do you wish to remain here? I will see if the innkeeper has a respectable position for you."

She eyed him suspiciously. He adjusted himself in the chair, leaned back against the door, crossed his legs, and closed his eyes. It did nothing to remove that tantalizing image of her from his mind.

"And what will you do?"

"I will go to find your father," he said. "With or without that locket."

"Without, then."

"You've hidden it?"

"I have."

"Good. I was afraid someone came in here, abused you, and stole it."

She was silent a moment. He refused to look at her to judge her thoughts.

"You thought that?" she asked at last.

He nodded. "I'm glad I was mistaken."

Another silence. This stretched on so long he began to think perhaps she'd taken his advice and dropped off to sleep. Finally she spoke again.

"Do you really think the locket will help you find Papa?"

"I will find him eventually."

"But it would be easier with the locket."

"Yes. If it indeed contains that list of conspirators, it's only logical to expect that he will go to one of them now. It's why he left the locket with you, I'm quite certain. He hoped you would use it to follow him."

"So naturally you hope *you* can use it to follow him."

"I do. Those men must be brought to justice."

"I could simply give it to you, you know."

"I know you could. And I could just as easily force you to tell me where you hid it, then just take it for myself."

"But you're a gentleman."

"No, I'm tired. Now go to sleep, Miss Darshaw."

There was another pause before she spoke again.

"I will give it to you if you take me with you to find my father."

"No. You'd only get in the way. On purpose."

"If you're only going to find him eventually, then I'd rather it be sooner and with me present. Take me with you and I'll provide the locket."

"No. Go to sleep now."

"And will you be going to sleep now?"

"Eventually."

"Sleeping in a chair isn't very comfortable, is it?"

"It will do."

"It will not. You'll be miserable. Promise to take me with you and I'll give you the locket *and* I'll invite you to share this nice comfortable bed."

Hell, it had been all he could do not to take her up on her offer the first time she made it. Now he was nearly lost. But her offer came with a price. Could he possibly consider it, consider taking her with him? *No, of course not.* For her own sake he couldn't.

Still, she was right about it being dashed uncomfortable in this damn chair. He certainly would not mind climbing into that rented bed, and the fact that she was in it only made the notion that much harder to ignore. Did he dare?

All she asked was that he promise to take her. Promises were easy to make, and passing the night in bed with the luscious—and practically naked—Miss Darshaw would be just as easy. A man with only half a brain would have no trouble taking her offer and even less trouble breaking his promise in the morning.

He could only hope that after one night in Miss Darshaw's bed he'd still have half a brain left.

SHE KNEW WHAT SHE WAS DOING. AT LEAST, SHE HOPED she did. Lord Lindley was not someone to be trifled with. It had taken quite a Herculean effort on her part, but she was almost convinced she had not failed. He was going to take her offer and make use of her tonight.

He wanted her—she hoped to heaven she had read that right in his eyes. Perhaps it was the pink stays. Perhaps it was that he finally decided he'd get no better offer elsewhere tonight. Perhaps he simply felt some measure of pity for her.

She hoped that last was not the case. How mortifying that would be to have the man realize how much she truly did want him. She was appalled to even admit it to herself.

But it was true; she wanted him. She was anxious about the whole thing, of course, but she wanted him. She had never felt actual desire for anyone before, and she found this new sensation exhilarating and terrifying at the same time. Lindley would initiate her into the ways of the world, and she wanted that so very badly.

She just hoped Madame was right and that Lindley would make this first encounter endurable. She would hate to begin her career as a whore with a man who turned out to be a brute. It was foolishness, of course, to hope for a night that would give her fond memories she could smile at long after daylight dawned and harsh reality took over. But that's what she wanted with Lindley. It seemed somehow quite wrong to pray for such a thing, but she did anyway.

Madame had indicated Sophie could count on the man giving in to sleep after a certain measure of exertion. She was not naive enough to pretend she did not comprehend what that meant; she would have to be a very active participant if she were to ensure that this level of exertion was attained. And she doubted Lindley would be content to get there by simply chasing her around the room. Heavens, but she had no idea what it would truly take to satisfy Lord Lindley.

Well, she had a vague notion of what it entailed, of course. But beyond the basic understanding of parts involved, however, her education was still a bit incomplete. She hoped that would not prove a fatal hindrance to her plan. Just as she was hoping for a satisfactory reaction to tonight's efforts, she couldn't help but wish he might end up with fond memories of her, as well.

The front two chair legs thumped down onto the floor, and her eyes shot up to meet his. Lindley was staring at her. Oh heavens, he was like a wild animal that had been hunting all its life. She was a pet rabbit left alone in the woods. She shuddered.

"Careful, Miss Darshaw, or I'm likely to assume your words constitute a proposition."

His eyes were dark with desire. She shuddered again and wished she could have blamed it on fear or disinclination. It was neither. It was eager, raw anticipation.

"Of course it was a proposition, my lord," she said, after just enough pause to steady herself. "I'm inviting you to join me. In bed."

It sounded preposterously bold, yet he retained his place in his chair. Was he refusing her? *Again?*

His voice was painfully calm when he spoke. "I have no desire whatsoever to take you up on that offer, Miss Darshaw."

Oh, but this was tragic! He did not want her after all. She was mortified. The man would rather sleep in a chair than entertain himself with her. Oh, she could just wither up and die right now.

But then a smoldering smile touched his lips and he continued.

"Unless, of course, you understand that I've no intention of sharing your bed and behaving in a gentlemanly fashion. If you let me anywhere near you tonight, Miss Darshaw, I promise you sleep will be the very last thing either of us care about."

Oh, thank heavens. He did want her! Perhaps she could continue living, after all.

"I've never yet seen you behave in a gentlemanly fashion, my lord," she said, casually adjusting the covers around her although she knew her hands trembled. "Why on earth should you think I'd expect that now?"

He was out of his chair and looming over her in a heartbeat. Goodness, what had she done? His very eyes were devouring her, making her weak, and he'd not so much as laid a finger on her. What in heaven's name would happen when he did?

She could hardly wait to find out.

It would seem she did not have to. Long before she was ready for it, Lindley swooped down on her. His whole being overpowered her, overwhelmed her in sensation. She could feel the strength of his will, taste the salty sweetness of his lips, quiver under the touch of his hands, and sense the surge of desire in her own soul she'd tried for so long to deny.

She wanted this man to do whatever he would with her tonight. Papa was just an excuse—his salvation really had nothing to do with what she'd offered Lindley. She had no choice but to admit that to herself now.

No choice, she realized, because her body was reacting in force to everything Lindley was doing. His hands slid over her skin; her hands raked desperately over his. His mouth covered hers and compelled her to moan with the urgency and ecstasy that just this much union produced within her. Her lips sought to consume a bit of him for herself. He pressed her into the soft bedding, and she clung to him, pulling him closer and hardly noticing that the room began to spin as her body begged for the breath she'd forgotten to take.

He pushed the covers back from her and his rough palm stroked the nearly naked flesh at her thigh. Oh heavens, how had she gone so many years without feeling such things? She arched herself into him, nipping at his lips, his chin, his neck. If she could have inhaled the man she supposed she would have, but her body was telling her there were far more efficient ways of bringing him quite fully inside her being.

She reached for the fastenings at his trousers. Thank heavens instinct was so strong on these matters. Perhaps moments like this would be more awkward for a properly raised miss, but she'd spent the last several years in Madame's brothel. She may not have been privy to the details of human congress, but her mind had certainly understood the basics long enough for her to have subconsciously formulated her plan of attack.

And indeed, she did have a plan for Lindley. She planned to get him naked. Oddly, though, he didn't seem quite as enthusiastic about her plan as she felt.

"What is it, my lord?" she asked when he pushed slightly away from her.

He was looming over her, just inches separating them. They felt like miles.

"You intend to put some effort into this, I see," he said.

"You would rather have me lie back and contemplate the laundry?"

She wasn't at all certain what he was about, but he smiled. "I would rather have you enjoy yourself, Miss Darshaw."

"As I would like for you to enjoy yourself, my lord."

"Then we'll need to dispense with all this 'my-lording' and 'Miss-Darshawing.' I should think at least we should consider ourselves on a first-name basis by now."

She wasn't at all pleased with this unwelcome shift from indescribable bliss to banal conversation. What the devil was the man blithering on about? And how on earth could he expect her to call him by his first name?

"You seem unconvinced, Miss Darshaw," he said, then dipped his head to kiss her softly on the throat.

Ah, yes, that was far better than conversation. She murmured something by way of encouragement, so his kiss continued. He shifted his weight onto one elbow and used his free hand to find the delicate silk edging of her costume, sliding his finger along it with just enough pressure to allow her breasts to spill out. Not that they'd been particularly contained. She'd fabricated the garment so that the stays would provide a tidy shelf to prop her bosoms up into what, she assumed, would be the most enticing—and tenuous—position with just the slightest slip of silk to cover them. Based on Lindley's reaction, she'd well accomplished that enticement goal.

Her bosoms thanked her. She sighed as the air hit them fully, causing her nipples to pucker. The sigh quickly turned to something more like a moan when Lindley's lips trailed from her neck down to a tingling peak.

Clearly her sounds and her arching provided the man more encouragement. He continued his oral worship of her nipple while at the same time he sent that blessedly free hand down to pass tenderly over her belly and then slide down to where the silk cords made a netlike pattern at her thigh. The sensation of his hand skimming over the mesh, brushing against her skin, was quite dizzying.

And of course there was no silk over that very sensitive place just at the juncture between her legs. He continued to let his fingers wander over her thigh, creeping slowly until they came dangerously close to that private area where no one had ever been. She squeaked when he brushed her there so gently she almost thought she had imagined it.

"If you are not ready at this point to send me back to my chair, then you simply must allow that we use first names, Miss Darshaw."

She tried to answer but couldn't seem to find any breath. Lamely, she shook her head.

"No?" he said. "But you do seem to enjoy this, my dear."

At "this" the man had the nerve to actually touch her. *There.* And yes, oh yes, she did enjoy it. Still, she could not speak, so all she could do was to shake her head.

He stopped touching her altogether. "Then I will go back to my chair."

"No!" By God, she found her voice at that. She grabbed his arm. "Stay. Please."

"Are you certain that's what you want, Sophie?" he asked, pushing back the strand of hair that had flopped in front of her face in her rush to keep him from leaving.

"It is, my lord," she said.

He shook his head. "Then you must play by the rules, my dear. First names."

"But I cannot!"

"Then I'm afraid it's the chair for me."

"No, please. I want you to . . . to . . . well, I *want* you."

She felt the heat rise to her cheeks. She was blushing. Heavens, what a thing for her to admit to him! Yet, she could hardly take it back. Besides, it was true. Lindley could certainly not have ignored the fact that she'd been pawing at him with a fervor that matched his own.

"And I am incredibly glad to hear it," he said, leaning in to kiss her lips once more.

He tasted like every dream she'd ever held—and more. He tasted like all the things she had ever wanted and yet been denied, like something she would regret for a long, long time, yet she had no idea of giving him up just yet. The time for leaving would come soon enough. Right now, she let herself sink into his kiss and melt into his arms.

"Sophie," he said in a voice full of air and of passion.

"My lord," she replied the same way.

Now he pulled away again. In fact, his hands left her so quickly she fairly dropped back onto the bed.

"Damn it, we've moved beyond my bloody title!"

"But I . . ."

"When I call you by your first name, you are to return the favor," he explained as if she were an ignorant child.

She rather felt like one. "I know, but I simply cannot!"

"Why? Because you can't forget that you're the daughter of a criminal, some little nobody who spent the last four years of her life in a bloody brothel? Do you believe I'm so full of myself that I don't care who's moaning under me in my bed? Or is it more? Perhaps you refuse to call me by my name because this is nothing more than your way of keeping me occupied while your father puts more and more miles between us. Perhaps you would find it easier to keep hating me if you refused to speak my name aloud in the throes of passion. Is that it, Sophie?"

"No! Truly, my lord, it isn't any of that. It's simply that . . . Er, there will be *throes*?"

"Of course there will be throes! Can you doubt that already?"

"Well, you know, of course, that women do talk to one another, and I did live in a brothel. It's just that my understanding is that these so-called throes are, er, optional."

"You mean nonexistent."

"Well, the gentlemen seem to experience them."

"Of course they do. They're bloody pigs who go there to use those girls for their own pleasure and not care one jot whether it's pleasurable for them."

"Er, you seemed to show up there quite frequently yourself, my lord."

Perhaps she shouldn't have said that. His expression became hard and unreadable when she did. Drat, but she really, truly should not have mentioned such things. It was more than a little distressing to let herself think of Lindley spending time with any of the more sophisticated, competent ladies in Madame's employ.

"And have you ever heard any of Madame's ladies complaining after time spent with me?" he asked after a pause.

She thought for a moment. Actually, she could not precisely recall any of the ladies mentioning anything of their time spent with Lindley. She was not even aware which of Madame's lucky women had been afforded such a treat. Clearly those who had never saw reason to complain about it.

"No, my lord. I have not."

He smiled at her. "Then you, my dear, have nothing to worry about tonight, do you?"

Oh yes, she most certainly did! She'd already discovered how remarkably easy it was to lose herself in this man's attentions. The night was still young and she was already beyond hope of regaining control over her emotions—or her behavior—where Lindley was concerned. Indeed, she had much to worry about.

"I'm not worried, my lord," she lied.

"Then say my name."

"I can't!"

He touched her face. "Why not, Sophie? Is it so very hard to see me as a man and not simply as a title?"

She would have answered him but he was kissing her

again, searching her soul as his lips commanded hers. Once again, she was lost. She ran her fingers through his thick hair, dark as night and cut in the height of fashion. His shoulders were broad and firm. She moved her hands to grasp his coat, holding him as if he might disappear.

His kissing and caressing went on until she found herself breathless and aching for more. For a heartbeat she was aware of her position, the shameless way she arched herself against him and let all her sensitive parts be put out plainly on display. Normally she would have been self-conscious or appalled to find herself this way, but with Lindley touching her here and nuzzling her there, she found she could only wish he were as scantily clad as she was. Once again she reached for the trouser fastenings. This time he assisted, tugging at his shirt to release it from his trousers, loosening his cravat until it slipped off.

"Your coat, my lord," she said, trying to help him with it.

The cut was so precise, so expertly done that it was no small feat for Lindley to slide his muscular arms from the sleeves. He did though, and when he pulled the shirt up over his head to reveal a torso that belonged more on a Greek god than an English gentleman, Sophie found herself completely at a loss for words. Yes, oh yes, she had much to worry about tonight.

Rather, she had much to worry about *tomorrow* when all this was in her past and Lindley's kisses and chiseled body were only a memory she might pull out on long, lonely nights full of fond regret and aching solitude. For now, however, this chiseled body was right here in front of her and, by heavens, she was going to take full advantage of that.

"You're smiling, Miss Darshaw."

"I thought we were onto first names now, my lord."

She realized what she'd said after she said it and cringed, waiting for him to demand she take her own advice. He did not, however, but merely laughed.

"Indeed we are, Sophie, and I'm determined we are to become better acquainted yet."

Yes, she thought she might like that. She forced her eyes to leave his wonderful body and focus on his equally wonderful face. The man was perfect, and there was even an unexpected kindness showing in his eyes that helped ease the missish nervousness she still had lingering in the back of her mind. Madame was right; Lindley *did* know what he was about and he would make this encounter more than merely endurable. Sophie would have to remember to give her former mistress a huge thank-you for encouraging her to disgrace herself this way.

Chapter Twelve

Lindley was content to take a moment or two just to gaze. Sophie was lying before him on the bed, her warm, rounded breasts exposed like two perfect pearls and her eyes glittering with passion. She was gazing at him, too. He saw the approval in her eyes as she studied him, took in his shoulders and his chest and anything else she chose to stare at. If his trousers had come off she'd have had a hell of a lot more to look at, too. He'd been hard and ready for her since the moment he left that blasted chair.

But now her eyes met his and he knew she was as ready as he was. It irked him that she would still refuse to call him by name, but he supposed he'd find a way around it. A mutually agreeable way. He'd *make* her call him by name. Indeed, the way the girl fairly panted for his touch and arched her delicious body toward his as he leaned in to hold her, he doubted he'd have to work very hard to get the response he wanted. She was more than willing; she was eager.

Which of course hinted that this was not her first foray into the world of sexual pleasures. He found himself somewhat annoyed by that but reminded himself that he should not be surprised. She'd not lived the protected life of a gently bred lady.

She'd had to do what she could to get by, to grasp what bits of happiness she could when she had the opportunity. Apparently she'd grasped some before he'd come along. He should be thankful that she knew what was to come and looked forward to him with desire and excitement rather than virginal fear and trepidation.

Still, he would certainly do what he could to ensure she would always remember him as superior to any others.

He moved to her and began by kissing her between the breasts. Clearly she found this acceptable, so he continued, paying due respects first to one lovely breast and then to the other. She murmured and writhed all the while his fingers ran over her body, touching her and stroking her, enjoying learning their way around her. The tangled wisps of honey-colored hair at the juncture of her legs teased him, and he only hoped he'd be able to keep himself in control long enough to assure she would long think back to this night as the most enjoyable hours of her life.

She reached again for his trousers, but he put her off once more. At this point, he felt it might be better for both of them if he remained in them a bit longer. For far too many months he'd focused solely on his duty to justice. This impatient young woman was such a delightful change in pace for him that he half feared he would embarrass himself if he wasn't somewhat careful. Clearly, she had an even more profound effect on his person than he'd expected. He couldn't say he didn't like it, but he had to admit he wasn't entirely pleased with this desperate—and juvenile—need to impress her.

At the same time, however, he sure as hell was going to enjoy himself with this female. Whatever it was she did to him, he knew she was not the only one who would leave this bed with fond memories. When morning finally came and they were forced back into their lives, he suspected he'd be doing so with an impertinent smile on his face.

Reveling in the scent of her and the softness of her skin, he trailed his kisses down to that delicate navel. She was ticklish and giggled a bit as he paused there, then continued his exploration. He listened as her breath caught when he brushed the curling wisps of hair, then let one finger gently stroke the soft folds beneath. He moved lower so he could kiss her there, just above the most sensitive spot.

A slight tremor rolled over her body, and he felt the blood pound in his veins. She would respond to him easily, and he would certainly respond to her. He teased her with more caressing and tormented himself with more kisses. He wanted to taste her, to sample all of her, but he needed to take his time. They had all night, and he was determined to go slowly for her.

She was breathing in jagged little gasps, twisting her body to be more accessible to him. He was grateful for her efforts. The more she reacted to her desire, the more it stoked his own. He'd wanted her badly before; now the wanting blazed nearly beyond his control.

"You're so beautiful," he said, dragging his ministrations away from her nether regions and reaching to coil that loose strand of blond hair at her slender neck around his fingers. "Eudora was a fool to let you leave her employ."

Her only reply was a sigh. Then another gasp. Then a moan. His hand had gone back to her tender folds, and she was rocking against him, so close to her climax that he could almost feel it with her.

Damn it, he needed to feel it with her. Hardly skipping a beat, he undid his trousers. He'd hoped to take longer for her, to think more of her pleasure than his own, but his desire had gone far beyond wanting at this point. He needed to plunge himself into her and feel her around him, to ride the passion as she did. He needed her to become his.

Without warning he pressed her legs apart and pushed himself into her. God, but she was hot and wet and so damn tight. It was as if he'd never felt this before, never found fulfillment inside a woman until now. He gave up all pretense of self-control and lost himself in the overwhelming sensation.

He thrust himself deeper, pushing again and again, overcome at each movement by the wave that was building up, ready to crash over them at any moment. Part of him wanted to prolong the ecstasy, but the greater part of him drove harder and harder, desperate for release. Everything he'd ever needed was right here, surrounding him, sharing the same oxygen and begging him to . . .

It was too much. He gave up the fight as passion overwhelmed him and he collapsed onto her. Drawing in air and fighting to keep from crushing her, he groaned from the last waves of his climax. He felt himself pulsate into her, pouring his seed recklessly in a way he usually would not have allowed.

Always before caution had ruled his passions and he'd been careful with his partners. With Sophie he'd not been so diligent. He'd forgotten there could be consequences. Lord, but she'd been so amazing he had forgotten everything but her.

He leaned in and kissed her.

She moaned under him, and the sound was enough to set his blood pounding again. Ah, but he'd known all along there was something special about Sophie Darshaw, hadn't he? How fortunate they both were that there was still a long, dark night ahead of them.

Carefully, he moved to the side, propping himself on his elbow. He hated to pull out of her, to separate from such a blissful joining, but it was time to see to her comfort. He slid carefully away.

She moaned again. It was not the right kind of moan, either. He knew that because it was followed by something a bit like a whimper and something very much like a wince.

Oh God, was she in pain?

"Sophie?"

"Thank you, my lord. That was quite, er, nice."

Nice? That's how she would describe what had just happened between them? *Nice?* No, by heaven, it was a good deal better than *nice*.

Unless he'd been such a brute as to only care for how things had gone for him. Had he, perhaps, been a bit too quick? Had he, somehow, finished ahead of her and not thought twice about it? Lord, he suddenly hated himself.

"If you wish, we do not need to stop," he offered, sliding his hand to the inside of her thigh. "If you'd like to continue, we could—"

"No, no!" she replied quickly, turning herself slightly away from him. "That was fine, my lord. Quite fine."

But of course he knew it wasn't. Why was she not snuggling next to him, curling her body toward his and cooing into his ear? Why did she press her legs together, covering herself the way her daring little costume could not? He'd satisfied his share of women over the years, and none of them had ever behaved like this.

Damn, could it possibly be that this had been a disappointment for her?

"Sophie? What's wrong?" he asked.

She didn't reply but turned her head to face the wall on the other side of the room. He knew that meant trouble. Why he should care so much, he did not know. But he did care; he cared immensely.

He reached out to brush her cheek. "Tell me what it is, Sophie."

"It's nothing, my lord."

"Rubbish. It is something."

"No, I'm fine."

"You're not."

"Of course I am."

"You are not. You're crying."

She didn't reply. He was right, though. He'd felt a teardrop on her cheek. He could see her body shudder as she struggled to hide whatever it was that tormented her.

"Please, Sophie. Talk to me. I can't stand to see you cry."

"I'm sorry, my lord. I don't mean to."

"But you are. What is it, are you hurt?"

There was a most disconcerting pause before she answered. "No."

It was not convincing. Dear Lord, had he truly gotten so wrapped up in the moment that he lost control and actually hurt her? That was completely unlike him. He'd always prided himself on such things as self-control and caution. Had he really been such a brute as all that?

He'd meant to do nothing but give her the same measure of mind-numbing enjoyment he was finding. He wanted to amaze her, to satisfy her, not make her cry! Honestly, he was certain he hadn't gone beyond the bounds of generally acceptable bedroom behavior. How had he hurt her? It wasn't as if she'd been an untried virgin and he should have . . .

Oh no. Realization slammed him as if he'd walked into a wall. By God, it was *exactly* as if she'd been an untried virgin, and he most certainly should have treated her far more gently than he had. She'd told him the truth when she said all she'd done for Eudora was sew. She'd been an innocent after all, and he'd treated her like . . . like . . .

He'd treated her like a whore.

No wonder she was crying. Despite the fact that her body indicated she'd much rather be left alone, he could not help but reach for her and gather her into his arms. She allowed it. He held her close and pressed a kiss into her silky hair.

"I'm told the pain does not last for long," he whispered.

"I'm not in pain, my lord."

"I don't believe you."

"Well, there may be a small discomfort, but it's hardly noticeable."

"So you would deny that you were a virgin?"

Another pause. "You could tell?"

He decided not to indict himself by answering that. "I should have believed you. I could have made it better for you."

"*Better?* Oh, I very much doubt that, my lord. Truly, it was . . . spectacular."

Well, he couldn't help but feel a bit smug at that. It wasn't every day a man's prowess was rated "spectacular." But then again, if he'd been so very spectacular, why was Sophie crying?

And she was still crying; he could feel her sniffling. He would have loved to convince himself it was tears of joy for his spectacular performance, but something told him that was most likely not the case. She was genuinely upset, and for the life of him he couldn't imagine why.

"Come, Sophie, won't you tell me what it is?"

Now she shook her head. "Honestly, my lord, I don't—"

"You've forgotten the rules, my dear," he interrupted, hoping a bit of levity might help her mood. He kissed her shoulder and held her tighter, too. "Certainly we've earned the right to first names by now."

"Yes, I suppose so, my lord, but I—"

"Then say it."

"I cannot."

Botheration. Why was the girl being so obstinate about this? He wanted to hear his name on her lips. How could it be asking so much of her?

"Why, Sophie?" he asked because he simply could not contain the admission. "I want to hear it. Why is it so impossible for you to speak my given name?"

Finally she replied, "Because I do not know it, my lord."

Oh. She did not know his name. Well, of course she would not. How would she? Unless she had asked Eudora after him, which he suddenly realized he was intensely disappointed that she clearly had not. Damn, why had he assumed she knew his name?

And here he had badgered her about it. Blast it, but he was a brute. The poor girl had given him her most precious asset and she hadn't even known his name. Well, he would give it to her.

He leaned forward, turning her so she would face him and bringing his lips close to hers. Indeed, he'd wanted his name on her lips. Now he would have it.

"Richard," he breathed. "My name is Richard Durmond."

He kissed her lightly, as chaste as a saint, then waited for her response. Her whisper caressed him in return.

"How very nice to meet you, Richard Durmond."

By God, that sounded just as enticing in her quiet, freshly kissed voice as he'd hoped it would. If he wasn't so determined to see to taking better care of her after his spectacular lapse in self-control, he'd be eager already to find out how his name sounded as she moaned it aloud in a moment of passion. Now that would be something spectacular, indeed.

But he could wait. For her sake, he would let her rest. He would be patient.

At least, as patient as a drowning man could be. Truth and reality seemed to pour over him from all sides. As he lay there, holding Sophie and tenderly stroking her velvet skin, he realized just how hopeless things were.

Tonight he had taken her virtue; tomorrow he would take her father. There was little chance of him ever hearing her speak his name again without cursing him. Indeed, spectacularly little chance of that.

SOPHIE CONCENTRATED ON KEEPING HER BREATHING slow and steady. *Breathe in, breathe out.* Her shoulder hurt from where it pressed into a lump in the bed, but she didn't turn. The inn was silent, and Lindley was so close she could feel him breathing.

He was not touching her, though. After they'd . . . well, afterward . . . she'd had quite a struggle to calm herself down. Lindley did an honorable job of attempting to comfort her, but really all that did was make her feel even worse. Lord, what had she done, thinking she could play at this, then simply go back to Madame and forget all about him?

She would never forget Lindley, never forget wanting him. Or having him. It made the future—even if she did manage to rescue Papa—terrifyingly bleak. It would be a future with no Lindley, and the very thought of that now threatened to send her back to unstifled sobbing.

Eventually she had managed to extricate herself from Lindley's too-comfortable embrace. She feigned exhaustion, yawning and sliding away from him and making it very clear she was ready for sleep. He hadn't argued.

He'd turned to face the other way, and here they'd stayed. She was certain he was asleep. Apparently he'd exerted himself enough. *Odd.* The girls at Madame's often made it sound as if such a thing could take literally hours. Surely they had not been at it that long. Then again, how could she say? When Lindley was making love to her it was as if the whole universe simply ceased to exist. For all she knew, it could be days later. Dear heavens, how was she to go on, knowing she'd tasted paradise and would never come close to it again?

Yet she had to go on. There was no other choice. Papa needed her, and Madame had made things clear. There was nothing to do but what needed to be done.

Very slowly and very carefully she shifted position. He did not stir. *Good.* She gingerly slid out from under the covers and lowered her feet to the cold, worn floor. He still did not move, so she continued. She left the bed, rising and pulling her shift off the bedstead where she had left it earlier.

She'd intentionally left her clothing scattered around the room, hoping Lindley might find that provocative. He had, so she smiled as she tiptoed to them and cautiously gathered them up. Piling them neatly on the washstand, she managed to get herself out of the silk mesh costume and slip into her shift. Then the stockings. Then her usual, more appropriate stays. Then her faded gown.

She'd been dressing herself alone for years now, ever since

she'd lost Mamma. She'd modified the fastenings so that she could do them herself. She supposed self-pity would have her wonder how many more lonely years she'd be doing just the same, but she refused to allow it. Now was not the time for self-pity. Now was the time to act. And acting meant leaving Lindley behind.

Her pack of belongings waited just behind the washstand, so she pulled it out. All was intact; the locket was still hidden inside. She was ready to leave. All it would take was just to walk away. Lindley would wake hours later to find her gone. She would meet Madame as planned and never have to face the man again. The locket would be out of his reach and Papa would be safe.

She turned to allow herself one last glance at him sleeping soundly where he had so recently kissed her and caressed her all the way into blissful abandon. She was glad she'd at least had the good sense to say thank you. Now did she dare leave the slightest whisper of a kiss on the way out? No, she'd better not. Her legs were weak, and despite her best efforts to pretend otherwise, she had indeed been much affected by his lovemaking. To touch him again would be a torment too pleasant to allow herself.

If he woke and ordered her to stay, she doubted she'd have the strength to resist. Best to leave while she could. She took her gaze from him and headed for the door.

"What, no kiss before you go, Miss Darshaw?"

She jumped. He was not asleep! Good heavens, had he been awake this whole time, watching her dress? How very rude.

"You should have told me I'd woken you."

"But you didn't. I haven't slept."

"You sounded like you were sleeping," she remarked, not quite certain what to do at this point.

"As did you. I take it the locket is in that pack there?"

"No. I've hidden it elsewhere."

He bolted up out of the bed, still bare from the waist up. She couldn't help but stare at his supple muscles.

"It's no use lying to me, Sophie," he said. "I've no more stomach for it. You were leaving me."

"Yes."

"Even after some damned rogue assaulted you on the street this evening?"

"I'll be careful."

"You'll be murdered! Or worse. What are you thinking, heading out there alone?"

"I have to find my father."

This couldn't come as any surprise to him; he would have guessed by now what she was planning. What would he do to keep her from going?

"I thought we were going to do that together in the daylight," he said simply.

"I changed my mind."

She could feel his eyes on her, condemning her, yet she still could not meet them.

"You looked inside the locket, didn't you?" he said after another pause.

"What?"

"While I was seeing about my carriage. You looked inside the locket and you have some idea where to find your father. That's the whole reason for this sudden desire to seduce me, isn't it?"

"Seduce you! Really, sir, I hardly seduced you."

"You were waiting in here in my bed, half naked when I returned!"

"And if you recall, you said you preferred to sleep in a chair."

"And still you got me into your bed, didn't you?" he continued. "You seduced me, Sophie. Admit it."

"I will not!"

Instead of escalating the argument, he suddenly shook his head. The man even had the gall to laugh at her. She didn't think that was very nice. This was a serious matter, after all.

"Oh, Sophie, you do amaze me," he said.

Her heart skipped a beat when she glanced up to catch him looking at her the way he was, but she forced herself to remember what was truly at stake. Or perhaps she was realizing it for the first time. She stood to lose much more than just her father. Lindley was perilously close to robbing her of her heart.

He touched her face, and she wondered if perhaps it was too late, already.

"Silly girl. You seduced me so you could take that locket and go find your worthless father."

Yes, very well, he was right about that. Still, she didn't think it quite fair to say she had actually "seduced" him. As she recalled, he did a fair amount of seducing her right back.

"But there's something you should know," he said, cupping her face in his hands so she had nothing to do but gaze up at him. "I've already lost too many people I cared about. I won't lose you."

Heavens, but did that mean he cared about her, too? She suddenly couldn't breathe.

"Run to your father if you like," he went on. "But I will always find you."

Oh. His caring only went so far as he cared about capturing Papa. She could have cried at her own foolishness.

"But keep in mind, my dear," he added, still touching her and standing so close she could smell the sweet scent of him, "I may not be the only one looking for you."

She swallowed. "All the more reason I need to find my father."

"Not without me, you don't."

"But you'll just haul him to the gallows! I cannot allow that, my lord. I've got to go find him . . . alone."

"And I cannot let you put yourself in danger like that."

"How do you intend to keep me here, bound and gagged as your prisoner?"

He actually smiled at the suggestion. "Are you trying to seduce me again, Sophie?"

"Er, no . . ." *But is it having that effect anyway?*

"Then we will go together. In the morning."

"No, I don't want—"

"It's not about what you want, Sophie! It's about what's right and wrong."

"As if you know anything about what's right and wrong for me, my lord."

"I know it was wrong for you to throw away your virtue for that man," he said, staring at her in a way that made her very self-conscious. "He is not worth it."

She shook her head and hoped to heaven he wouldn't see

the tears welling up in her eyes. "He's my father. He's all I have."

"Damn it, Sophie, you deserve better."

His arms went around her and pulled her in close. The warmth of his skin against her was intoxicating, and it didn't even dawn on her to put up a fight. She willingly sought out his lips when he leaned in to kiss her. The urgency and desperation was every bit as strong now as it had been before he'd joined his body with hers in that terrifying abandon that had so thoroughly driven her wild with pleasure. Dear Lord, but she wanted him again and again and again.

She let him pull her tighter, engulfing her with his being. She slid her arms around him, too, raking her fingers up over his solid frame and burying them in his thick, dark hair. She kissed him as if it would save her life. It was heaven, it was bliss, it was . . .

"What the hell . . . ?"

Lindley pushed away from her. Something clattered to the floor at their feet. Sophie glanced down and realized what had happened.

"Oh no!" she cried, scrambling down to scoop up her pack that had been forgotten, wedged between their bodies.

"What on earth do you have in that thing?" he asked, stooping to help her.

She quickly shoved everything back as best she could. Oh heavens, but it would be dreadful if he found some of these particular contents! She would much rather have him simply take the locket than to see the rest of her possessions.

"I swear, something stabbed me," he said. "Are you an assassin, Miss Darshaw?"

"No! It's merely my sewing things, my lord."

At this point he picked up her scissors that had spilled out. "So I see. And just what else is it you sew, my dear? I was quite taken with that article you wore for me earlier tonight."

She tried to prevent it, but the man was too quick for her. He snatched up her pack and stood with it, peeking inside. She grabbed for it and it tumbled out of his hands, dumping itself neatly on the bed. Oh, dear heavens, but everything scattered about, right there in plain view.

Lindley stood there, and slowly his left eyebrow came up.

His lip did the same. Sophie felt her cheeks go warm. He reached down and extracted a scrap of amethyst velvet from the assortment. He rubbed it between his fingers and turned to smile at her.

"This looks familiar. I take it you crafted those pantalets you were so eager to get out of at Fitzgelder's theatrical event?"

"Er, I was testing them. They didn't work."

He kept staring at her with that sly smile as he ran the fabric slowly over his lips. "Indeed, they worked for me, Miss Darshaw. Your display behind that screen had me mesmerized."

"Yes, well, I need to put these things away."

But he blocked her path, reaching past her to push aside the various swatches and pin rolls until his hand fell on something she rather wished it hadn't. And it was not the locket.

It was the ghastly strap-on article she'd been working on for one of Madame's more, er, adventurous clients. He picked it up to examine it. She could only pray he'd not realize what he held.

"What is this?"

"Ah, that? Er, a pincushion."

He cocked his head to one side. "No, I don't think so."

"It's nothing!" she said and dove for it, hoping to rip it out of his hands. She missed.

"Nothing? It looks very much like something."

He held it up at eye level, and there was no doubt what it was. A series of straps with buckles fell limply about while the main object of the item did not. She'd crafted it of very soft leather over a wooden dowel and filled it with sawdust. No, it did not fall limp. She winced.

"What are you doing with something like this?" he asked.

"Put that down. It isn't yours."

"I'll say for damn sure it's not mine!"

"Then put it back. You have no right to rummage through my things."

Of course he went right on rummaging through her things, with more vigor than ever now. He dropped the strap device down beside the velvet and pin rolls and proceeded to extract what appeared to be a roll of gauze.

"Are you making bandages now?" he asked.

Of course he did not believe her when she replied in the affirmative. He shook out the little roll and his eyes got large. So did his grin.

"Ah, indeed this would cure any man's ailment."

"It's a nightgown," she said, as if calling it that would make it any less daring.

"I see. But where is the rest of it? It would seem parts of you will be a bit chilly at night."

And he was right. The top line of the bodice was made to fit below the breasts, and the front of the gown was slit all the way from the bosom to the bottom. Except that the garment hardly went all the way to the bottom. It ended in a flirty ruffle just at the thigh. And, of course, it was almost entirely sheer.

Though this invisible nightgown was hardly as shocking as that leather device with the straps, she still wished he had not seen it. She had sewn it to her own measurements, and it felt a bit too personal to have him studying it the way he was. The man was well acquainted with her body by now and could easily be imagining her in it. That was a bit unnerving. His smile, though, said she ought to be enormously flattered.

"I tell you, Miss Darshaw, you do have the most interesting sewing supplies. Let's see what else you need in order to keep up with your mending, shall we?"

Her protests fell on deaf ears as he let the nightgown flutter back onto the pile and moved on to scrutinize the next item at hand.

"And this is . . . ?"

"Also not yours." Nor was it hers. She was not at all interested in wearing a hooded mask with rabbit ears. One of Madame's usual patrons, however . . .

"It's very, er, cute. Go ahead, why don't you put it on?"

"Because it is not finished, my lord," she announced, reaching for it. "It still has pins in it."

She yanked it away from him and he got caught by one. He swore in pain and pulled his hand back. She felt immediately guilty.

"Oh! I'm sorry. Let me see that," she said, grabbing his hand without thinking and pulling it up into the thin light from the window to look at it.

A tiny spot of blood grew at the little scratch her pin had made on his thumb. She dug a handkerchief from her pocket and applied it, dabbing the blood and hoping he would not be too angry with her. He was an absolute beast for going through her private things, but she hated that he'd been hurt by it. A tentative glance up at his face, however, proved she'd not harmed him too badly.

"On second thought," he said with a chuckle, "I'm rather grateful you did not put this on. I prefer seeing your face just as it is."

Oh, bother, but she knew she was blushing again. How ridiculous she was to fall victim to his flattery. Still, it was easy to let herself believe the man. His impossibly blue eyes were exceedingly sincere.

"It's not mine," she explained, babbling like an idiot in the hope it would keep her from tumbling into his arms again. "It's for someone at Madame's. She tells me what her special clients like, and I make it for them."

He picked up the strap device again. "It would appear some of her clients have unusual tastes."

"Put that down. No one is to know of such things. Madame counts on me for discretion."

"Yes, I can see why. I imagine her clientele would prefer that no one know of their certain, er, tastes."

"They prefer it very much. Now please let me put my things away."

"And not learn what else you have hiding in here?"

"There's nothing else."

"There's a certain locket."

"Why are you so sure it's in there?" she asked.

"Because I know for a fact it's not on your person."

She couldn't help but blush even more deeply at that. Yes, he would know that, wouldn't he? He'd done a fairly in-depth search of her various parts. No locket.

"And I doubt you would leave it here for me to find," he continued. "So you must have put it in this pack with all your other, er, items."

"Very well, yes. You're correct. I put it in there, in that little roll with my needles and thread."

"Now see? You are capable of truth telling."

"I'd rather just tell you where it is than have you ransack everything. I need all those items to be intact. When I get back to London Madame will pay me nicely for them."

"I don't doubt it!" he said with more of that infernal chuckling.

He found the sewing roll and began to carefully unfold it. She was grateful he didn't send her needles flying or her buttons rolling across the floor, but it still felt very wrong to have him go through her items. She'd built her life, her dreams, on that little pack. To have him searching it this way now was quite disconcerting.

"Ah, here it is," he said when he found the locket, as she knew he would. "So, what clues to your father's whereabouts does it contain?"

"I don't know. I didn't look."

"More lies, Miss Darshaw?"

"It's the truth! I thought there would be ample time to search it when I left, when there wasn't so much risk you might find it."

"Well, why don't we look inside it together, shall we?"

His large hands cradled the locket, studying it briefly before attempting to hinge it open. The thin chain wove between his elegant fingers and the gold appeared warm in the dim light. Any moment now he would possess the information that would help to damn her father. She was helpless to just stand and watch.

Yet as he pried at the locket, nothing seemed to happen. His brows came together in frustration and he moved with the locket to stand nearer the window where he could get additional light from the night's bright moon. She followed.

"It's sealed," he said after a moment.

"Sealed?"

"I can see the hinges, so this locket was initially made to open and shut. However, it no longer opens. It's been sealed."

"Then it's no wonder Mr. Fitzgelder was in such a bad mood when I came upon him in that linen cupboard. He was holding the locket at that time. He must have been struggling to open it."

"Well, unless he had a hammer in there with him, there was little chance of him getting it open."

"Really? Do you think it must be destroyed to open it?"

She tried to peer around him to see the locket. Her eyes kept getting distracted by the awe-inspiring expanse of his muscular back and his well-toned arms and shoulders. Indeed, no locket on the planet could possibly be as fascinating as that view.

"I hope not," he replied. "I was under the impression this locket was useful in more ways than as just a carrier of secrets. Destroying it would likely not prove helpful."

"What do you mean?"

"I mean that if we want to discover what is inside, we'd best find a way to open it very carefully. This locket is more than a locket. It's also a key."

"A key? To what?"

"I don't know. But your father does, Sophie. And I will find him."

"How, if we cannot open the locket?"

"Oh, we'll find a way to open it. Hell, I'm sure I can find something to pry it open. Perhaps we could use—"

He was going for her scissors, and she cringed at the thought of those expensive blades being bent or dulled on this infernal locket. Fortunately for her scissors, though, he was interrupted. Someone knocked softly at their door.

He sent her a questioning glance, as if perhaps she'd been expecting someone. She truly hoped she was not! How dreadful if Madame thought to come and check on her, to find out why she had not yet left. It would complicate things enormously.

She shrugged for Lindley. He returned the action, then went to the door. She was left to bite her lip and hope things were not about to get uncomfortable.

There was a man at the door. Lindley didn't open it very far, but Sophie could hear his voice. She did not recognize it, though clearly he spoke in the accent of one who was somewhat familiar with the lower elements of life. Still, Lindley seemed on good terms with him, so she forced herself not to worry.

Until one simple word caught her ear. *Loveland.* She heard it plainly and knew just what it must mean. This man had found Papa. She was an idiot not to have realized right away where he would go. Of course, they were so close to Loveland already. She should have been working actively to take Lindley away from this area, not lure him into staying!

The earl shut the door and turned to her. His expression was dark.

"That was my man," he announced. "We need to leave here. Now."

And travel to Loveland to apprehend Papa once and for all? She couldn't allow it. She had to delay him, to somehow get word to Papa and warn him.

"No!" she argued. "We can't. You said we should stay until morning. It's too dangerous to leave now."

"And Feasel just informed me it's too dangerous to stay. Fitzgelder has dispatched more of his minions. He's directed them to this very place. I need to get you away from here. Now."

"To this place? He's sent them here and not to . . ." She stopped herself before she made matters worse by as much as confirming Papa's whereabouts for him.

"And not to *where*, Sophie? Why would you expect Fitzgelder to send his men somewhere other than here?"

"Well, I simply thought that . . . er, that he might . . . that is . . . Well, I heard your man make mention of some place, and I simply assumed that must be where you would say Mr. Fitzgelder directed his men."

"Loveland?"

"Oh? Is that what he said? Yes, I suppose that might be what I heard, though I don't know the place, I guess I just assumed that, er, perhaps you meant, well . . ."

Now he was laughing at her again. "It's getting late and surely you need some rest, my dear. Please, don't embarrass yourself by pretending you don't know about Loveland. I'm well aware you used to live there."

"You know that I . . . ? That is, I don't know what you're talking about, my lord."

"Gather your things. I need to get you to safety."

She frowned, not quite certain she could believe him. "But what of . . . ?"

"What of Loveland? No, I'll not be taking you there. That is, of course, where your father would be though, correct?"

"Why, I haven't the slightest idea! No, of course he'd never go there. It's probably not even still standing. I'm sure someone must have pulled it down by now, sitting empty as it's been."

"Thank you, I'll take that as confirmation that he is there."

"But that's not what I said!"

He laughed again. "Yes you did, my dear. Truly, you are an abominable liar."

"That's not what you said earlier. You accused me of lying repeatedly!"

"I'm not saying you don't lie; I'm just saying you do it very badly. Now hurry, if you want to bring your, er, things, collect them now."

It was obvious the man meant business. One way or another he was leaving here tonight. By God, she knew she'd better go with him if she had any hope of protecting her father. And truthfully, if Mr. Fitzgelder's men were coming here, she would much prefer to be elsewhere.

And maybe, just maybe, she could find a way to work this in her favor. She reorganized her things into her pack and commented in an offhand fashion.

"If you really believe my father might be at Loveland—although I don't know any reason he might have to go back there after all these years—then perhaps I can be of assistance, my lord."

"Oh? And how is that?"

"I know a shortcut! Yes, if you let me direct you, I can take you to Loveland in half the time and then you could—"

"Oh no, that's not going to work, my dear." He took up her pack for her once it was reassembled. "You'd have me off on some wild-goose chase, and that's the last thing we have time for."

Drat. He figured her out.

"Besides," he went on, taking her elbow and leading her toward the door. "Your father is not at Loveland. Not yet. My man already sent someone to look there."

Chapter Thirteen

Sophie had insisted on bickering with him the whole way to the back of the inn. It was as if she actually wanted to wake everyone inside. Perhaps she had. Perhaps she was hoping she might create enough disturbance to allow her another opportunity to try and leave him.

Well, it didn't work. And if it had, she'd have been without the locket. He'd placed it securely in his own breast pocket, and there it would stay until they found something that might help pry it open.

The yard behind the inn was not large, and the mews row was right there, allowing guests to stable their animals and store their carriages close at hand. Convenient, he had to say. And much safer for them than having to traipse all over town to locate tools and his carriage. With luck, this endeavor should take very little time.

But then something very much like a shadow caught his attention. There, at the corner of the stable building at the far end of the yard. He'd been sure he saw a form, a human form, darting just out of sight. And this time it was *not* Feasel.

He held up his hand to motion for Sophie to stop where she was, still in the doorway just about to step outside. She didn't get the message and came trotting out, slamming into him from behind. He sighed. Well, the figure was gone. Perhaps whoever he was, he hadn't seen the foolhardy chit yet.

"Come here," he hissed, grabbing her arm and pulling her back against the building, into the shadows.

"What is—" she started, but he put his hand over her mouth.

Her eyes flashed and glared at him, but she didn't fight. With a nod of warning he tentatively removed his hand. She didn't screech at him for his rough behavior, but at the same time there was nothing about her that said she wouldn't promptly bite him if he did that again. He leaned toward her, one hand on either side of her shoulders, effectively pinning her there against the night-cooled wall of the inn.

"There was someone out here—a man—hiding at the far end of the stable," he whispered to her.

Her glance darted around nervously. "What was he doing?" she asked.

"I don't know, it could have been nothing, but I didn't want him to get a good look at you," he explained. "If he's one of Fitzgelder's men, he was sent here after you to get the locket."

"Well, considering the way you are manhandling me, don't you think if he notices us he'll assume you've managed to get it from me? Perhaps he'll go after you now."

All the more reason to be quick about things. Cautioning her again—for all the good it would do—he led her quietly toward the stables. He kept a close watch on the shadows but did not detect anything. If someone had been there, he was gone now.

He managed to find a stable hand to help ready his carriage. Despite keeping one eye on Sophie and one eye on his work, it was not long before his horses were stamping in their harnesses, anticipating what would come next. They seemed nearly as impatient as Sophie.

He helped her up into her seat, then hoisted himself in beside her. The stable hand waved them on their way and pulled the door shut behind them. Lindley slapped the reins and the horses jolted into action. If anyone had been watching them with malicious intent, they would soon be left behind. There had been no other carriage or waiting horse saddled and ready. They were safely away.

"I believe that stable hand was glad to be rid of us," Lindley said, introducing casual conversation as Sophie stared impassively ahead. "I had the feeling we interrupted something there."

"It's rather late; I'm sure he was looking forward to taking his bed."

"Unless his bed was that pile of fresh hay piled in the corner of the room with the suspicious lump of canvas that seemed to wiggle inexplicably, I doubt that was his intent."

"What do you mean?"

"I believe our young man was not entirely alone when we found him," Lindley said with a chuckle. "I had the idea the boy was entertaining a ready mort."

"A *what*?"

He chuckled at her naiveté. "I think we interrupted him with tonight's convenient little tail."

"Convenient little tail?"

"Oh, you know, some easy mab who doesn't mind a roll in the hay."

"Some easy mab?"

Could she truly still be this innocent that she did not understand?

"He had a *woman* in there, Sophie," he explained carefully.

"Oh, I know what you meant, my lord. And what lovely names you have for her, too."

He recognized sarcasm when he heard it. Very well, he supposed he had been rather free with his use of colorful language. She clearly did not like it.

"I'm sorry," he conceded. "I should watch my tongue."

"Whyever should you need to do that? It isn't as if there are any ladies present or anything, merely convenient tails or valueless mabs."

"Now see here! I never claimed she had no value. By my guess, her gentleman was eager to get back to making full use of her value."

He had to smile at his own turn of phrase. Sophie, however, did not seem to find it so humorous.

"Oh, so he's a gentleman, is he, while her only value is to be used for sport?"

"It's merely a phrase, Sophie. What the devil are you talking on about?"

"I simply would like to know what criteria you used, my lord, to pass such judgment on that poor woman. Was she wearing a sign, perhaps?"

"By deuce, Sophie, I never saw one hair of her. How should I know whether she wore a sign?"

"Yet you quickly assumed she was not a respectable person."

"She was waiting in a pile of hay to shag a stable hand. I'm fairly certain she was not a royal princess."

"She could be his wife."

"I don't know many wives who would willingly brighten their husband's filthy workplace in such a way. Really, Sophie, why are you ranting on about this? Those were nothing more than words I used to describe what I assumed was going on."

"Oh. So you would use similar words to describe me."

"No! Good God, of course I would never."

"Why, because I made myself valuable in a borrowed bed rather than on the floor of a barn?"

Ah, so that was what had her in a flap. He should have realized it, should have been more sensitive. Of course she would be concerned about how people would label her now. He had been very much a party to her crossing that line between respectability and commonness.

Well, Sophie Darshaw was far from common. As long as he had breath in him, he'd see that no one so much as hinted at impugning her character. She was above all that, despite what she'd done tonight. Or what she'd been wearing when she'd done it.

He put his thumb on her chin and tipped her face so she would look at him. "No, Sophie. I would never use words like that about you. And I promise, I will be much more judicious in using them to describe anyone else in the future. Will you forgive me?"

She shook his hand off and stared straight ahead. Damn it, but since when did he need forgiveness from some slip of a girl simply because she'd disapproved of his language? He did not much like the feeling.

At last she gave absolution, and he could finally breathe.

"Well . . . I suppose you meant no real harm."

"No, I assure you I did not. I spoke without thinking."

"You excel in that, it would seem."

Indeed, she was correct. It did seem he'd been saying and doing quite a few things without thinking of late. He hoped rushing Sophie out into the night like this was not one of them. He needed to believe she—and the locket—would be safe.

SOPHIE SCOOTED AS FAR OVER TO THE EDGE OF THE seat as she could. She recalled the way Lindley had flipped the young stable hand what looked like quite a goodly sum for such a simple thing as readying a carriage. Perhaps that was how things would go for her, too. Lindley would use her until he was through, pass her a handful of coins, then leave. And then she would be a real, honest whore.

She would have no reason at all not to allow Madame to introduce her to gentlemen. And she would accept money for it. She may be riding in a stylish phaeton tonight, but she'd be a fool not to remember where this was all leading.

"Where are we going?" she asked.

"Where would your father most likely be if he is not at Loveland?"

"I don't know," she replied. "I've thought him in the grave for years. How do I know where the man spends his time after a day and a half of reacquaintance? I thought you were going to get that information out of the locket."

"If you don't mind, I'd like to get some distance between us and whoever was spying on us from behind the mews. I didn't notice any other carriages around, so I'm hoping he's not prepared to follow us."

He was right, there hadn't seemed to be any other conveyances at the ready. *Good.* That probably meant Madame's plan was going as expected and she was waiting with Annie just out of town on the south road. All Sophie needed to do was get herself away from Lindley.

"Perhaps we should not go together," she said, desperate to

think of something reasonable that might serve her purposes. "Perhaps I should wait here and you should go, leading him astray."

"To what purpose, Miss Darshaw?"

"Well, it would confuse him."

He looked at her as if what she'd said was even more ridiculous than she knew it was. "And I suppose you'd like me to hand you the locket while I'm at it?"

"Well, you could, you know. That way if he followed after you and your oh-so-inconspicuous carriage it would be safe and he could not get it."

"We will stay together, Miss Darshaw," he announced. "You, me, *and* the locket. Once we are a safe distance, perhaps we will find a place to stop for the night, and there we can see about opening it."

"With what? I thought you needed to hunt down something to . . ."

He bumped her with his elbow as he reached behind to take something long and pointy out of his pocket. She heard fabric tear as he produced it.

"Damn!" he swore, pulling up what turned out to be an awl. He must have found it in the stable, probably used for leatherwork on some of the tack. My, but wouldn't she have loved to have had something like that when she was fabricating the rather vulgar little strapping device Madame had ordered!

"That's lovely," she said.

"Yes, but it ripped my lining," he grumbled.

"I can repair it," she said without really thinking. "Do you believe this will break open the locket?"

"We don't wish to break it, Miss Darshaw," he said, readjusting himself in his seat and driving the horses quickly out of the yard. "As I said, it is not merely a locket."

"Yes, you said it is a key of some sort."

"That's right. I'm given to believe that by some manipulation, it is a literal key."

"Well, it certainly looks like no key I've seen before."

"Agreed. I assure you, once I am convinced Fitzgelder's henchmen are not hovering over us with murder on their minds, we will take a good, thorough look at this locket."

"That you are holding on to and do not trust with me."

"You were trying to take it and leave, you may recall."

Indeed, she did recall that. She also recalled, however, *why* she was attempting to take the locket and leave him.

"Because you are trying to use it to drag my father to the gallows, you may recall."

"He will have a fair trial."

"Which will undoubtedly merely prove all the things you've said about him, my lord. And *then* he'll be dragged to the gallows."

He was silent. The carriage rumbled through the sleeping village until after a minute or two he pulled it to a halt. Had he finally grown so weary of her arguments that he'd decided not to honor his agreement, not to take her with him to find Papa? Heavens, would he put her out here, at the side of the road?

But of course she could be glad for that. It would free her to go find Madame and continue with her original plan. Yes, it would be a good thing if Lindley abandoned her.

So why was her heart pounding and her breathing so suddenly difficult?

"Well, here we are at a crossroads, Miss Darshaw," he said.

She glanced around and realized he was not speaking figuratively. They were, indeed, at a crossroads. Three roads intersected at this point, going off in several directions. Lindley could direct them north, which would take them toward Loveland where there was a very strong possibility Papa might go for refuge, or they could go south, which would take them toward the advancing Fitzgelder contingent but also toward her planned rendezvous with Madame; or they could angle back on the third road, which seemed to veer off to the northeast. She had no idea what lay along that road.

"Which way do we go?" she asked, not sure which answer to hope for.

"We wait," he replied. "I sent Feasel out to . . . ah, there he comes now."

As if on command, hoofbeats could be heard approaching. Sophie made out a man rapidly approaching them from the south. She hoped Lindley was not mistaken about his identity, as they were very much alone and exposed here.

Apparently he was not. The man greeted them and Lindley called back. He sounded remarkably cheerful, considering they were being forced to flee in the night for their lives. *Men.*

"So, what have you found for me, Feasel?" he asked when the man pulled his horse to a halt beside their carriage.

"Nothing that plans to kill you tonight, milord," Feasel replied. "My man down here on the south road says he hasn't seen anything come this way since after dark. Word earlier was no sign of the Frenchy or any of Fitzgelder's thugs on the north road, either."

"I'm fairly certain we saw at least one of those thugs back at the inn," Lindley grumbled. "I'm only hoping he doesn't follow us."

"That's what I'm here for, milord. You get yourselves on to safety—I just came by some troubling news."

"Oh?"

"Tom just sent me word that Fitzgelder left London. He's on his way here."

"What, Fitzgelder himself?"

Sophie couldn't help but shudder at that thought. Was her horrible former employer that desperate to do away with his cousin, or was he more concerned with finding the locket? If so, he'd obviously be after *her*.

Lindley didn't seem any more thrilled by this news than she was. "Keep an eye on him, Feasel. We know he's up to no good."

"He's not getting by us, milord."

"I want to hear what he does, where he goes . . . who he sees."

"Of course," Feasel said. "And where will you go?"

Sophie decided that was an excellent question. Where would they go? Was anywhere safe?

She worried for Madame. Feasel said no one was seen on the south road—Madame should have been there waiting for her by now. Surely his men could not have overlooked two women and a baby waiting at the side of the road. Had something happened? She glanced up to Lindley.

His expression was unreadable. "We'll go to Haven Abbey."

Sophie frowned. Where on earth was Haven Abbey? She

did rather like the name, though. Hopefully it would be prophetic.

Feasel nodded. "Need an escort there?"

"Any reason you believe we need one?" Lindley asked.

His man eyed him, then slid a glance in Sophie's direction. He grinned. "No, sir. It appears you have things well in hand. Nothing should be out to bother you on that route, and I'll make sure there's no one that follows."

So just how far away was this Haven Abbey? Sophie watched Lindley for some sign of a clue. Her concern must have showed on her face, because Feasel chuckled under his breath and gave a polite bow in her direction.

"Don't you worry, Miss Darshaw," he said. "His lordship will get you there safe and out of the cold night air in no time."

So Lindley's hired man knew her name. She wasn't quite comfortable with that. What else did the man know about her?

Lindley seemed eager to be on their way, so he and Feasel exchanged a few words planning how soon they could expect to hear from him regarding Fitzgelder, and Lindley reminded the man how important it was that no one know where they were going.

"You and Tom," Lindley instructed. "No one else."

"You can count on us, milord," Feasel said. "It's all going to be over soon, and we'll see those bloody murderers hang. Er, beg pardon, Miss Darshaw."

Sophie glared at him. There were two sides to justice, and she needed no additional reminder that she and Papa were on the wrong one.

"Miss Darshaw is as eager to see an end to this as we are," Lindley said. She glared at him, too. "She'd very much like to know her father's whereabouts, so be sure to keep me informed."

"Of course, milord—so long as the two of you don't mind the interruption," Feasel said with a knowing wink.

Sophie rolled her eyes.

"I'm sure we'll manage," Lindley said.

Feasel simply laughed. "Oh, I know you'll manage. I just hope you don't lose track of things and forget what we're all about here."

"Shouldn't you be off about some business or other and let us be on our way?"

"Business it is, milord," Feasel said, touching his dirty cap and nodding toward Sophie. "Good night, Miss Darshaw."

With reassurances that all would be well and with Feasel's word that they would not be followed by Fitzgelder's unsavories, Lindley's man left them and they were, once again, alone. Except for the dozens of questions racing through Sophie's mind.

"I'm sorry," Lindley said as the carriage rocked into motion. "I didn't mean to give him reason to think anything untoward would be transpiring between us."

Sophie shrugged. "It hardly matters, my lord."

"It *does* matter."

"He knows my name," she remarked, changing the topic. "How?"

"He works for me. When there are things I need to know, Feasel is the one who finds them out for me. I've had him following you since you left Eudora's employ."

"What? You've had him following me?" *The nerve of the man!*

"You can hardly blame me," he said, directing the horses to veer onto the road that went off toward the northeast.

"I most certainly *can* blame you," she said. "It's very rude to spy on people."

"I couldn't be sure you weren't working with your father, a part of their whole network."

"I believed my father was dead."

"I know that now, Sophie. Six weeks ago I did not. And you have to admit, leaving the security of Eudora's and going to work for a cretin like Fitzgelder did seem a bit suspicious."

Indeed, she could practically laugh at that. "Hardly suspicious, my lord. Foolish, is what it was. I left in the hopes of working my way into a more respectable position, if you can believe that."

"Yes, I can believe that, Sophie," he said. "You are not cut out for the sort of life you have. But no fear. I'll set you up so that you never have to worry about going to work for someone like Fitzgelder or even Eudora again."

She heard the words but still had no idea what to make of

them. His eyes were focused ahead on the road, so there was no way to read them to learn what he meant. Was she to become his mistress? It was a disheartening thought, becoming that sort of woman when for so long she'd dreamed of respectability, yet a part of her was thrilled at the notion. A very big part of her, actually.

"You keep saying you'll set me up. What do you mean?"

"Well, would you like a house? You should have a house, a nice house in Town, on a fashionable row."

A house! So he would make her his mistress. She would have a house, she could dress in fine clothes, she would be safe from the likes of Fitzgelder, and her nights would be spent paying for it all in the sweetest way imaginable. True, it was not respectability, but it was a far sight better than any hope she'd had so far.

Still, it would all come at a price.

"And will my father be allowed to live there with me, sir?" she asked finally.

He did not answer. He merely kept his eyes on the road ahead, though she did note his gloved hands clenched the reins just a bit more tightly. That was answer enough.

"I didn't think so," she replied for him.

She knew how she had to reply to his most tempting offer. It was simply not tempting enough.

"I'll not be needing you to set me up, then, after all, my lord."

HE COULD SEE THE FEW DISTANT LIGHTS THAT REPRESENTED Southam. How long since he had been here? Too long. Fortunately, he doubted he would run into anyone he knew as they made their way through town. His destination lay just to the south of there. *Haven Abbey.* This visit was long, long overdue.

Sophie had ridden in silence most of the way, giving in to sleep finally, and now she was propped snugly against his side. She'd gamely tried to stay awake for the hour's ride, but about five miles ago slumber won her over. Her last angry words had been fueled by concern for her father.

He knew what it was to love someone like that. He'd have

done anything to save his family. He'd have easily thrown away his virtue or honor or ridden off into the night with a veritable stranger if it had saved them their fate. Yes, he could understand Sophie's feelings.

She loved her father enough to waste her virginity on an enemy.

Damn, but he wished that's not what he was to her. She was not just a bit of trash to be used and thrown away. She had the air of quality to her; she was more than just some unwanted orphan who'd fallen into Madame's brothel. She was special; he'd always known that, seen it all over her the very first time they met. She deserved so much more than her lot.

She should have been allowed to wait, to fall in love with someone capable of returning the feeling. Her first experience should have been with someone who could cherish her and promise her a future, some happiness. All he could promise was that he'd soon be gone from her life. And he'd take her father with him.

It seemed so unfair. If there was any way it did not have to be like that . . . if he could just keep his arm around her, pull her tighter to him and assure her all would be well . . . but of course that was not the way it would go. He had his duty, and she had nothing.

No, that was not entirely true. He was in a position to see that she did not end up with nothing. When it was safe, he would find a way to look after her, even if he had to do it anonymously. He'd see that she never had to go back to someone like Fitzgelder or that damned brothel. Hell, what was Eudora thinking to have this innocent crafting such things as those items he'd found in her pack?

Sophie should be making fine things for proper ladies, not wasting her time and her skill on frivolities for Eudora's deviant clients. That's what he'd do. He'd set her up with a shop. Sophie would be mistress of her own life from now on; he'd see to it. The next time she shared her bed with a man, it would be one of her own choosing for no other reason than that she cared for him.

And if I ever lay eyes on him, I'll murder the bastard.

Damn it, he had no right to think that way. He was busy wishing Sophie well, not plotting some unknown person's murder. If she found a man to make her happy, why should he not want that for her? He *did* want her to be happy.

He just did not want her to be happy with some other man, that was all.

Oh, hell. He wanted to keep her for himself, didn't he? All for himself. Well, that was a bloody shame. The man who hauled her father off to Newgate would never be worthy of such an honor. A sobering thought, indeed.

He tooled his carriage through the vacant streets of slumbering Southam. Dark visions of a lonely, Sophie-less future swarmed him, and he did not like them one bit. Damn it, of all the accessible women in the world, why should Miss Darshaw be the one to capture his fool attention this way? And now that he'd had her why was the attraction even stronger than before? That, certainly, was out of the ordinary for him.

But then again, there was nothing ordinary about Sophie. He adjusted his arm slightly, just so he could feel her wiggle against him as she slept. She'd been so determined to avoid this, to sit primly in her seat keeping inches between them. How furious she'd be when she woke to realize he'd been holding her this way for miles. He smiled just thinking of the delightful little fit she'd likely throw.

That line of thought, of course, led him to wonder what he would end up doing to appease her, and that line of thought, of course, led him to imagine all sorts of peaceful alternatives to argument. That line of thought, of course, led him to find his trousers becoming most uncomfortably tight. Lord, but he'd have to find a new line of thought right away.

It was almost a relief, then, when a stray dog ran up and began barking at his carriage wheels. His horses skittered nervously, but he held them from bolting. The dog yelped when it took a spoke to the jaw, but it backed away and the horses settled.

"What is it?" Sophie asked, stirring and pushing herself groggily away from him.

She turned to look around, gaining her bearings. Damn, but her bodice pulled tight against her lovely bosom when she twisted her lithe body that way. The trousers were not getting any more roomy.

"Just a dog," he answered. "Nothing to worry about, my dear."

At that moment the dog made one last lunge at them, this time his teeth aimed for one of the horses. The carriage lurched and Sophie fell against him. Her hand fell onto his thigh as she tried to steady herself. Good God, but he did like her touch.

"Oh my," she exclaimed. Good God, but he did like her voice. "We didn't run over the poor thing, did we?"

"No, it's fine," he said, patting her hand where it still rested on his leg. Good God, but he did like comforting her. "We missed him."

She pulled her hand away. *Damn it.* She seemed more interested in the dog that was now running off with its tail between its legs.

"Where are we?" she asked as the barking subsided.

"Southam," he replied. "Haven Abbey is very close now. You should be settled into a warm, comfortable bed within the half hour."

And how he liked the sound of that, too. She seemed a bit skeptical.

"And what is this place, this Haven Abbey?"

"Oh, I'm sure you'll like it," he said, not at all certain that would be the case.

He wasn't even sure he himself would like it. Not now. Not without Marie or little Charles. Not without the people he had most loved. He couldn't imagine the house—a place he'd spent dozens of Christmases and family holidays—to be nearly the warm, welcoming home he'd once loved. Yet given the circumstances, he could think of nowhere else to go.

He hoped it would not prove a mistake.

"But what is it? A friend's home?"

"Not quite," he said, and then realized an interesting irony. "I suppose it's like Loveland."

"What?" she asked, looking startled.

"Haven Abbey was my grandmother's home," he replied.

He turned on the road leading south out of the village and missed the vague comfort of Sophie's body nestled against his. She was back to her prim distance now, with no mention whatsoever of having fallen asleep on him earlier. He supposed he'd humor her and not make mention of it, though he certainly wasn't quite able to forget it.

"So was this the home of your maternal grandmother, or paternal?" she asked, clearly for the single effect of making polite conversation.

"My mother's mother," he replied. "I spent many happy days here, as you must have with your own grandmother at Loveland."

She seemed unimpressed. "And was your grandmother a courtesan, too?"

Now he laughed. "Don't think you can shock me, Miss Darshaw. I'm afraid I've learned all about your sordid history as I've studied your father."

"I'm not certain I like that idea, sir," she said.

"I know that your grandmother was the mistress of a previous Lord Dashford, and this is why you are a cousin to the current viscount at Hartwood. I know that your mother was raised at Loveland and then left to become an actress. She married your father after he came over from France, and in your younger years you traveled with them. Then you came to stay at Loveland until after your father's death, when you went to live with your mother in London and fell on hard times. Your grandmother has been dead some years now, I believe. I'm sure you miss her very much."

"Yes, I do."

"Though I wonder, why did you not seek out help from your cousin?"

"Evaline? Oh, but she wasn't able to—"

She stopped herself, as if she'd said something scandalous. Yes, he supposed she had. The fact that she was not only cousin to Dashford but to his new bride was surely not a matter of public knowledge. At the wedding the new Lady Dashford seemed to have been hesitant to discuss such things, and he could understand why. It was not everyone who relished claiming a relative that dwelt for years in a brothel.

"Yes, I know you are cousin to Lady Dashford as well. Not very many people know that, do they?"

"What? I've not had the pleasure of meeting Lord Dashford's new bride."

"But of course you have. He married your cousin, Evaline Pinchley."

Her mouth hung open. He could scarcely believe it, but this seemed to be entirely new information for her. Well, he was glad to be the bearer of happy news.

"Yes, it's true," he said. "They were married just a few days ago."

"Indeed, I was aware it was Lord Dashford's wedding that you and Lord Rastmoor had attended," Sophie said, her brow wrinkling as she tried to make sense of things. "But how can it be he married Evaline? No one was to know about her!"

"Yes, I gathered that. Her mother was born to your grandmother well before her liaison with the old Lord Dashford, wasn't she? Though your mothers were half sisters, they were not raised together, were they?"

Sophie shook her head. "No, they weren't. Evaline's mother was sent away, brought up elsewhere. Her connection to Grandmamma was not well-known, and she was able to marry a respectable man. My cousin was allowed only limited contact with any of us, though she and I were quite close at one time."

"She abandoned you when she found out you ended up at Eudora's?"

"Oh, no! She . . . that is, I was too ashamed to tell her where I was. She had enough of her own troubles once her parents died. We haven't seen one another in years now."

"Well, perhaps you will find a way to reunite at some point."

"Good heavens! She's a lady now. She can hardly acknowledge me."

"Is that why Dashford never helped you all these years? You weren't good enough for him?"

He'd always rather liked Dashford but would gladly throttle the man just now. It should have been Dashford's responsibility to look after his cousin, even if her mother was born on the wrong side of the blanket. He shouldn't have left her struggling there in a brothel all those years.

"I've never been well acquainted with the current Lord Dashford," Sophie said. "By the time I came to live with Grandmamma he was away at school, and then Papa died and

Mamma needed me in Town, and then Grandmamma died and we had nowhere else to go . . ."

"And you never asked Dashford for help, did you?"

"No. Of course not."

Indeed, that sounded like something that would make sense to her. The woman may have lived in a brothel, but she still held her head high, he'd give her that. She wanted to make her own way, not live off of charity from some relative she hardly knew. He supposed on some level this was commendable, but he could not approve. Not for her.

"Damn it, Sophie, you should have gone to him."

"Don't scold me. I did as I saw fit."

"And look where it brought you."

She folded her arms across her chest and huffed. "Yes. It brought me here. With you."

That stung a bit. He knew what she meant. She'd been looking after herself, even under the nose of that bastard Fitzgelder and after years living in a brothel. She'd done well, he had to admit, all things considered. Until he'd come along and ruined her.

All the more reason, then, for him to see that she was cared for from here out. The foolish, headstrong chit was going to discover he could be just as stubborn as she. And he was bigger.

Chapter Fourteen

They left the main road to turn onto a narrow lane. In the moonlight, Sophie could see the outline of a house ahead . . . no, it was not a house. It was a castle. Good heavens, was this Haven Abbey? It was ancient, with a turret at one end and ramparts along the roof. Not at all what she had expected! Where on earth was Lindley taking her?

"Is this it? This is your grandmother's home?"

"Not very much like Loveland?"

"No, not very. Good heavens, does your grandmother still live here?"

"No," he replied. "She's been gone years now."

"I'm sorry."

"Yes, so am I."

"But the grounds are maintained," she said, noticing what appeared to be careful plantings along the way and the silhouette of hedges trimmed neatly. "Is someone living here?"

"I keep a staff to look after it."

"You must love this place."

"I haven't been here in three years."

"I see. Is that when you lost your grandmother?"

"No. It's when I lost the rest of my family."

"Oh."

She didn't know what to say to that. He'd made mention of it before—that he'd lost his family and her father had been partially responsible. She hadn't let herself think of it, hadn't wanted to care. But now it was impossible. She did care.

This had been a home; his home. He'd had family here, obviously more than just his grandmother. Had he been married? Heavens, had there been a wife, children? Dear Lord, but she hadn't let herself imagine that before now. It was unbearably painful to think what he might have lost.

Sitting here beside him now, arriving at this place he'd been afraid to return to for three years, she could feel the hurt emanating from him. No wonder he would have spent his life seeking justice. No wonder he'd had so little inclination to show Papa any mercy. She knew the anguish of losing loved ones. She could only imagine the torment of knowing they'd been murdered.

He likely never intended to come here again. It was only the threat on their lives that gave him reason now. The threat on *her* life.

"Thank you for bringing me here," she said. "I know you would have preferred not to."

"It was the most practical solution," he said. "But don't thank me yet. We still have to see whether or not we can rouse someone to let us in."

At first she thought he was teasing. After waiting as he pounded at the enormous front door for several shivering minutes, however, she began to realize he had not been. Finally there was a sound from inside. Someone was approaching.

The door creaked open just the tiniest slit. A wizened face peered out—an old man with a nightcap. The one blue eye Sophie could see scanned her quickly, then moved on to Lindley. It widened immediately.

"Good evening, Wimpole," Lindley said, grinning at the old fellow. "Care to let us in?"

The door flung open with more force than she would have expected an elderly man to muster after having just been dragged from his bed. Sophie could see him clearly now, his shirt tucked haphazardly into his breeches and his stocking feet shoeless on the stone floor. In one hand he held a taper, in the other what appeared to be a broom.

"Doing some late night tidying, are you?" Lindley asked as the old man stepped back to invite them inside.

"Someone's rapping at the door in the middle of the night, milord. One never knows what to expect. Could be footpads or vandals, you know," the old man said.

"And you will stave them off with a broom. Ah, Wimpole, it has indeed been far too long."

He clapped the man on the back. Despite his frail appearance, the old man seemed quite happy to take abuse at his master's hand. Apparently three years' absence had not dimmed whatever fondness existed between them. It was very sweet and heartwarming, and Sophie felt herself grossly out of place.

A presence on the staircase suddenly made herself known. Sophie glanced up to see a rather tall, narrow woman in nightclothes with a heavy wrapper pulled tight around her. The lady's cap was askew and her graying hair poked out at odd angles. Still, the delight on her lined face made her appear less severe than Sophie guessed she would have otherwise.

Lindley noticed and reciprocated her smile. "Ah, Mrs. W. You're looking lovely as ever."

She glided down, balancing her taper in a shaking hand. "I'd look even lovelier if a body could sleep at night. Whatever are you up to, dragging us from our beds at this hour?"

"I'm sorry," Lindley said. "You know I wouldn't if I had any other choice. The truth is, er, we've come into a bit of trouble."

At this both sets of elderly eyes turned Sophie's way. Indeed, she could only imagine what they must be thinking. She felt her face go warm. So just how on earth was Lindley going to explain this? More specifically, how was he going to explain *her*?

"You recall my friend, Dashford, don't you?" Lindley went on. "Well, this is his cousin, Miss Sophie D'Archaud."

She was quite surprised to hear her name spoken that way, in the actual French that Papa had been born with. All her life they'd gone by Darshaw as a part of Papa's intention to fit in better here in his new homeland. The way Lindley spoke it now, however, it was as if it were something noble and respectable. She rather liked the sound.

"Miss D'Archaud, this is Wimpole and his dear wife," Lindley said in a tone that sounded very much as if their sudden arrival at this hour was entirely normal. "They have looked after us here at Haven Abbey since before I was born. You may trust them with your life."

Sophie gave a polite nod and smiled as best she could. Really, how was she to present herself a respectable lady, worthy of claiming connection to the likes of Lord Dashford? Surely these very competent servants would recognize the truth. A young woman traveling alone at night with a gentleman like Lindley was bound to raise an eyebrow or two. She felt it very safe to assume that they would, well, assume. Even now Mrs. Wimpole was studying her quite thoroughly, and Sophie could not say her expression was especially approving.

"I need you to take extra heed for Miss D'Archaud's comfort," Lindley said as if he truly cared for such a thing. "And we must be discreet. I'm afraid poor Miss D'Archaud has been through quite a harrowing experience."

Sophie glanced at him. By heavens, what on earth was he going to tell these people about her?

"She was recently kidnapped at the hands of a cruel, cruel man, you know. We must look after her until it is safe and she can be returned to her cousin."

Well, at the mention of a harrowing experience and a kidnapper who merited repeated use of the word *cruel*, Mrs. Wimpole's disapproval faded instantly away and an eager need to hover seemed to take over. She moved immediately to Sophie's side and placed an arm over her shoulder. Actually, after riding all night in the damp air, it felt rather nice to be hovered over by an understanding female. Or at least one who craved a good story.

"Good heavens! The poor little thing," the woman said, maternal concern simply oozing from her. "Whatever could have happened to you, my dear? Come, you'll need something hot to drink and we'll tuck you into bed right away. You can tell good Mrs. W all about it."

Sophie glanced up at Lindley. She was not quite sure what he expected from her at this point. Should she give in to the hovering and let herself be ushered up to bed? Somehow she'd rather expected that . . . well, that Lindley would be the one ushering her to bed. But now she was to be treated as some sort of delicate maiden who required hovering? Would he allow such a thing?

"Go with her, Miss D'Archaud," he said, nodding toward her as cool and polite as if they had just been introduced in a ballroom. "A good rest will do you well."

"Yes, my lord, but . . . er, where will you be?"

"Don't you worry," he said, and now he spoke as if she were little more than a worrisome child. "I'll be nearby. You'll be safe."

Yes, but would she be alone? It appeared so, as he did not follow when Mrs. Wimpole started leading her toward the staircase. Lindley seemed content to remain here below, laughing with his man, Wimpole, and discussing what was to be done with the horses. The stone steps seemed particularly cold and unwelcoming as she trailed Mrs. Wimpole up them, wondering how on earth to answer the woman's myriad questions.

Wherever had they been? Had the kidnapper asked a ransom for her? How did it happen that Lindley was the one to rescue her? Didn't she fear catching her death out in this night chill? Would she prefer to sleep in the blue room or the yellow? The only good thing about all of Mrs. Wimpole's questions was that she hardly paused long enough between them for Sophie to mumble an incoherent one syllable answer. She knew, however, eventually she'd be expected to supply some additional information about this imaginary kidnapping Lindley had so rashly invented.

As they reached the top of the stairs, thankfully, she noticed something that might just serve to deter the woman's inquiries. Family portraits hung gallery-style. Ah, but what beloved retainer could resist a few well-meaning comments here?

"What lovely paintings," Sophie said, catching the woman midquestion. "How well you've looked after them. They seem almost alive."

Indeed, at the head of the stairs was a quite handsome portrait of Lindley, himself. Clearly he was more than a few years younger, probably just out of school, but already his blue eyes showed the same confidence that defined the man now. His strong jawline and godlike features were richly portrayed in all their perfection.

Beside that portrait hung one of a very pretty young woman. Far prettier than Sophie could ever hope to be, in fact. The woman's hair was a rich chestnut brown, and her ivory skin seemed to glisten on the canvas. The most striking thing about this portrait, however, was not the woman, but the child she held in her arms.

A young boy, it appeared. His mop of curling dark hair fell almost into his crystal blue eyes. The child seemed to smile out at the viewer, his expression full of joy and mischief. Even though so small, he clearly felt quite at ease with the world, ready to attempt anything that might suit his fancy. In fact . . .

Heavens, the boy looked very much like Lindley.

Oh dear, had she found his wife and child, immortalized in oil and positioned beside him in this hallway? Of course it must be. The reality of it slammed into her soul. To realize just what the man had, in fact, lost nearly took her breath away, and she felt her legs go weak. These were the people Lindley had loved—the ones her father had helped to murder. The tragedy of it all threatened to overwhelm her.

"Ah, that's our Lady Marie with little Charles," Mrs. Wimpole said, giving a reverent sigh.

"So very sad," Sophie could only breathe.

"Oh, did you know them?"

Sophie shook her head, suddenly eager to be done with the portraits and lock herself in her room, away from such painful reminders. "No, but I have heard . . ."

The servant nodded. "Yes, I suppose everyone heard. The house has never been the same. In fact, I have worried for his lordship. For years it appeared he would not come here again."

"It's very hard to lose our loved ones."

"So young, and leaving his lordship behind all alone like that," Mrs. Wimpole said, opening one of the many doors along the corridor. "Ah, but I'm glad to see he's taken to helping others now. So tell me, just how did our Lindley come to be your champion, Miss D'Archaud?"

"Well," Sophie said, stepping into an enormous, cold room

and wishing Mrs. Wimpole's taper did more than simply send shadows dancing around them. "He simply, er, happened along at the right moment, I suppose you could say."

The older woman nodded, putting the taper on a table and bending over the grate. "Yes, sometimes fate does things that way, doesn't it?"

Not often for me, she thought about saying, but she held her tongue. No sense getting Mrs. Wimpole primed for another barrage of questions. There had been far too many of them already, and none of them had answers she wanted to think about.

"Get yourself into bed, dear," the woman said as she glanced up to catch Sophie yawning. "I'll fetch some tea."

"Thank you." She only hoped she'd still be awake by the time it arrived.

"DID YOU MANAGE TO ROUSE OLD BEN AND GET HIM to tend to the horses, sir?" Wimpole asked when Lindley returned from the stables.

It had taken far longer to rub down the horses and clean up the carriage than expected, and Lindley brushed at the muck on his boots. They were a lost cause, he feared. It seemed very likely that all of him would smell of horse forever.

"How long has Ben been looking after everything on his own?" Lindley asked. "The poor fellow ought to have some help out there."

"Oh, we don't need much, my lord," Wimpole replied, helping Lindley out of his damp coat. "There's just the one carriage when we need it, and we don't need it often, so Ben is hardly overworked."

Lindley draped his coat over his arm and eyed the abbey's butler. The man must be nearing seventy, at least. Why had it not dawned on him that the staff here at Haven Abbey was aging, that he ought to see about setting up their pensions and finding a relief staff?

Because he'd been happier to forget Haven Abbey existed altogether, of course. For the sake of his own pain he'd completely forgotten about theirs. It was inexcusable.

"And what of you and the missus, Wimpole? How are you getting along, rattling about in this old ruin all on your own?"

Wimpole shrugged. "We have the dailies, my lord. You've been very generous with allowances, and your steward keeps an eye on things for you. The grounds are kept well, and we've shut up most of the house. We're getting by, sir."

Indeed, but getting by was hardly what he wished for such loyal retainers. No, the Wimpoles were more like family. As much as any of the family he had left, at least. They deserved better.

"You've certainly done a far better job of tending to things around here than I have, Wimpole," Lindley acknowledged. "I'm sorry to have neglected you."

"You've had other responsibilities, sir. And now it seems you've taken on some others, eh? That pretty little miss is awfully lucky you found her."

The man had a suspicious sparkle to his eye and just the hint of insinuation in his voice. Yes, of course the man must be curious. Who wouldn't be, a gentleman showing up in the middle of the night to a home he hadn't visited in three years in the company of a beautiful young woman he claimed had been the victim of a kidnapping? Only a fool would not expect to answer a few questions.

"Miss D'Archaud has been the victim of unhappy circumstance, and I am only too glad to have made myself useful to her," Lindley said diplomatically. "Fortunately, I was able to remove her from the unhappy circumstance before she was very ill treated."

"Yes, how fortunate. Pity, though, you could not have made it the additional hour to her cousin's home, milord."

"Hour and a half, at least," Lindley corrected just a bit too quickly.

As if it made a difference. Clearly Wimpole knew as well as he that Hartwood was not very far. Why had he not simply gone on there? Why had he brought an unaccompanied lady to his family home like this? It was already such an ungodly hour, what were another few miles if it meant protecting Miss D'Archaud's invented honor?

And damn it, but now that he'd made the girl respectable

gentry, how was he supposed to explain spending the rest of the night energetically making himself additionally useful to her up in her bed?

He wasn't, of course.

"Miss D'Archaud may not be entirely out of danger yet, Wimpole," Lindley explained. "I did not feel the road to her cousin's home would be safe for us at this hour. Haven Abbey was a much better choice given the circumstance."

"Of course, milord," Wimpole said with that still-annoying little smirk. "Would you have me dispatch word to her cousin, or would you rather we wait until you can be sure all is safe?"

"Let's wait, most definitely," Lindley replied.

"As you wish, milord."

It did seem as though the man was *milording* him more than was absolutely necessary, but Lindley decided he was far too exhausted to bother with further explanation. Much better just to say good night and be done with it. Surely by morning he would be in a better frame of mind for explaining Sophie to his hired man.

"There's no need for you to lose any further sleep on my account, Wimpole," Lindley said. "Why not head back to your bed? I think I'll visit the brandy decanter for a few moments before taking myself up to sleep."

"You're certain there's nothing more you need, sir?"

"No, Wimpole, I'll be fine."

"I see. Well, the missus said we ought to put you in the green room, sir."

Yes, that made sense. He'd rather taken that as his room over the years. He wondered how he was going to tactfully ask which room Sophie had been placed in.

"I believe Miss D'Archaud will be in the rose room," Wimpole volunteered.

Lindley was most grateful. "Fine. Good. She should be very comfortable there."

The old man nodded, bowed slightly, and turned to go. He paused at the door.

"It's good to have you back, sir."

"It's good to be back, Wimpole."

With that, his man actually smiled, then politely left Lindley alone. The huge house was deathly quiet. And dark, as well. The single taper Lindley had kept to find his way hardly did the job. Odd how a familiar place such as Haven Abbey could take on such an alien appearance simply because of the dark.

He made good on his promise to visit the brandy and downed a few swallows before heading up the broad staircase. The darkness was heavy, and every sound made him jump inwardly. His taper flickered, sending eerie shadows dancing across the walls and ceiling. He didn't realize he was doing it, but he must have been clutching the stair rail. It gave him a splinter and he swore.

Faces at the top of the staircase became visible in the candlelight. His face. And Marie's. He'd forgotten their portraits hung here, along with several other Durmonds. Strange that these portraits could be all that was left of them. The silence and chilling darkness added to the strangeness of it all.

He should not have come back here. It was still too painful. He should have found somewhere else to take Sophie.

But where? He believed Sophie's claim that she'd never been close to Dashford. Would the man have eagerly welcomed them at Hartwood, in the middle of the night? He couldn't know. But clearly they would not be safe on the road to London, not while Fitzgelder was on his way to collect the damn locket. No, for Sophie's sake he'd done the only safe thing he could do. He'd just have to be man enough to walk past these portraits and ignore the blasted sensation of his soul being ripped from inside him all over again.

He wondered if he'd be man enough to walk past Sophie's room, as well.

Damn it, he needed her. He needed to be certain she was well, that she was safe and comfortable here. He needed the warmth of a living body tonight. He needed it to be hers.

The rose room. He stood at the door and listened, hoping Mrs. Wimpole was long gone and Sophie was alone. All he heard was the emptiness all around him and the blood pounding in his own veins.

Almost silently, he knocked. Then held his breath to wait. Finally, a sound from inside let him know he'd been heard. He breathed a sigh of relief as if the simple act of rousing Sophie would save him from the many ghosts that roamed these halls.

SHE KNEW IT WAS LINDLEY WHEN THE SLIGHT RAP came at her door. It had seemed ages since Mrs. W got the fire in the grate, helped her undress, then left her to sleep. She'd begun to believe Lindley would not come to her.

Of course, until she let him in she would really not know if he had merely come to bid her good night or if he had more interesting things on his mind. She tossed the covers back and dashed for the door. She was somewhat out of breath when she flung it open to find him there, his hair damp and tousled, his coat thrown over his arm, and his eyes dark with midnight and desire.

"I take it you were not sleeping?" he said quietly.

"No, I was waiting . . . er, to fall asleep, I mean. Waiting to fall asleep."

"Then I'm glad I did not wake you. May I come in?"

Oh, dear heavens, yes! "Very well, I suppose so, if you like."

Apparently he did like. He pushed the door open and stalked into the room. His presence seemed to fill the place up, where it had felt cavernous and empty before.

"You're not wearing anything from your personal collection, my dear," he said when she had shut the door and they were alone.

The room was dim, lit only by the flickering candle he held and the shuttered lamp she had left burning on the bed stand. Still, she could read the hunger in his eyes and the heat in his expression as he let his gaze roam over her. There was no point in feeling self-conscious. She would never tire of being the object of his attentions.

She did wish, however, she could forget about that dratted Marie person. It was embarrassingly painful to admit how jealous she was. Lindley might want her now, but down deep she knew she was just a poor substitute for what he really wanted. She could never replace what he'd lost.

She could, however, take advantage of the situation now.

"I wasn't sure you'd come, my lord," she said. "To see me, that is. Come to see me, I mean."

"Of course."

"But as you are here . . . perhaps you might look at something for me."

He smiled at her. "Oh, most definitely, Miss Darshaw. I will most definitely look at something for you."

Chapter Fifteen

"Er, the window, sir," Sophie said, thinking of something quickly.

"You need me to look out the window?" he asked.

"No, that is, I need you to help me shut it. It's open a bit, see? I'm afraid I might get cold in the night."

"Ah, we don't want you cold in the night, do we?" he said.

There was a sliver of moonlight trailing in through the window, and now that they stood there in it, she could see his face plainly. He was smiling, and he didn't for one minute believe she needed his help with the window. *Good.* She needed him for something far more important.

"So, my dear Miss Darshaw, what shall we do to ensure you stay adequately warm and comfortable all night long?"

He was standing very near her, and she moved even closer. "You have some suggestions, my lord?"

"Indeed, I do," he replied, still with that knee-weakening smile.

But just when she thought he might pull her into his arms, he stepped away. For some inexplicable reason, he walked away from her. Worse, he wasn't even moving toward the bed. Instead, his eye seemed to be on the bureau across the room.

"What you need is some more appropriate clothing."

What? She was ready to throw herself at his feet, and he was concerned with appropriate clothing? Why on earth had he come to her if he was not interested in warming her himself? If she didn't want him so very badly just now, she was sure she would be quite infuriated with him.

"I was hoping to warm myself with something a bit more, er, *in*appropriate."

"Then I'm certain we shall find just the thing. In here."

He grabbed her pack where she had left it on the bureau. Ah, now he was moving in the right direction. He tossed the pack onto the bed, pulling it open to investigate the contents beside the flickering taper.

Her knees were still weak, but this time she was the one smiling. He did want her.

"Let's see, this one has proven its worth," he said, taking out the pink silk knitted article, then he set it aside to extract the white gauzy gown in miniature proportions. "And of course there's this."

Yet he set that one aside, as well, and kept looking. What did he expect to find? Oh, please not the hood with the rabbit ears. She really did not find that item alluring at all. Although, perhaps Lindley had some ideas for it she had not thought of . . . No, he set it aside with a roll of his eyes. But what else was he looking for?

"Oh, now this has definite merit," he said at last.

He'd gotten to the very bottom of her pack. What had he found? She wasn't sure she recalled any other clothing she'd been working on for Madame, and she doubted the strapping device was to his liking. She frowned, trying to recall what else he might discover when he pulled out the white satin cords.

Ah, yes. She'd forgotten about those. Madame had given her strict instruction—they were to be soft, tied with a tight loop at one end and a loop something very like a noose at the other, and made in two pairs. It was not made to slip around the neck, however, but over the hands and feet, one pair for each. Madame had been rather sketchy regarding the purpose of these articles, and Sophie did not ask.

"I have no idea what Madame intends for those," she said.

Lindley seemed perplexed. "Hmm, yes . . . what would they be used for?"

"Well, she told me one pair should be made to slip around the wrists while the other is for the, er, ankles."

He studied the cords as if trying to determine what possible use Madame might have had in mind. Odd, considering Sophie had rather expected Lindley to know much more about this sort of thing than she did. Well, perhaps it was a good sign that Madame still kept some secrets from him. Perhaps that meant he had not been so very involved with activities at the brothel.

"Let's see," he began, seating her on the bed and taking up her hands to try the noose ends of the smaller cords to see if they fit. "Sit here, my dear. Now, perhaps if we try this . . ."

Gently he tightened the soft cord around her wrists. Indeed, she rather enjoyed the feel of his skin against hers, but she could not imagine what this little length of cord could possibly do regarding pleasurable intimacies.

Before she could voice her confusion, though, Lindley swooped up one free end of the cord and looped it around one of the bedposts. She cried out, startled, but he quickly grabbed up the other, reached past her, and looped that one on the other bedpost. The surprise of it all knocked her over. Next thing she knew, she was lying on the bed, her arms spread wide and held in place by the cords. As she struggled the nooses tightened on her wrists. She felt helpless.

Lindley was smiling over her.

"The others for your ankles would be used the same way, my dear," he said. "Then I would be free to do as I saw fit, and you could do little but lie here and enjoy."

She wasn't sure she liked the sound of that.

"And what if I don't enjoy, sir?"

"Then clearly I am doing it wrong."

He leaned in at that point and kissed her neck, in the soft, vulnerable spot just where he would have found her pulse beating furiously. Ah, so he had lied to her. He *did* know what these cords were for. And yes, she likely *would* enjoy whatever he decided to do to her while she was helplessly bound this way.

She supposed she did not have to let him know she enjoyed

it, though. Tricking her this way was not fair play. She would not let him know he had won so easily. Yes, she could certainly give him a bit of his own. Such a skill might come in handy in her future, as a matter of fact.

"So when, exactly, am I supposed to begin enjoying?" she asked.

The kisses stopped.

"I see you intend to be difficult," he said, tugging off his cravat. "You know what we do with difficult children."

"Children, sir? Surely you don't do any of this with children!"

He sat back on his heels, kneeling beside her and frowning.

"Honestly, Sophie. You wanted to know what the cords were for, so I am showing you. Won't you play along?"

"Tied up this way I hardly have anything to play with, my lord."

Now he smiled again. "Ah, but I do, my dear. Yes, I most certainly do."

At that he leaned over her again and played with the edge of her shift, pushing it down low over her bosom, teasing her with his touch. Repeatedly his fingers brushed her nipples, yet they never lingered. She squirmed. It would be difficult to pretend for very long that she did not enjoy this game.

She gave what she hoped sounded like a bored sigh. "Seems such a shame that all I can do is lie here and let you do all the work."

He didn't even pause a moment as his kisses and teasing continued. "Lucky for me this is work I enjoy."

Indeed, she enjoyed it very much, too. A sigh escaped her that was anything but bored. Well, if he was content to keep her passive and still, she supposed she would not argue. Not yet, anyway.

His hands glided over her, traveling down to her thighs. She felt her shift sliding up as his fingertips tickled against the sensitive places inside her legs and up over her belly. He carefully avoided any areas that would send her over the edge into sheer delight, but he certainly brought her close. She struggled to be still, not to pull against the bindings.

"Will you be still, my dear, or must I bind your feet, as well?"

"No, I'll be still. It's just that when you touch me there . . ."

"Here?"

"Yes! Yes, that's the spot. I'm afraid I rather lose control."

"Good."

Now he paused his caresses long enough to pull off his shirt. Once again the man's solid, muscular body took her breath away. Oh, but she wished she could touch it, touch him, and feel the warmth and power beneath his skin. She writhed with agonized pleasure when his hands went back to stroking her thighs.

"You aren't being very still."

"You aren't making it especially easy for me to keep still."

"Then how about if I do this?"

His hands clamped over her legs, just below her knees. Before she could ask what he was about, he spread her legs apart and brought his face in close to kiss her—down there. She would have most certainly wiggled more than she did if he had not held her so tightly, keeping her from sliding away from him as the first wave of pleasure rocked her. He was lapping at her sensitive center and she was nearly undone immediately.

She thought she might have made some sound, some groan of bliss, but she could not be certain. All she knew was that in such a very short time he had reduced her to a nearly senseless mass of jelly, helpless in his control. And there was nothing she could do for him in return.

Unless, of course, she got out of these frustrating cords.

"Please . . . you have to stop!" she panted.

He did.

"Undo the cords, please. Quickly!"

He did that, too.

"What is it, Sophie?" he asked, sounding dreadfully concerned.

She started rubbing her wrists as if they hurt. Then she suddenly became aware of the state of her shift. Her bosoms were hanging out at the top and it was pulled up high on her belly to reveal her bottom portions. She quickly moved to cover herself.

"No! Don't look at me like this!"

"What is it? What is wrong?" he asked.

"Turn around; don't look at me, my lord."

He did as she asked, clearly confused by her sudden change in attitude. She was rather proud of herself, actually. He may have had to tie her up to control her body, but she was learning just exactly how much control she could wield over him simply by speaking a word or two.

He had his back to her, still demanding to know if she was hurt or what he could do to help her. She smiled and pulled the cords off her wrists, widening the little nooses just a bit.

"Give me your hands," she asked, keeping just a hint of desperation in her voice.

Again, he did exactly as she commanded and reached behind him, offering her his hands. In one quick move she slipped the cords over him, tightened them, and wrapped the remaining cords around his arms, successfully binding his hands together behind his back.

"There!" she said in triumph. "This should help enormously."

She grabbed him by the broad shoulders and pulled until he toppled back onto the bed beside her. Without pause she swung her leg over to straddle him and keep him there, bound and pinned beneath her. It was his turn to become the victim in this little game he'd taught her.

"Now, my lord, how do you like being on the other side?"

He shifted just slightly to adjust his hands beneath him and gave her a wicked grin.

"I like it very much. Now that I'm your prisoner, what will you do with me, Miss D'Archaud?"

She pondered that. "I think to begin with, I shall do this."

She leaned in and nipped first his left nipple and then his right. He drew in a short breath for each one, and she knew she was becoming more and more adept at this sort of thing. My, but she did like it!

She moved so that now her legs were straddling his thighs. His trousers were pulled tight against him; she could see that their playtime had made him hard and ready for more. She wanted more, too. She unfastened his trousers and decided to help herself.

The man was magnificent. For a long moment she sat back on her heels and just stared. Then she slowly reached to touch him. He was soft as velvet and firm as granite. What a fascinating combination.

He moaned when she wrapped her hand around the heated flesh. It was an invigorating feeling, to be holding him in such an intimate way. To think that he trusted her so! Especially as he knew she had so little experience with this. She found herself somewhat flattered by it all, but the desire surging within her did not allow much time for contemplation.

She knew what she wanted—and she was going to take it. Cautiously, she bent to kiss him on the very tip of his manhood. He growled.

"By God, you're going to kill me, my dear."

"It's more difficult than one might expect to be tied up and helpless against such torture, isn't it, my lord?"

"You may torture me this way for eternity, Sophie."

Tempting, but she knew in fact she could not. She needed him too badly to let this go on that long. Clearly he was willing. She would have him.

Wondering if she was at all doing this correctly, she slid her body close to his. Kneeling above him, she couldn't help but glance into his face, hoping she would see encouragement there. She did.

"You really are a prodigy," he said with a smile that gave all the encouragement she needed.

She lowered herself slowly, feeling the fiery hot sensation of his manhood pressing against her. It was what she needed, what her body cried out for. She reveled in the slightest touch, moving and brushing herself against him, until both of them were breathing in raspy gasps. She could take it no more.

Moaning right along with him, she pressed herself down onto him. His body slid into her, warming her and filling her like nothing ever had. With a shiver of desire, she dug her fingers into the solid muscle of his shoulders, riding him as if she'd done this a hundred times before. Her body was primed and ready this time. She felt every inch of him, every wave of passion, every breath of flaming need.

At some point his arms were free, reaching for her, touching her face, her neck, her breasts, her back. She lost track of the passage of time and simply gave in to the motion, the sensation. He thrust himself up into her, deeper than she could have imagined and more wonderful than she could have wished for.

She cried out his name when the ecstasy hit her, more powerful and breathtaking than before. He pulled her to him and held her against his chest as her body rocked and writhed with the passion. She struggled to breathe and didn't care if she did.

Before she was completely back to earth, though, he shifted. Still holding her, he rolled onto his side and then laid her on her back. She blinked up at him.

"You got free, my lord."

He smiled. "No, my dear. I'm far from free. You tie knots no man could possibly undo."

And then he was moving inside her again. She would not have thought it possible, but desire raged to a wildfire in her and she was, once more, sinking into the heated oblivion of wave after wave of thrilling climax. She held him as if she might float away on it.

Finally he growled out her name. She was clinging to his back, choking out her own incoherent cries of passion. He dropped down onto her, then rolled to his side, keeping her caught against him with one powerful arm. She wriggled tight against him, filling her lungs and waiting for the room to stop spinning.

"Well. So that's what those cords are for," she said when she could finally speak.

"Yes," he said, tucking her close and chuckling as he kissed her hair. "And I hope you learned your lesson about keeping people bound against their will."

Oh, she'd learned a lesson well enough. One she would gladly study again and again with him, if only fate would grant her that chance.

IT WAS MORNING. THE BIRDS WERE SINGING OUTSIDE the window, and bright sunlight streamed through the gaps in the elaborate drapes. Dust motes glittered like minuscule gems. The air was fresh and pure.

And Lindley felt like hell.

He threw his legs over the side of the bed and just sat there.

Sophie still slumbered behind him, as peaceful as a child and as beautiful as an angel. He hadn't meant to still be here with her; he'd planned to steal back to his own bed long before daylight. Somehow, it simply had not happened. He'd stayed. Surely the servants would have noticed by now.

Why? He'd left many women after nights of passion; why had he not left Sophie? Because he'd felt as if leaving her would tear out his soul, that was why. What in God's name was wrong with him?

He wanted her. He wanted to stay with her, to make love until reality disappeared and there was nothing more to do but be happy. It was foolishness, of course. Happiness had no place between them. He knew that. He had his duty, and she had hers. His was to resume his hunt for her father; hers was to protect and defend the man.

It was a bloody shame, but this was just the way things were. It would be pointless to prolong the inevitable. He needed to leave. When she woke he would be gone and they would be enemies again.

Damn, but perhaps this truly would leave him a man with no soul. He felt hollow and cold already.

He padded softly around the room, gathering his clothing and cursing at their rumpled state. Really, he was cursing his own weakness. He should have never given in to temptation last night. He would be tired all day from the sleep he'd lost.

As if sleep was all he'd lost. The emptiness inside assured him that Sophie was not entirely alone there in that bed. A part of him remained with her. It would always remain with her. And she would never know it.

That was a blessing, he supposed. She would never know how leaving her this morning destroyed him. He could at least hold on to that little measure of pride.

He looked atrocious: his clothes were just thrown on and he hardly cared. He would find time to right himself later. For now, he needed to get away from her before she woke. Before he lost his nerve and begged her to let him stay.

For one insane moment he thought about leaving the locket for her, but force of will won out and he took it with him. Now he'd become a thief. Well, perhaps a handful of coins would ease his conscience. He took out his purse and dropped it onto her pack. He may have used her like a whore, but at least he'd paid her well. She could hate him more for it if she liked, but she'd earned that wage and should have it.

Grabbing his boots, he silently let himself out. The door squeaked on its hinges, but Sophie did not stir. He left her behind and pulled the door to behind him. It clicked shut, slicing whatever ties he'd still had to his decency. She would never know what it cost him to leave her today.

Making his way downstairs—which took him through the gauntlet of disapproving family members gazing with reproach from their portraits—Lindley found a bench and began working at his boots. He'd carried them rather than make a sound and wake Sophie. Yes, he was that much the coward.

"Will you be wanting breakfast, milord?" Wimpole asked, appearing from somewhere.

Lindley grimaced. The thought of treating himself to food only served to turn his stomach. He did not deserve the luxury of food.

"No," he replied. "I'll be wanting my carriage. I have business to attend this morning, Wimpole. It cannot wait."

"You'll be paying a call on Lord Dashford, I presume," Wimpole said with an all-too-easily-understood grin. "I rather hoped that's the way it was for you and the young miss, milord."

So the man had him rushing to offer for Sophie now, did he? *Damn it.* Of course that's what would be expected. He'd introduced Sophie as a proper lady. The household staff was bound to know he had not treated her like one last night. Naturally they would expect him to do the right thing.

Well, he would not correct Wimpole's assumption. Sophie deserved to be treated well during her stay here, and leaving the servants to believe she would soon be their mistress would ensure that. Lindley owed her that much, at least. He would shelter and protect her as long as he could. Haven Abbey would do until he could make further arrangements for her.

"See that Miss D'Archaud has everything she needs, Wimpole," Lindley directed, dodging the man's obvious but unexpressed questions. "And since we are not certain what danger still exists for her, I'd like it if you and the staff could keep her indoors. Safe. No matter what."

He hoped that might serve to deter Sophie from running away anytime soon. He had no doubt that would be her first objective, but he could trust Wimpole to see that she was retained here. For added measure, he'd get word to Feasel that the girl was to be monitored at all times. From a distance, of course.

Wimpole was all too eager to promise they'd take good care of the girl, and before Lindley could rethink his plans he left. He spared one glance over his shoulder as he drove away. Haven Abbey was bright and beautiful on this morning. How could the place appear so peaceful when everything about it caused such chaos inside him?

He guided the carriage out onto the main road. A rustle in the brush off to the side caught his attention, and before he could even react he heard his name called out. He let out a frustrated sigh.

"Damn it, Feasel, must you always be jumping out at me like this?"

"Didn't get enough sleep, milord?" his man replied with a smirk, jogging up to the carriage.

Lindley reined in his horses and frowned. "My sleep habits are hardly your concern."

Feasel laughed. "I take that back, milord. Sounds more like you got a little too much sleep, if you know what I mean."

Yes, he knew what he meant, damn him. As if his relationship with Miss Darshaw was something to be bandied about on the street.

"What news do you have for me, Feasel?" Lindley asked, making it very clear he was not about to be badgered about what did—or did not—go on last night.

Feasel took the hint, cleared his throat, and got on about their business. "No news from Tom yet on Fitzgelder's whereabouts, but it's early still. Foolish lad probably found some snug little port to drop his anchor last night. I expect to be hearing from him anytime now. Then I'll tan his randy little hide."

Bother, but it was inconvenient the boy saw no need to rein in his passions any better. With Fitzgelder on the prowl this was not time to let their guard down. Still, Lindley supposed he could hardly fault the lad, not after giving in to his own Achilles' heel last night. Somehow they'd get by until Tom decided to do up his trousers and make himself useful again.

"Well, don't tan him so much he's no good to us, Feasel," Lindley advised. "I'm heading up to Loveland today, and I'm counting on Tom to find his way there in case I need him."

"I'll head up there with you, milord."

"No. I need you here. Keep an eye on Miss Darshaw."

Clearly Feasel felt this task was beneath him. "Oh come, sir. You can't think she'll be much of a threat to us now, after all this?"

"Of course she's no threat! By God, Feasel, you'll stay here and see that she stays at the abbey and no one gets to her." Lindley hoped his tone conveyed the gravity of his intentions. Feasel was a good man, but he would not be high in Lindley's favor if he allowed any harm to come to that young woman.

"I see, sir," Feasel replied, and Lindley believed he truly did. "She will be safe."

"Good. I'll send help for you when I can. When you are in contact with Tom, have him come after me. You know the way?"

"Well enough, sir," Feasel assured. "So the girl told you her father would be at Loveland, even though our people have seen nothing of him there?"

"He's not there *yet*, Feasel. He will be."

"Very well, milord. But what if—"

Feasel's words were cut off by pounding hoofbeats. Lindley instinctively reached for the pistol he had tucked on the floor near his feet. Feasel pulled a lethal-looking knife from his boot. Neither was needed.

The rider hailed them as he approached. It was Tom.

"Well, here he is now, milord," Feasel said, clearly loud enough for Tom to overhear. "My own precious get, the useless moll-monger himself."

"It's good to see you, Tom," Lindley said, hoping any hide-tanning could wait until he was gone. "Your father was just saying he was hoping to hear from you at any moment."

"Well, he's hearing from me now, and I've got something to tell ye, sir," Tom said, somewhat breathless from his ride, or perhaps the fury in his father's eyes.

"Come to brag of your night's debauchery, are you?" Feasel asked.

"No, sir!" Tom replied. "I've come to tell ye what I saw, heading on the north road."

"Fitzgelder?" Lindley asked.

"No sir, he ain't been through Warwick yet, though I was lookin' for him all the night long."

Feasel grunted dubiously at that.

Tom continued. "It was some actors; a whole pack of them, milord."

"And did the actresses distract you with their great big—"

This time Lindley did the interrupting. He knew exactly what Feasel thought his son had been doing, but he did not wish to get in the middle of a family dispute. Especially not over such things as great big, er, distractions.

Tom barely took time to frown at his father. "No, sir. I didn't see any actresses. Well, not any young ones, anyway. This was a troupe of mostly men. And, milord, they was heading on up toward that place you told us your man D'Archaud might be going."

Well, but this did sound promising. "The actors were heading to Loveland?"

"Aye, sir," Tom replied. "And at least one of them was speaking French, too!"

By God, that was good news indeed. If D'Archaud had been looking for some of his old friends to hide him, a troupe of French actors would be the first place Lindley ought to look. My, but how convenient that Tom was a randy young sort and happened to be out and about at all hours to notice the troupe.

"Good work, Tom. How long ago did you see them?"

The young man shrugged and his mop of sandy hair flopped onto his forehead. "It wasn't yet daylight, sir. Papa left word where I'd find him, so I got myself out here as quick as I could."

That would have been an hour ago, at least. From Warwick it was just over an hour's ride to Loveland. D'Archaud and his friends were quite likely there already. Damn, but if they found what they wanted and then left, Lindley might lose track of them yet. He was not about to let that happen.

"Then we have no time to waste. Tom, you head back to Warwick and follow them up to Loveland that way. I'll go from Southam and come around from the east. If we get to Loveland and they are not there, we will know they must have gone on north."

Tom nodded. The boy might be easily distracted, but he wasn't slow. He'd follow up on his end of things. Lindley could trust him.

"And what of me, milord?" Feasel asked.

"You'll stay here."

Feasel looked almost hurt. Did he truly think Sophie was so very unimportant to any of this?

"I need you, Feasel," Lindley said. "She's got to be kept safe."

"Very well, milord. I'll remain here."

"Thank you."

Lindley honestly could not ever remember thanking the man for anything and meaning it this much.

"Are we riding hell-for-leather, sir?" Tom asked.

"Most definitely," Lindley replied. "Er, if your mount can take it."

"Aye, sir. He don't look like much, but he can move."

"Then let us be on our way."

Tom grinned like a child in a sweetshop. He spurred his horse forward, gave his father a nod, and was off in a cloud of dewy dust. Lindley gave Feasel a nod of his own, then urged his pair into motion. D'Archaud wouldn't know what hit him. It would all be over soon. Justice would finally be served.

Somehow, though, Lindley found it hard to match Tom's enthusiasm.

SOPHIE STOOD AT THE WINDOW AND WATCHED. SHE'D given up battling the tears. By now they were flowing freely and there was little she could do except an occasional dab.

He was gone. She'd heard him this morning. He'd climbed out of bed, dressed silently, insulted her by leaving behind an embarassingly large pile of coins, then left. She could do nothing but stare out the window and watch his beautiful carriage glide elegantly down the lane.

He had the locket, of course, and all she had were a few sordid memories. Anything that had been beautiful and precious between them had been destroyed by his actions. He didn't even wake her to say good-bye.

Now Papa would meet justice, and she would be free to go beg Madame to take her back. She was well qualified to be far more than a seamstress now. Perhaps fate would be kind and she'd die young, as so many girls did.

But first, she'd allow herself one last vanity. She'd throw herself down on Lindley's soft bed and have a good, sniffling cry.

Chapter Sixteen

A knock at the door woke her. Apparently after shedding every tear in her body she'd fallen asleep. No telling how long she'd been that way. She should have tried to find a way to leave, to warn Papa that Lindley was coming, or at least to see about arranging her own life. The last thing she wanted was to stay here, trespassing on Lindley's goodwill as if she had any right to it. As if she wanted it.

But now someone was rapping at the door. A servant, most likely, come to evict her from the premises. Wimpole and his wife had been friendly and accommodating last night, but surely by now they realized what she was. Lindley's ridiculous story of her kidnapping and legitimate connection to Dashford was thin at best. Of course no one would truly believe it, especially as they must have noticed the man spent the entire night in her bed.

She did not belong here. This was his family home, not some shameless love nest where he might stash a ladybird now and then. She needed to leave, and surely now that he was gone, his servants would easily agree. She was glad, at least, the sunlight streaming in through the window assured her it was still early in the day. As she recalled, they'd passed through a village nearby. There would be plenty of time to make her way there. Perhaps the coins she'd earned on her back last night would be enough to buy her a seat on the coach back to London.

Straightening her clothes, she wiped the last trace of tears and went to the door, determined to keep some measure of dignity. The housekeeper might know what sort of woman she was, but Sophie certainly did not have to act like one in front of her. She would tell Mrs. Wimpole she was already packed to leave and ask direction to that little village.

She opened the door, and the words died on her lips.

"Annie?!"

And there, beside Annie in the corridor, was Madame herself, holding Annie's babe and smiling as if this were the grandest reunion of her life. Well, it certainly was the oddest. What on earth was Madame Eudora doing in Lord Lindley's family home?

And there was Wimpole with a very nervous Mrs. Wimpole.

"See, Wimpole?" Madame said with one of her dazzling smiles. "I told you there would be no trouble. Miss Darshaw and I are dear, dear friends."

"Yes, er, Miss Eudora, but his lordship didn't say anything about you visiting . . ."

Wimpole was clearly as confused by everything as Sophie was. Still, he did seem to know Madame by name. What was she to make of that? She glanced at Annie, hoping for some sort of explanation. All she saw was an uncomfortable anxiousness in her friend's eyes. Well, at least Sophie wasn't the only one feeling a bit off balance by all of this.

But Madame seemed entirely at ease. She propped the babe more securely in her arms and brushed past the others, making her way right into Sophie's room as if she belonged there. Indeed, she glanced around the place and smiled.

"Thank heavens someone replaced that dour old wallpaper. This room was absolutely tomblike."

Sophie did all she could not to let her mouth drop open and her jaw hang slack. By heavens, *did* Madame belong here?

"Come along, Annie," Madame called behind her. "Mrs. W, bring up some tea, will you? The young ladies and I have so much to catch up on."

"But Miss Eudora, what will his lordship say?" Mrs. Wimpole muttered, sounding quite beyond exasperated.

"Richard will be more than happy to find me here. Trust me, Mrs. W. The feud is long over and Richard has welcomed me back to the fold. I've only now decided to accept his most generous offer."

The Wimpoles did not seem to quite believe that, yet they did not argue. Obviously, whatever the relationship was between these elderly servants and Madame, it was not one of strangers. Sophie hoped Madame had every intention of explaining.

"Now, how about that tea?" Madame said with another smile.

Mrs. Wimpole paused slightly, then gave a grudging little curtsy. Wimpole gave a nearly inaudible grunt, but both turned and made their way from the corridor. Annie scurried into the room behind Madame. Sophie shut the door.

"So," Madame began, fairly tossing the babe to Annie and turning to run her approving gaze up and down Sophie's drab appearance. "Lindley had you here in *my* bed, did he?"

Sophie's jaw dropped. *Madame's bed? Good heavens!* What was she supposed to say to something like that?

But apparently Madame didn't expect a response. She went on perusing the room, touching things, studying things, and smiling in a way that was far from dazzling.

"Although I suppose Marie had my bed replaced years ago. I suppose I forget how much time has actually passed . . ."

Madame's leisurely way of examining the room was very off-putting. Sophie glanced at Annie, but she was consumed entirely with nuzzling her cooing child. All else was silent and tense. Even the air in the room felt strangely unbreathable.

"You've been here before, Madame?" Sophie asked when she could stand no more of the silence.

Madame laughed. "Not for years. Tell me, do you find it to your liking? I would imagine Haven Abbey is quite luxurious for you, dear Sophie."

"I've only been here a few hours, Madame," Sophie replied.

"Oh come now, Sophie. Can you not tell me you would give almost everything to live in a place such as this? Can you just imagine it, being mistress of such a home?"

Madame laughed again, a shrill sound, almost like breaking glass.

"No," Sophie replied, stepping closer to Annie. "I can't. I could never see myself as mistress of such a place."

"Of course you can't." Madame sighed, turning from her perusal of a needlework pillow. "That's always been your trouble, Sophie. You have no idea what you could attain if you'd only reach your hand out to take it."

Personally, Sophie felt she'd reached out and taken quite a lot lately. Whatever did Madame mean by that, anyway? It was all so confusing.

Mrs. Wimpole arrived at the door with their tea. She let herself in, and Madame ordered her about sharply, directing her to place the tray on the table near the window and then leave them. The woman complied, but Sophie was quite certain there was mumbling under her breath as she left. She couldn't really blame her. Something about Madame's demeanor was, well, demeaning.

"Come, Sophie," Madame said abruptly. "We'll let Annie get the tea ready. Let me show you some of the abbey."

"But won't the tea be cold, Madame?"

"Nonsense. Mrs. W always brings it too hot anyway. Walk with me, Sophie. Annie knows what to do."

Annie nervously stroked and fussed over her child, but she assured Madame she would prepare the tea. Sophie noted the woman's hands were shaking. *Good heavens, why should that be?* But Madame took Sophie's arm and looped it around hers, not giving her much choice but to walk beside her out into the corridor.

"So, dear Sophie, tell me what you think of my fine home here," Madame said.

"*Your* home? Er, it's very lovely," Sophie said, wondering what else she could say. Madame's words were shocking, to say the least.

"It's not lovely," Madame corrected. "It's archaic. It's drafty in the winter and far too huge to keep up with. Why, I daresay there are rooms in this moldering castle that no one has visited in years. It's ridiculous that it has sat virtually empty all these years. Now I . . . I would have done something with it."

Sophie stared at the floor and let Madame lead her. Everything inside her screamed out that something was very, very wrong.

"You seem a bit nervous, Sophie."

"Er, I suppose so, Madame, but . . ."

"You are afraid Lindley might not approve of my being here?"

"Well, frankly . . . yes."

Madame snorted. "Silly girl. You have no idea. Obviously he has not told you who I am, has he?"

"I thought I knew who you were, Madame," Sophie replied cautiously.

Madame clicked her tongue and shook her head. "To think, little Sophie, I'd begun to suspect he actually cared more for you than just what he could get between your legs. Clearly I was wrong."

Well, that was more than insulting.

"All Lord Lindley has ever truly been interested in has been capturing my father," she happily informed her former employer. "Any, er, other interest was purely due to my own talents for distraction."

"Ah, suddenly you've become an expert in feminine wiles, have you? Really now, Sophie. If you were such a grand distraction for the man, why did he rush off the very minute the sun rose this morning?"

Bother. How on earth did Madame know what time Lindley left her today? And truly, what business was it of hers? What was this woman's relation to Lindley, anyway?

"His lordship is highly motivated to capture my father," she replied.

"Oh? And does he suddenly believe he knows where he might find your father?"

"He has some idea, I believe."

"Did you tell him?" Madame asked.

"Of course not," Sophie said. "I have no idea where to find my father. And even if I did, why would I tell Lindley?"

"You would not have had to tell him if you gave him that locket."

At this Sophie could only stare at the woman. How could Madame know of the locket?

"Oh, don't pretend you don't know about it," Madame said, pinning her with a gaze like daggers. "I'm aware you took that locket from Fitzgelder, my dear. Did Lindley lure you into giving it to him? Or did you fancy yourself in love and just hand it over voluntarily?"

"I most certainly am not in love with Lindley!"

"Then you still have the locket?"

"Er, no . . ."

"So you gave it to him."

"I did not!"

"Then who has it, Sophie? Honestly, did you simply lose track of it? Something so important to your family and you lost it?"

"I did not. I . . . er, my father has it."

This clearly surprised Madame, but Sophie could not tell if this was in a good way or a bad way.

"Your father has it?"

"Yes. Of course."

She wasn't quite certain why she lied. Silly, but Madame's odd behavior and accusations were making her feel like a scolded child. She should not have to take it from this woman. Not after Madame withheld information about her father all those years, after she showed up inexplicably here and threw the servants into a fluster, after she accused Sophie of willfully handing her father over to the enemy and then had the absolute nerve to suggest Sophie might actually be in love with the man!

"Did your father tell you why this locket is so important?" Madame asked.

"It's believed to contain a list of conspirators," Sophie answered.

"I see. And is that all he told you?"

"The locket is also a key."

Now Madame nodded her head, silently contemplating things. What things the woman might have to contemplate Sophie could not guess, since it was clear nothing she'd told her about the locket appeared to be new information for Madame.

"So your father told you about the treasure," Madame said.

"Treasure? There is a treasure?" Good heavens, what on earth was the woman talking about now?

"Of course there's a treasure," Madame said with a toss of her head. "And now that your father has the key and Lindley does not, this means I hold all the cards in my hand."

"Er, what cards are those, Madame?" Sophie asked, her head swimming with all this new information.

"Well, *you* for one, my dear," Madame said.

Her painted lips spread into a broad smile. This time it was not dazzling, but something more like the expression on a cat after finding the lid off the creamer. Except that on a cat, that expression was likable.

"Ah, but look, Sophie," Madame went on, turning her attention toward the paintings around them. "It is the family portrait gallery. Did you see these?"

"Yes, they are lovely. Lord Lindley had a beautiful family."

"*Had?* Ah, so he told you what happened."

"He mentioned some of it," she admitted. There was no need to tell Madame that Lindley's sole reason for confiding in her was so she could realize her father's part in his suffering.

"I suppose by telling you all his sorrows he gained more of your sympathy," Madame said.

"Of course he has my sympathy. To lose a wife and child would be dreadful."

Madame seemed amazed she did indeed know so much of Lindley's past. Sophie felt just a bit smug, but Madame's wicked smile wiped some of that away.

They had paused before the portrait of the young woman with the child. Madame was staring at them. Yes, Sophie had guessed right. This was Lindley's family, and Madame knew them, somehow.

"Of course you recognized the painting. The child certainly did favor Lindley, did he not? And Marie was quite lovely, wasn't she?"

"Yes."

"Of course you realize someone like you could never hope to take her place."

Sophie felt her eye twitch. "Yes, Madame. I know exactly who and what I am."

"Good. That's a lesson you've long needed to learn, my girl."

Oh, she'd learned it, indeed. She'd learned at the hands of

an expert. A bag of coins and an empty bed was proof of her passing marks. It was a lesson she'd never, ever forget.

HIS ANGRY STOMACH RUMBLED, AND LINDLEY HAD TO admit he was exhausted. Perhaps he should have eaten something before he'd run off this morning. But how could he? The longer he'd dawdled at Haven Abbey the more likely he was to give up on his goal altogether. It was hard enough to leave when he did.

As it was, his hurried departure had done little to further his goal. He'd made it to Loveland and stole quietly up to a low ridge overlooking the cottage. Indeed, smoke curled from the chimney and the two theatrical wagons Tom had reported were right there in plain view. Tom, however, was nowhere to be found. Frustrated, Lindley had been forced to leave Loveland and go looking for him.

He didn't dare try to confront D'Archaud on his own, not with those actors in residence. If his quarry had indeed joined his friends at Loveland, Lindley could count on them to put up a fight. There was too much at stake for D'Archaud to give up without one.

He cursed as he abandoned Loveland and went on to Lack Wooton, the last town Tom would have to pass through on his journey from the west toward Loveland. He hoped he would find the boy there. He prayed he would not find trouble.

Really, though, he wished he might find some food.

Unfortunately, the little village of Lack Wooton lacked several things. Any decent place to find a meal, someone who might represent local constabulary, or any evidence of Tom Feasel. Damn that boy, but he seemed to have simply disappeared. Lindley found himself wavering between cursing the boy for his incompetence and worrying that something dreadful must have happened along the way.

Had Tom run afoul of that greedy bastard Fitzgelder or any of his henchmen? Lindley very sincerely hoped not. Then why had the young man not turned up? Lindley had trusted him with delicate information. He needed to know Tom could be trusted.

Well, trustworthy, dead, or not, the boy was simply not to

be found. The longer Lindley dawdled here the more chance that D'Archaud would get what he came for and leave Loveland. Lindley had no clue where the man would go from there. He needed to go back to Loveland and watch, waiting for the right opportunity to take the man.

But he could not do that alone. If Tom was not to be found, he'd simply have to recruit someone else. There seemed to be but one place to do that: the only tavern in the village. Well, he had no choice but to make his way inside. He needed food and he needed to find able-bodied men. He doubted he'd find much of either in this place, but it would have to do.

Besides, he had the distinct feeling he was being watched.

Since the minute he'd rolled into town in his fashionable—and noticeable—phaeton he knew he was being, well, noticed. He was used to that. But the longer he was here, making his way through the village until he could find an establishment to leave his carriage where he might be relatively certain it would still be there when he got back, the more he began to feel that he was being watched by someone other than just the curious villagers. He didn't much care for it.

"Lookin' for something 'ere, are ye, milord?"

Lindley glanced up to find a rather dirty little man sidling up to him just before he reached the tavern door. He recognized him. This was one of Fitzgelder's friends, one of the men he'd sent out almost a week ago to assassinate his cousin.

"I'm looking for some food, as a matter of fact," Lindley said. "But what of you? Weren't you supposed to be, er, taking care of something for Fitzgelder?"

The man smiled. His teeth looked even worse in the bright June sunlight than Lindley remembered from that candlelit hallway. He smelled a bit worse for the wear, too.

"I did my part on that, you can bet I did," he said. "How could I help it if the two muckbrained coves I hired to do the job ended up getting themselves bludgered to ol' Nick?"

"I see you're horribly distraught over it, too," Lindley said. "But I'm sure your employer understands that was hardly your fault."

The man simply shrugged and held the door open for Lindley. "He ain't happy, but he's got more for me to take care of now, and I don't plan on letting him down."

"Not going to hire the work out this time, are you?"

"No sir, I'm taking charge of this one myself."

The man patted his pocket, indicating he held something there that was connected to whatever this latest request from Fitzgelder was. He ushered Lindley into the dark, low-beamed tavern and indicated they should move toward a table at the far end of the room. Lindley gave his eyes a moment to adjust to the dim light and then let the man lead the way.

"In fact," his unkempt companion went on to say, "this time I'm making sure things go the way they're supposed to. I've got me some new help, and this time it's someone I think even you might approve, milord."

At that the man pulled out a knife and jabbed it up against Lindley's side.

It was a warning, clearly, for had the man wanted to gut him right there Lindley had not been prepared to defend himself. Damn it, but he knew what sort of lowlife this was. Why in St. Peter's name did he let his guard down? If the jackanapes killed him he'd have to admit he'd practically deserved it.

But the man didn't kill him. Likely he was causing untold damage to Lindley's coat, but there was no bloodshed—yet. Lindley allowed himself to be forced down into a chair.

"This time you're a part of the job, milord," his captor hissed. "And looky who I've got helping me."

Holy hell, it was Tom. Tom Feasel stepped out from behind a huge, black beam and smiled sheepishly at Lindley, holding up his gun so Lindley knew it was there.

Well, this was not turning out to be a good day. At all.

"What the devil is going on?"

"Your young friend here," the man said, pressing the knife uncomfortably into Lindley's side and jutting his chin up to indicate Tom's direction, "tells us you've been traveling with that little whore who's got a certain bit of jewelry what doesn't belong to her."

"I see my friend has been keeping closer watch over me than I've been of him," Lindley said, letting Tom see just how disappointed he was in the boy.

"So where is she?" the man asked.

Damn it, but he shouldn't have left Sophie alone there. If Fitzgelder thought for one minute she still had that locket in her possession, her life would be forfeit. Well, Lindley would just have to hope this buffoon was the only one this close to Haven Abbey. Tom clearly would be able to show the man the way, but if Lindley could convince them they had no reason for going there . . .

"I took what I wanted from her and left her along the way," Lindley said. "Like any other whore, I found if I paid her enough she'd give up anything for me."

He had no idea it would bore a hole deep into his chest to speak this way about Sophie. Yet, if it might save her, he'd plow right through every vital organ he had. He looked his uninvited companion square in the eye.

"I took the locket, if that's what you're looking for."

The man immediately shoved his free hand directly into Lindley's pocket. It was the wrong pocket, fortunately. Lindley shoved him off and was rewarded by the unnerving sound of the finest Bond Street tailoring being ripped beyond repair. *Damned cretin.*

"I don't have it on me, you mutton-head," he said. "With pickpockets and the likes of you prowling about, do you think I'd carry it in such an obvious place as my coat pocket?"

He wished he'd thought a bit more about pickpockets and thugs when he'd tucked it into his coat pocket earlier. Right now he could only hope this man was as easily misled as he was malodorous.

"Ye'd best be telling me where it is then, milord," the fool said, but he kept his hands out of any more of Lindley's pockets. "It ain't yers."

"And it won't ever be *yers* either, if you keep plugging that ruddy knife into my side. Now act like a civilized creature and we can discuss this."

The man seemed to consider it. Lindley was very nearly about to become very uncivilized himself and relieve his captor of the bloody knife—taking his chances that Tom wouldn't actually shoot him—when the man miraculously complied. He stepped away from Lindley and took his knife with him. It was, to say the least, a relief.

"I've got it put somewhere for safekeeping," Lindley said.

"Then how about if you take us there and get it for us?"

"Why, so you can take it back to Fitzgelder and he can get the treasure?"

This gave the man pause. Ah, so the mention of treasure caught his attention. Tom, however, didn't seem quite so affected.

"What treasure?" the man asked, his grip on the knife going progressively more limp.

"Didn't Fitzgelder tell you what that locket is?" Lindley asked. "It holds the secret to a treasure. No? He didn't tell you? Oh, then I suppose he doesn't intend to share."

He very much hoped he hadn't made a mistake by mentioning the treasure, especially since he knew little else about it. His information regarding that damn locket was patchy at best. If Fitzgelder knew more—and obviously he did or else why would he have had that locket to begin with—it would be dangerous to let him get his hands on it again.

That locket was Lindley's last link with D'Archaud. Without it he had nothing to bargain with and no hope of tracking him down again. He needed the locket, and he needed to get back to Loveland. And even more, he needed to know Sophie was protected from all of it. This bloody ruffian appeared to be standing in the way of accomplishing any of those goals, unfortunately.

"I'm not giving you the locket." Lindley crossed his arms in front of himself.

Yes, it made him appear obstinate and selfish—which was exactly the image he hoped to portray—but it might also add an additional layer should this cutthroat decide to shiv him and take his chances hunting the locket alone. If Tom decided to use that gun, however, he doubted crossed arms would make much difference.

"You'll give me that locket or I'll ruin this pretty cravat by making you bleed all over it," the man growled.

Now the knife was more or less aimed at his throat. What sort of establishment was this that knife-wielding patrons could partner with gun-hoisting youths and harass the nobility? Aside from the three of them, the tavern seemed to be completely empty. In a small town with only one such facility,

Lindley had to credit this to forward planning by Fitzgelder's man. So they had expected him all along, had they? He'd walked right into their trap.

Well, he could play their game. He'd come entirely too far these last three years to be thwarted now. And he was in a foul, foul mood just now.

"I've been hunting that treasure for myself," Lindley said, practically spitting the words. "I'll be damned if I hand it over to you and this . . . this traitorous pup."

"You will hand it over!" the man said, shoving his knife yet closer.

"You ought to do as he says, milord," Tom suddenly piped up. "He ain't one to tease with. Mr. Fitzgelder said we've got to get that locket, so we've got to get that locket, over yer dead body or not, milord."

"Well, if my body's dead, then who's going to be telling you where to find that locket?"

Now the man with the knife smiled at him. "There's a pretty little whore what might do just that. With a wee bit of persuading."

Lindley's blood heated at the very mention of it. These two lobcocks might just be foolhardy enough to kill him, then not even bother to check his pockets before they ran on to find Sophie. And Tom, damn him, would know right where she was.

"No. Leave her out of this."

"Ah, so ye've taken rather a liking to the handy moll, have ye?" The odiferous man pressed in closer on Lindley. "She must have some fine talent indeed. I wouldn't mind finding out about that myself."

"Very well. I'll give you the locket."

Now Tom seemed surprised. Lindley hoped the other man wouldn't recognize this. He'd given in too quickly. He should have put up more of a fight, since that was clearly what Tom expected. Truthfully, though, Lindley hated fighting. It mussed the clothes and wasted a good deal of time. Besides, if he had any hope at all of keeping Sophie safe he could hardly do it dead. Any idiot knew one unarmed man against a thug with a knife and a boy with a pistol did not represent fair odds.

He was simply biding time until he might even these odds just a bit.

"Very well. I'll take you to the locket," Lindley announced.

"So ye've come to yer wits." The thug chuckled as if it had been his clever bullying that convinced Lindley. "Let's go. Take us where ye've hid it."

"It's this way."

Lindley began to lead them back toward the door they'd just entered through.

Tom coughed. "Er, Hutch, don't you think we'd be safer to go out the back? We might've paid off the staff in here, but ain't there bound to be some bodies walking around out there he might call out to for help?"

Damn the clever boy.

"Hmm, yeah, there might be at that, my boy," the thug said, his knife coming up to poke Lindley just below the chin. "Good thinking. Come along, milord. We're going out the back. And if ye think ye can raise a scene, ye'd best think again. I've gutted better men than ye and gotten away with it, I have. Don't think I ain't above doing ye right where ye stand in broad daylight."

"And what proof do I have that you won't *do me* right where I stand one second after I give you the locket?"

"Ye've got my word."

"Ah, strangely enough, I'm not reassured," Lindley said. "How about if we find a compromise? You put that knife down, and we'll go get the locket together. Just the two of us. Unarmed."

"Ye're bloody looby if you think I'll agree to that!" Hutch-the-thug appeared honestly insulted by his suggestion.

"Very well, bring the knife, but leave the boy here."

"The knife *and* the boy are coming."

"Then you'll not be getting that locket."

"Then ye'll be getting a bright red necktie!"

"Hutch," Tom said, interrupting at a rather convenient time. "It's a small place here. We go sticking his spoon in the wall and someone will know. That won't help get us that locket, and Mr. Fitzgelder ain't going to be pleased."

His words seemed to have the right effect. Hutch stopped raging, and the knife stopped pressing into Lindley's skin.

Thankfully, he could almost breathe again. He didn't want to, though. He was too busy listening to Tom, trying to decide where the lad was going with this.

"His lordship ain't going to give us no trouble," Tom went on. "He's too soft and cared for to put up a fight. You lay down that knife so he can think straight, and I'll keep my gun on him. We'll take him to get us that locket, then let him on his way. He ain't telling nobody what we're up to; he can't. He don't want nobody to know he's been hunting French treasure and taking up with that whor . . . that girl."

What the devil was the boy up to? He knew Lindley was hardly soft or overly cared for. He knew for a fact Lindley would love nothing better than to tell the authorities everything he knew about the locket, the treasure, and this bastard ruining his clothes with his damn knife. So what was Tom doing?

Could it be possible the boy was having second thoughts about turning on him? That was rather a welcome thought. Still, he had no intentions of intervening in the thrashing his father would no doubt give him when this was all finally over.

But Hutch apparently saw reason in Tom's words. He chewed his fat lip a moment or two and then nodded. "Very well. I'll put down the knife, but Tom keeps his gun on you, Lindley. You try anything at all, and he blows a hole in you big enough to stuff in both bollocks and a boot."

Lindley thought about asking for clarification on whose bollocks, exactly, but decided not to bother.

"Don't worry, Hutch," Tom said, but his defiant young eyes were very clearly focused on Lindley. "I know what I'm doing. You can trust me."

By God, Lindley hoped he interpreted that right.

"Get us that locket, then," Hutch said, tossing his knife onto a nearby table.

Lindley nodded at Tom. "Very well. We'll go this way."

Tom stepped aside to allow Lindley to lead the way, but Lindley leapt sideways instead. He grabbed up the knife from the table where Hutch had laid it and whirled on him. All Tom had to do was shift slightly so that instead of training his gun on Lindley, now it was aimed at Hutch's heart. Thank God, he did.

"Do I snuff him, sir?" Tom asked.

Lindley paused just long enough to watch the thug sweat. "Hmm, no, I think not. Not here, anyway. Let's take him out back."

"Very good idea, sir."

Yes, Lindley had to agree that it was far better than the original plan. He much preferred any plan that left him still breathing in the end. Perhaps he would ask Feasel to forgo that thrashing, after all.

Chapter Seventeen

Sophie felt even more out of place in the bright boudoir when Madame brought her back to it. They had not walked far, just up one end of the corridor and then to the other before Madame decided it was time to return for their tea. Still, it was easy to see Haven Abbey was a beautiful place from a beautiful time in Lindley's life. Sophie knew she had no right to be here.

"Well, it appears Annie has our tea ready for us," Madame said, not bothering to keep her voice down although it was very clear that Annie was now quietly rocking her child to sleep.

The young woman was sitting in a beam of sunlight, holding little Rosie close. If the situation had not been so very unconventional, the pair would have made the most lovely portrait. But unlike the subjects gracing those portraits in the corridor, Annie and her child were not very likely to ever be immortalized that way. A sad, heartbroken whore and her fatherless child were not very much like Lady Marie and her bright-eyed little heir. Especially not considering that Annie was very much alive while Marie was not.

"Shall we sit, Sophie?" Madame asked.

"I poured for you, Madame," Annie said with a sober gravity that was completely beyond anything tea deserved, ready or not ready. "Your cup is on the left."

Madame led them to the little table where Mrs. W had placed it. There was only one empty chair in the room, so Madame took it and motioned for Sophie to sit on the bed. Annie was in the other chair, near the window, her arms wrapped tight around her slumbering babe.

"Annie, would you come join us?" Madame asked.

"Certainly I can take her tea to her," Sophie said, reaching for a cup.

But Madame nearly slapped it out of her hand.

"Annie will join us. Sit down, Sophie. Annie, which cup have you poured for dear Sophie?"

Sophie could hardly see what it mattered which cup was for whom. As if Madame needed to disturb Annie from her comfortable place and risk waking the babe. Sophie could certainly have put in her own milk and sugar; Madame had not needed to order Annie to do it. Yet Annie was already rising from her seat, carefully laying her child on a little pallet she had prepared in the corner. The babe stirred only slightly, so Annie left her to come quickly to their little grouping at the tea table.

"This one is for you, Madame," Annie said, indicating a cup and then pointing to another. "And this one is for Sophie."

"And what of you, Annie?" Madame asked.

"I do not think I like tea just now, Madame," Annie said.

"Ah, I see," Madame repeated. She placed her own cup back onto the tray.

It was the most bizarre exchange. If it hadn't been regarding nothing more than half-cold tea, Sophie would have been tempted to believe it meant something quite momentous. She was, however, glad to see the babe slept on and did not wake.

"But Sophie likes tea," Madame announced. "Come along, dear, do not insult Annie. She went to great trouble to make it just as you like it."

They were both watching her intently. Sophie picked up her cup and smiled for Annie.

"Thank you. I'm sure it is just fine," Sophie said, taking a sip and finding it to be, as Madame predicted, just the way she liked it. She smiled at Annie and sipped again.

"Very good," Madame said, rising. "I should go and confer with Mrs. W as to what we shall be having for dinner."

"Dinner?" Sophie asked. "Will we be staying as long as that? I rather expected we would be on our way to London."

Annie squeaked a bit. That also seemed as if it should mean something, but as Sophie did not speak Squeak she couldn't imagine what it might be. This whole day was quite beyond comprehension.

"London? Oh, but it seems as if Annie is not as eager to return as you are," Madame said. "Fortunately for her, then, I should mention I have pressing business in the area. I'm afraid we will be staying a bit longer, my dear Sophie."

"Business, Madame?" Sophie asked.

What business could Madame possibly have here at Haven Abbey? Especially with Lindley gone?

"So, ladies, please drink your tea and relax," Madame said and rose with an elegant flourish. "Annie, you're very welcome to drink mine, if you like."

"No," Annie said, staring at her hands in her lap. "I think I am not thirsty, Madame."

The older woman laughed. "Yes, I supposed you might not be. But Sophie is. See that you take plenty of the stuff, my dear. And I expect to find you resting when I return. Annie, it would be well for you to see that she rests."

"Yes, Madame," Annie said. "I understand."

With that, Madame glided out of the room, and Annie dropped quietly to sit in the chair she had vacated. She seemed to glance up at Sophie with an expression of hopeful anticipation when Sophie raised her teacup to her lips. It made her a bit self-conscious, but Sophie smiled and sipped. Anything to help ease Annie's obvious nervousness.

"You should take some tea, Annie," Sophie said to break the awkward quiet. "You look as if you did not sleep well last night."

"No. We did not, I'm afraid." Annie looked away from her, studying her lap instead.

"Did you leave the inn as Madame planned and go to wait for me? I'm so very sorry I did not join you. I wanted to, but Lindley insisted on . . ."

Annie glanced up, and her soft brown eyes held such concern Sophie wished to heaven she'd not been the cause of any worry for her friend. Yet she knew she had been.

"He did not . . . er, he was not unpleasant toward you, Sophie?"

Sophie blushed. "He was not. You need have no fear on that count."

"I am glad. If only . . . well, I wish Madame had not asked that of you."

"I wish *you* had not had to wonder what happened to me. Did you wait out on the road very long?"

Now Annie was looking at her lap again. "Er, no. Madame was concerned for you, so we stayed in the inn. We realized Lindley took you away, but then there was a fire!"

"Good heavens, a fire?"

"It was put out quickly, but we were forced to move our things to the inn across the street for the night. Rosie was quite upset by it all, and I was overly worried for you."

Sophie took another sip of her tea and patted her friend's hand. Oddly, her aim was off and she missed it the first time. Perhaps she truly did need rest as much as Madame seemed to believe.

"You are a good friend, Annie. I would do anything to help you and Rosie make a better life. You know I would."

She supposed she'd mostly meant the words rhetorically, but Annie was watching her closely now. Too closely. It made her somewhat uncomfortable, in fact. Perhaps she'd insulted her friend by bringing up such a painful subject.

"Do you really mean that?" Annie asked.

"Of course," Sophie assured her. "You've been like a sister to me, Annie. And I love little Rosie as if she were my own niece."

Now Annie's eyes grew shiny and somewhat red around the edges. She appeared to be blinking back tears. Sophie reached out again and this time took her hand.

"I am so glad you found me here, Annie."

But Annie shook her head and began mumbling. "Don't be, Sophie."

"Of course I'm glad you're here. Why, look at Rosie sleeping so soundly, and here you are giving me such excellent tea."

To show just how grateful she was, she took another hearty gulp of it.

Yet Annie simply hung her head and mumbled all the more. "I never told you, Sophie. I wanted to, but . . . oh, I should have told you."

"Told me what?" Sophie asked.

"I'm not your sister, Sophie."

Now Sophie laughed. "No, of course you're not really my sister, Annie. I know that."

She took another sip of tea but nearly spit it out when Annie spoke again.

"No, but Rosie is."

"What?" Sophie asked quickly, the room seeming to sway around her.

"I never told you who my lover was, Sophie, because he begged me not to. He said you were only safe if you knew nothing about him. But it's true; Rosie's father is also *your* father."

Sophie could barely grasp the words. What was Annie saying? *Papa* was her lover? Tiny little Rosie was her *sister*? Well, that was unexpected news. Good heavens, it was enough to make her head spin. In fact, her head *was* spinning.

Or maybe it really was the room.

What was going on? She knew she was still sitting quietly on the bed across from Annie, but suddenly Sophie felt as if her head were floating off her body and soaring around the room. Her hands shook, slopping tea.

"Here you go, Sophie," Annie said, leaving her chair to come to her side. "Drink some more. It will help."

She did drink, but it did not help. In fact, it made things worse. She found she could not focus on Annie anymore. It began to appear as if there were two Annies, and Sophie was quite certain that had never been the case before.

Oh no, this had happened before! At the surgeon's house, when Papa had given her something to drink. *Drat it all.* She'd been drugged again! She tossed the teacup away, but of course the damage had been done.

"I'm so sorry, Sophie," Annie was saying, pushing her slightly so that she fell back into the soft bedding. "I had no choice. Madame threatened me—she'll send Rosie away if I don't do everything she asks of me."

Sophie felt the darkness closing around her, as she floated into a warm, soft oblivion.

"Sleep, Sophie," Annie was mumbling, her voice far, far away. "It's for your own good. Your father will help if he can. I know he will."

Sophie wanted to laugh, but that would have taken so much effort. Instead she simply muttered, "You and Papa are too well suited for each other."

"IS HE DEAD?" TOM ASKED.

Hutch lay face-first in the mud in the deserted alleyway behind the tavern.

"No, I didn't hit him that hard," Lindley replied. "He'll wake up wishing us dead, I don't doubt. You've made some pretty unsavory friends here, Tom. I daresay you won't want them finding you anytime soon."

"Damn. I was hoping he might trust me awhile longer," Tom grumbled.

"Why in God's name would you want that? Your father didn't send you out to pry information from him this way, did he?"

"No, sir. I've been doing some things my father don't quite know about."

"I see. And obviously running around with thugs like this is one of them."

"This is one of Fitzgelder's men," Tom said. "But I wasn't going to help him get that locket back to Fitzgelder, I swear to you, milord."

"Here, help me tie him," Lindley said, noticing a tangle of twine discarded among a pile of refuse. "You can explain to me later how you came to be with such a character."

"Actually, sir . . ." Tom said, taking up the twine but then putting it back down. "I'd rather not explain things, if I can possibly avoid it."

"Yes, I'm certain you would rather. Hand me that twine."

"He's going to be all over angry with you, sir. You ought to just let me kill him."

"I'd rather you not have blood on your hands on my account, Tom. I'll just have to take care he doesn't find me."

"He'll hunt you, sir."

"I can look after myself."

A light seemed to go on behind Tom's eyes. "Unless he thinks I killed you, milord!"

"You killed me? Now, you must excuse me if I don't rush into believing that's a marvelous idea."

"If you was dead, milord, these dogs of Fitzgelder's would give up the chase. We could fake your death!"

Well, when put like that, Lindley had to admit the boy's idea had some merit. It had a few holes, too.

"And what will he do when he wants to search my body for the locket?"

Tom frowned. "Oh. I suppose he would insist on that, wouldn't he?"

"Yes, I'm sure he would, and then . . ." But Lindley paused. "Although if he believed the locket was someplace other than my corpse, perhaps he wouldn't need to see a body. We would be free to go find D'Archaud while these others think me dead."

"Aye, that might do it, milord."

"Very well then, Tom. You may tell our friend Hutch when he wakes that you led me to trust you just so you could get information about the locket, then you murdered me and disposed of my body. Think you can convince him to take that news to Fitzgelder?"

"I can do it, sir. But where would you have me tell him that locket is?"

Lindley thought for just a moment. "Tell him . . . tell him I posted it. To my dear friend Madame Eudora."

Tom was momentarily surprised, but then he smiled. "Yes, that should do nicely, milord. I think that's damned genius."

"Thank you, Tom. Now hurry. I suspect we don't have long before your partner there wakes up. We've got to make things look as if you rid the world of my poor body."

"Can I say I threw you in the river?"

"It's not much of a river here, is it, Tom? No, something far less worthy of my station, I should think."

"How about a hay cart? Can I say I tossed you up into a hay cart and hid you there and the driver left with it for Coventry?"

"Hmm, perhaps . . ."

"Or manure, sir? Perhaps you are in a load of manure carted off to parts unknown? Surely he'd be disinclined to hunt for you there."

Lindley had to laugh. "Very well. Manure it is. I should think Fitzgelder would get particular enjoyment from that notion."

"Indeed, especially as he will think it gets him nearer to that locket. He is determined to find it, sir. He said you would probably get it from the girl, so he sent us after you, but I heard him say he's got someone taking care of her just in case."

Lindley's lip curled at the thought of Fitzgelder "taking care of" Sophie. Thank God he'd left her somewhere safe. Still, even knowing she was secure in Haven Abbey with Feasel keeping guard, Lindley could not be at ease. Not until this was over and he had proof enough to see Fitzgelder hanged. All he needed for that was to find D'Archaud.

"And what of word from Loveland?" Lindley asked, leaving Hutch propped against a discarded crate. "I still do not know if D'Archaud has met up with those actors."

"I wish I had news for ye, milord."

"I'll just have to go back there and keep watch until you can join me. You'll be well enough here until then? You can handle yourself with this ruffian when he wakes?"

"I'll be fine, sir."

"Then let's set our stage, shall we?"

The boy nodded energetically. "I'm looking forward to it, milord."

Lindley wasn't sure how he ought to take that.

HER ARMS FELT SO HEAVY, AS IF A GREAT WEIGHT RESTED on them. She tried to pick up her head to look around, but it seemed her whole body was pinned to the bed. She could barely even open her eyes.

But she had to, for some reason. She knew she had to open her eyes, move her arms, get out of this place. Where was this place, anyway?

It was all a blur. Was Lindley here? He would know what was wrong; he could help her. She tried to look for him, but her silly eyes just would not open for her. Papa? Was he here? Nothing made sense.

A soft hand touched her forehead. It felt cool, and she wished it would linger, but it did not. She heard voices.

They were close by, hovering over her. Were they angels? The one voice was so soft, so pretty . . . it could have been an angel. But no, angels would never sound so sad. The soft hand was touching her again, lifting her head up off the pillow. My, but how could such a soft little hand be so very strong to lift something so enormously heavy as her head?

It seemed ridiculously silly, and Sophie wanted to laugh. She was laughing, perhaps. But there was no sound. Just the sad, sad voice near her head.

"She's sleeping, Madame. She doesn't need more," the voice said.

"Give it to her, Annie. We can't have her waking up and making a commotion. No one needs to know about this. Not yet, anyway."

This voice was not so sad. Not very sweet either. She decided she very much did not like this voice, though it seemed she could almost recognize it. If only her eyes would open, but they would not. That suddenly seemed very funny, too. Yes, perhaps all of it was a great joke and she was laughing.

Still, though, she would have expected to hear it.

The soft hand put something to her lips, and she had to swallow or else choke on the bitter liquid that was poured down her throat. *Tea?* My, but what dreadful tea they had in this place. She wished they did not force it on her this way. Grandmamma would be appalled at such manners!

And then it seemed very funny again. Oh, what a lovely day this must be for her to find everything so inordinately humorous. Wouldn't Lindley love to hear about it? She would have to tell him.

But where was he? She should have heard his voice by now. He should be here; she was quite sure she'd been looking for him. Why wasn't he here? She needed him here.

"She's calling for someone," the sweet, sad voice said. "Lindley, I believe."

The other voice gave a grating laugh. "Let her call for him all she wants. He won't hear her. I paid good money so that he won't hear anything ever again."

Nothing was making sense. Why would Lindley not hear

her? The harsh voice said he could not. Had something happened? Yes, she seemed to recall she'd been worried over something . . . something important. But what was it? Was it Lindley? Was he in some sort of trouble?

She choked as more liquid was poured into her mouth. Her head was so heavy, and now the room seemed to be moving, perhaps carrying her away to somewhere else. Yes, somewhere else would be lovely.

Oh, she hoped they would have better tea wherever she was going. And Lindley. It would be so nice if he were there with her. She wanted Lindley with her so very badly. And she'd really like to laugh, but she just couldn't. Nothing at all seemed remotely worth laughing at suddenly.

SILENTLY LINDLEY MOVED CLOSER. HE'D BEEN KEEPing watch over Loveland several hours now, and so far nothing seemed to be happening. The actors were indeed in residence, and they seemed perfectly content to stay. There was no sign of messengers coming or going, and certainly no sign of D'Archaud.

Was the man gone? Was he not coming? Or could he already be there, hidden in the house? In the daylight Lindley had been afraid to get close enough to find out. But finally night had fallen, and he decided it would be safe enough to draw nearer.

Now he was as close as he could get. He laid his hand on the old whitewashed wall of the cottage and crept behind a mountainous lavender that seemed almost to burst from its bed. There was a window just above. Lindley inched his way up to peer through.

Inside a fire glowed, and he could make out several men lounging about. D'Archaud was not one of them. *Damn.*

Ah, but their voices did carry. One man in particular was quite jovial and boisterous. And French. Lord, but that man was French.

He rattled on in English, carelessly tossing out phrases here and there that gave away his heritage. When the group spontaneously broke into song, this one sang in French. A middle-aged woman came in to join them and was dragged into a dance until she nearly tripped over the feet of one of the younger men. Everyone laughed and wine flowed. Actors, indeed.

Yet there was no sign of Sophie's useless father. Lindley wondered if perhaps he had already missed D'Archaud, if he'd been here, discovered the treasure without the use of that locket, and left his friends behind to celebrate their portion of it. Could Lindley have been so close only to have lost the man? D'Archaud could be halfway back to France by now.

Approaching voices startled him, and Lindley practically dove for cover behind an overgrown rose. Who on earth could be coming? Riders on horseback from what he could hear. He strained to listen.

Two riders trotted up to the cottage and dismounted. Lindley dared to peek out and was a bit disappointed to find not D'Archaud there in the moonlight, but two servants wearing Dashford's livery. What in the devil could this be about?

One servant held the horses and another went to the house. He knocked politely on the front door. The squatters inside were suddenly quiet. The man knocked again, and this time Lindley could hear footsteps. How would these actors take a visit from Dashford's men? He slipped one of the pistols he'd retrieved from his carriage out from its place at his waist.

The voice of the Frenchman sounded at the door. Apparently he'd chosen to greet these servants as guests rather than fight. Lindley listened.

The servant informed the Frenchman that this cottage was owned by the viscount Dashford. It appeared Dashford had heard the troupe of actors had come to stay here and had a request. Instead of booting them out on their ears, it seemed his lordship would very much like the troupe to come to his home in the morning to provide entertainment for some guests the lord was hosting.

The Frenchman agreed without hesitation and asked the servants to please send their gratitude to his lordship for the hospitality. It was all very polite, and in minutes the two Dashford men were back on their way to Hartwood. Lindley was alone in the darkness, wondering what this was all about. What on earth would make Dashford insist on hosting these actors as entertainment for his guests?

And just what guests could those be? Certainly the house had been quite full when Lindley was there for the wedding several days ago, but hadn't the poor man been able to get his bride alone at this point? Lindley was fairly certain that if he himself ever did get around to taking a bride he'd not want a houseful of guests—and certainly not actors!—three days into what ought to be a rather enjoyable honeymoon.

No, if he had the opportunity to get Sophie all to himself in his big sprawling home, he'd certainly not want to waste any time with . . .

Good God, what was he imagining? Sophie in his house? Certainly not. He couldn't do that. A gentleman did not bring that sort of woman into his home. Haven Abbey was one thing, but to bring her to Durmond Park, his family seat? It was not done. Someday he'd have to keep a proper wife there, not someone like Sophie.

And then the panic hit. *A proper wife?* Hellfire, he could never be happy with the sort of wife he'd be expected to take one day, some blue-blooded diamond who'd been raised since birth to be more interested in her place in society than her place in Lindley's heart. He knew a lifetime being shackled to someone proper and appropriate was expected of him, but Lord, the idea was depressing. How could he ever be content with someone like that, someone who was not . . . damn it, someone who was not Sophie!

By God, if he was going to install some pretty young wife at his ancient family home, it was going to have to be Sophie Darshaw. And he was sure as hell going to spend an awful lot of time there with her. No acting troupe would be needed.

He slumped back against the wall and ignored the rose thorns that poked him in various places. He was hopelessly in love with Sophie, wasn't he? How on earth did that happen? Certainly he'd been attracted to her right from the start. What red-blooded man wouldn't be? Certainly he'd enjoyed his time with her, taken pleasure in their passion . . . that was all to be expected. But to fall in *love* with her? Well, that was quite another matter.

And it irked him to no end when he realized he'd done nothing to encourage her to feel the same way toward him. Hell, he'd left her alone to come all the way out there and drag her father off to the gallows! Damn it, but he'd only given Sophie reason to hate him. That hurt.

Well, starting now he would be changing his plans. He'd do everything in his power to make up for what he'd done, how he'd treated her. He'd somehow find her father and . . .

Footsteps interrupted him. He realized he was no longer alone here in the yard. Through the roses he caught a glimpse of a figure moving quickly, approaching the cottage from the narrow lane that led out to the main road.

It was a young man on foot, as far as Lindley could tell. There was no sign of livery, and everything about the man's halting movements said he was hoping to avoid detection. He dashed up to the front door and let himself inside without knocking. Lindley slid back up to listen at the window.

The young man made his presence known inside right away. Instantly the actors made a great fuss over him. Apparently his arrival was an unexpected pleasure for them. Lindley was glad when the party filed into the room nearest him, just inside the window.

He eavesdropped shamefully; it only took a moment to make a startling discovery. The newcomer was not a young man. It was a woman—the same actress who had been in Fitzgelder's house, who had posed as Sophie's husband. As to where she'd been in the time since they were divided at the posting house, he had that answer quickly.

She'd been at Dashford's. She made no mention of Rastmoor, and Lindley wondered what she'd done with him. It was not a mark in her favor that the Frenchman seemed so happy to see her. Lindley was still trying to puzzle out that relationship when another piece of news caught his attention.

The actress announced that Fitzgelder was at Hartwood. He apparently was one of the guests Dashford would like the actors to entertain. To their credit, none of the actors sounded exactly thrilled to hear that name. Neither was Lindley.

After some nervous debate, the Frenchman calmed his troupe and told them he would handle things. The older woman in the group herded everyone to the kitchen for something she had been cooking, and little by little the noisy group filed out of earshot. He waited a moment before moving, just to be certain he would not be detected.

Fitzgelder is at Hartwood. Damn, but somehow while Lindley had kept Feasel guarding the abbey and Tom had been scheming in Lack Wooton, their dangerous quarry had slipped past and gone on to Hartwood, of all places. This was news indeed. What could have taken him there? Did he expect Lindley to go there with the locket? Perhaps he'd not gotten word yet that Lindley was dead. Or perhaps Tom had failed and their ruse had been found out.

Damn, but where was Tom? He glanced at his pocket watch. It was getting late. What should he do? *Hell.* He knew what he should *not* do.

He should *not* sit here waiting for D'Archaud when Tom was somewhere risking his life to save Lindley's skin and Sophie was alone back at Haven Abbey. By God, he was a fool. He knew exactly what he should do.

First, he would find the boy. Indeed, the lad had helped him, and now he must need Lindley's help. Lindley would go back to Lack Wooton. Then he would find out what Fitzgelder was doing at Hartwood. Perhaps Dashford was in danger. The man was his friend; Lindley could hardly sit idly by. He had a responsibility to the living as well as the dead.

The truth came barreling at him, and Lindley was forced to admit he'd made a monumental error. He'd been stalking the wrong prey. D'Archaud was not his target. Whatever the man had done in the past, he was not the orchestrator. Even if he had been Fitzgelder's willing assistant, his capture would gain Lindley nothing. Lindley needed to let go of the past and focus on today. He needed to let go of D'Archaud.

Then maybe, by some miracle, Sophie might find a way to forgive him.

Chapter Eighteen

Sophie pulled the bedcovers up closer and realized her whole body ached. Heavens, but she felt as if she'd been sleeping for ages. She cracked her groggy eyes open and realized by the darkness around her that, most likely, she had been.

Good heavens, what time was it? Last thing she recalled was . . . She had to think for a moment before her mind could clear enough for her to remember. What had she been doing just before . . .

The tea! Lord above, but Annie had drugged her tea. Yes, Sophie could remember that now. And worse . . . she remembered Madame. Sophie's memory was hazy, but she could quite clearly recall Madame's voice, speaking horrible things about Lindley. Dear God, Madame had claimed Lindley was dead!

Sophie jerked up to sitting. Her head throbbed. Her stomach churned. She blinked into the darkness, hoping it was all a dream. Of course it wasn't.

"Sophie, what is it?"

She glanced over to find Annie sitting nearby, one dim taper glowing beside her. She looked awful; her face was pale and her eyes were red and swollen. Gracious, what had happened? Sophie's heart pounded.

"Lindley . . . is he . . . ?"

Annie shushed her and came to sit on the bed beside her. "You must keep quiet, Sophie. No one must hear you."

"Keep quiet? But Madame said . . . and you drugged my tea . . . and . . . where's Rosie?"

"Madame took her," Annie said. "She only allows me a few minutes at a time with her."

"Why?"

"Because she knows I hate what she's doing. She knows I'd never cooperate if Rosie's very life didn't depend on it!"

"Her very life? What on earth is Madame doing?"

"Please, Sophie, you've got to remain quiet. I assured Madame I would not allow you to wake up. She believes I gave you more, er, tea this evening so you will sleep through the night."

"She's forcing you to drug me?"

"Hush, yes."

"But why?"

"So you will not cause any trouble for her or ruin her plans."

"And her plans involve . . . murdering Lindley?"

"I'm so sorry, Sophie. Madame believes he has that locket she wants and . . . well, there are some very bad men who do whatever she says."

"She sent someone to . . . to kill him to get that silly locket?"

"It's hardly a silly locket, Sophie! Hush, now. She should be coming to check on you any moment. No matter what happens, you must let her think you are asleep."

"I need to get away from here. All of us—you, me, and Rosie. We've got to go help Lindley."

"Sophie, we're trapped here in a castle! Even if we could get away, where would we go?"

"I don't know, but I can't sit by and do nothing, not if there's a chance . . ."

"There's not. I'm sorry, Sophie. We just have to do as Madame says until she gets what she wants."

"And that is . . . ?"

Annie was quiet a moment before she replied. "She wants your father's money."

"That's absurd. My father doesn't have any money! Don't tell me that's why you became involved with him. You thought he had money?"

"No! Of course not. I fell in love with your father before I knew any of this. But it's true; he's a very wealthy man."

"Annie, he's been dead for years . . . How could he have any money?"

"I don't know; he won't talk about it and . . . and I haven't seen him for weeks now. But I do know that locket is the key to some sort of treasure. Madame wants it."

"And she's willing to kill Lindley for it."

All this time she'd thought Madame and Lindley were . . . friends. How could the woman turn on him so? Sophie's head ached, and she felt weak as a child. Madame was not at all the woman she thought she'd known. She and Annie simply had to find a way out of there. Perhaps they could . . .

"Listen . . . I think I hear her coming!"

Sure enough, Madame's voice was just outside in the corridor, directing the servants. The bedroom door opened half a heartbeat after Sophie dropped back down onto her pillow and shut her eyes. She listened while carefully keeping her breathing low and regular.

"Yes, yes, the girl is fine," Madame was saying as she breezed into the room.

"His lordship meant for us to look after her," Mrs. Wimpole said on her heels, with more than a little annoyance in her tone.

"Well, look at her," Madame said. "See? She's fine. I told you, she's very tired. Annie's been sitting with her. Now, go away and stop buzzing around like an unwanted bee. When I have need of you, I'll ring."

Mrs. Wimpole huffed, but Sophie heard the door shut and only one set of footsteps continue in. Madame's, no doubt. She could feel the woman's eyes on her, probably looming over and assuring herself that Sophie was, indeed, well. And unconscious.

"She appears to be breathing," Madame commented.

"Yes, she's quite comfortable," Annie said.

"She's not going to wake up anytime soon, is she?"

"No, of course not. The laudanum seems to agree with her."

Sophie heard Madame chuckle. The nerve of the woman to chuckle over her when she was pretending to be insensible! And to think Sophie had once looked at Madame Eudora as almost a second mother. Well, as of right now she did not get along with her mother. At all.

"Good. That will be of use when our guest arrives from London."

"What?" Annie said, and Sophie recognized the concern in her voice. "Who is coming from London?"

"Oh, just a gentleman who's been, shall we say, interested in meeting little Sophie. I owe him a favor, so I sent him word that he ought to pop in for a visit. I expect him first thing tomorrow. Sophie should be adequately, er, pliable by then."

"Oh, Madame! Please, you cannot do that to her. You know her father will do as you say. He'll pay that ransom, I know he will."

Again, the older woman chuckled. "Oh, I have no doubt he'll pay. After all, I've got his entire family right here in the palm of my hand, don't I? He'll give me what I've asked for—eventually. Why should I not bring in a little additional profit in the meantime?"

"But she's not . . . Madame, you know she's innocent."

This time Madame's laugh was more than a mere chuckle. It was like a guffaw, as a matter of fact. Sophie was quite miffed, and it was all she could do to keep herself silent and still.

"Don't be so naive, Annie! She's been traveling with Lindley. I assure you the man has sullied our little dove. More than once, I would imagine. Indeed, the girl is well primed for her eager visitor."

"But you told her father you would look after her! That she would be safe if he paid you quickly."

"Honestly, Annie, your sentimentality is sickening. I thought we agreed you would do exactly as I say in exchange for me not tossing your child off the ramparts."

Annie squeaked in horror at the very thought of such a

thing. Sophie could hardly believe her ears—Madame was a monster! Good heavens, how could she never have realized just what the woman was capable of? Well, Sophie was simply going to have to save them all somehow.

"Stop your whimpering," Madame said. "I want you to stay in here tonight to see that Sophie stays nice and quiet. When your little brat starts hollering again, I'll have that useless housekeeper bring her in for you. I can't abide the way that child interrupts my sleep every night."

"I could get her now," Annie offered.

"No, you will keep an eye on Sophie now. Remember, Annie, do as I say and things will go well for you. If you choose to do something foolish, however . . ."

"Yes, Madame. I understand."

"Good. I always knew you were a smart girl, Annie."

"Thank you, Madame."

Annie sounded as if her heart were broken. Madame's footsteps went toward the door, and Sophie could hear it open. She did not stir even though her neck was at an odd angle and was beginning to ache dreadfully. She waited what felt like an eternity before finally she heard Madame march out into the corridor. The door shut behind her and all was silent. Annie let out a halting breath.

Sophie waited just a few moments to make sure Madame would not come back, and then she sighed, too, stretching her arms and moving her head to get the kink out of her neck. Oh, but what a mess they were in! Madame was waiting for Papa to somehow pay a ransom? Surely that would never happen. She had no idea where Madame and Annie got any notion Papa had money, but she was quite certain they were mistaken. No ransom would come to rescue them.

"I didn't know Madame was planning to invite someone here, Sophie."

"I can't imagine who it would be."

"I can," Annie said. Sophie did not miss the dread in her friend's voice. "That man who used to ask after you all the time."

"Who on earth was that?"

She wished it had been Lindley. Judging from Annie's tone, however, she knew it was nothing like that. Lindley had only been interested in her because she was her father's daughter. Whoever this man was, he obviously had other things on his mind. Good heavens, but what on earth would she do if Madame's friend showed up and expected, er, these other things? Her flesh crawled at the very thought.

"His name is Warren," Annie said. "I believe Madame calls him Captain. He works for the government in some capacity, but none of the girls like him. He has certain preferences . . ."

Annie didn't finish that statement. She didn't have to. It was common knowledge that Madame prided herself in accommodating certain preferences. She paid Sophie good money to create articles to facilitate some of these. Usually these special clients were harmless, although she'd heard whispers of some who weren't. What on earth did Madame have in mind for her?

"I don't know what to do, Sophie," Annie went on. "Perhaps it would be better for you if you did take the laudanum."

"No! Heavens, Annie, I will not simply lie down and give up. There must be some way out of this."

"But how?"

How indeed? Sophie's mind raced, desperate to think of something they could do. But what resources did they have? They were two women and a baby. How were they to slip away undetected in the middle of the night? Madame had her sources; she would find them in a heartbeat. And she'd be furious!

Oh, if only Sophie could believe Lindley were somewhere out there thinking of her, wondering about her. But of course she could not even know if he was still alive. She prayed that he was, but even then she knew he would be no help to them. That little purse full of coins told her she had fulfilled her purpose for him. Lindley—if he did survive Madame's schemes—was through with her.

She needed to think of Annie, of little Rosie. She needed to find their way out of this. She needed a plan, she needed courage, and she needed to believe Lindley was safe, out there somewhere thinking fondly of her. Indeed, there were a great many things she needed right now.

Apparently, what she needed most was a miracle.

There was a knock at the door and both women jumped.

Sophie quickly fell back into her pillow, adjusting her covers approximately as they had been minutes ago. This time she kept her head turned so that she could crack her eyes open just slightly to see who might be here to make life yet more complicated for them.

Annie took a deep breath and went to open the door. It was Mrs. Wimpole with Rosie.

"Miss Eudora sent for me to bring her to you," she said, cradling the fussy baby and glancing in Sophie's direction.

"Thank you," Annie said, smiling as she took the child. "I'm sure this is all we'll need tonight. Madame said I am to sleep in here to keep an eye on Miss Darshaw."

"Oh? And why exactly does Miss D'Archaud need so much attention?" Mrs. Wimpole asked. "It isn't normal for a healthy young woman to sleep so much. Should I call for a doctor?"

"No!" Annie said quickly, doing her best to settle Rosie, who very obviously did not care for all this conversation and would much prefer a meal. "She's fine. Really, you may go to your bed now."

But Mrs. Wimpole didn't leave. "His lordship was quite worried for Miss D'Archaud. I'm not at all convinced he would be pleased to find that you and Miss Eudora have got her in that bed there like a prisoner. Now step aside and let me look in on her myself."

"No, it truly is not necessary . . ." Annie said but cut herself off before Rosie's crying could get out of hand.

It would not do at all to alert Madame to this confrontation. Sophie half expected to find the woman charging into her chamber at any moment. Mrs. Wimpole did not back down. Her feet shuffled just slightly as she moved toward the bed and laid her hand on Sophie's forehead. Sophie pinched her eyes shut tight.

"See? She is perfectly well," Annie said.

"Then why does she not rouse herself with all the commotion your child is making?" the housekeeper inquired. "I'm no fool, miss. I know what sort of person Miss Eudora has become, and I have my suspicions about you. I can see that you are up to no good where Miss D'Archaud is concerned, and I know his lordship wouldn't stand for it. I've got half a mind to call for the magistrate."

Oh, wouldn't Madame just love that? The magistrate would probably throw them all out into the dark. Madame would be furious, then little Rosie truly would be at her mercy, and it seemed mercy was a trait Madame was sadly lacking. No, Sophie certainly could not let the woman call for the magistrate.

"Please do not send for the magistrate," she said, pushing the covers aside and sitting up.

Annie made her familiar squeaking sound, but Mrs. Wimpole jammed her fists into her hips and glared at Sophie in the flickering candlelight.

"So you're not asleep," she said.

"No, but Madame must believe I am," Sophie announced. "Please, Mrs. Wimpole. We need your help."

The woman eyed her, raising one brow and waiting for an explanation. Sophie cleared her throat before giving her one.

"Madame Eudora plans to murder Lord Lindley."

She thought the servant would deny any such possibility—it sounded absurd even as Sophie said it. But the woman did not. She merely kept her stern gaze directly on Sophie and waited.

"Go on," she said.

"Madame wants Lindley dead so she can take something he has," Sophie explained as quickly as she could. "And she is holding us here for ransom from my father. Annie is . . . er, my stepmother."

Well, that sounded even more absurd. What could it mean about her life when the truth had become far more unbelievable than a lie? So far, though, Mrs. Wimpole was still listening. Apparently she wasn't quite ready to discount Sophie's claims and toss them out into the night.

"What can I do to help you?" she asked finally.

By God, those were wonderful words. Sophie breathed in relief and smiled.

"Thank you, Mrs. Wimpole," she said. "First, could you tell me, what exactly do you keep in that rather formidable tower I saw as we arrived?"

LINDLEY PULLED SOPHIE CLOSE, HOLDING HER WARM body and enjoying the feel of her skin against his. She moaned and was agreeable to his advances, snuggling against him and sighing with pleasure. He wanted to bury himself in her, to hear her breathing his name in ecstasy, and then keep her here with him like this forever. He knew all he had to do was speak the words.

Yet it was as if his voice would not come. No air could enter his lungs. The more he tried to speak, to cry out his love and his intentions for her, the tighter his lungs became. Sophie began to slip away.

His fingertips dug into the bedding for her, but he just couldn't reach her. She was simply gone, suddenly and painfully. He tried to call her back but still he was mute as death.

And then he woke up. He'd been dreaming, hadn't he? Yet it was a dream too close to real life. He was alone and Sophie was gone.

Damn, but he had not meant to sleep so hard. He'd taken this room over the shabby public house in Lack Wooton simply to rest and refresh himself. He'd not meant to spend the night dreaming of things that could never be. What had he missed as he slumbered? Anything might have happened.

D'Archaud might have joined the actors at Loveland by now, and Sophie may have left Haven Abbey. Tom may have never found his way back, and Lindley might very well be completely on his own today, with thugs out looking to kill him and Fitzgelder's plan playing out at Hartwood.

By God, he'd had no business sleeping. A cold, hard dread settled in Lindley's stomach. Something was wrong; he just knew it.

Worse, he knew it involved Sophie. He had to get to her. He'd have to give up on everything else. Sophie was all that mattered now. There was no time to waste. Lindley dressed and called for his carriage as quickly possible.

He was just climbing into the carriage when Tom appeared. Lindley was glad to see the young man still among the living, and even more glad to see him alone. There was no sign of the thug he'd been with yesterday or any other of Fitzgelder's unsavories.

"Milord!" Tom called out, waving as if there might be any chance Lindley did not see him across the yard. "I have news. From Haven Abbey."

That cold dread turned into ice. "What is it? What has happened? Is Miss Darshaw well?"

"She's gone, milord!"

"What? Gone where? What have you learned?"

"I went to my father, to see if he had encountered trouble," Tom said, his winded horse dancing beneath him. "As I was with him, though, a rider left the abbey in the night."

"What rider? Who was it?"

"I followed him to learn that very thing. Turns out he's one of Eudora's boys."

"Eudora? Why should she have anyone at Haven Abbey?"

"Because she's there herself, milord."

Lindley could scarcely believe it as Tom explained what he'd learned. Eudora had arrived at the abbey yesterday, shortly after his departure. From what the rider said when Tom caught and questioned him—and Lindley had no doubt Tom and his father did a thorough job of that—Eudora had known Sophie would be there and she'd gone to get the locket. She was planning to hold Sophie until D'Archaud collected his treasure and would ransom the girl rather than see her put to work in the brothel.

He half believed Eudora would do such a thing, too. Surely his loyalty to her should have prevented such thoughts, but for some reason it did not. He could not help but fear Sophie was in very real danger, indeed.

"But there's more," Tom added.

"What more? Spill it."

"Well, it seems Miss Darshaw has taken off."

"She's left the abbey? Damn. Where would she go?"

"I don't know. She was there one minute, and the next thing Madame knows she's gone somehow. Eudora's angrier than you can imagine—worried she won't get that ransom now."

"She's a fool. D'Archaud hasn't cared much what happened to his daughter over the last four years; why should she expect he'd suddenly be willing to pay ransom for her? Damn! What is the girl thinking, running out in the middle of the night?"

"The man said Madame seemed to think she was off to find you."

"Me?" He was remarkably flattered at the idea of it. Could Sophie really have run away, hoping to find him?

"To warn you, sir. Apparently, the girl is under the impression yer own dear Eudora is planning to kill you."

"That's ridiculous."

"Is it?"

Well, Lindley found he had no answer to that. Hellfire, this whole thing was spinning rapidly out of control. What the devil was Sophie up to? And an even better question, what the devil was Eudora up to? He'd strangle the woman if he found any of her threats against Sophie were true.

Obviously, though, Sophie felt they were sincere. She felt that enough to go running out into the night. To rescue him.

God, but he did love that woman. Now, however, he simply needed to find her and pray it was not too late to tell her. But where would she go? He'd certainly not left word telling anyone where to find him. How could she possibly have thought to know where to look?

Ah, but she knew he was after her father. She would simply go where he expected her father to go. And that would be Loveland.

And the temporary residents of Loveland were scheduled to visit Hartwood today. With Fitzgelder. Damn, if Sophie joined up with them she could be walking directly into the very last place she would wish to be.

"Very well then, Tom," Lindley said, pulling on his gloves and taking up the reins. "I'll find her. You go back to your father. Tell him he's needed—he's to look for me first at Hartwood and then at Loveland."

"And me, sir?"

"Get some rest. Stay near the abbey and let me know if Eudora makes any move."

THE DOOR AT THE BOTTOM OF THE ANCIENT, WINDING stairway creaked. It echoed against the damp stone walls. Sophie glanced nervously at Annie. The sun had risen nearly two hours ago, yet they'd heard nothing from below, from the rest of the house. It was as if this tower room were a hundred miles away from Haven Abbey rather than attached and looming over it.

After endless footsteps had sounded on the stairs, a light

knock came at the door. It was the agreed upon signal—two sets of two short raps. Sophie breathed easier. Mrs. Wimpole was bringing their breakfast.

She hoped.

The door to their little room moaned as Sophie swung it open. Mrs. Wimpole was there, huffing from her march up the stairs. She held a tray with breakfast.

"Perhaps we should arrange for you to give the signal knock at the door below, Mrs. Wimpole," Sophie suggested, taking the tray and ushering the servant in.

"Safer this way. You keep this door bolted tight, my dear. Miss Eudora has been in a rare fit since you turned up missing in the night. Don't open this up for nobody."

"But surely if Madame sends someone up here to look for us they'll realize someone has bolted it from inside," Annie said, nervously repositioning Sophie's pin rolls where she had them set out on a rugged little table.

"If anyone asks I'll tell them this room hasn't been used in years, that the hinges are all rusted up and can't be opened," Mrs. Wimpole said.

Sophie frowned. "Will that be enough, do you think, to keep anyone from hunting up here?"

The older woman smiled. "She's convinced you went off after Lord Lindley, and I gave her plenty of reason to believe it, miss. I told her you were inconsolable yesterday morning when he left. I told her just what you told me to say, that you knew where he was going and you wanted to go after him. She's well certain that's what you've done, although . . ."

"Yes?"

"I'm afraid she's every bit as certain that you won't be finding him, miss. It seems she fully believes his lordship has already met with some . . . mishap."

"How does she know? Has someone come to bring word?"

Sophie could feel the blood pounding in her head. Oh, but she simply couldn't let herself think of this, of the possibility that Lindley was . . . No, it just couldn't be. He *had* to be well, out there somewhere searching for her father.

"No, no one has arrived, but Miss Eudora sent one of her servants out last night."

Sophie frowned. Annie had told her they traveled with Madame's driver and one young man who seemed to be quite devoted to Madame, fetching and delivering messages for her and whatnot. So just what message could Madame be sending, she wondered.

"When she discovered you gone, she called her young man and sent him off," Mrs. Wimpole explained. "I don't know where."

Sophie glanced at Annie, but it seemed she had no idea where the man might have been going. She shrugged. "To warn Captain Warren, perhaps?"

It was as good a guess as any Sophie could think of. "Yes, that could be."

But Mrs. Wimpole seemed especially perplexed. "Captain Warren? You know of him?"

"Yes, he's a, er, friend of Madame's," Sophie said, modifying the details just a bit.

"Oh, he's far more than that," Mrs. Wimpole said. "He's her son."

"Her son?"

"You did not know that?"

"No, Madame never mentioned she had a son."

Mrs. Wimpole shook her head and sighed. "She was so young when it happened, the poor dear. Seduced by an older man, she was. She ran off with him before she was even out of the schoolroom, and then he cast her aside before she'd birthed his by-blow. Her family was forced to turn their backs on her shame."

"Her own family refused to help her?"

"You can be sure it was not what anyone wished for. Miss Eudora did not make things easy for them, sorry to say. Oh, but it broke her mother's heart."

Somehow Sophie had never thought of Madame having a mother, or any family, for that matter. The very thought had never entered her mind. It was as if Madame had always simply been who she was when Sophie came to know her—a fading beauty making profit off the weakness of men.

Now a whole new person was being presented to her. She was suddenly becoming aware of the woman under Madame's charming façade: a woman who had loved and had suffered abandonment, had done the unthinkable in order to care for her fatherless child, had made her own way and watched her family turn their backs on her. It was no wonder she was cold and deceitful underneath it all.

"You knew her mother?" Sophie asked.

Mrs. Wimpole nodded. "I was her maid all those years Miss Eudora was home. Such a pretty girl . . . We all expected her to marry well, as her sister had done."

"Her sister . . . ? I'm afraid I don't understand. What is Eudora's connection to this household?"

Mrs. Wimpole sighed. "I'm not at all surprised his lordship hasn't told you. A gentleman can't very well go around telling people that his aunt is the owner of a . . . er, of a . . . of a place like that."

His *aunt*? Eudora was Lindley's *aunt*? No, Sophie supposed he couldn't go around mentioning that. Still, as she was one of the residents of a place like that, she could have thought Lindley might tell her of his connection to Madame. The fact that he hadn't was just one more indication of his disinterest.

She glanced over at Annie. Oddly enough, her friend did not at all seem to be surprised by this new information. Perhaps, then, it was not so very new to her.

"Annie, did you know about this?" she asked.

Annie seemed hesitant to answer, but finally she did. "Yes, when we were traveling here yesterday Madame told me. She seems to still hold quite a good deal of anger toward her family, though they are all gone now."

"But she has only ever seemed on good terms with Lindley," Sophie said. "Often he'd come to visit, and Madame always seemed more than happy to see him. I thought . . ."

Sophie stopped herself. She had not meant to mention her own familiarity with the brothel in front of Mrs. Wimpole. Drat. So much for clinging to the fantasy of being the respectable Miss D'Archaud.

"I thought that their relationship was a friendly one," she finished, deciding the truth had been bound to come out eventually and hoping it did not alter Mrs. Wimpole's wish to aid them.

"I doubt that before the tragedy he even knew he had an aunt," Mrs. Wimpole said, thankfully overlooking Sophie's admission. "His mother would have never told him. Likely he learned of it from old family records as the poor man was putting things in order."

"But if he has been kind to her since then, why should she seek to harm him? Truly, I was certain I heard her plotting his murder. She sounded quite happy about it, as a matter of fact! What sort of aunt could do that?"

"She's evil in her core, Sophie," Annie said, tucking her daughter's blanket more snugly around her. "Whatever Eudora has been through has made her hard and cruel."

Mrs. Wimpole clucked her tongue. "It was a cruel thing she did back when she was a girl of just seventeen, treating the family honor as if it were nothing, flaunting her affair with a married man and then making a public spectacle of herself when she took off with him. It was cruel, and it sent her mother to an early grave."

"Sometimes love makes people do horrible things," Annie said quietly.

Sophie kept silent. She knew she certainly had no room to disagree with that statement. Mrs. Wimpole, however, seemed to have acres for disagreeing.

"Love makes people better," the older woman declared as one who'd had decades to think on it. "Any sort of love that makes people destroy their family and throw away their lives is not any sort of real love, if you ask me."

"But why would she wish to destroy Lindley?"

Annie had the answer to this.

"Because of your father, Sophie. That locket truly is the key to some sort of treasure, and your father knows where it is. If Lindley gets him first, Eudora will never get her hands on that money. And she wants it badly."

"And," Mrs. Wimpole added, "she'd be the last surviving heir to Haven Abbey."

Good heavens, was that true? Indeed, with all of that, it seemed Madame had ample reason to kill her own nephew. Sophie's heart turned over in her breast. What if Madame had already succeeded?

"Then Lindley may already be . . ." She couldn't bring herself to finish the sentence.

"And likely she'll do the same to us if we interrupt her plans," Annie added.

"Well, I do not intend to sit idly by and not interrupt them," Sophie announced. "Mrs. Wimpole, I have my own plan."

The woman smiled. "Whatever we can do to help you, miss, my husband and I are willing. You can count on us."

"Good. The first thing we must do is to kill Annie and little Rosie."

Mrs. Wimpole actually went pale at that. Annie chuckled.

Sophie quickly corrected herself. "Rather, what I mean to say, we must first convince Madame that Annie and her child are dead."

Mrs. Wimpole only regained a bit of her color and frowned in a most disapproving fashion. Sophie held up the little bundle she'd been sewing much of the night. From a distance it looked quite convincing. Someone who did not investigate too closely might believe it was, indeed, a small child.

Sophie smiled at the older woman and hoped she would not balk at the risky and macabre scheme she and Annie had come up with in the night.

"This is why I asked if you had any spare fabric or old clothes," Sophie explained. "I'm hoping that very shortly someone will discover that poor Annie has taken her child and leapt from the walls of the castle into the moat. There is still a moat around the rear of the building, I believe?"

It took a moment, but finally Mrs. Wimpole showed faint signs of a smile. "Yes, miss. There is. It would surely be a most horrible way to end one's own life."

"I certainly hope Madame feels the same way and is not at all tempted to closely examine the bodies."

"I will see to it she does not," the housekeeper said. "Now, start on your breakfast before the little one wakes up again. You can tell me what I must do, and I should be making my way back down before Miss Eudora wonders at my absence."

Sophie was only too happy to do as instructed. With Mrs. Wimpole approving of their scheme, it was just a matter of time before she might be able to leave here and go to warn Lindley. She prayed it would not be too late.

They had hoped by convincing Madame they had already escaped in the night she might not be hunting close by for them. The ploy was to let her believe Sophie had gone after Lindley. This would give Sophie time to construct the effigies of Annie and Rosie, then have them dragged from the moat. When Madame was informed of the "find," they hoped she would stop hunting for Annie altogether. Annie could simply stay here, hidden safely away in this ancient tower with her child until Papa could come for her.

It was an ambitious plan, to be sure. Much could go wrong. But for the life of her—and considering she had nothing but her skill with a needle and a hope that God still heard her prayers—Sophie could think of no other way. She simply had to make this work.

She had to find Lindley and keep him safe. Even if it meant Papa's freedom . . . or his life. Indeed, perhaps she was no different from Eudora, after all. She loved a man she could never have; loved him enough to risk everything she claimed to care about.

Chapter Nineteen

Lindley knew what it was to lose everything he'd ever cared about. He was experiencing it all over again and his gut wrenched at the thought. But one thing he knew: anger was not helpful. He'd learned that three years ago when he was presented the lifeless bodies of his family. His whole family—his mother, dearest Maria, little Charlie who was growing to be such a fine boy, his best friend Charles . . . everyone he truly cared about. Yes, he'd been angry then, and it had done nothing good.

It was only when he'd been able to tamp that anger down and use his brain that he'd been able to make some headway. He'd recalled things—little things like words and phrases that had popped into conversation—and was able to take them to the Home Office. Captain Warren asked him to be of use to them in their efforts to ferret out the men who had orchestrated these and other horrific murders, and he'd agreed without hesitation.

Three years ago tensions had still run high between the English and the French. Napoleon was still a viable threat. England still had men in sensitive positions, dangerous positions, monitoring the enemy. If their identities became known, those men could—did—lose their lives.

And apparently, others—women and innocent children—along with them.

Damn it, the anger was threatening to overtake him once more. He would not let it. His priorities had changed now. He was not hunting D'Archaud. He was after Sophie—anything he did to Fitzgelder or any of the others involved in those past crimes would be done not to avenge the dead but to rescue the living. Sophie must be saved.

First, though, he'd have to find her. He'd gone to Hartwood only to see no sign of her there. The acting troupe was nowhere to be seen, and Dashford's stuffy butler had refused to give any word on anyone's whereabouts. It wasn't until Lindley found a stable hand to rough up a bit that he learned Dashford had taken his friend Rastmoor out riding. Toward Loveland.

So the action would be taking place there, after all. He urged his horses even faster now as he left Hartwood behind. Loveland was five miles—he could travel that in no time. If Sophie was there, he would find her. He would protect her if it was the very last thing he did with his damned life.

And it seemed it might very well be.

Two hotheaded grooms were following from Hartwood. What the hell did they want? Lindley pressed his horses faster, hoping they would not injure themselves on the rutted road. He did not have time to waste dealing with Dashford's servants. Damn it, but he'd always considered Dashford a friend. It was deuced frustrating to think the man might actually be an enemy.

And Rastmoor, too, it would seem. Lord, but this was a frustrating mess. Whatever was transpiring at Loveland, he needed to be there in time to sort it all out. That would mean he'd need to outpace these bloody servants.

The men were closing in on him fast, but just up ahead Lindley saw another group of riders and wagons directly in his path. Damn, he would have to pull his phaeton up sharply if he hoped to avoid a collision. And he most heartily did hope for that.

His horses were aware of the danger and followed his commands perfectly. They didn't shy or tear off the road in panic, and he managed to pull them under control rather expertly, if he did say so himself. By now he was close enough to the other travelers to recognize them: two wagonloads of actors accompanied by Dashford and Rastmoor riding astride.

The grooms came pounding up behind him. "Watch it, sir!" one of them called to Dashford. "He might be armed!"

Well, that didn't do much to convince Lindley his friend Dashford was guiltless in all this and simply out for a quiet ride in the morning air. Clearly the grooms were aware of dangerous happenings if they suspected Lindley of being armed, which of course he was.

"What's this about, Lindley?" Dashford questioned.

Lindley smiled cheerfully for his friend. "I stopped at Hartwood to see you and was told you were out here."

One of the grooms spoke up. "When he left, her ladyship thought it might be a good idea if we came along, too."

"Did she now?" Dashford said.

"I say, is something going on that—" Lindley said, then stopped short when his gaze fell on the man in the rear wagon. "You!"

It was D'Archaud, sitting there glaring back at him.

"Lindley, you dog. What in the bloody hell have you done with my daughter?" the man shouted, scrambling to get out of the wagon. Three of the nearby actors worked to restrain him.

"I was hoping to find her here with you, D'Archaud," Lindley replied calmly, tamping down his own fury. "Am I to take it she's missing?"

"I'll murder you!" D'Archaud declared loudly. "What have you done to her?"

Rastmoor seemed clueless to the significance of the situation here. He was practically laughing when he spoke. "I see you've been busy making friends wherever you go, Lindley."

"And just what, exactly, did you do to this man's daughter?" Dashford asked, as clueless as his companion.

Lindley gave up trying to rein in his anger. "I tried to keep her out of the mess this man is making of his life! Watch him, Dash, he's not to be trusted."

"Oh?" Dashford responded. "Some would say you aren't, either."

It seemed no one here was to be trusted, and immediately the subject of the treasure came up, with various parties accusing each other of wanting to steal it while others claimed they had exclusive right to it. Really, the whole scene was a waste of time and rather difficult for Lindley to follow. He knew one thing, though. That damn French treasure was the key to everything.

So, the loud, flamboyantly dressed actor must be D'Archaud's partner in all of this. Lindley studied him. Aside from the tasteless, garish clothing he wore, the man had an undeniably superior bearing about him. And he was clearly French, although for some odd reason today the man spoke with the most hideous Italian accent Lindley had ever heard. The others kept calling him Giuseppe, but he strongly doubted that was the man's real name.

This must be the one who helped D'Archaud amass the so-called treasure. Warren had said it was earned by years of payment from the French for activities they carried out on English soil, spying and ruining good men's lives. Likely they found it easy to hide their identities and cover their tracks by posing as humble actors, traveling here and there as they conducted their clandestine treachery. No wonder they had eluded the Home Office for so long.

And now somehow, when they had come to retrieve their hidden treasure, Dashford and Rastmoor had gotten involved. Yet where was Fitzgelder during all this? And even more important, where the hell was Sophie?

The garish Frenchman suddenly turned his attention on Lindley. "He's after the treasure, too."

Dashford was visibly annoyed. "I'm afraid you're just going to have to wait your turn with it, Lindley," he said, patting the metal box he was holding across his lap. "Your friend D'Archaud back there got his hands on it first, but I claim right of ownership for my wife. Just what claim do you have on it?"

"That's the treasure?" Lindley asked.

"Don't get any ideas," Rastmoor warned.

Lindley frowned. "*That's* the treasure? Odd. I rather thought it would be bigger. I suppose I shouldn't be surprised, though. Those French . . . they always exaggerate."

Dashford seemed surprised by this. "French, you say? The treasure is French?"

"Indeed. I know little about it, but I do know it's French."

Dashford seemed to ponder that a moment, then shrugged. "Well, no matter. Our friend here"—he gestured toward D'Archaud—"has graciously informed us of where we might find at least one of the keys needed to open the box. Since the box was hidden in my wife's property, and since the presumed holder of one of these keys is currently a guest at Hartwood, we are headed back there to see about opening it. Perhaps it did indeed come from France, but it's in England now."

"You already have one of the keys?" Lindley asked. Thank God! Did this mean Sophie was there and they still believed her to have the locket?

"Not quite," Rastmoor said. "It's en route to Fitzgelder, we believe."

Damn, Fitzgelder. So he was the guest at Hartwood with some knowledge of the locket, was he? Just what did that mean for Sophie?

"Are you certain of that?" Lindley asked.

"Not at all," Dashford replied.

"Well then, who has the other? Two are required, I believe?" Lindley questioned.

"Sadly, that one belonged to an actress," Dashford explained. "One Julia St. Clement."

Ah, this was a surprise. Lindley knew the name. The St. Clement chit was an actress who had broken Rastmoor's heart some years ago, the one he was still not entirely recovered from, poor sap. Hellfire, but for the first time Lindley realized he could actually empathize with Rastmoor's misery.

"If the St. Clement woman had it, this would mean it is already in Fitzgelder's possession, wouldn't it? She was, after all, his wife, wasn't she?"

"Yes," Dashford said.

"No," Rastmoor said.

Everyone looked at him, but he offered no explanation. Lindley decided he would remedy that later, when there was less of an audience.

"At any rate," Dashford went on, "Fitzgelder is in my possession. Lindley, what do you say to returning with us to Hartwood? My grooms, of course, will see that you encounter no difficulties on the way."

Lindley recognized that for what it was—Dashford's warning. No one trusted anyone in this motley little group, yet they were all traipsing back to Hartwood in hopes of finding the key to a treasure. Oh, but this was bound to be interesting.

Upon their arrival, the gathering at Hartwood was an absolute fiasco. Lindley paced angrily, cooling his heels in the upstairs room Dashford had assigned to him, too frustrated to think straight. By God, they'd gathered D'Archaud, the bloody Frenchman, Dashford's wife, and even Fitzgelder together all in one room and still Lindley had no better idea of how to find Sophie.

He had learned, however, that the Frenchman was in fact D'Archaud's brother-in-law, that the young actress who'd posed as Sophie's husband was in fact the Frenchman's daughter, making her Sophie's actual cousin—although it seemed neither of them knew it—and that same actress was also the very Julia St. Clement whom Rastmoor had been grieving all these years. Apparently she was not dead, nor had she ever been married to Fitzgelder. It was all very convoluted and confusing.

Fitzgelder, for his part, did seem very much interested in killing her now. The bastard was in a foul mood and seemed very much interested in killing practically everyone, as a matter of fact. Dashford had enough sturdy footmen standing guard to assure them this would most likely not happen.

To top it all, however, the damn locket Lindley had been flaying himself over stealing from Sophie turned out to be bogus! When he dramatically produced it in an effort to speed this process along so he could get back to the business of locating Sophie, the damned Italian-Frenchman declared this was the wrong locket. Apparently Fitzgelder had not gotten a chance to examine it thoroughly before it was dropped into Sophie's apron, so all this time they'd been chasing a locket that, in fact, held no value. Somewhere along the way it had been switched, and the real one was still at large.

Nothing was going well. Dashford was storming because Rastmoor had brought his not-dead-actress-whore into this house, Rastmoor was fuming because he'd gotten word his young sister had fallen prey to Fitzgelder's seduction, and everyone still seemed to eye Lindley as if he was perhaps the greatest villain of the lot. And still his Sophie was missing.

It was almost a relief when the whole blasted party disbanded and Dashford sent everyone up to refresh themselves in rooms he assigned them. Lindley could certainly use a moment or two to consider things. Damn, but he needed some answers and he needed them now.

First, he needed to lose the two liveried watchdogs Dashford had placed on guard over him. They loitered in the corridor, just outside the room where Lindley had been ensconced as luncheon was being prepared. He opened the door and called to them.

"I say, it's bloody dull around here. Where is everyone?"

The servants exchanged glances, then seemed to acquiesce they had no instructions against speaking to the prisoner. One of them cleared his throat and spoke in lofty tones.

"I'm sure when it's convenient, his lordship will entertain you."

Well, that didn't do anything to dislodge them. He'd have to be a bit more specific.

"What about those actors? One would think a whole bloody troupe of bloody actors could provide some bloody diversion."

Perhaps if he overused the same offensive word enough he could annoy them into letting him escape. Lord knew he was finding it annoying. They, however, were of sterner stock.

"They are down in the kitchen with the servants, sir."

Well, at least that answered one question. And, it gave him an excellent idea. *Bloody* excellent, in fact.

"In the kitchen? Well, what sort of bloody household is this where some dirty actors off the street get bloody fed before their betters?"

Ah, yes, he was succeeding. He caught one footman rolling his eyes.

"Her ladyship said some luncheon is being prepared and will be brought up to you, sir," the man replied almost eloquently.

"I'm bloody particular about my food, young man. How do I know what sort of conditions your cook keeps in her bloody kitchen? By God, this is a bloody outrage! I'm an earl, bloody dammit, and I'll not stay penned up here like some bloody cooped chicken!"

He stormed out into the corridor, fussing with his cravat

and giving every evidence of being a self-centered prig. The watchdogs moved toward him, but as the only threatening thing about him was that he might insult their attire or use the word *bloody* a dozen more times, they simply followed as he passed. Not entirely what he had hoped for, but it was progress in the right direction.

He needed to find D'Archaud. He assumed the man would be with the actors, in the kitchen. And, truth be told, he was a bit hungry.

He proceeded with his unwanted entourage, getting lost a time or two and finally having to ask them for bloody directions. They patiently escorted him to the kitchen, located in the rather mazelike lowest level of Dashford's sprawling home. Lindley had to admit he was rather more partial to his own estate, so very well designed and symmetrical. But, to each his own, he allowed. Dashford and his new bride seemed content enough here. Somehow.

He found D'Archaud sitting with the other actors, busily devouring cold meat. Once the man caught sight of Lindley, he gave every impression of suddenly wanting to devour something more along the lines of the earl's liver. Well, that was fine with Lindley. He'd love nothing better than to go fist to claw with D'Archaud. Throttling that man would be a pleasure.

Except that he'd already decided to put Sophie's wishes ahead of his own pleasure. *Damn.*

"I hope someone's seeing to lunch for your daughter, D'Archaud," Lindley said, not bothering to hide his sneer. "Wherever she may be."

D'Archaud threw his stool back and would have lunged at Lindley but for his brother-in-law's intervention.

"Now, now, this is hardly the place for it," the Frenchman muttered.

"I'll kill him, St. Clement," D'Archaud hissed. "You would, too, if it was your daughter he'd run off with."

"You left her in a bloody brothel to fend for herself, D'Archaud," Lindley growled, and this time he used that word accidentally.

"That gave you no right to treat her as your personal whore, Lindley!"

Well, that was too much. He could not stomach the man speaking that way about Sophie. He dove for him, forgetting his vow of tolerance and planning to rip the man's throat out.

The footmen stopped him. Between footmen, actors, and shrieking kitchen staff, Lindley was unable to so much as harm a hair on D'Archaud's useless head. Neither was D'Archaud able to lay hands on him, either.

"Enough!" St. Clement announced in his bellowing accent. "D'Archaud, tell him what you know."

D'Archaud clearly disapproved of that notion. "What? But he's—"

"Kill him later," St. Clement ordered. "For now, he wants to help Sophie."

D'Archaud's face puckered into a sneer of disgust, but his fists unclenched and he met Lindley's eyes square on.

"You want to save Sophie?" he asked.

"I do. And as much as it nauseates me to think it, I intend to let you go free, D'Archaud."

D'Archaud gave a rude snort. "Why do I find that so difficult to believe, monsieur?"

"What do you know about Sophie?" Lindley asked, ignoring the man's scorn. "Where is she?"

D'Archaud swore in French. "She's been taken by Eudora and held for ransom."

The man suddenly seemed deflated, sinking back into his seat and half knocking it over again.

"That's why he came here," St. Clement said, stepping close to his brother-in-law's side. "He wanted to find the treasure to pay the ransom and save his daughters."

Lindley was caught by that last word. "*Daughters*, D'Archaud? Plural? You have more than one daughter out there in danger?"

"Yes, I do," the man declared. "And a wife, too. Well, she'd have been my wife by now if that damn bitch would have allowed it."

Lindley was fairly certain he knew what bitch D'Archaud meant, but he asked anyway. "Eudora?"

"Yes, Eudora. She's been using my family against me for years. She and her damn puppy, Fitzgelder."

The pieces were finally falling into place. It seemed perhaps D'Archaud had not abandoned Sophie in that brothel as much as Eudora had manipulated him into leaving her there. His cooperation ensured Sophie's well-being. Indeed, somehow he found the man's outrageous claims oddly believable.

After all, everything he said appeared to corroborate Tom's story that Eudora and Fitzgelder were somehow partnered in all this. And hadn't Eudora been the one to tell him Fitzgelder would be expecting a package several days ago? The package that contained the locket.

Of course this had all been about the locket. Eudora had been hunting this treasure right from the start. She'd been using everyone around her as tools to get it.

"Damn her," he said under his breath, then looked over to D'Archaud. "When was the last you heard from Eudora?"

"Yesterday," D'Archaud replied. "I was to find the treasure, then give it to Fitzgelder to take to her. She indicated she was holding my family where I would never find her."

"Yes, she was."

"Was? What do you mean, *was*?"

"I mean I just got word this morning that Sophie has escaped."

"Mon Dieu!"

Now St. Clement rejoined the conversation. "*Escaped*? You mean, she is safe?"

"I mean she is missing," Lindley clarified. "Eudora does not have her, but apparently no one else does, either."

"But there's no telling what could happen to her!"

"I can think of several things that could happen to her," Lindley said. "None of them pleasant. First of all, I need to know just what we're up against. Do either of you have any special friends out wandering the countryside who might run across her?"

Both Frenchmen shook their heads.

"Fortunately I do, so I'm hoping they find her before anyone else."

"Such as Fitzgelder," D'Archaud said. "He has a whole army of rogues waiting to catch any one of us off our guard. Surely if Eudora has lost Sophie, Fitzgelder's *mercenaires* will be looking to find her."

"Then clearly I need to have a little chat with Fitzgelder,"

Lindley said and realized he was quite looking forward to it, actually.

"I'll go with you," D'Archaud said.

"No. I need you here," Lindley instructed and then glanced over his shoulder at the two footmen still standing watch over them. Fitzgelder was upstairs, locked in his room with instructions that he not be allowed to leave. Lindley would just have to go up and pay a visit, and Dashford's orderly footmen would simply get in the way of conducting business.

"Keep them here," he said softly.

The Frenchmen nodded. Suddenly they went from being his enemies to his accomplices as St. Clement leapt to his feet and announced in his grandest accented tones yet that he and his marvelous players would like to perform scenes both comic and tragic to amaze and enrich Dashford's kitchen staff. Lindley stepped aside and watched as the troupe instantly jumped into action, moving furnishings and captivating the household staff with their dramatic efforts.

It took no more than ten minutes before a howling King Lear had even the watchful footmen entranced in theatrical fascination. Lindley slipped out the back of the room and found his way to the staircase. Indeed, Fitzgelder was going to have something to answer for.

SOPHIE WAITED FOR WHAT SEEMED HOURS BEFORE SHE heard the first sounds of approaching voices. Tucking herself deeper into the shadows, she hid behind the crumbling stone wall that marked off a sort of picturesque garden. She had crept down from the tower and ducked out a rear door that clearly had not been used in decades. Indeed, this whole end of the abbey was long fallen into disuse, and Mrs. Wimpole had assured her there would be little reason for Madame to take note of Sophie in this area.

So far the woman had been right. Their plan had been put into action, and Sophie was simply awaiting her chance at escape. All that remained was to create enough distraction that Sophie could make her way from this overgrown garden to the nearby stable. Mrs. Wimpole promised there would be a horse for her.

She'd eaten as much luncheon as she'd been able, but her stomach was in knots from nerves. So many things had to work just right in order for this to succeed. Now all she could do was cross her fingers and watch.

If she craned her neck just right and pushed aside a branch or two of the heavy boxwood, Sophie could see the moat. Any moment now she might expect . . . Ah, yes. There was Wimpole now, accompanied by an old man who must be the groom she'd been told would assist in this deception. On cue, the men started pulling something heavy from the moat just as Sophie could hear Mrs. Wimpole's cries in the distance.

"This way, Miss Eudora!" the housekeeper was saying as she came into view leading a reluctant Madame. "See? Oh, how dreadful! How awful!"

Madame stopped following the woman a good thirty paces from the men and their soggy bundle. She wrinkled her nose and watched the men intently before asking, "Is it her?"

Mrs. Wimpole checked the large, Annie-shaped form that was slowly being hauled up onto the bank. The woman's gown, now muddied and dripping, was unmistakable. The bedraggled wig they had made from the sacrifice of Annie's own dark locks did exactly as it was intended; it hung every which way, obscuring the crude facial features Sophie had fashioned and giving the object a feel of authenticity she had been nearly afraid to hope for.

By heavens, Sophie had done a most excellent job of creating a faux-Annie, if she did say so herself. She could be absolutely proud of her craftsmanship if the whole thing were not so very disturbing. My, but with Mrs. Wimpole weeping and wailing over the form, the scene could very easily be mistaken as something horrible. Sophie wondered if perhaps she ought to worry for herself, thinking up such a dreadful scheme.

But it was working.

"See, Miss Eudora, here is the child," Mrs. Wimpole called out, stooping over a smaller bundle that lay some feet away. "They found it just minutes ago. Such a sad, sad shame."

Eudora took a step forward as if she might go to Mrs. Wimpole and investigate the body herself, but the old man from the stables coughed loudly over his labors with the larger "body."

"Must have happened sometime in the night," he announced loudly. "Looks like the fish have had plenty of time to start taking meals off of 'em. Won't make for a pretty funeral, that's fer certain."

Well, that was more than enough to stop Madame in her tracks, Sophie was happy to see. The woman took another three steps back and pulled her wrapper up around her nose, as if the stench of death was already offending.

"Well, this is none of my concern," she said coldly. "Silly fool, to go and commit suicide like this. Wrap them up and put them somewhere. And for God's sake, don't bring them into the house!"

"Should we contact the magistrate?" Wimpole asked.

"Heavens no!" Madame ordered. "Do nothing, do you hear me? Warren should be here any minute. We'll wait to see what he would have us do."

Mrs. Wimpole nodded and dabbed her eyes. Sophie had to smile. The woman was every bit as accomplished an actress as Miss St. Clement. Perhaps when all this was over Sophie could find her missing friend and introduce the pair.

But now was time to concentrate on the work at hand. Mrs. Wimpole kept Madame busy with recounting the horror of discovering such a terrible thing here in the abbey moat, and Madame's man came rushing out to be near her and offer his services. They were not needed, of course, which was a good thing since Madame ordered him not to soil his hands with such work, anyway.

The important thing was that he was here instead of keeping watch over Madame's carriage in the stable or standing guard at the front of the abbey. This gave Sophie the chance she'd been needing to slip away undiscovered. She'd best take advantage of it while she could.

She took one last look at the morbid scene beside the moat and shuddered. Thank heavens it was only a sham. She'd left Annie safe with Rosie half an hour ago, hugging and kissing them both good-bye with a promise to keep herself safe and bring Papa back soon to collect them. Mrs. Wimpole assured her all would be well, and for the first time Sophie had hope that might indeed be the case.

She had done all she could here. Now, all she needed was

to rescue Papa and see that Lindley did not end up dead. Surely after facilitating this, that much would be easy.

LINDLEY MOVED QUICKLY THROUGH THE HOUSE, AVOIDing any area he thought might be peopled at this hour. No one seemed to notice him; it appeared the actors were doing their job well below and had attracted the attention of all the household staff. *Excellent.* This would give him ample opportunity to slip upstairs and visit Fitzgelder.

"My lord!" someone called.

Lindley cringed and turned slowly to find Dashford's butler approaching. "I have been looking for you."

Damn. "Oh?"

"A letter arrived."

What? "For me?"

That was odd. Who the devil knew he was here? He took the paper the man extended to him. A quick glance at the seal told him this was from the Home Office. Very strange.

"It arrived yesterday," the butler explained. "Apparently the sender thought you might still be a guest here after the wedding. Lady Dashford had instructed us to send it back today, but now that you are here I can give it to you directly."

"Thank you," Lindley said.

The butler seemed content to have done his duty so he bowed and went on his way. Lindley was left to wonder what information Warren could possibly be sending him that it was so urgent to follow him to a wedding in Warwickshire. He ducked into the nearby dining room to read it in private.

Someone had gone to great pains to see that the seal on the folded letter did its work without fail. Lindley feared he would tear right through the paper trying to remove it, so he grabbed up a knife and pried carefully at the unnecessarily large spot of sealing wax. Finally he had it up and unfolded the letter.

By God, it was everything they needed to convict Fitzgelder. There were names and dates and an itemized list of the charges Warren was ready to bring against the man. Oddly enough, there was no mention of D'Archaud. It seemed everything from petty larceny to murder to crimes against the Crown was laid right at Fitzgelder's awkward feet. The letter was as a gift from heaven.

Lindley folded it and didn't even realize he still had the knife in his hand until he'd left the room and was already halfway up the staircase to go confront the annoying bastard who had cost Lindley so very, very much. He reminded himself he needed to find out what Fitzgelder knew of Sophie before he killed him. Er, before he turned him over to the proper authorities. He tucked the knife up his sleeve.

The corridor at the top of the stairs was empty. Silently Lindley approached the door to Fitzgelder's room. How would the man react to his visit? Did Fitzgelder still think him a friend, or did he realize by now the truth of the matter? Knocking and alerting the bastard to his presence might only serve to allow the man time to arm himself. Lindley would much prefer his visit to be a surprise. Noiselessly he knelt before the door and withdrew the knife. Rather handy that he'd thought to bring it.

As quietly as possible, he worked the lock. With the merest whisper of a click, it opened a hair's breadth. He casually returned the knife to his sleeve, stood, and readjusted his coat. Even while contemplating murder, a gentleman wanted to appear in good form. He touched the knob, and it turned easily. The door swung open with an ominous creak.

"What the hell . . . ?" Fitzgelder yelled, lounging on the bed in his stocking feet with a book, of all things. He was caught completely off guard.

"Shut up. It's me," Lindley announced, stepping inside the stuffy room. "And I believe I have something you might be interested in."

"Well now," Fitzgelder replied. "It's about damn time."

Damn, but the man unrattled quickly. Lindley pulled the door shut tight and moved toward the oily bastard. He dropped his voice.

"I've a letter from some friends of mine," he said, slipping it out of his coat and letting Fitzgelder take a good look at the crest emblazoned on the paper. "It concerns you."

Fitzgelder understood, and he didn't like it one bit.

"Brutus. And to think I believed you nothing more than an

entertaining popinjay," the bastard said, shaking his head. "I should have listened to Eudora. She told me to keep an eye on you."

Lindley saw the fire blaze in his eyes and the gears turn in his head, desperate to figure out an escape. Let him fret. There was no escape for the mongrel now.

"There was an attack on some innocent women along the road a few days ago," Lindley explained.

"What do I care about that?"

"You don't, I'm sure. What's important to you, however, is that the attack was actually intended for your cousin, Anthony Rastmoor."

Fitzgelder went back to his book. At least, he pretended to.

"As I've seen my cousin recently, I'll assume it failed."

Lindley smiled. "Yes. Miserably."

"Pity."

"You might be saddened to hear that one of the attackers was killed on the road, in fact."

Saddened was obviously not what Fitzgelder felt. "I'll send a card to the widow."

"The other was killed later, though," Lindley went on. "Presumably to keep him silent. It was too late, however. He survived just long enough to give testimony that the attack had been orchestrated by you."

"Good help is so hard to find these days."

"And they were able to connect this attack to others. Truly, Fitzgelder, you should have taken care to cover your tracks better."

True, Lindley's friends at the Home Office had likely used less than pleasant tactics to get the would-be highwayman to talk, and of course they had to trace his contacts back through two or three other petty thugs before they finally were able to connect him to Fitzgelder, but the results were favorable. According to Warren's letter, there were at least two connections to known criminals who had been involved in traitorous activities involving payment from French loyalists and schemes targeting English agents. Fitzgelder would not be going free anytime soon.

But perhaps Fitzgelder did not have to know that just yet.

"So I am here to make you an offer."

Fitzgelder eyed him. Obviously he was intrigued, so Lindley continued.

"I am in a position to, er, misplace some of the evidence against you, should you be agreeable to providing some information I need, of course."

"Why should you want to make bargains with me?" Fitzgelder asked.

"Because I want Miss Darshaw, you snake," Lindley said, having to hold himself back from ripping pieces off the man. "I know you have your petty thugs prowling everywhere, and I wonder if you just might know where she could be."

Now Fitzgelder laughed. "Eudora's little whoring seamstress? You can't be serious, my friend. You would turn me loose for *her*?"

"I would. Eudora took her before I was quite finished with her, as a matter of fact."

Fitzgelder seemed to think this was the funniest thing he'd heard. "Oh, Lindley, you must think me a fool. It's that bloody treasure you're after, isn't it? Well, Eudora won't let you have it. Or that Darshaw chit, either. She's got a vested interest in that one, I'm afraid."

What was that to mean? Of course Eudora would want the treasure—money had always been that woman's chief motivator—but what of this special interest she had in Sophie? Surely she couldn't be that devoted to the girl's sewing abilities that she would never let her be parted from her?

"You see, Lindley," Fitzgelder began with a patronizing sigh, "it's like this. Eudora's in love with the girl's want-wit father."

"That's ridiculous."

He had never seen any indication of it. Surely Fitzgelder was mistaken. Eudora did not . . . But then again, he'd completely misread Eudora's involvement with Fitzgelder, too, hadn't he? D'Archaud had claimed his dealings with Eudora had gone on for years; perhaps there had been more there than he'd mentioned.

It certainly could explain his claim that he had another daughter with a woman Eudora had refused to allow him to marry. Indeed, unrequited love had certainly caused people to behave oddly throughout the centuries. Yes, the more he thought about it the more he had to admit Fitzgelder's assertion held water. A woman scorned was capable of doing any number of cruel things to the object of her misplaced affection.

And threatening to force his adult daughter into the most vile form of human slavery would certainly fit that bill.

"So where do I find them?" Lindley asked.

"Well, Lindley, let me tell you," Fitzgelder said, sighing again and shutting the large volume he'd been reading. He hung his legs over the side of the bed and yawned, the lazy bastard.

"Yes?"

"I don't think Eudora would appreciate it very much if I told you."

"Damn it, Fitzgelder, I have no time for this. I—"

But Fitzgelder swung at him without warning. Lindley ducked just in time to keep the sharp corner of that heavy book from smashing into his face, but he caught enough of it with the side of his head to throw him off balance. He staggered.

Whirling, he lunged at Fitzgelder, but the smaller man stooped low to avoid his advance. When he came up, he held one of his discarded boots in his hand. Lindley saw it a fraction of a second too late. Fitzgelder flung the boot and landed its heel right into the back of Lindley's head.

Pain seared through him in a jolt. The room went dark, and Lindley had but one last thought.

Thank God Sophie wasn't here to see this. It was damned embarrassing.

Chapter Twenty

She supposed it should not have taken half a day to find her way to Loveland, but Sophie had not been there in years. She'd made a wrong turn. Or two. But at last, she was through the tiny village where she remembered visiting the baker with Grandmamma. Loveland could not be far.

Findutton-on-Avon seemed little changed since her last visit, although there were signs of a recent and damaging flood. Still, it was enough the same for her to find Grandmamma's road without too much difficulty. She began to recognize the scenery as she plodded along on the ancient nag the old groom had left saddled for her.

It had not been a comfortable ride, but she was happy to be free of Madame. Her nerves were on edge, though, and more than once she'd imagined someone following. Always, though, it turned out to be nothing. She was well and truly escaped. Now if only she could be so certain that Lindley fared as well.

Worry for him and guilt that she might be too late had clung to her all day. She tried to console herself with thoughts of Papa, but it was no use. Lindley's smile, his fiery touch, his elegant confidence . . . these had all seeped into her and taken over her heart. She could think of nothing worth living for if Lindley had not survived.

Of course she knew better than to believe there might be some place for her in his life if he still had it, but as long as he breathed there was just the tiniest hope that somehow, someday she might find her way back into his arms. Even just a moment or two would be better than nothing. She wondered if Annie might understand such a feeling.

Perhaps not. Annie seemed assured that Papa returned her feelings. Sophie supposed her situation was somewhat more like the affair that had brought Madame to ruin all those years ago. Except that Sophie did not have a fine home or noble family to dishonor. Indeed, Lindley had brought her far more salvation than ruin. Her story was nothing at all like Madame's.

Besides, Madame had gone on to prosper from her hard lessons learned. Sophie knew beyond all doubt, now that she was being completely honest with herself, that she could never willfully give herself to other men for something as unimportant as money. Whether he wanted her or not, she belonged solely to Lindley. She would gladly starve before pretending she could go to anyone else.

She rounded a bend and came over a gentle rise. There was Loveland before her, just as it was in her memory. Yet, it was different, of course.

Gone was the cheerful, carefully maintained garden that Grandmamma loved. Certainly the area was bursting with flowers of all colors, but they were growing in disarray, with weeds choking and dividing them. The whitewashed walls of the cottage were marred by time and weather, and a clear line ran around the perimeter of the house where the river had left its bank and flooded the place. Sophie could nearly weep to think what the interior must look like.

It dawned on her that she should spend less time wandering through her emotions and more time cautiously observing. Was she alone here? Were Papa or Lindley anywhere nearby? What of their enemies? She guided the horse slowly toward the yard, the area between the cottage and the little stable beside it.

Dismounting, she poked her head into the stable. All was

silent and empty. There was no sign of habitation. Odd though, the ground seemed newly rutted as if by several sets of carriage wheels and many prints, both human and horse. How old were these tracks? Was she alone, or had she come too late?

She stood there, unsure of what to do next, studying the tracks and trying to calm the pulse that pounded in her veins. Too late . . . perhaps it was as she feared. Papa had been here, Lindley had arrived, but she was too late. Madame had done as she planned.

Her horse flicked his ears. Sophie glanced nervously around. No, she didn't see anything, but there was a sound. Yes, behind the stable. She heard it again; it was not imagination.

Leaving her horse to nibble at the weeds that sprouted everywhere, Sophie slung her little pack over her shoulder and moved silently to the corner of the stable. She pressed herself against it and slid around to the back. Taking a deep breath, she leaned forward just enough to peek around. If anyone were there, she was taking a great risk. Still, she had to know.

And she was glad she did. There, serenely munching on grass, was Papa's horse.

So he was here! *Thank heavens.* Papa was here, and he'd left his horse behind Grandmamma's stable so that no one would . . . Wait, why would Papa simply leave the horse untethered and unconfined? Surely he would worry the creature might wander off, unless . . . unless something terrible had happened.

She turned on her heel and ran toward the cottage. The heavy front door was unlocked and flew open for her. She dashed inside. The air was musty and damp yet smelled of recent cooking. Someone most certainly had been here. It had to be Papa—she *had* to find him.

Yet every room she ran to was empty. She found a hole in Grandmamma's bedroom floor where someone had intentionally ripped the flooring apart, but there was no other sign of violence. No sign of Papa or Lindley, either. She began to panic.

And then she heard the front door slam shut. Footsteps sounded on the staircase. Was this a good thing? Or should she be very, very afraid?

* * *

HELLFIRE AND BLOODY DAMNATION. LINDLEY'S HEAD was throbbing. By Jupiter, but Fitzgelder most certainly knew how to swing a boot. Slowly his eyes focused on the room around him and took stock of his situation. At first glance, it did not look good.

For starters, he was lying on the floor with his hands bound behind him. Second, his feet were drawn up and tied to his hands. Aside from the fact this twisted posture must be wreaking havoc on his seams, it was mortifying to think that he had been completely vulnerable while Fitzgelder took the time to do this to him. What else had the blasted bastard done?

Glancing down, he discovered the coup de grâce. Bloody hell, the mongrel had rubbed bootblack all over his cravat and tied the thing in an absurdly feminine bow. *Botheration.* He did not have time to hunt down another just now! Still, he had to admit the little ruffle Fitzgelder tied at the bottom was expertly done. He would have never thought the man capable of such a touch.

It hardly made Lindley feel any more charitable toward him, though. Fitzgelder would pay. Oh yes, he certainly would. Just as soon as Lindley dragged every scrap of information out of him that might help in finding and protecting Sophie.

Shifting his body slightly, he was able to find just enough slack in the cords that bound him to curl his fingers up toward his wrist. Thank God, that knife was still there. Idiot Fitzgelder, did it not dawn on him that Lindley had used some sort of tool to pick the lock and let himself in here? He should have looked for it.

Most fortunate, however, that he did not. It took some effort, and by now his body ached from the awkward position on that hard floor, but eventually he had the knife in hand and it was a simple matter of cutting through the cords. Well, perhaps it was not quite *simple*, but eventually Lindley got himself free.

He stretched, climbing up to his feet and shaking his limbs to fully waken them. How long had he been out? He did not notice any marked change in the amount of afternoon sunlight streaming through the window, so he hoped that meant there was still time to collect Fitzgelder and stop him from whatever he had planned.

His head ached screamingly, and he felt the goose egg that sprouted up where the boot had struck. If he had the time, he'd request something cold to place over it, but there was no time. He would just have to get by.

Letting himself out into the corridor, he found it empty as before. This allowed him to retrieve the pistol he had hidden in his room earlier. He should have simply kept it on him, yet probably if he had Fitzgelder would have seen fit to use it. Still, he cursed himself for underestimating the bastard. It had been incredibly naive of him to think Fitzgelder would have cooperated. Even knowing Warren had this information, he was every bit as determined as Eudora to get his grimy hands on that treasure.

All Lindley wanted was Sophie.

Pistol hidden behind his coat, he made his way downstairs. He ducked round a corner as a pair of giggling housemaids scurried by. They didn't seem to notice him, so busy were they reliving the delightful moment of theatrical entertainment they had apparently just left in the basement. That was good news. Apparently St. Clement's troupe was still performing. This meant Lindley could not have been unconscious long.

"My lord!"

Hellfire. It was the butler again.

"Yes?"

"There is someone here for you. He's waiting at the door. He says his name is Feasel."

And so it was. The butler escorted him to the door where Feasel waited nervously, practically wringing his hat in his hands. Lindley could not like that one bit. He met the man, thanked the butler, then stepped outside to see what bad news Feasel might be bringing him now.

"I know you wanted to be informed, so I'm informing ye," Feasel said. "Miss Darshaw has left the abbey."

"I know. Tom met me early this morning. He must have told you I knew, else how would you know to find me here? Didn't he make it back to report to you?"

"He reported back, indeed, but then we found out Miss Darshaw wasn't really gone like we'd heard."

"What?"

"She's sly, that one. It seems she made Madame *think* she and that other gal was run off, but really she was hiding someplace. She didn't really take off until later, once Madame already had her man out hunting her elsewhere."

Indeed, that was sly.

"Where is she now?"

"I sent Tom on to watch over her, keep her safe. I knew that's what ye'd want."

Yes, it was. He only hoped Feasel understood how badly he wanted it, that keeping Sophie safe was really all that mattered anymore.

"Where is she? Was she going to Loveland?"

"I don't know, sir. Tom was following, though."

Of course Loveland was where she'd go. Lindley knew her goal would be her father. Unless she knew her father was here, at Hartwood. Was it possible she was on her way here, now? But Fitzgelder was here, too, and on the loose, thanks to Lindley.

"You've got to find her, Feasel. I'll talk to Dashford, see if he will spare some men to—"

"Wait, sir. There's a bit more you should know."

"What? What more is there?"

"There's Warren, sir."

"Warren? Yes, yes . . . I got his letter. He's finally gathered enough evidence on Fitzgelder so he's—"

"He's following Miss Darshaw, too."

"What?"

"He arrived at the abbey with a couple of thugs. He was very angry to find out she was gone, so he and his thugs took off after her. I heard them say Loveland, sir. They know about Loveland, as well."

"Warren was at the abbey? What the devil took him there?"

"Eudora, I'm afraid, sir. It seems . . . Well, it appears he's her son."

"Captain Warren is Eudora's son? Impossible!"

"Well, that's the way it looked to me, sir. He was calling her 'mum' and she was scolding him for taking so long to get there. I don't know, but the two of them are up to something not good. Not good at all!"

"You must have misunderstood. It simply cannot be."

Although, for the life of him Lindley could not think of a single reason this could not be, other than the obvious fact he did not want it to be. Truth was, he'd heard Eudora had an illegitimate child all those years ago. It was one of many family secrets surrounding her. He'd merely never wondered where that grown child was today, never imagined he might even know the man.

And, by God, it certainly would explain how Eudora seemed to know so much about Lindley's comings and goings, how she'd known he was coming to Dashford's wedding when he was certain he had not told her. Warren had known. If what Feasel said was true, then she could have easily gotten that information from Warren. And all variety of other information, as well.

It was rather frightening to think of what information could be shared between those two, as a matter of fact. Warren had privileged connections to high-ranking government persons. Madame had the most intimate connections to many of these same people through their patronage of her establishment. Damn, but if Warren and Eudora were to combine their efforts, they could blackmail and control a good number of very influential people! Lindley knew for a fact she was capable of it; he just never dreamed someone like Warren could be a party to it.

And they'd have had free use of Fitzgelder's network, as well. Indeed, they could have been using him to do their dirty work all this time, and now that the treasure was within their grasp, he would take the fall for them. If so, why had Warren needed Lindley all this time?

Perhaps he hadn't. Perhaps all of this had been part of the game, using Lindley to gather information on Fitzgelder's contacts so Warren could use them against him when it was convenient. All along Fitzgelder had played into their trap, further implicating himself and trusting they would protect him when really that had been the furthest thing from their minds. And Lindley was an unwitting party to every bit of it.

It was staggering to think what this could mean, what it said about that horrible tragedy three years ago. What it might mean to Sophie if they felt she knew too much! Hell, she'd lived in that brothel for years. She could very well be privy to these underhanded dealings. Now that she was out from under their watchful eye as they prepared to spring their trap on Fitzgelder and get away with murder and treasure and all of it, she would be seen as a very valid liability.

Damn, he'd known Feasel could not have been bringing him *good* news. He simply had no idea it would truly be this *bad*. It was almost bad enough to not be believable.

Almost.

"Very well, Feasel, we will assume the worst. If Warren is working with Eudora, then that changes things a bit. We are going to need help."

"Yes, sir. I was hoping you'd see it that way."

"But there isn't much time. You try to find Tom. I've got to locate Fitzgelder, then head to Loveland and search for Miss Darshaw. If you and Tom find her before I do, by all means, keep her safe. And keep Warren away from her!"

Feasel actually had the nerve to laugh at that. Lindley supposed it did sound a bit obviously possessive. Well, hell. He *was* possessive. Sophie Darshaw was his, and even though he'd always thought of Warren as a friend, he wasn't about to take any chances with her. Especially as the more he thought about it the less likely it became that Warren truly was a friend.

"I'll do my best for her, sir."

Feasel went on his way still chuckling. Well, Lindley wasn't so giddy. Too many things had gone from black to white—or vice versa—overnight for him. What he thought he knew didn't seem so solid right now. He wasn't even certain he could count on Dashford or Rastmoor for help.

All he knew for certain was that wherever Sophie was, she was in danger and he was not there to help her. That hurt.

He stepped back into the house and caught his reflection in a mirror. Immediately he understood why Feasel had been laughing. Lindley was clownish. His head was swollen and misshapen from Fitzgelder's boot attack, his cravat spotted with bootblack, his coat dusty and askew, and there was that inexcusable bow wagging under his chin for all to see. He had truly never looked more ridiculous.

Nor did he have the slightest inclination to tidy up. Sophie needed him. Who cared what sort of fool he must look like?

SOPHIE STOOD IN GRANDMAMMA'S UPSTAIRS BEDROOM and listened as the footsteps approached. They were heavy, large. *A man's footsteps.* Was it Papa? Lindley? Or any of the numerous people she most certainly did not wish to run into just now? Her heart pounded and her breath caught in her throat.

She could not be found here, alone, armed only with needles and pins and a few sundry items she'd rather leave hidden in her pack. She glanced at the window and for a wild moment thought about leaving that way. But as she reminded herself she could not fly, it seemed another exit was in order. Ah, she recalled the secret passage!

Quickly she scurried into Grandmamma's tiny dressing room. As a child she'd played in there and imagined all sorts of adventures. It seemed the most romantic thing in the world to live in a house that had secret passages. She only hoped that all these years later her memory was not faulty.

There she found it, the almost invisible latch that would open a narrow panel that served as a door. Surprisingly, it swung open noiselessly. Sunlight from the room behind her fell onto the floor, and Sophie could see inside enough to know that things were very much as she recalled them.

A small landing and then a wooden staircase led down. She slipped through the panel and pulled it shut behind her. Everything went dark.

Did she dare tiptoe down the stairs? She wasn't sure. The wooden steps had been ancient when she knew them. Were they still sturdy enough to carry her down to the stair landing at the kitchen? Or should she perhaps try to go farther, all the way down to that damp, musty cellar where Grandmamma would occasionally send her to retrieve potatoes or apples in the winter?

She would prefer to avoid that. The mildew and spiders had been bad enough when Grandmamma was here to look after the place every day. She guessed the spider population in the cellar had probably not diminished in the years since Grandmamma's passing. Perhaps she would be safe enough right here, concealed behind the secret panel two steps away from daylight and two floors away from spiders.

Yes, that sounded best. She held her breath and waited. The footsteps were close now, on the first floor and coming into Grandmamma's bedroom. Hopefully it would turn out to be only Papa, and she could rush out and throw herself into his arms. Or even better, perhaps it was Lindley, and she could race out throw herself into *his* arms. Until she knew for certain, though, she would rather wait.

She strained her ears. The man appeared to be studying the room, moving toward that hole in the floor she had discovered. She heard sounds as if he were investigating that area. Then he swore. His voice was completely unfamiliar to Sophie, but whoever he was, he showed an expert grasp of colorful language.

Either he was a lover of preservation and was furious to see the destruction of a fine floor or he expected to find something hidden beneath it that was now gone. Sophie suspected the latter. And she was very happy not to rush out and throw herself into his arms.

But what could this stranger have been looking for? Did Grandmamma leave something behind here? Something hidden under her floor? No, she was certain the old darling would have told her if there was some sort of hidden treasure in . . .

Oh, but could this be the treasure everyone else was talking about? She hadn't believed such a thing, but perhaps it was real. Papa's horse was just outside, and there was a hole in the floor here that this foul man was cursing to every level of hell and back . . . Could this possibly add up to mean the story of treasure was real? Did Papa really have a treasure that Madame was trying to take from him?

Then heavens, where was he? She'd found no sign of Papa beyond his abandoned horse. If he'd taken the treasure, why had he not taken his horse? She was quite certain he'd rather liked the stubborn animal. Something must have happened to him.

And then she heard the house creak. Only, it seemed a bit loud for just the ordinary creak of tired beams in a tired old building. The man in Grandmamma's bedroom must have heard it, too. His footsteps went silent and he cursed again, much softer this time.

Now there were more footsteps, running up the stairs. Sophie had to cover her mouth to keep from letting any nervous sounds escape. She clutched her pack to her, praying the scissors didn't fall out and announce her presence as they'd done at Fitzgelder's house.

Oh, she had scissors! Indeed, those could be a formidable weapon, couldn't they? She dug carefully into her pack to wrap her fingers around them. Just in case.

THE GARDEN OUTSIDE LOVELAND LOOKED LIKE A REGular livery. Three horses, all saddled and ready, wandered aimlessly about the gardens. One seemed particularly thrilled to have found a rose trellis with flowers in full bloom, one looked suspiciously like an old nag he'd seen in the stable at Haven Abbey two nights ago, and the other was an attractive beast that was freshly lathered from a long ride. This one he recognized. *Warren's.*

Lindley pulled his own horse up to a halt and dismounted quietly. He couldn't believe any of the men Warren might have brought along with him rode either of these others. But who was Warren meeting here? He held his pistol at the ready and decided to be especially cautious as he entered the cottage to find out.

He heard Warren upstairs. The man was not taking pains to be silent, stomping around and then cursing as if it were a second language for him. There were no other voices or footsteps he could detect, but he trod very carefully as he made his way up to the first floor. Near the top, his foot slipped and he was forced to transfer his full weight rather quickly.

The stair tread creaked violently.

Warren ceased stomping and cursing. Lindley knew the man had heard him. Damn, he'd lost his element of surprise. It appeared he'd lost his element of D'Archaud, as well. The man had accompanied him from Hartwood, then claimed he knew a secret entrance into the house. Where was he now?

Lindley would simply have to face Warren alone. Sophie's

life might depend on it. Praying for luck and an unarmed Warren, Lindley charged up the rest of the steps and into the bedroom from where the sounds had been emanating.

He found the man ready and waiting for him. With a pistol. It rather matched the one Lindley had. It appeared they had a stalemate.

But who had Sophie?

"If you're here to get the treasure, Lindley, you're too late," Warren said. "It's gone."

He waved his gun in the direction of a rough hole made in the floor when someone had pulled several boards up. Lindley nodded. Yes, D'Archaud had told him he'd found the box under the flooring.

"You're too late. I'm afraid the treasure's already been located and divided between the owners."

Warren grumbled. "Owners? What, you shared it?"

"No, it's not mine. It belongs to two gentlemen from France."

"D'Archaud," Warren said, hissing the name as if it were another curse.

"And his brother-in-law, Albert St. Clement. He's an actor; perhaps you've heard of him."

"Yes, I've heard of him." Warren was clearly disgusted by the very thought of it all. "So what did they give you to buy your blind eye? How much did it cost them to make you turn your back on justice, to let them keep their ill-gotten spoils while your family rots in their graves?"

"Those are not ill-gotten spoils, Warren, and I think you know that. That treasure belonged to D'Archaud from birth. He and his sister's husband brought it with them when they fled the Terror. They hid it to keep his greedy brother from following and taking it from them."

"Lindley, don't tell me you believe that? Clearly they invented that story."

"It's the truth, Warren," Lindley said.

And he was correct. His departure from Hartwood had been delayed by the unfortunate discovery that Fitzgelder had taken everyone hostage. Lindley had been forced to lend a hand in his apprehension while D'Archaud and St. Clement explained their situation. The real locket contained proof of

D'Archaud's claims—and eventually provided access to the treasure. That little box Dashford had carried held nothing more than the final clue to its whereabouts. The actual treasure itself, when they found it, would have never fit in a dozen such boxes. And every bit of it was honestly obtained.

Sophie, when they found her, would come to discover she was quite a wealthy young woman. That was, provided they *did* find her.

"Not that I expect you to know much about such things," Lindley added.

"So you are content to let the damn Frenchies have their treasure, are you?" Warren asked, his pistol still aiming Lindley's way.

"It is their treasure, Warren. They have every right to it; they and their daughters."

"Ah, so that's how it is. You'd rather use D'Archaud's whoring daughter to get at it. Yes, she's a ripe little tart. I wouldn't mind using her for a few things, myself."

Well, that was beyond enough. Lindley leapt at Warren and decided he'd much rather personally rip the man's windpipe out than waste the lead on shooting him. Unfortunately, Warren clearly disagreed. He tried to bring his pistol into line to fire, but Lindley was too quick for him.

The gun hit the floor half a second before the men did. Lindley found himself rolling and throwing fists in an effort to gain an advantage. His longer arms and greater weight soon gave him that, and in no time he had Warren pressed into the hard wood floor. Both pistols were flung just out of reach. He pinned his opponent there, determined to pry information out of him any way he could.

"Where is Miss Darshaw?" Lindley growled.

"In my bed wearing a smile," Warren replied with a sneer.

"If you want to walk away from here, Warren, you'd better start telling the truth."

"Oh, but I thought we were friends, Lindley."

"I've heard we're a damn sight closer than that, cousin!"

"You heard that, did you?"

"Is it true?"

"Does it pain you to realize you share the same blood with a whore and a bastard?"

Lindley released his hold on Warren just a bit. Not much, but a bit.

"What pains me is to think someone I trusted has been using me for his own gain all this time. And that's what it's been, hasn't it? I was not helping bring justice so much as I was covering your tracks as you betrayed your own country."

Warren eyed him, his breathing labored as Lindley still pressed him into the floor. "You've become quite perceptive, cousin. It appears you hardly need an answer from me."

"You still have not told me where Miss Darshaw really is."

"Because I don't know where your little moll really is," Warren replied.

Lindley was tempted to believe him, until something clattered on the other side of the wall. He could see in Warren's eyes that he was as surprised by it as Lindley. Someone was there, just through the tiny dressing room. Although, from where Lindley was perched on his newfound cousin's chest, he could see through the doorway, and the small room appeared surprisingly empty.

He didn't have long to puzzle over it, though. Warren took advantage of this momentary distraction to twist his wiry frame, tossing Lindley off to one side and scrambling out from under him. Lindley lunged to get back in control of the situation, but Warren was quick. He grabbed the closest pistol and made it up to his feet.

Lindley was left kneeling ten feet in front of him. Any untrained idiot could shoot a man at ten feet. Warren was an accomplished soldier. Now it was Lindley's turn to curse.

"Damn it, Warren, put the gun down."

"But then how on earth will I be able to shoot you, cousin?"

Lindley was about to launch into a touching homily about the tragedy of bloodshed between family members when what appeared to be the back wall of the little dressing room flew open and a shrieking female form came bursting through it. *Sophie.* Thank God she was unharmed!

She wouldn't be, however, if Lindley didn't do something quickly. As soon as she took in the situation, she cried out and immediately launched herself at Warren. Lindley dropped to his side and rolled in the direction of his gun, lying against the leg of the bed. His fingers wrapped around it just as he heard

Warren's pistol go off, the jarring sound echoing in the house and driving shards of ice-cold dread straight into Lindley's soul.

In one movement he swung the gun around to train it on Warren while grabbing the bedstead to pull himself up onto his feet. Sophie was—thankfully—still making a good deal of noise. So was Warren, actually, as he tossed down his spent weapon and tried to fend off her attack. He staggered and tripped, falling down beneath the woman while she pummeled away at him with a blunt object of some sort.

Lindley rushed over to help. Warren groaned. The blunt object thudded against his skull, his face, the rest of his body. Sophie had become a force of nature with this oddly lethal weapon, its dangling straps lashing at Warren with every blow she landed.

By Jupiter, it was that obscene leather object from her sewing pack! Warren was being soundly defeated by a seamstress with a buckle-on dildo.

Lindley had to try desperately not to laugh as he kicked aside Warren's discarded gun and carefully held his own aimed at the man's black heart. He stooped slightly to grab Sophie and pull her away.

"That's enough. There's no need to kill the man, my dearest."

"But he was going to shoot you!"

He allowed himself one blessed look at her before turning his gaze back on Warren. "Yet you did not allow it. Are you injured?"

She seemed to pause for the first time and consider this. "Er, no, he missed me. You?"

"I'm fine," Lindley replied, delighted she was so concerned for him. "Everything is fine."

Sophie didn't seem entirely convinced. She eyed her victim suspiciously. "So this is Captain Warren?"

"It is. Although I doubt he will be for much longer. I suspect his superiors will not be glad to learn all he has been involved in."

Indeed, Lindley knew he himself would not be glad at all. He'd rather hoped his suspicions about Warren's involvement in his family's death and the other criminal activities would prove to be false. The man's behavior today seemed to offer proof they were not. Eudora and her son had much to answer for.

Right now, though, all Warren seemed interested in doing was sneering at them both, clearly looking for his chance to escape. Lindley had to do something to prevent that. Damn, but where the hell was D'Archaud?

In the dressing room where Sophie had been, apparently. Following her path, D'Archaud appeared at the rear panel wall and stepped into the room with them.

"Papa!" Sophie squealed, flinging her arms around the man, the dangerous item in her hands slinging wildly.

D'Archaud noticed it, glanced over at Lindley with a frown, then eyed Sophie.

"Er, Captain Warren was going to kill Lindley, so I used this on him," she said, then added, "as a weapon. I'm afraid I rather dropped my scissors down the stairs while I was hiding."

D'Archaud glared back at Lindley. Sophie must have recognized the tension. The makeshift weapon dropped from her hand and hit the floor with a noisy, jingling *thunk*.

"She's really quite impressive with it," Lindley said, for lack of anything better.

Judging from D'Archaud's glower, he should have come up with something better. That was probably not the right thing to say to the girl's father. *Oh well.* Lindley was not interested in discussing that right now, anyway. They had business to attend.

"Help me restrain him," Lindley ordered. "Where the hell were you anyway, D'Archaud?"

"Secret passage," the man replied. "It comes all the way up from the cellar. Sophie, *ma belle*, help us find something to tie this *canaille*."

Sophie glanced around, then dashed back to the secret passageway. She returned in an instant carrying her familiar pack. Lord, but Lindley was glad the girl carried that thing with her everywhere. He did wish, however, D'Archaud were not watching so very closely as she dug through the various contents.

"Here, use these," she said quickly, pulling out the soft, knotted cords.

Indeed, they would work perfectly, so Lindley grabbed them from her, jerking Warren's hands behind his back and binding them tightly.

"By God, I can see why you were so determined to find that girl again, Lindley," Warren said, only half mocking.

Lindley pulled the binding even tighter. He glanced over to find Sophie smiling. She caught him noticing and she blushed. Hell yes, he was determined to find that girl again. And never let her go.

But first things must be taken care of. He dragged Warren toward the hallway.

"Come along, cousin. Let's take you to someone who can decide what to do with you."

Warren had a few suggestions for what Lindley might do with himself, but nothing that aided in bringing the foul-mouthed bastard to justice for his crimes. Lindley led the small group downstairs to the cozy entry hall. That was as far as they could get, however. The front door was blocked by Eudora. He almost wondered why he had not expected this.

"Hello, Auntie," he said. "What brings you here?"

Unsurprisingly, she raised a pistol toward him.

Lindley sighed. "Oh, don't tell me you've come to kill me, too?"

"Don't be silly, Richard. I came to kill *him*."

With that she pointed her gun past Lindley and took aim at D'Archaud. It was clear she was not making idle threats. Everyone moved at once as Eudora leveled the gun and fired. The sound reverberated in the small area, and Lindley dove to protect Sophie. This turned out to be precisely the direction D'Archaud was moving, as well. They collided—with poor Sophie in the middle—and the force of it caused the whole group to stumble in various directions.

Warren, however, stumbled to the floor. His eyes were wide, and the sudden stain that appeared on his coat just above his left breast indicated where the ball from Eudora's gun had gone. She shrieked and ran to drop by his side.

"Georgie!"

"What the hell were you aiming at, Mother?"

But Eudora didn't answer her son. She looked up at D'Archaud and fairly screamed at him.

"I hope you're happy now! After everything I've done for you, Philip. I looked after your daughter; I fed her and kept the men off her—well, most of them. I even let your precious Annie stay in my house, bearing your brat! Well, perhaps you'll know how I've felt all this time. You claim you wanted to marry her? Now you never will! She took your squalling by-blow and jumped off a roof, she did. They fished them out of a moat just this morning."

Lindley could only assume Eudora was referring to D'Archaud's woman and that other daughter he'd mentioned. From the man's face this news was devastating. *Poor bastard.*

"It's not true, Papa," Sophie said quickly, laying her hand on her father's arm. "Don't listen to her. We faked it all. Annie took Rosie into hiding, and I sewed effigies. That's what Madame saw them pull from the moat. Annie and the babe are quite well, really."

D'Archaud appeared very much relieved, but Eudora was furious. She left her bleeding, groaning son and leapt up to her feet as if she might dispatch Sophie with her bare hands. Lindley stopped her, digging his fingers into her elbow until she winced. He likely would have done more, but yet another interruption arrived on scene.

Feasel and Tom came rushing in through the doorway. Well, Feasel rushed. Tom rather limped.

"You found the bugger, eh?" Feasel said, noticing Warren. "He's not quite dead yet, though."

"Not quite," Lindley replied. "But what happened to you, Tom?"

"We ran into Warren's thugs along the way. Took care of them for you."

Warren moaned.

"Many thanks," Lindley said. "Now how about helping me drag him out of doors? He's bleeding on the flooring."

They were just hauling Warren and his cursing mother out into the yard when that blustering French actor, St. Clement, rolled up in a wagon with three young men from his troupe. He nodded toward D'Archaud, smiled at a confused Sophie, then hopped down from his perch to come slap Lindley on the back.

"When I found out where you and D'Archaud had disappeared to, I was worried you might need my help. I see you've got it all in hand, though."

"Monsieur, er, St. Clement?" Sophie asked, clearly overwhelmed by everything.

"Ah, but you must call me uncle now, my dear little Sophie," the man said.

Now Sophie looked even more confused, her perfect brow wrinkling as she struggled to make sense of things. Lindley could hardly wait to explain it all to her, to see her smile when she realized life would be forever better for her. To assure her she would never again have to rely on someone like Eudora, or ever find herself alone. He would sweep her into his arms and tell her that . . .

But it was D'Archaud who explained things.

"It is true, *ma petite*. Albert is your uncle—his wife was my sister, Louise. He saved us and brought us here during the Terror in our land. Oh, but I have so much I can finally tell you, *chou-chou*!"

The man linked his arm around Sophie and pulled her away from Lindley. She was so happy to find her father and so amazed by what he was saying that she seemed to have even forgotten Lindley existed. It wrenched at his heart, but he realized it would be wrong to expect anything more from her just now. She'd been through so much; if he truly cared for her, he'd allow her some time to adjust to so much shocking revelation.

Besides, he had his own matters to attend. His own family needed attention. Particularly Warren, as Lindley decided he'd rather see the man live than let him bleed out on the dirt.

"Can I offer the use of a wagon and some able arms for lifting?" St. Clement said.

Lindley accepted. With the help of the actors, he managed to pry the suddenly doting Eudora off her grown son long enough to pile Warren into one of the large theatrical wagons. He was losing a great deal of blood and seemed to have given up the will to struggle against them, but the wound appeared high enough in his shoulder that Lindley expected he would not die from it. Not today, at least.

Lindley forced Eudora back into the carriage she'd arrived in and placed a burly young actor on the box with the driver, instructing them both that heads would roll if Eudora did not make it safely to Hartwood. He hoped Dashford wouldn't mind if Lindley interrupted his honeymoon just a bit longer to see that the proper authorities were notified and took possession of the mother and son schemers. It was handy that he'd left Fitzgelder there safely in custody, too.

All that remained was for D'Archaud to retrieve his Annie and their child from Haven Abbey.

"She must be so worried," Sophie said as she and her father joined the rest of the group in the yard.

"I'll take you there just as soon as things are settled at Hartwood," Lindley offered.

D'Archaud was not content with that answer. The man took one step forward, placing himself partially in front of Sophie. Lindley understood. He was keeping her from him, protecting her as he should have done all along.

"Sophie and I will go now, milord. You have no objection?"

Hell yes, he had objection! But he couldn't very well keep Sophie from taking her father back to his Annie and infant. No, they should not be forced to wait for that reunion.

"Take my carriage," he said, realizing that would leave him to ride one of the pitiful creatures that still grazed on the Loveland garden.

D'Archaud appeared grateful. Lindley supposed he could understand the man's rush—yet here he was helping escort Sophie to the conveyance that would take her miles away while he remained here to handle the most unpleasant business of handing people he cared deeply for over to the authorities. Damn, how he hated these turns of events.

He did, however, manage to position himself perfectly for helping Sophie up into her seat before D'Archaud could assume the task. She took his hand politely when he offered it but did not look at him. She still carried her little pack under her arm, he noticed. He would have to go find those missing scissors and give them back to her at some point. Perhaps the binding cords, too.

He lifted her up to step into the phaeton and wanted so much more than just this casual touch. It simply felt wrong to allow her to leave this way. How could she be so cool, as if nothing had happened between them? He held her hand much longer than was appropriate.

Finally she was forced to look at him, to send her gaze down his way and let his eyes capture hers. Could she read on his face all the things he wished to say? Could she see in his eyes any of the things he felt?

"How shall we return your carriage to you when we are done, sir?" she asked, breaking the silence between them.

His first instinct was to reply "naked," but good sense won out and he refrained.

"I'll find you," he said instead. "I will always come for what is mine, Sophie."

She looked away now and tried to pull her hand back. He held on.

"*You* are mine, Sophie," he added, just in case she might not yet understand.

She kept her eyes on her lap, but her cheeks colored beautifully.

"Yes, my lord. I am."

He let her have her hand back. Her father had pulled himself up into the seat on the other side, and clearly she was uncomfortable discussing this in front of him. Lindley didn't mind.

She'd told him what he needed to know—her heart belonged to him. Good God, but he'd had no idea he'd needed that so badly. It was as if that dark, empty place inside of him was suddenly flooded with light. Sophie was his.

He could cling to that until they were together again. And then he would make sure it was forever. Smiling like a dolt, he gave D'Archaud a friendly nod and stepped back to let the man drive away with his horses, his carriage, and the future Countess Lindley.

Chapter Twenty-one

Sophie stared at the blank page, holding the pen carefully but not knowing what mark to make on the paper. It was the finest paper she'd ever seen, and it seemed a shame when her hesitation produced nothing more than a blot. *Drat.* Did she toss the page into the grate and waste another? The writing set was a gift from her cousin Evaline.

Dear Evaline—at last there was a chance to be close again. Papa was a noble-born Frenchman, and taking on his true name meant Sophie's past could be virtually wiped clean. With their new connections, Sophie had been presented to society as everything proper and respectable. Lord Dashford backed up Papa's claim that he and Sophie had been living peacefully with friends all this time. So far it appeared no one was questioning them. Perhaps Papa's hefty new bank account had something to do with that.

Never in her wildest dreams could Sophie have imagined her good fortune. Seemingly overnight, her life had gone from a dreadful, dirty existence to being full of family and friends, all healthy and secure with bright, shining futures dawning on the horizon.

She'd been reunited with Evaline just two days ago. The

viscountess and her new husband had come to London to meet her as soon as Papa had secured his portion of the treasure with the bank and found them a decent place to live. Julia St. Clement had come, too, and fairly glowed with excitement as she talked of her upcoming wedding to that dratted Lord Rastmoor she'd claimed to have hated.

Papa and Annie were set to be wed soon, too. Sophie would lose a dear friend yet gain a step-mamma and a sister. It was all a bit much to take in.

And still . . . the one thing she wanted more than all was missing.

Ten whole days had gone by, and she'd heard nothing from Lindley. Nothing—no note, no message, no visit. It was as if he'd forgotten her completely.

And it wasn't as if he hadn't been in Town. No, she had read in the papers that the man had brought an infamous whore to justice and discovered treason within the Home Office. It seemed he was quite lauded for his efforts, bringing testimony to the court even as early as last Friday. Indeed, he was in London for a week and had done nothing to contact her.

So she'd decided to contact him. But what could she say? Perhaps his parting words to her had meant nothing, but hers had meant everything. Whether he wanted her or not, she was his. She would never be anyone else's.

But how could she put that on paper? She wanted him so badly. Must he leave her to beg? She wasn't asking for much from him, just a bit of his time. If he didn't intend to make her his mistress, at least surely he could not be opposed to an occasional meeting? She would be discreet.

Bother. How did one craft a polite letter inviting a man for an impromptu tryst? Papa would only be gone until this evening. Her window of opportunity was rapidly narrowing. If she did not get this letter drafted and sent on, she might never have another chance. Papa was meeting with his solicitor now, setting the last details for taking a country house somewhere. He would be carting them all off to the country, and she would never see Lindley again.

She scribbled furiously on the paper. At a time like this she supposed there was simply no use for propriety. If she wanted to entice Lindley before it was too late, she'd best be direct.

He would either respond favorably, or he would not. Either way, she would have done her best to try.

Her letter was very nearly complete when a rap at the front door of their home interrupted. As she'd planned ahead and given the servants the afternoon off—then proceeded to pay the housekeeper to leave after the woman claimed not to want a day off—there was no one available to answer it for her. *Drat.* With all of Papa's business dealings lately she supposed this could be something important. Surely word would get back to him if someone had come and found the house empty. She'd best answer it and get rid of the visitor quickly.

Wiping at the ink on her fingers, she stalked to the door and tried to make a happy face. She was becoming rather proficient at that, smiling for everyone with all the wonderful things going on around her, yet secretly withering inside as every hour passed without any sign of Lindley even so much as remembering her. She patted her hair, hid her emotion, and pulled the door open.

Lindley. Dear heavens, he looked even more wonderful here at her doorstep than he had in her dreams last night. Or the night before. Or ever.

"Good afternoon, Miss D'Archaud," he said, removing his hat and smiling in a way that completely robbed her of breath.

She simply stared at him. He held his hat in one hand and a package in the other.

"May I come in?" he said after a pause.

She stepped out of the way. It was the closest thing to an invitation she could muster in her weakened state.

He entered, walking past her and then helping her shut the door when she merely stood there gaping at him. She knew he must think her a fool, but for the life of her she could do nothing more than stand and gawk. Lindley was here! He'd come to her!

"Er, you were expecting someone else?" he asked after another pause.

She shook her head.

He smiled. "Well, I'm glad to hear that. So, would you like to invite me into the drawing room?"

She nodded.

He stepped into the drawing room where she'd recently

been working. Apparently she forgot to follow, because a moment later he came back to the entryway and took her by the hand.

"Perhaps you should come with me," he said.

She nodded again and let him lead her obediently. Lord, what a ninny she was! Surely he would tire of her and leave if she didn't find her voice soon.

He placed his package on a table and his hat on top of it. Then he waited for her to speak. After listening to the clock tick on the mantel for far too long, however, she still could not quite remember how to do so.

"Your father is out?" he asked, standing in the center of the room and rocking on his heels.

More nodding. At least she could do that much.

"Your stepmother-to-be?"

Papa had insisted on propriety. Annie and Rosie were staying with Annie's family in Town until the wedding in two weeks. The family was quite happy to have them, considering Papa had been rather free with his money as a way of showing gratitude. She thought it was completely unjust that the family should prosper now after having done nothing for Annie when she'd been forced to seek employment with Madame, but it made Annie happy to think in some way she'd redeemed herself for her mother and younger siblings.

Of course it would require the use of speech to convey all this to Lindley. Instead, she simply shook her head. Drat, but if she could have spoken she would have cursed her faulty tongue.

"So Miss D'Archaud is all alone this afternoon," he remarked.

Emphatic nodding.

"And just what have you been doing to amuse yourself, my dear?"

Ah, but this she could answer! She dashed to the desk and snatched up the letter she'd been working on. Heavens, but her heart was pounding. Did she really have the nerve to give it to him? But if she did not, he might leave, and she could never forgive herself for that.

As it was, he might refuse her and leave anyway. Did she dare? She dared.

She handed the letter to him and tried not to let her hand shake. He looked at it, his eyes following the hasty text while his expression was unreadable. What was he thinking? What would be his response? Did he find it shocking, unseemly? Would he scold her and storm out? She waited.

"You wrote this letter?"

She swallowed and cleared her throat. "Only just, my lord."

"It is addressed simply to 'Dearest R.' I pray to God that stands for Richard, Sophie."

"It does." Her voice was still weak and pitiful, but at least she was forming words.

"I'm glad, seeing as this letter is apparently an invitation for your R fellow to come and spend an afternoon in 'certain familiar pursuits,' as you put it. Would you care to explain what those might be, Sophie?"

Heavens but he was trying to embarrass her now, wasn't he? She supposed that ought to leave her a bit miffed, but the most adorable smile teased at the corner of his lips, and she just couldn't be. Surely if he was playfully teasing her she might still cling to some hope.

"I was hoping you might recall them, my lord."

"There's no need, Miss D'Archaud, as you've so politely gone and listed a great many of them here," he said, glancing back at the letter and raising an eyebrow.

"No one wants to be misunderstood, sir."

"Indeed, there can hardly be any misunderstanding your intent. Lord, but you're marvelously thorough in your descriptions."

"My intent is to be thorough in everything I do today," she said, feeling brave enough to smile for him.

"Although I do believe you spelled *punishment* with too many *N*s, my dear."

"Then perhaps I need some correction, my lord."

She expected him to make a witty reply, but he did not. He just stared at her for a long moment, then swept all rational thought right out of her when he dropped the letter, crushed her into his arms, and kissed her. It did not take rational thought to kiss him back with every part of her being.

"Ah, Sophie, it's been an eternity. God knows how I've missed you."

She clung to him, pressing herself against him as if that could, in some way, keep him here with her forever.

"I thought I might never see you again," she whispered. "That's why I was writing that letter. Tomorrow we leave for Kent."

"I know. I hope you like it there; I've always thought it quite lovely."

"I don't want to go!"

She pushed herself away from him just enough to look up into his face. She was simply going to have to pluck up the courage to beg.

"What?"

"I want to stay here. With you."

"With me?"

"Oh, I don't mean that you'd have to keep me in any sort of fashion, or make any actual arrangement," she said, trying to explain herself quickly so he would not bolt out the door with his hand on his purse and his eye on his freedom. "I can still sew; I would support myself. If you've changed your mind you would not need to set me up as your mistress, but—"

"My mistress, Sophie? You would have me install you in Town as my *mistress*?"

"Only if you want to, of course."

He was holding her tightly, his eyes searching hers. "Well, I don't want to. Damn it, Sophie. Is that what you want? I should buy you fashionable clothes and set you up in a fine home where I can visit two days a week and let you take other callers in between?"

"No! Heavens, no. But when we left Loveland that day I thought that's what you said . . . that I belonged to you. I assumed you meant to keep me, but—"

"Good God, Sophie. That's not what I meant at all."

The conviction was evident in his voice. Lord, but she'd made a complete cake of herself, hadn't she? Whatever he'd said—or meant to say—that day in Loveland, she'd certainly misconstrued it. Oh, but how mortifying!

Before she could pull away from him to go hide under a rock, though, he pulled her closer. Indeed, being pressed against his solid chest as he stroked her hair was certainly better than crawling under a rock, but she was no less shamed by her pretentious assumptions. As if a man like Lindley could wish to keep someone like her for a mistress.

"I would never insult you that way, Sophie," he said, and she felt his lips press against her head. "Besides, I won't be here in Town very often. I'll be away in Kent, spending time with my wonderful wife."

She couldn't help it. Her face popped up so she could stare at him. "Your *wife*?!"

"Of course."

"You mean . . . you plan to marry again?"

"Yes I plan to . . . what do you mean *again*?"

"I mean, well, Eudora told me how devoted you were to . . . Marie."

"Damn Eudora. Of course I was devoted to Marie, but I was never *married* to her!"

"Never married? But I saw her portrait . . . and there was little Charles, and . . ."

"And Marie was my *sister*. She married Charlie Cardell, my best friend from school days. Their son was my nephew, Sophie."

"Oh," Sophie said, making sense of it now and realizing Eudora had purposely misled her out of simple spite and cruelty. Horrible woman.

"Charlie worked for the Home Office," Lindley said. "Though I'm afraid I was not thrilled with my sister marrying so far beneath her. I tried to find Charlie a more prestigious position, but he refused. He loved what he did, and he told me he'd just uncovered a plot to sell information to the French and claimed one of the men he was after frequented Eudora's nunnery. He learned Eudora was my aunt, though she'd been estranged from the family for years. He asked if I would contact her, forge some sort of connection that perhaps he could use to find information. I told him no."

"But you were quite friendly with Madame," Sophie said. "I noticed you visiting often, as a matter of fact."

"Did you now?" he said with a smile that declared he rather approved of her notice. "But that was only after someone waylaid Charlie's carriage, killing him and everyone inside: my mother, my sister, my nephew. I knew it must have something to do with his investigation, so that's why I befriended Eudora after all those years of pretending I didn't know I had an aunt living that lifestyle in London."

"Oh."

"It doesn't paint me to be very noble, does it?"

"You couldn't have known," she said, laying her hand on his face. "And you've certainly done everything humanly possible since then to make it right."

"I grieve for them every day, but I'll never make it right."

"You found those that caused it, didn't you?"

"Yes, it appears Warren was the mastermind, after all. Eudora was working with him to extract information from her clients. She was the connection to Fitzgelder."

"And my father?"

"In the wrong place at the wrong time. Whatever your father has done in his past, Sophie, he was not a party to murder. I'm sorry I let Eudora trick me into hunting him. He spurned her, so she wanted to punish him. Which brings me back to the subject of your misspelled letter, my dear. Were you quite sincere when you wrote it?"

"Oh yes! I sent the servants out for the day, and Papa said he will be gone until evening. So as you see, we have plenty of time for . . . proper spelling."

Rather than kissing her again or getting down to the business of completing some of the activities mentioned in her letter, Lindley reached into his pocket and withdrew his watch.

"Sorry, my dear, but I'm afraid we have less time than you think. Your father only allowed me half an hour, and I fear we've already used most of that up in idle chatter."

"What do you mean? Papa is with his solicitor arranging for our new home."

He shook his head. "No, he's with *my* solicitor. It is *my* property he plans to move you to in Kent."

"Your property? But why?"

"Because he refuses to grant me permission to ask you to marry me until I have properly courted you and proven myself a worthy man, that's why."

She could not even comprehend his words. She merely stared and waited for him to explain.

"He wants you to feel you have a choice, Sophie. And you do, you know. You are a woman of means now. You have connections, in England as well as France. You will be able to choose any husband you want."

"But I'm no one! I can't really be a lady, not with my history."

"That was Sophie Darshaw. Now you are Sophie D'Archaud, of noble blood and gentle breeding. No one needs to know how you spent the last few years of your life."

"Or that my grandmother was a courtesan, or that my mother was an actress, or that my father was accused of murder, or—"

He wrapped her tightly into his arms. "You're right. You've got a dreadful past, and you'd best grab the first man you see. Just to sway things in my favor, I'm going to blindfold you."

"Oh, now that does sound promising!"

"And just promise me you will at least consider my proposal, Sophie. I know we've had a rather irregular relationship so far, but I can promise there's nothing irregular about the way I feel for you. I love you, Sophie, whether it's Darshaw or D'Archaud. And I would be the happiest man on earth if you'd consent to being my wife."

She pretended to think about it. "Well, would your wife be expected to behave in a polite, wifely manner all the time, or would she still be allowed some room for, er, creativity?"

"Creativity? Yes. Hell, yes."

"I see. Then in that case, sir, hell, yes it is."

He smiled broadly and nearly crushed her. "I'll never let you regret it."

"But perhaps you might wish to let me breathe a bit," she wheezed.

He released his hold and stepped away from her. "You're right. And your father should be here soon, so perhaps now would be a good time to open the package I've brought you."

She was confused, but he handed her the box and she carefully undid the strings. Placing it back on the table, she opened it.

"My scissors!"

"I retrieved them for you."

"Yes, and the binding cords as well," she said, pulling them out and feeling her face go warm at the memory of that night at Haven Abbey.

She was surprised at the next items she discovered. The velvet pantalets had somehow reappeared.

"Those I found particularly intriguing," he said.

She shook her head. "They chafe."

"Pity. They were one of the few items in your collection I did not fully get to enjoy."

"Ah, don't think I haven't sewn anything else these past ten days, my lord," she said.

He grinned like an eager child. "Oh? You have made something new?"

"Indeed I have."

"Is it as tantalizingly creative as the others?"

"More so," she replied, stepping into his arms and looking up into his dark, passionate gaze.

"Is it wildly alluring?" he asked, stroking her hair.

"Terribly."

"Is it somewhat scandalous?"

"Dreadfully."

It appeared this time he was at a loss for words as she tiptoed to press her lips against his.

"And I can hardly wait to see you in it, my lord."

Keep reading for a preview of
the next historical romance
by Susan Gee Heino

Paramour by Pretense

Coming soon from Berkley Sensation!

Chapter One

London, England
May 1820

The candlelight was lovely, and Penelope knew hers was the prettiest gown in the room. She also knew this was not by any accident. Her brother spared no expense in his desperate efforts to get her married off. The only thing good about Anthony's efforts was that this gown he'd paid for was the exact shade of blue to complement her necklace. Indeed, she did love this necklace.

She put her hand to it, enjoying the feel of the warm gold and the smooth stones set into place to form the stout body of a beetle. Not just any beetle, though. This was a scarab—an amulet fashioned by Egyptian hands many, many centuries ago. Indeed, she'd paid a pretty penny for it. No doubt Anthony would scold when he realized that's where all her money had gone, but she could not care. This was the finest piece of her collection.

She'd hoped whatever magic it might still contain would work to ward off the suitors her brother wished for, yet it appeared Anthony's power was far greater than even that of the sacred scarab. Suitors had been hanging on her all night. Pity none of them actually suited her.

Mercy, but it had been nearly impossible to get rid of them.

She'd managed, however. It had required her agreeing to stand up with Puddleston Blunk for the entire Country Dance, and there were fourteen couples to work through before she could finally claim exhaustion and send the lout off to procure her a lemonade. Now she was alone. If she didn't dream up a way to disappear soon, though, he'd return and she'd be stuck with Puddleston on her arm until Mamma showed up to pry him off. And Mamma would likely not do that. Mamma said Puddleston Blunk was a good catch.

Heavens, but if there was ever a time to decide on a plan, it was now. She had no intention of catching someone like Mr. Blunk, by accident or on purpose. There were other things she wished to do with her life, and all she needed was Mamma's permission and a healthy pile of her brother's money. So far both of those had been elusive.

Oh, it wasn't as if she hadn't come up with a plausible scheme. Indeed she had, just this very afternoon. But it was somewhat outrageous. Risky, even. Did she dare consider it?

She glanced nervously around Lord Heversham's crowded ballroom. Nothing out of the ordinary; no one she did not know. If she did have any hope of carrying out her plan, none of the men present would fit her purposes. Her eye fell on the row of young ladies seated with their chaperones against the far wall. Those were the plain girls, the girls with poor connections or even poorer dowries.

Her quiet friend Maria Bradley was there. She looked miserable. Penelope would have given nearly anything to have joined her there on that wallflower row. Oh, if only she and Maria could trade places. How cruel fate was to truss Penelope up in a beautiful gown and surround her with suitors when any one of these young ladies might so much rather be in her satin shoes.

Then again, it hadn't been fate at all that had done this to her. It had been Anthony. If he could just listen to reason! She did not wish to marry. She wished to travel to Egypt and dig for mummies. Was that so very much for a woman of three-and-twenty to dream of? Apparently it was, because both her brother and her mother became nearly apoplectic at the very mention of it.

Which was why she had tried to soothe them by announcing her hope to go there and meet the well-known Egyptologist Dr. Oldham. They'd exchanged several letters, and she'd found him fascinating. Perhaps she might even consider marrying him.

She had expected Anthony to find this acceptable, since he seemed so very keen on seeing her foisted off on someone else. She thought her mother might approve of her interest in someone so scholarly and mature as Dr. Oldham. Neither was the case. Mother had to call for her salts, and Anthony declared he'd burn in hell before he allowed his sister to drag the family name through mud—well, more mud, as he put it—and go chasing off to Egypt after some fortune-hunting Lothario. They'd ordered her to cease all communications with the man and confiscated her letter writing paper. Honestly, was that even legal?

If Anthony would but listen to her! Couldn't he see that sending her to Egypt would only make her more responsible, more respectable? She would have a purpose, meet educated people, and fill her idle time with noble, scholarly pursuits. The longer she was forced to dance around here in London like a mindless ninny, the more desperate and unpredictable she would become. Surely no mere husband could remedy that.

If only there were some middle ground, something between wasting away in genteel uselessness and being married. Something that could take her out from under Anthony's wing, yet not shackle her to someone else. But what could that be?

An engagement, she supposed, was halfway between. But she'd tried that before. Three times now she'd been engaged, hoping that would buy her some leeway, that as an engaged woman she'd finally be allowed to make some of her own choices or pursue her own goals. In each case, however, she found it provided her even less freedom. And by now Anthony would recognize another engagement for what it was—a ruse to escape his rule. If she tried that route again, no doubt Anthony would call her bluff and drag her immediately to the altar with whatever sap she'd chosen and make it final. That would not help her at all.

Unless, of course, Anthony might not call her bluff. What

if this time she procured a fiancé Anthony did not approve? Ah, that was the scheme that had invaded her mind earlier and would not quite let go, despite its outrageous ridiculousness. Still, she could not help but wonder . . .

If she found a fiancé so unacceptable, so objectionable, wouldn't Anthony's brotherly concern cause him to intervene? And if he truly felt he must intervene, wouldn't it stand to reason he might see fit to put some distance between her and the object of her misplaced affection? Perhaps given the choice between seeing his dearest sister wed to some ogre or gone off to Egypt, Anthony might just choose Egypt. She knew she certainly would! All it would take was careful planning on her part, and selecting just the right man to play his part.

This was where her scheme hit a snag. A big one. Where on earth would she find such a fiancé? Someone so dreadful that even Anthony would not want her to keep him, yet at the same time there would have to be something about him that Anthony might think truly interested her. The scheme would never work if Anthony did not fully believe she wanted the fellow.

So just what would this wantable, objectionable man look like? Certainly she'd never seen anyone like that, not in the tight, dull circle Mamma and Anthony kept her in. But perhaps her sister-in-law, Julia, might know someone who . . .

A blustering shout interrupted her imaginings.

She couldn't quite see over the crush of ball-goers, but she could certainly hear there was some sort of racket going on near the door to the ballroom. Drat, if only she were a bit taller! Finally something interesting was occurring and she could not see it.

She pressed through the crowd to get a closer look. There was, after all, no way she was going to miss ogling at what might be her only bit of excitement all Season.

Whispers and scandalized murmurs breezed through the pack around her, but she could not hear enough to get the gist of things. She could, however, begin to pick out a few words here and there from the loud male voice shouting over the hushed din. Indeed, things were getting more than interesting. She ducked under Lady Davenforth's enormous bosom and pressed past Sir Douglas MacClinty's portly abdomen. No one noticed her, so she kept on, moving slowly toward the front of the room. Mamma would surely have a fit, but Mamma hadn't seen her so far. She could gawk as blatantly as she liked.

"It just isn't seemly, sir!" the blustering male voice was saying.

"Yes, it seemed a bit unusual to me, too," another male voice said.

This was a deep voice, a voice with tone and texture that Penelope was certain she'd recognize if she ever heard it again. It was a good voice, warm and amused and certain. She could picture the man it belonged to as smiling while he spoke. She could imagine he had a glint of mischief in his eye.

She could also tell he was more than a little bit drunk.

"But for shame, sir! You had your hand on my wife's, er . . . arm!" the first voice stormed.

"No, sir," the second man corrected. "I had my hand on your wife's, er, bosom."

The crowd gasped. Someone—most likely the blustering gentleman—choked. The man with the warm, amused voice said nothing, despite all the tumult around him. Penelope decided she simply must get a look at this person.

There was a chair against the nearby wall, so she scooted herself to it and hoisted up her skirt. Surely with all the fuss these gentlemen were causing no one would so much as notice a woman with strawberry ringlets standing atop a chair, would they? Of course not. Up she went, steadying herself by grasping on to the nearby fern propped securely—she hoped—on a plaster column.

Ah, now she could see the men. The first was very much as she expected, red-faced, jowly, and well, blustering. The other man was a different story. She drew in a surprised breath.

For all his cultured tones and textured warmth, the man appeared very unlike his voice. She expected someone dashing and rakish, someone who lived by his wit and reveled in the stimulation of intelligent conversation, among other things. Someone who appreciated fine spirits and looked down on his nose at lesser men. A dandy even, who was sought after and used to being admired. That was how he had sounded, at least.

What she saw when her eyes fell upon him was something quite different.

By heavens, but the man was a hermit! He was unkempt, with dirt in his hair and whiskers on his face several days old. His clothes were a disaster. If he had been dressed for mucking a stable or plowing a field, he would have been only slightly overdone. The man was a positive horror!

And now he noticed her. She clutched the fern for support as his eyes locked onto hers. When he smiled, she thought she felt the chair shift beneath her feet.

"If you'd let me explain, Burlington," he said to the blustering man, although his eyes remained fixed on Penelope. "I was trying to say that you have reached a hasty conclusion where your wife is concerned. I was walking into the room as she was walking out of the room, and we merely collided. There was nothing more than that."

"But you were alone with her. Your hand was on her . . . Well, don't think I haven't heard of your reputation, sir."

"Yes, yes. I daresay everyone has heard of my reputation and this is hardly going to rectify that, is it? Oh well. I assure you, in this instance, at least, I am innocent."

"I ought to call you out!" the first man blustered on bravely.

"Well, I suppose I could shoot you on a field of honor if you insist, but I really would so much rather not. My head is going to be bloody ringing enough in the morning as it is."

The crowd laughed at that, and the red-faced man went even more red-faced. He seemed to realize he was running out of practical reason to continue his blustering, but it was obvious he wished to continue. He glanced around nervously and at last was reduced to giving his disheveled companion a frustrated sneer.

"Since my wife would be very much distressed at the thought of a duel, I shall let you go this time."

"Ah, Burlington, that's terribly kindhearted of you."

"But watch yourself, man. And do what your uncle sent you to town for in the first place—find yourself a wife and leave everyone else's alone."

The hermit only gave half a smile at this advice. "Isn't it thoughtful of my uncle to keep all of London so well informed of my endeavors."

"If your endeavors did not breed scandal and dishonor at every turn, no one in London would give a fig for them. Watch yourself, Lord Harry, unless you really don't wish to live long enough to make use of that title your unfortunate uncle will be forced to leave you one day."

"Oh, that ruddy title. I tell you, Burlington, there are plenty of other things I'd very much rather make use of." Again, his eyes fell on Penelope, and for just a moment she felt as if she might have an inkling what the man meant—and she did not mind it.

"But I also tell you," he continued, turning back to his grumbling confronter, "your wife is not one of them."

With that, Lord Harry nodded at those around who still observed their altercation, then he gave Penelope a special nod all her own and departed. He turned on his heel and abandoned the assembly. Penelope clenched the fern so tightly she was left with nothing more than a handful of tiny green leaves. The dratted chair was still moving. She was sure of it.

"Penelope!"

This blustering screech was her mother's. Penelope started and very nearly fell off her precarious roost. Bother. Of course Mamma would appear now and discover her this way.

"Oh, hello, Mamma," she said, as if standing on chairs in someone's decorated ballroom was perfectly normal. "I thought I saw a mouse."

"More like a rat," her mother said, glaring in the direction Lord Harry had gone. "You pay no attention to that man, Penelope. Harris Chesterton might be heir to the Earl of Kingsdere, but he's hardly fit for polite company. And here you are gawking on a chair? Honestly, Penelope, what can you be thinking?"

Honestly? Well, she was thinking she'd just discovered the perfect fiancé.

HARRIS CHESTERTON LEFT LORD HEVERSHAM'S HOUSE empty-handed, but he couldn't help but smile. True, he'd not actually gotten what he'd come for, and yes, he had been caught prowling about the bowels of Heversham's home when he should not have been there. And of course he'd very nearly gotten dragged into a duel with that blubbering fool Burlington—not to mention what he'd had to endure with that prying Lady Burlington—but still the night had not been a total waste. He'd seen something that changed his life.

That girl, the one who stood on a chair. Ah yes, he'd seen her quite clearly. He couldn't actually recall much of what she looked like, but he'd noticed something about her. She was wearing the scarab.

The Scarab of Osiris. He knew it instantly, had held it in his hand and felt the smooth gold, the carefully carved insect form, the warm amber orb at its head that fairly glowed like the sun. It was a beautiful piece. And it was stolen.

He knew, because he'd been the one to steal it.

After it was originally stolen from its place in a dead pharaoh's tomb, of course. He'd been merely trying to return the thing, along with several other treasures that had been looted from their rightful place and brought here, to England, where they did not belong.

Oh, certainly, he did not begrudge the legitimate men of science and conservation who worked within the proper authority to responsibly excavate and preserve antiquities to be shared with the world. He simply had a bit of a problem with the wholesale pillaging of one nation's culture and history to fund the luxurious tastes of a few private citizens in another. The young woman on the chair was a perfect example of that.

She was just another of these well-bred simpletons who were hungry for gold and sparkling things without ever stopping to wonder at the meaning, the history, the eternal significance of pieces like that scarab. No doubt she'd lined someone's pocket well, probably with more thought to how the lapis lazuli of the scarab's wings matched her blue eyes quite remarkably than to any concept of the hopes and dreams of its ancient creators.

Damn. Harris could do little but kick himself. What an idiot he was to fail so miserably at keeping these articles safe. And just a matter of days before he'd needed to give his reclaimed collection back to the people who'd asked—no, demanded—it returned.

But now that he knew where at least one piece was, perhaps he could track down the rest. Perhaps he could save these priceless treasures after all. And perhaps that would save his friend, Oldham. Indeed, far more than a friend.

First, though, he'd have to find a way to locate that woman. It wouldn't be an entirely unpleasant task, he had to admit. The scarab did bring out the blue of her eyes quite remarkably, now that he thought about it.

"WE WILL HAVE NO MORE OF THIS EGYPT NONSENSE," Anthony, Lord Rastmoor, declared, silencing Penelope when she tried to protest the morning after the dance. "It's all I can do to keep you under control here in London. I can't even imagine the havoc you might wreak traveling off to some foreign land on your own."

"But I wouldn't be alone," Penelope protested to her brother. "I would be traveling with Mr. and Mrs. Tollerson. They've been friends of the family for ages. They'd keep close watch over me."

"Mr. and Mrs. Tollerson can't even keep close watch over their own teeth. They are far too old to keep you on a leash, Penelope. You'd run all over them. Look what happened when I left you alone with mother and you nearly became prey to that loathsome Fitzgelder."

Oh, he just loved to bring that up, didn't he? And he never seemed to have the facts right about it. Totally unfair.

"That was five years ago, Anthony," she reminded. "And as you recall, I was quite in control of things where Fitzgelder was concerned."

He merely snorted at her for that. "Just as you have been with your subsequent three fiancés, I suppose."

"I never really intended to get engaged to any of them, Anthony. The first one was a misunderstanding. The second one tricked me, and the third . . . well, I'm not entirely certain what happened there."

"It is always one disaster after another with you, isn't it?"

"But it's never my fault! Anthony, if you'd simply give me a chance—"

"No. If you want to go to Egypt, little sister, then find a husband. Let him take you there. Let him try to keep you from knocking over the Sphinx, or whatever ruddy mess you might make of the place."

He was serious, she knew. But where on earth in all this sea of London foppery and English propriety did he expect her to find a husband who might have the slightest inclination to go to Egypt? She did not run with an especially adventurous crowd. He and Mamma had seen to it the young men she met were all properly dull and impossibly proper.

Very well, then. If a husband was what it would take to get to Egypt, then a husband she was going to find. Well, a fiancé, anyway.

She would implement her plan. She'd thought to give begging and pleading one last try this morning, but since that had clearly failed, she had no other recourse. Anthony had pushed her into it.

Now, all she had to do was find that dreadful gentleman from last night. And really, the morning post had already helped her along in that. The Earl of Kingsdere, as it turned out, was hosting a ball in honor of his own birthday. She and Mamma had received an invitation. They would accept, of course.

Surely the man's heir—the very hairy Lord Harry she had seen last night—would wish to help his uncle celebrate the occasion, even if he was a hermit. She only hoped he would not be forced to shave. True, he had seemed to be hiding rather nice features beneath that scruff, but Anthony would surely hate him more if he remained woolly.

Penelope smiled for her brother over her breakfast. "Very well, Anthony. Your word is law. I suppose there's nothing more to be said on the matter."

"There isn't."

Silly Anthony. He actually believed he was correct.